Thurlow's
WAR

by

Alex Rosenberg

Library and Archives Canada Cataloguing in Publication
Rosenberg, Alex, author
Thurlow's War / Alex Rosenberg

Issued in print and electronic formats.

ISBN: 978-1-998501-32-8 (paperback)
ISBN: 978-1-998501-33-5 (ebook)

Cover Design: Paul Hewitt
Interior Design: Richa Bargotra

Warpath Press
Toronto, Ontario, Canada
www.warpathpress.com

1

Flying is the only kind of freedom that ever seemed complete to me. Pull up off the runway, the propeller shoveling the air away behind you, moving effortlessly in any direction at the whim of your wrist on the joy stick, letting the throb of an engine dominate your whole body as you open the throttle, mixing the air with more and more kerosene, gliding though the whispering wind as you feather a prop and dead stick into a layer of cloud. It was always the same rush of freedom.

Every time.

Then comes the instant the transcendent thrill is completely destroyed by terror. You see the line of machine gun tracer move into your wing root, announcing itself too late. You've entirely missed the enemy pursuit plane boring in, and you're going down for certain. That's when the prey's instinct overtakes the predator's conceit, and you hold a gasp, waiting to see if the evasive snap roll works, waiting to see if you'll survive.

It works and ten minutes later you're basking in the freedom again, oblivious to the lesson you should have just learned. That's how narcotic flying has always been to me.

Anyway, flying's been a drug for me since a day in the summer of 1924. I'd spent a year's savings from my paper route for a 15-minute joyride in a barnstormer's Curtis Jenny. The biplane had dropped down in a farmer's field just at the edge of

Waterloo, Iowa. I'd already been in love with aviation and knew the lore of every American ace, not just Rickenbacker and Frank Luke. I knew the pursuit fighters they'd flown in the Great War, right down to the numbers on their tailplanes. This would be my first chance, maybe my only chance, to fly. I spent the whole day on the field, trying but failing to find something, anything the taciturn pilot could be induced to talk about, each time he climbed out of the cockpit. He'd just stare at me, holding me for a moment in the gaze of his deep blue eyes. His indifference to anything but getting his machine into the air was something I later came to understand.

———

I was flying wingman, parked right behind Jim Peak. We'd just crossed the Ebro when we were bounced by a half-dozen of the Condor Legion's best. The brand-new Messerschmitt Bf 109s opened up their cannon fire and then they almost caught up with it. That's how fast they came down.

Momentary terror and then reflex. We broke and went straight for the patchy clouds just below us. Our Russian P-16s were solid ships, but they only matched up against the Messerschmitt fighter when we could cut tighter circles behind them. I know. I'd managed the trick twice in the months since the new German fighters had arrived, flown by Germans fighting for Franco's Fascists. I didn't paint any swastikas to number my kills below my name on the fuselage, though. It didn't seem to be good taste. How quaint.

Breaking through the clouds at about 800 feet suddenly I could see the tracer rounds bite into the cowling over my engine. The German plane was so close I thought he was going to ram. I hadn't fooled him for a minute and this close to the ground I was going to have to level off and get shot out of the sky. Suddenly my propeller was feathering. I looked down at the airspeed indicator and knew a stall was coming. Then I saw the smoking oil streaming from my cowling. The German had seen it too. He climbed a little and was banking back and forth to watch me break up and bail out. I didn't want to give him the satisfaction, but there was no choice.

I jumped clear, pulled the cord and settled down to observe the arid pastureland along the banks of the Ebro. To my surprise the plane descended pretty much in one piece, hitting the ground before the engine fire had a chance to spread along the fuselage. The Messerschmitt was watching too. When the fighter hit the ground in a copse of trees divided by a farm track, the German flew off. Those were the days before pursuit pilots had to worry about being strafed in their 'chutes.

I landed on the brow of a hill rolling down a half mile of scrub and rock-strewn field to the wood, where my ship had come down. It wasn't visible in the copse, but it was sending up a blackish smoke signal from the fire that must have been putting itself out. I gathered up the 'chute and began hiking down to the plane, hoping to save some gear that might help me get away. It took longer getting there than I expected.

No landing gear down, the plane had pancaked a few feet before being stopped by a eucalyptus tree that was now leaning over it as if to shade a large bovine. I reached inside the cockpit for my side arm, a British Webley service revolver, a map case, the musette bag we all carried, with the flask of brandy and the nice little Retina camera issued for reconnaissance pictures. It wasn't good for that job but it was all they could give us. And the Retina was great for sightseeing snaps.

It was late afternoon of a sunny day in early October, and I thought I'd have a chance if no one noticed the smoke before it got dark. I'd wait till dusk, torch the plane, and hotfoot it back towards the Ebro river. Figured I'd worry about crossing it if I ever got that far.

I was sitting against the tree trying to enjoy one of those very harsh Spanish fags, when I saw the dust cloud. It was rising behind a large black, open topped car coming down the narrow track at speed. There was a double set of wheels in the back. It had to be a military vehicle, a German one at that. It began to slow and soon was close enough to make out the three-pointed star on the hood. I beat a retreat deeper into the stand of trees and slid down behind a fallen eucalyptus trunk.

The car came to a stop beside the fuselage of my P-16 and the driver—a German soldier—pulled up the handbrake and hopped out to hold open the passenger door. A tall figure in a flight suit unfolded himself out from under the low canopy over the rear seat. He was obviously a pilot, probably the one who'd shot me out of the sky, come to gloat over his kill.

He walked around the wrecked plane, read my name painted below the windscreen, then climbed into the cockpit. He sat there for a few minutes. I saw the ailerons on each wing flick up and down and tail go left and right. He was obviously treading on the pedals and feeling out the joystick. The man climbed out, went back to the staff-car, pulled his own camera from the back seat and took a picture of the P-16. The driver reached for the camera, wanting to take a picture of the pilot with the downed plane, but he shook his head.

Maybe the lens of my camera sent a glint into his eye, because the pilot raised his head and scanned the eucalyptus trunks. He saw me, crouched in their shade, holding the camera and winding the film advance. Then, motioning towards me in a peremptory gesture, he spoke in English to the driver. "Take that camera." The drive looked from the pilot to me, now standing forty feet away among the trees. He obviously didn't understand English. The pilot pointed at me, and then holding his camera, shouted, "The camera" as if making his English louder would make it understood by the German. The order now understood, the man began to advance towards me.

I stood, slung the Retina to my shoulder and pulled my Webley from its holster. "Tell your man another step and he's a fallen hero of the Condor Legion." The German had already stopped. My revolver swiveled toward the pilot; I spoke to him. "Now, get in your staff car, take your driver, and go back where you came from."

More tamely than I expected, the pilot stepped to the running board and mounted the back seat. The driver seemed happy to comply with my wish as well when, from the back seat, his passenger pointed to the driver's wheel. The big staff car roared to life, and the transmission found its reverse gear in a muffled grind. Soon enough the car was raising a dust cloud behind it.

That night Franco's Fascists launched their offensive on the Ebro. It turned out to be the longest and biggest battle of the Spanish Civil War. In the end, it took me almost a month and some good luck to get back across the river. When I finally did, the good guys were well on their way to losing the battle and the Civil War.

I guess I finally admitted to myself that month I spent on the run that the Republic would lose. I was hidden by stalwart *campesinos*. They were still loyal to a government selling itself to the Russians in the vain hope of getting enough equipment to hang on to some remnant of Spain. Cold nights in the November dark of a farmer's hovel, I had plenty of time to think. I'd left the US Army because I wouldn't accept the discipline. But because they wouldn't be disciplined either, the Spanish Republicans—

the good guys—were going to lose. I'd already watched its factions killing one another on the streets of Barcelona. The conclusion was inescapable. By the time I'd scrambled across the Ebro back into the ever-shrinking Republican redoubt, I knew that the next fight I got into, I was going to take orders, whether I liked them or not. That meant joining someone's regular army and staying in it. The one thing I couldn't do was stay neutral.

———

Almost a year later, in the fall of '39 I still had several rolls of film from my year and a half in Spain when I ran in to Robert Capa in Paris. He was back from China and not yet the most famous war photographer of the century.

I was sitting on the terrace of a café near the Odeon on the Left Bank. Looking up from my *Paris-Soir*, there he was, dropping himself at the chair opposite. Robert was the kind of person you were always glad to see, even after his photos from Spain made him a little arrogant about his first brush with fame.

"Willy Thurlow." The English was colloquial but the pronunciation Hungarian. He smiled his handsome face, the eyes bright below the darkest brows. The thick black hair was still unruly in a way that women couldn't resist smoothing down. I'd seen it happen a hundred times in Madrid. I made my face take on a mock grimace. Everyone knew I went by 'Will' and hated 'Willy.' Capa knew too. "Glad to see you made it out of Gur!" This was the internment camp, actually a concentration camp, the French had rigged up for the thousands of refugees who'd poured across the border when Franco finally defeated the Spanish Republic in early '39.

"Never even saw the place, Bobby." Small revenge, everyone called him 'Robert.' I shook my head. "American passport. Just waltzed into France like a tourist."

"Now there's a war on here, you going back home?" The Second World War was already three weeks old and Poland almost completely overrun by the Germans.

I nodded. "Nothing for me here. Maybe the Army Air Corps will take me back. They're going to need pilot instructors, if we're dragged into this war." It was then I looked down at the folded copy of the Paris *Herald Tribune* he'd put down on the table. There, below the masthead, was a photograph of Charles A. Lindbergh, in a double-breasted suit standing at a lectern with a hand in the air. Robert was talking, but I was too distracted by the picture to listen. Picking up the paper I began to read the article. Seeing my absorption, he stopped. Lindbergh had given a speech the day before, demanding that the US keep out of the war.

I put the paper down. "What you'd expect." Robert pointed at the picture. "Even got a medal from Herman Göring last year."

I looked at him quizzically. "Medal?"

"Yup. Caused an uproar. Don't you remember?" He picked up the paper and opened it. "Read the rest of the article." I skimmed it quickly. In October of '38, a few weeks before the "Cristal Night" firebombing of almost every Jewish synagogue in Germany, Lindbergh had toured German air force bases, accepted a decoration from Göring—the Commander Cross of the Order of the German Eagle. And he'd refused to return it.

"Well, now I know why I missed this news. Last October, when it was happening, I was on the lam in Spain, shot down by a German fighter, trying to make it back to Republican lines. Took more than three weeks, hiding, traveling at night, swimming that damn river in the middle of a pitched battle."

"Were you on the Ebro?" Capa knew the battle there was the Republic's last gasp.

I nodded. "Snapped a lot of photos too, just like you taught me."

I'd stirred a professional curiosity. "Can I see them?"

'Sure, if you can develop them for me."

He shook his head. "You mean you haven't looked at them yourself. You don't even know what you've got?" I could only nod. His return smile was condescending. "Look, bring them round to my place and I'll develop them. If there's anything worth selling, I'll pass them on to my agency. Could be a couple of hundred francs in it."

"Okay, but I'm sailing on the *Ile de France* in two days."

"It's a long shot but if anything you got pays off, I'll wire you the money when you get to New York."

The next day I took six 35mm roll of film to Robert's flat. I stood behind him in the bathroom as he developed the pictures, one after another. The roll started with snaps of a girl I'd known in Barcelona, obligingly candid ones, then a couple of me standing on the wing of the Russian P-16 I'd flown with my name below the cockpit. There were enough shots of German bombers flying low and people headed for bomb shelters, along with a truck carrying Republican soldiers fists raised in salute. The last roll began with a dozen pictures of a tall blond guy in a German flying suit standing over the wreck of the same plane, a German staff car in the background, a Luftwaffe sergeant next to him. Then there were the campesinos who'd gotten me back across Republican lines.

Robert made two copies of each frame and gave me a complete set. I told him how to reach me in New York. He'd keep the negatives for his agent.

Ten days later the *Ile de France* docked at pier 88 in New York. It had been a long crossing. She'd zigzagged much of the way worrying about U-boats. Second class passengers like me were subjected to a thorough customs inspection. The line moved slowly down the gangplank into the somber shade of the vast shed and across the floor to the customs agents in their white military caps. When my turn finally came, I flung my cases up onto the table with a little too much show of annoyance. The pair of inspectors looked at each other, grimaced and began unbelting my cases. I knew what they were looking for. Like a lot of people leaving Paris, I'd stopped at the English language bookstore on the left bank, Shakespeare and Co, for as many titles by Henry Miller as were available. I was bringing back *Tropic of Cancer* and the just published *Tropic of Capricorn*, neatly wrapped in a brown parcel marked *Emilie Bronte, Wuthering Heights*. The wrapping didn't fool the inspectors for a moment. The younger of the two lifted them out and put them aside. They continued to rifle through my clothes until one of them came to the manila envelope with the photos Robert Capa had developed. He passed the envelope over to the older man, who looked at the picture on top of the stack and set the envelope beneath the two book parcels.

I knew I didn't have a leg to stand on when it came to the books, but why would they want the photos? "Sir, those are just pictures, personal photos."

The younger inspector was already belting up the case he'd inspected. The older man ran a piece of chalk across the side of the one he'd examined. Then he looked at me sternly. "Pornographic pictures." Turning towards the people waiting behind me, he shouted "Next."

Lindbergh didn't make any more speeches for a year. But then he made three, on coast-to-coast radio hook-ups, condemning Roosevelt, the Eastern Establishment and the Jews for trying to railroad the country into the European war. It hadn't been much of a war any way. Once Poland fell everyone sort of sat on their hands. The Brits called it "the phony war." The French thought it was a joke, *drôle de guerre*," and after their *Blitzkrieg* on Poland, the Germans described it as *Sitzkrieg*. But then in May, Germany attacked in the west and by the middle of June, Paris was occupied. I never did hear from Robert Capa again, not till four years later, back in Paris a few weeks after he went ashore on Omaha Beach in Normandy. It was V-mail, shipped all the way to me at an air base in New Guinea.

2

The name Rankin didn't mean anything to me. We'd met before, though I hadn't remembered. Either he had a better memory than me or the file in his hands had reminded him. Thin, grey hair, parted down the middle, Captain Rankin, US Army, was a prune of a man, probably itching, certainly perspiring, under a tunic shiny from too many pressings, and a Sam Browne belt splitting leather at the buckle across his chest. Evidently, he hadn't been able to replace either, not on his Army pay, since returning from France with Pershing after the Great War. How long had he been a captain? A decade or more? I was feeling sorry for him when I sat down.

Before him on his desk that hot day in late June 1940, was my letter applying for reinstatement in the Air Corps at the rank I'd left it—captain. Beneath it was a maroon file folder from which a half-a-dozen flimsies protruded in three directions. We were sitting in an office in one of the temporary War Department buildings on either side of the Reflecting Pool between the Washington Monument and the Lincoln Memorial. They'd been temporary since the Great War. People had taken to calling it The First World War once the Germans had invaded Poland eight months before.

"Your application will get serious consideration, Mr. Thurlow." Those where his parting words but his look as I rose was "Not a chance!" The salutation, Mr., instead of Captain, made it clear what his recommendation to General Arnold would be. "Hap" Arnold was chief of the Air Corps.

First, Rankin had taken me through a tour of my four years in the Air Corps. I hadn't done any more than my share of drinking and carousing at March Field in California. There was little enough to do out there in the orange groves fifty miles east of Hollywood, nursing flying cadets in and out of a succession of underpowered trainers. But now it conferred a series of blots on my Army copy book.

"Why'd you leave the service in '36?"

"Finished my 4 year obligation." I gestured at his folder. "Knew I wasn't going to get a promotion anytime soon. Got tired of the spit and polish I suppose."

"And now you want back in? Why?"

"There's a war coming, captain. You know it. I know it. I want to serve my country." All this got from Rankin was a smirk.

I'd prepared a lot of answers to the questions I knew he would ask about flying in the Spanish Republican Air Force. Turned out they were easy, too easy—how long had I served, where and when, which unit, what kinds of planes. My answers probably didn't matter.

"Did you support the Spanish Republicans?"

"No interest in politics, sir. I did it for the money."

"I'll bet. Paid a lot better than the Air Corps, eh, Thurlow?"

"Yeh, about $1000 a month." This was at least three times a captain's salary.

Rankin shook his head. "You know you can lose your US citizenship for having served a foreign power in time of war."

I couldn't resist contradicting. "Don't think so. I didn't join up in the States, and last I checked we're not at war with Spain. Signed a peace treaty with them in '98, right?"

He smiled grimly and closed the file, smoothed out the wrinkles in my letter with his palm. Then he spoke again. "Your problem Thurlow, is you're not very good at following orders."

I replied firmly. "There's nothing in my record about insubordination sir."

"I see you're not wearing your West Point class ring, Mr. Thurlow." He proffered his—a large gold one engraved with the Military Academy shield. "I was a couple of classes ahead of you. But I remember you pretty well." I said nothing. What was he getting at? "You must have been ordered to stay away from the nigger a hundred times." Now I understood. "But you wouldn't listen…You ate with him, you marched drill with him. I'll bet you would have roomed with him if you could have shared billets."

I remembered the four years in Coventry—the silent treatment—that Ben Davis had suffered as the only black cadet at West Point. His father was the sole Negro officer in the entire army. Ben Davis was bent on following in his footsteps. He had entered the academy a few years after me. Ben had been one of the very few, like me, who wanted to join the Air Corps. That's what first made us friends.

"Staying away from Davis? Those weren't orders from the TAC, sir." This was the title of the Army officer in charge of each company of cadets at West Point.

"They were orders from your superior cadets, Thurlow. You didn't care for those orders. So you didn't obey them." He was right of course. I'd told the cadets who issued them that they were against Army regs'. Now those cadets and their friends were officers in the US Army, where they could enforce them.

Rankin was silent for a moment. If he was waiting for a reply, an excuse, an apology, I couldn't bring myself to offer one. I too sat there silently, turning my gaze from him to the Reflecting

Pool outside his smudged and sooty window so he couldn't see the anger in my eyes.

Rankin wasn't finished of course. He was going to make his position very clear. "So, first you showed up as a nigger-lover at the Point, and then you fought for the Commies in Spain…No interest in politics, right?" I wasn't going to admit it but Rankin was right. Ever since I'd been a kid, I'd taken sides in history—the Blue against the Grey, when the other kids romanticized the Lost Cause of the Confederacy, the Sioux against the cavalry, when Custer was still a hero, the Iowa homesteaders and ranchers against the railway trusts.

But befriending Ben Davis, going to Spain, it hadn't been politics, not really. It was flying. But I wasn't going to explain myself in any way that would satisfy Rankin or the US Army. All I'd ever really wanted to do was fly, that and get an education.

My people couldn't pay for me to do either, farming someone else's 160 acres of corn west of Waterloo, Iowa. Not the way farm prices were going, right through the '20s. The only way I was going to do either was an appointment to the Military Academy. My father didn't like the idea. He'd raised me to be suspicious of authority—the railways, the banks, the Chicago grain markets. But West Point was the only way I could get an education and fly.

Is it politics if you're always on the side of the little guy, the one who draws the short straw? Right through my experience, it was always the little guy getting the shaft. I was finally sure the army wasn't for me in the summer of '32.

I was sitting in a darkened movie theater with a hundred other cadets, watching the newsreel before the feature. The chief of staff, MacArthur, had the troops attack the shanties of homeless veterans who'd come to Washington and camped out for months asking congress to pay the cash bonus they'd been promised for service in the Great War. Warm and dry, well fed and comfortable, the cadets watched the action unfold on the screen. They began whistling, hollering abuse at the miserable vagrants and down at the heels ex-doughboys cooking their meager meals around campfires before their squalid little paper carton shacks sinking into the Anacostia mud. Then the audience began to cheer the bayonet wielding squads pushing the wretched scarecrows away from their hovels, torching the little they owned, donning gas masks and firing tear gas grenades. I rose and left the movie theater. *Why don't the good guys ever win?*

I resigned my commission first chance I got, in the summer of '36. But I still had to fly, and not crop dusters. I'd read about the Frenchman, Malraux, who organized mercenary pilots to fly obsolete planes for the Spanish Republicans. It didn't seem like politics to me. They just looked like good guys, and at first it looked like they could win.

So I got a passport and left for Spain, hoping to join them. Malraux's unit was washed up even before I'd gotten there. But by then the Russians had begun supplying modern fighters. All the government needed was pilots who could fly them to sweep Franco's planes from the skies. We owned the air till the Messerschmitts arrived in '38.

Was it politics flying for the good guys?

"No interest in politics?" Rankin's question hung in the air between us. He was sitting there, beating a pencil against his blotter, waiting for a reply. Finally I had to say something. "Look, sir. The Air Corps needs experienced pilots, even if it's just for training. The Germans are overrunning France. We'll be in this war soon."

He shook his head. I'd said the wrong thing. "Politics again, Mr. Thurlow?"

"Captain, I've had two years' experience flying some of the most modern ships in anyone's air force, including ours. I can teach pilots what I know, save lives in combat."

A tight smile formed on Rankin face. "We're not fighting anybody, Thurlow. And with any luck we won't be anytime soon." He rose. The interview was over. There was nothing more to say. I had to get up too. No hand shake was proffered. Instead just the words uttered mechanically, "Your application will get serious consideration, Mr. Thurlow."

———

It was a long walk up Wisconsin Avenue to the Willard Hotel. I was going to have to check out quickly if I wanted to stretch the money I had left. But not so quickly that I couldn't afford the walk, just to think things through. I needed work, I still wanted to fly. I hadn't ever flown multiengine planes, so the airlines were out. Were the aircraft companies hiring test pilots? There were flight schools springing up too. How about Canada, the RAF, or the Royal Canadian Air Force? Were they recruiting Americans? The advantage I had, looking for a job flying fighters was I could prove I wouldn't funk it. I'd faced death enough times in Spain to know fear wouldn't stop me. After the first spasm of terror, reflexes took over. Trouble was I'd have to tell recruiters I'd flown in Spain.

The desk clerk turned to get my room key, and found an envelope in my box. "There's a message for you, Mr. Thurlow. He handed me my key and the letter. I glanced at it, Willard Hotel stationary. Not mail, someone had dropped by and written a note. I moved off towards the elevators and opened the envelope as I walked along. It was written with a fountain pen in blue ink with a fine woman's hand.

Dear Mr. Thurlow,

Will you call on me at the China Development Finance Corporation at Dupont Circle at your convenience. Mr. T.V. Soong, my principal, wishes me to place an opportunity before you.

Sincerely yours,

Mai Ling-Chen

I'd noticed the National Press Club building across the street from the Willard. I turned from the elevator and made my way to the club's reading room. It didn't take much research to learn that T.V. Soong was the brother-in-law of the Chinese president, Chiang Kai-shek. Soong was at the center of a financial web that controlled most of China's foreign trade. Suspected of a lifetime of shady dealings, he was the head of his country's military purchase mission to the US. One way and another, China had been at war with Japan since 1931, with the president's family profiting mightily from the opportunities for corruption. Now in 1940, having fought the Japanese almost to a stalemate, China was trying hard to secure American arms and US involvement. The Japanese had made it easy for the Chinese to win American sympathy, repeatedly attacking US Navy patrol boats in Chinese waters, then signing up with the Germans and Italians, finally invading French colonies in Indochina.

Dupont Circle was a ten minute cab ride way. The China Development Finance Corporation seemed to take up the entire fourth floor of a six-storey building. Though I'd arrived without warning, apparently I'd been expected. The welcome was courteous. All I had to do was give my name and the man at the desk in the entry way knew whom I wanted to see. The smile suggested he may even have known why I was expected. He rose and said quietly, "Please come this way." I followed him over a deep carpet to an office door at which he knocked discretely and then opened.

Mai-Ling Chen was seated on a chesterfield in a large drawing room. She didn't look much like Hollywood's idea of a dragon-lady. Plump, middle aged, dressed only slightly more fashionably than Mrs. Roosevelt, she rose, held out her hand and gave me her name in a flawless American accent. "I'm Mai Ling-Chen. Glad to meet you Mr. Thurlow. Thanks for coming."

I would have said 'Nothing better to do,' but it would have been true. She sat back on the brocade of tufted sofa, trying not to look inscrutable. She indicated a generous chair in the same fabric that made a corner with it. There was a decanter of whiskey with matching cut crystal glasses on the low table before me and she poured each of us three fingers without asking. I took the glass. One taste and I was in no hurry to get to the business she'd invited me to discuss. "I expected to talk to a Chinese lady, Miss Chen, but I didn't expect one who's mastered American English completely."

She smiled. "Aha, yes. I was at Mills College, class of '18. It's a small women's college across the San Francisco Bay."

I didn't think four years was enough to have gone native, or learn how to drink, but I let it go. "How can I help you, Miss Chen?"

"You know who Mr. T.V. Soong is?"

"A banker?"

She smiled at my caution. "Yes, and a close advisor of the president of the Republic of China. He has come to Washington to seek help in its defense against Japanese aggression." She stopped. "I didn't mean it to come out sounding like propaganda, Mr. Thurlow…"

It was my turn to interrupt. "Aggression's what I'd call it too." I wanted her to see I knew who the good guys were.

"Anyway, one of the things we need badly is pilots, especially pilots who can fly Russian planes." Now the penny dropped. It was almost as if she didn't have to go on, but I let her. "For several years our air force was heavily supplied by the USSR. And many of the pilots who flew the airplanes were Russian too." She stopped. "They've all had to leave."

I wanted to make things easier for her so I said the obvious. "Now the Russians are allied with the Germans and the Germans are allied with the Japanese. So, the friend of their friend can't be your friend anymore, is that it?"

"Exactly…" She stopped and then took the plunge. "That's where you come in, Mr. Thurlow. You flew Russian fighters in Spain. The very same fighters our air force is equipped with. Mr. Soong wants to offer you a contract to train our pilots to fly them."

I should have said *How did you know?* Instead, I just shook my head. "Sorry, but I'm trying to get back into the US Army Air Corps." The interview with Rankin hadn't gone well. But I thought there was still a chance, maybe not right away, but when things got worse and they started to need experienced men. Besides, there were other possibilities to explore, the aircraft companies, private flight schools, the RAF and the RCAF.

"The Chinese government will pay you more, much more than an officer's salary, even more than you were paid in Spain. And in gold, if you want it that way."

Did they know how much I'd been getting in Spain, I wondered? It didn't matter. I rose. "Sorry. No sale." Mai-ling Chen didn't get up with me. Instead she moved her hand across the brocade, smoothing out nonexistent wrinkles. Then she spoke. There was a hint of reluctance in her very California voice. "Mr. Thurlow, they won't have you, you know." I looked down and said nothing. "The Air Corps, the manufacturers, the flying schools, no one, and they'll stop you from flying for the British, too."

I was angry at her words. "You don't know that. I just had a War Department interview today, this morning. The Army hasn't made a decision yet. They couldn't have."

"I'm sorry. The matter has already been closed. Your meeting was just for show." She paused, held up her hand to forestall my 'How do you know?' "That's all I know. Mr. Soong has friends in the War Department. They told us, last week. That's why you were invited here."

The calm and finality of her tone convinced me. I sat down again. "Even if you're right about the Air Corps, how can they stop me getting a job flying in this country or overseas for that matter?" I addressed the question as much to myself as to Mai-Lin Chen.

"I don't really know. But when Mr. Soong says something, you can bank on it. Someone in the War Department is interested in you." She smiled. "I don't know who, but it must be someone Mr. Soong knows."

I smiled to myself. *So, flying for the good guys again?* T.V. Soong and his corrupt brother-in-law, President Chang weren't good guys, but 500 million Chinese people were worth fighting for.

Mai Ling-Chen took my smile for agreement. Her face became more serious. "One thing more, Mr. Thurlow. There are not many people with your qualifications. You must keep this matter secret. The Japanese will certainly try to put a stop to your work if they learn of it."

A week later I had a ticket on the China Clipper.

3

There's a lot of time to think between Honolulu and Manila, even if it's on a Pan Am flying boat. We were headed for Wake Island, the second leg from San Francisco, on the way to Midway. I was sitting at a window, hour after hour, watching the sun moving slowly towards the right side of an endless Pacific horizon, trying hard to understand what I was doing. Here I was headed from the losing side of one war to the losing side of another, bigger, longer, deadlier one. I guess I knew why.

The clipper was sailing along smoothly at 8,000 feet, much too high above the azure flatness of the Pacific to discern anything but a perfect mirror of the sky. The drone of the four engines was so even there wasn't even a rhythmic beat. Here I was in a white suit, sipping a martini in a reclining chaise. I wasn't living in the same world I had known just a few years before, flying open cockpit air mail bi-planes for the Army across midwestern winters. I shuddered, suddenly remembering the icy wind cutting through my body. It was a job no one wanted in 1934, the year I finished flight school, being the next victim of the Air Corps winter airmail runs. President Roosevelt had cancelled all the corrupt airmail contracts the previous administration had cooked up and given the Air Corps the job, but not the equipment to do it. There were crashes every week in 1934. Nobody wanted to fly the year I graduated from West Point. Nobody, except me and the Negro cadet, Ben Davis. I got the chance. He didn't.

The pilot's voice came over the speakers, speaking quietly under the drone of the four engines on the big wing above our heads. "Just crossed the international dateline folks. It's a day later…or is it earlier? One of the two." With a chortle he switched the speaker off. *Wiseacre.*

What did you want to rejoin the army for anyway? The letter from the War Department had come, just as Mai-Lin Chen said it would, a few days after my interview with Rankin: We regret…services not required… Inwardly I shrugged. *Whoever it was kept you out of the Air Corps, they were doing you a favor.* I knew that, but were they the same people who put T. V. Soong and the Chinese government on to me? And if so, why? What was in it for them?

Trying to think that puzzle through, I fell asleep. It must have been hours later when the pilot's voice on the intercom again woke me. "Folks, you'll be glad to see Midway down there. We'll come in from the west and be on the water in a couple of minutes." I pulled out my old Retina camera, hoping to take a snapshot of the spray off the sponson jutting out from the bottom of the fuselage. The pilot was still talking. "Our route from here to Wake Island was personally plotted out by Pan Am's official trail-blazer, Colonel Charles A. Lindbergh."

The Pan Am clipper, I knew, went all the way to Hong Kong. But my ticket ended at Manila, sixteen hours, two more take-offs and landings east of Wake. Then it would be a slow boat to China.

I was glad to be met at the Manila seaplane terminal by a dapper Chinese man in a white suit like mine, his snap brimmed hat the same shade: almost the "number one son" stereotype out of the *Charlie Chan* films. I hadn't expected to meet anyone and was wondering how to find my way to the Hong Kong steamship lines when he approached me and quietly spoke. "Mr.

Thurlow, please follow me." He was polite but peremptory and evidently felt no need to give me his name. My only case was awaiting me at the end of the quay and the customs procedures were perfunctory, once my guide passed a few American dollars to the agent.

Manila was teeming, a foretaste of China. Our ancient taxi rattled along past only a few docks and wharves before depositing us beside a tramp steamer. My companion got out, paid, and stood with me surveying the rust-stained hulk. "So sorry, but this is the best way to Hong Kong. The liners all stop at Kobe and you can't pass through Japan."

"Couldn't I have flown to Hong Kong? The Clipper is headed that way, isn't it?"

He frowned briefly. "Yes, you might have done. But there's no way to deplane at the Pan Am dock there without being observed. Much easier to slip in by ship." *Why would anyone care?* Then I recalled Mai Ling-Chen's injunction of secrecy. *Why would Japanese observers in Hong Kong even know I was coming?* My question answered itself. The corruption of Chiang Kai-shek's government put every secret up for sale.

I nodded my understanding and he led me up the gangplank, found a Mandarin speaking officer and handed me over. Only then did he smile. "Mr. Thurlow, it's only 700 miles by sea. She'll only take three days or so. Here is a chit for your hotel. Someone will come for you." He held out his hand, said "Good luck," turned, and left. The officer crooked his finger and led me below to a surprisingly pleasant cabin, not quite a stateroom, but one with port holes, a ventilator, and its own bath. As I unpacked it occurred to me that the island-colony of Hong Kong was cut off from China by Japanese occupation of Canton directly across a narrow bay. *How am I going to get past the Japs?* The Chinese had to know what they were doing, didn't they?

I was almost a week in Hong Kong, booked into a posh hotel, just another Caucasian in a tropical weight suit, hard to distinguish from a thousand others, wondering how I was to get to Chongqing, the new capital of the retreating Chinese government. That city, a thousand miles due north, was being bombed regularly by the Japanese, though no one seemed to be reporting it anywhere. There were flights to Chongqing every few days from Hong Kong. DC-3s would take off from Kai Tak airport, in the dark, at unscheduled times, to avoid or evade Japanese interception. Mostly they succeeded, but passengers were advised of the risks.

Hong Kong was a contrast between the neatness, order and tension of the European streets and the frenetic boisterousness of the narrow Chinese trader's alleys. The Brits were anxious about what the Japanese would do next. They'd just invaded the French colonies of Indochina. Would they threaten Hong Kong, Singapore? It was the sole topic of conversation along the gracious verandas overlooking Kowloon, the mainland suburb, across the bay. On the hotel terraces Europeans (and only Europeans) were served long drinks in the late afternoon by obsequious Indian servants in white dinner jackets. What the Japanese Army was up to didn't matter to the Chinese traders. They would carry on just as others were doing everywhere in Japanese-occupied China. This, at any rate, was what I was told by the Brits.

No one told me I couldn't, so one afternoon I took the ferry to Kowloon across the narrow bay. There I ambled through the markets, bazaars, entrepots, watching the push carts trundle by, eavesdropping on truck and barter in a pidgin of Cantonese and English I couldn't understand. I had to conclude the Brits were right. Mostly, these people were far too absorbed in mere survival to worry about which axis their world would revolve around. Their need to survive wouldn't take no for an answer. At every corner there was a hand stuffing some merchandize I didn't want down into my pocket, while the other hand was held up, rubbing four fingers against the thumb, demanding payment for goods received. After a while it was hard to stay good humored about this importunate tactic repeated over and over. It turned out to be a mild foretaste of life on the mainland.

———

It was just after ten o'clock one night that there was a quiet knock on my hotel room door. I was already in bed, looking forward to falling asleep with Yutang's best seller, *Moment in Peking*. It wasn't to be. I opened the door just wide enough to see a woman tricked out in the dress of a bar-girl. At first glance she looked Chinese, but too tall. I was about to tell her she'd knocked on the wrong door when she spoke. "Mr. Thurlow?" I nodded. "Please dress and pack your things." The accent was very British. I pulled open the door to invite her in, but she shook her head and closed the door before her. When I opened the door again, holding my valise, she turned and wordlessly began walking down the corridor to the lift.

Still wordless, she led me out of the hotel. No eyebrows were raised. She was evidently known by the desk clerks. Turning her head both ways along the dark street, she looked at a watch. A moment later a very small, non-descript sedan drove up. She ushered me into the back and slid in after me. The car moved off without a word to the driver.

I broke the silence. "We going to the ferry?" The airport was across the bay in Kowloon.

She shook her head. Then she spoke. "Have you been to Aberdeen Harbour? It's quite a sight, even at night" The car turned away from the harbor and began climbing curving roads upwards into hills invisible in the night.

"I haven't. What is it?"

"It's a city of hundreds of thousands of people who've been living on sampans for years, people born, raised, and died on the water, hardly ever standing on dry land." She fell silent. "Since the Japanese took Canton it's become even more crowded…"

The car now began a steep descent and I could see the moon's reflection, silvery on the waters below. "Are we sight-seeing, at this hour?" I didn't want to sound belligerent. It was dark in the car, and the dim street lamps shined on a silhouette of the woman who answered, "No. We're going to take a sampan up what Europeans call the Pearl River, to Canton."

I made the obvious reply. "Japanese-held Canton?" She only nodded. I added, "We? Does that mean you're coming too?" Again, only a nod. The car pulled off the main road and began crawling along a sea-wall. There in the lapping water were small boats, lanterns bobbing on their squat masts as far into the distance as I could see. Lashed so tightly, the junks and sampans swayed in unison with no water to be seen between. The rows of flat bottom hulls were still swarming with men and women moving from one to the next, their gaunt, drawn faces visible in the full moon and the wan lamps.

My guide opened her door. Before I'd managed to unfold myself from the cramped seat she'd grabbed my case and was leading me onto one of the floating rows. I reached forward to take the valise. She resisted. "Don't worry. I'm not going to steal it."

"Not what I'm worried about, sister." She released the bag reluctantly. "Look, if you're coming with me we might as well exchange names."

She turned again. "I know your name, Mr. Thurlow." Then she began moving again. She spoke as we picked our way along the boats. "I'm Wendy Anying. Wen, actually, but everyone calls me Wendy."

Speaking to her back I replied. "Pleased to meet you, Wendy. Call me Will." The words came out in a breathless rush as I lurched across two sterns loosely lashed together. Carrying the case in the uncertain light made balance-keeping even trickier on the sway of each boat. We must have walked across twenty or thirty of these skiffs, lighters, punts, long boats, reaching out into the harbor. In each there was a small stove still smoking from the evening meal, a tea pot perched above it. Around it men and women smoked, murmuring in the flickering obscurity of a kerosene lamp, paying no notice to passers-by trespassing their house-boats. My guide was moving faster than me and the distance between us soon widened. Her silhouette was easy to follow, tall and thin. I called out, "Wendy…Miss Anying." She stopped and I caught up. "Look, why are we taking a boat? Why can't I fly to Chongqing?"

"Those were my orders." She turned and strode off, balancing nimbly between the sterns. My footing was not so sure. I was beginning to lose her in the dark when we came to the last skiff in the long tongue of boats stretching back to the shore.

She dropped off the boat's stern down to the deck of a squat sampan, where she turned, waiting for me to catch up. As I arrived, an arm reached up for my case. There were two men on board, both elderly, both in faded brown threadbare padded jackets, stained and torn, closed with wooden spindles through loops, indistinguishable from all the other men I'd seen along the floating pier of boats lashed together. As I dropped into the sampan, one man cast off while the other busied himself with a small motor that coughed and seized a few times before beginning a quiet comfortable chug. We moved off, chugging into a channel and then out into open water. I sat down under a canopy amidships. Wendy was opposite me, lighting a smoke from the distinctive Senior Service package in her hand. She passed me the pack. I took one and leaned back, for a moment leaning my head out from under the canopy.

Finally at her ease she pulled the smoke in and let it exit through her nostrils. I did the same. "What now, Wendy?" The only dim light in the craft behind her, it was still too dark to attach a face to the name.

"We run up into the estuary, blend into the traffic and hope we don't meet any patrol boats."

"How much of a chance we will?"

"Not much. Only ever been stopped once and that was by a Chinese police boat working for the Japs. They took a bribe."

Chinese working for the Japs? I didn't understand. "Why would Chinese work for the Japs? Why would the Japs trust them?"

"Don't be simple minded, Mr. Thurlow."

I smiled, unwilling to be insulted. "Call me Will."

"Look, there are lots of Chinese who hate their own government, not just the Reds." I nodded and she continued. "Some are crazy enough to think China woud do better if the Japs ran things. There's a turn-coat government of Chinese, mostly the rich, running occupied China for the Japs. They don't have the man-power or the language to do it for themselves."

I nodded. "And when we get to Canton, what happens?"

"We'll find our way to an unguarded spot on the Japanese front lines and smuggle you across. Then it's just a long train ride to Chongqing." She dropped her smoke over the side, found a cushion and stretched out on her side of the sampan. Long and blue, the narrow silk dress shimmered like the shallow waves lapping up against our boat, as it made slow progress on a calm sea. Wendy saw me glance at the slit up the skirt that showed off a thigh, but she made no effort to hide it. "Let's get some sleep, Will." I was glad to hear her use my name. I stretched out and let the slight breeze of gentle sea air from the bow lull me to sleep.

4

Wendy was shaking my leg. I opened my eyes in the glow of an early morning sun just breaking the eastern horizon. "There's a patrol boat. We need to hide you." Her hand on my shoulder prevented me from rising. I rolled off the bench and, crouching, I scrambled into the small wheel house astern. There I sat, on the damp deck beneath the rudimentary controls of the boat. Doorless and with open windows front and back it was hardly a hiding place at all. Our motor cut out and soon I heard the louder sound of a more powerful engine than ours. Suddenly we were in the shadow of the patrol boat, a craft twice the size of our sampan. Looking up through the open entry I could just see the dark hull looming above us and hear a strident voice in Mandarin, not Japanese. Then I saw Wendy climb up a hemp ladder dropped from the patrol boat. Wedged between body and arm she was carrying the ragged cushion she'd been resting her head on.

I passed the next fifteen minutes in agonizing impatience, wanting to do something, knowing I could do nothing, lurching up a half-dozen times in a resolve that immediately dissolved. Standing under a lantern by our little wheel house, one of the two crew looked down at me twice, moving only his eyes left and right in a universal gesture of 'no'.

At last I saw a woman's foot, leg, and then torso make its way down the rope ladder. The patrol boat cast off and a few minutes later we were again making way up the narrowing estuary. Wendy came over to where I was still crouching. "Wait just a few moments more, Will. When they've pulled far enough away you can get up. She passed a half-smoked cigarette down to me. I wanted to take it as a gesture of intimacy.

We were sitting face to face again, under the canvas canopy amidships. "How did you get rid of them?" Now at last I had a look at her. A long face for a Chinese woman, with a square jaw, cheek bones shaped a distinct plane below the strong epicanthal folds of her eyes. The nose too was Chinese—small and slightly up-turned. She was beautiful, in a way that seemed effortless. The thick jet black hair fell evenly to a freshly cut flat plane at the nape of her neck. There was a glint in her large eyes, the dark brows contrasting with the very white teeth biting slightly at the full lips. But her look was worried.

"I convinced the captain, a Chinaman, we were just running opium from Hong Kong into Canton." 'Chinaman'—it seemed like a term of abuse, surprising in the mouth of a Chinese woman. Contempt, self-loathing? Was she mocking me?

"Opium? How did you do that?"

"I gave him 500 grams of the stuff?" So, that's why she'd carried the cushion up the ladder.

Wendy answered my unvoiced questions. "Sure, we're carrying a couple of kilos." She picked up another cushion. "Don't look so shocked. The Brits have been selling Indian narcotics into China for two hundred years or so. Finances the tea trade, don't you know." The last three words in a haughty British accent, perfectly delivered.

"But I thought you were a Chinese government agent, not a drug smuggler." My tone was harsher than I wanted it to be.

"I'm both." She was returning my tone with a hint of exasperation. "It's the only way to finance the work."

"Trouble is, a pound of opium wasn't enough." She grimaced at a thought. What else did she offer, I wondered? Then she told me. "I had to…offer my charms, to get rid of him."

Fury and shame rose up as suddenly I pictured the transaction in the patrol boat. She could see the flush spread across my face as the shame overcame my anger. I leaned towards her and hissed the words "He forced you…" I'd let this woman save me…that way. I wouldn't even think the words. Suddenly I was loathing myself.

"Calm down. It was business…the business I am supposed to be in." She was staring hard now, measuring my reaction. Had she gotten me back under control? "I'm worried, Will. The patrol boat captain knew your name." She paused. "That's why they didn't fly you out of Hong Kong. The Japs are looking for you. They probably would have shot down the plane if they thought you were on it."

I took a breath. "A DC-3 full of people just to get me?"

Wendy nodded. After a silence, she spoke again. "I've been going back and forth from Hong Kong since the Japanese took Canton. I've been stopped once or twice. Nothing like this ever happened. And now they know my name. Who are you, Will?"

"Just a fly-boy." I thought back to Mai Ling-Chen's injunction of secrecy in Washington. I wasn't going to say more. "Have other mercenaries come through this way?"

"No. It's pretty much just locals and intelligence agents like me slipping into Canton. No one is much interested, nobody asks questions. Bribery does the trick. It's expected. There's pretty much an established price for turning a blind eye. Even works with Japanese soldiers. But this is different. Somebody's looking for you. And they were told where to find you."

"Guess I owe you my life, Wendy." It was all I could say. She'd paid for it.

"We're not out of the woods yet. He took the opium, but that patrol boat captain's still going to pass on his suspicions…"

"What'll I do?"

"What'll *we* do, Will? You've gotten me in too deep to leave your fate to chance. What's so special about you? How come they're so interested in you?"

We were interrupted by one of the boatmen, who asked Wendy a question in Mandarin. She nodded and the other crewmember at the helm moved the boat out of the mid-channel and towards shore.

The Canton waterfront was much like Hong Kong's Port Aberdeen—teeming with lighters, punts, sampans, and junks, lashed together and stretching well into the current of the Pearl River. Though in morning light the scene was a sepia of greys, even the lapping water and the overcast sky.

Our motor turned over quietly as the boat carefully made its way to a low pier meant for touch-and-go landings. As we approached Wendy spoke. "Grab your bag. We need to get off quickly and blend into the foot traffic fast." Blend in? I was half a foot too tall and dressed all wrong.

The narrow alleyways began at the brackish, oil-slicked water's edge. They were dark and crowded. Men and women passed, all equally burdened with bundles tied at the top by rope. There was no room here even for the wooden cowls that spread a load to each side of one's shoulders. These porters' clothes varied from patched rags to traditional caftans skirting the ground, but the faces were all drawn, gaunt, weathered. A few of the men wore a long braid coming out of a hat, but the women's hair was lank and grey. There seemed to be no youth or hope or spirit among them. Their look was matched by the ramshackle structures that sagged beneath a half-dozen levels stacked high enough to keep the lane Wendy had chosen in perpetual shade. She walked ahead as quickly as the flow allowed. No one lifted a head even to notice me looming up behind her.

After enough turns that I'd completely lost my way, we began to mount a rickety almost ladder-like set of warn stair-treads to a fourth-floor doorway. It was at the back of a shabby wooden building that looked like it wouldn't stand up more than another few weeks. Before addressing the lock Wendy pulled a small flashlight from her purse and looked up and down the door jamb, obviously checking for markers she'd left to ensure the absence of uninvited visitors.

Inside she struck a match and lit a kerosene lamp to reveal a single room, crowded with clothes—dresses and underwear, jewelry strewn across small tables, a make-up stand, and a drinks tray. I advanced towards it and lit a Camel, then I offered her one.

Wendy shook her head. Then she kicked off her heels. "I'm going to take my clothes off now. Turn around if you don't want to watch." I wanted to watch but I gave her my back, then swiveling too soon I had a glimpse of her in the kerosene glow. She noticed without any mark of annoyance. Stepping into a one-piece boiler suit, she looked like an airman ready to fly. It was a look I liked. She pulled a small hard suitcase from beneath the bed and began pulling together clothing, make up, jewelry, a few pieces of paper and dropping them in it. Snapping the bag closed she spoke. "Let's go."

I rose, stubbed out my butt and said, "Where to?"

"Safe house a mile away. Too many people know I live here."

I straightened up and saluted, "Aye, Aye Sir," hoping she'd see the complement I was paying.

A few hours later Wendy and I were cooling our heels, trying to pass the endless daylight hours cooped up in a shuttered room well away from the docks. It had been thirty minutes or more from her *pied-à-terre*, up a labyrinth of lanes and alleys beyond the reach of the sun, slanting shafts of light through the smoke of a hundred thousand charcoal stoves. The place was just what we needed, except that right below the large rattan-shaded window, now filtering the wan daylight, was a truck loading supplies for the imperial Japanese Army.

We were finally in one place, sitting easily, at an angle, in two sagging lounge chairs. Wendy had climbed out of her coveralls and into a washed-out kimono sashed in a way that seemed to me calculated to be louche. Or was I just hoping? In the close humid air, I was down to my undershirt.

There was just enough light for us to search one another's faces, for each to begin to figure out who this person we were trapped with, for the moment at least, really was.

As I looked it became evident that Wendy was not exactly Chinese. She was Chinese of course, but there was something a little different about her. She was taller than the stereotype, her gestures and hand-motions weren't so restrained. Then I saw, as a beam of light crossed her face. The irises of her eyes weren't brown. They were hazel.

She was sizing me up as well. "So, tell me a little about yourself, Will, but no secrets, nothing I can give away to the Kenpeitai when they catch me." This was the Japanese military police, more than a match for the Gestapo.

"When, not if they catch you?" Perhaps I'd not heard right. Had she misspoken.

"If I keep doing this they'll certainly catch up to me."

"Stop, then."

"I can't. It's a drug, Will." She shrugged. "You didn't answer my question. I'd like to know a little about the kind of guy I might end up throwing my life away for."

I told her: Iowa, West Point, the Air Corps, resigning my commission, flying Russian planes for the Spanish Republic. Wendy didn't interrupt. When I finished she spoke. "I see why you came to China. You'll be disappointed."

"I was disappointed in Spain. Didn't stop me." We shared a conspiratorial smile. "You?" It was my turn. "What about you? Isn't there a song about you?" I was trying hard to think of it.

"I'm afraid there is. Noel Coward song. 'Half Caste Woman.' I'll sing it for you if you like." She leaned back in the large chair, looked into the shadow of the pitched roofing above us. Then she began in a quiet sultry voice, conjuring every image in the lyric.

> Laugh a bit, drink a bit, love a bit more,
> You can supply our need.
> Chaff a bit, think a bit, what's it all for?
> That's your Eurasian creed.
>
> Half-caste woman, living a life apart.
> Where did your story begin?
> Half-caste woman, have you a secret heart
> Waiting for someone to win?

She stopped, looking at me. I wasn't able to supply the next line of the lyric. She smiled and went on, quietly, breathlessly, languorously, as she leaned back again into the rattan chair, taking long drags from a cigarette between verses. It was as though each one told a chapter in her story.

Were you born of some queer magic
In your shimmering gown?
Is there something strange and tragic
Deep, deep down?

Half-caste woman, what are your slanting eyes
Waiting and hoping to see?
Scanning the far horizon
Wondering what the end will be

Down along the river
The sky is a quiver
For dawn is beginning to break.

Hear the sirens wailing
Some big ship is sailing.
And leaving your dreams in its wake.

Go to bed in daylight.
Try to sleep in vain.
Get up in the evening.
Work begins again.

Half-caste woman, living a life apart.
Where did your story begin?
Half-caste woman, have you a secret heart
Waiting for someone to win?

Half-caste woman, what are your slanting eyes
Waiting and hoping to see?
Scanning the far horizon,
Wondering what the end will be.

She finished and paused. "Back in Hong Kong they think he wrote it for me. But I was twelve when I first heard it. Been my song ever since. You'd think I'd tire of it, singing in the supper clubs since I was 16."

"Half-caste woman?" It was half a statement, half a question as I said it.

"My father was a Welshman, engineering officer on a P and O liner. That's what my mother told me anyway. There were remittances, enough to see me through a convent school over in Kowloon, but I never met him. Don't think I would have wanted to either."

"How'd you get into this racket?"

"Spying for General Cash My Check?" We both smiled. This was the American name for the president of the forlorn, embattled Republic of China. The Nationalist generalissimo Chiang Kai-shek was ever importuning America for money, ostensibly to fight the Japanese, while siphoning off enough money to keep him and his family in power.

"Why not, you're going to work for him, aren't you, Will?"

"And getting well paid." I replied. "What's your excuse?"

Wendy thought a moment and then leaned forward. "I joined the Communists early. But after '37 when the Japanese offensive really got going, it became clear they weren't going to fight the Japs, just lay low and try to survive. The only way I can fight the Japs is working for Chiang."

The silence between us seemed comfortable.

I'd only been in the company of this woman for less than a day, twenty hours or so. But now it dawned on me that whoever she was really, she was having an effect on me no woman, in fact no person, had ever had. It wasn't just that I'd never met someone quite so…what was the right word, *intrepid?* My first emotion, back on the sampan in the Pearl River estuary, had been admiration. She just knew what she was doing, every step, in command. I'd never experienced it so completely, not from anyone. But now those feelings had been replaced by something stronger. It was some combination of care and lust I had never felt before. Care, lust…and something more, a sense of companionship, alliance, union, *contra mundum.*

Sitting across from her in the long shadows of the shuttered windows, I wanted to reach out, touch her…on the arm, the hand, somewhere. But I couldn't. The words of the song came back to me, *Laugh a bit, drink a bit, love a bit more, You can supply our need.* I wouldn't treat her as a half-caste woman. I couldn't do anything but stare at her lovely face.

In spite of myself, I must have been looking at her the wrong way, because she rose from her chair, stepped over to mine and parked herself on the wide arm rest. Then she leaned down towards my face. The kimono opened to reveal a breast. I felt the thick black mane against my neck. She whispered "Sometimes it suits me, this job. Being a half-caste woman…" We never noticed the daylight fade into night.

Neither of us was really asleep when a gentle knock sounded at the door. Wendy rose, pulled the kimono over her body and opened it. There she spoke for a few moments in Mandarin to someone I couldn't see. The door closed and she turned to me. "Time to go." We dressed hurriedly and cases in hand, descended the several flights. There was another of those very small non-descript sedans, like the one we'd used in Hong Kong, where the back alley opened to a street just wide enough for a car that size. We clambered in, cases on our laps. "Where are we headed?"

"North and west, through the front lines. The Japs are thinly stretched. The driver will know a way though that won't cost much in bribes." I nodded. "Then it's the rail head at Qingyuan, about seventy-five miles from here." She was still in charge.

5

A week later we were in Chongqing. A million people in a city I'd never heard of, one edge layered with tenements sliding down a muddy bank into the Yangtze, the other pushing out to the overbuilt banks of another river, the Jailing. Later, flying off the military airport on a long spit of sand in the middle of the Yangtze I saw that the city was haphazardly spread across a range of hills, perhaps a thousand yards wide, hemmed in by these two great brown rivers. Each was a run of swift currents and inshore eddies, that together made Chongqing a seaport fifteen hundred miles inland from the Pacific.

Most of the city was pock-marked by the rubble from three hundred bombing raids over the previous three years. What still stood was a warren of alleys darkened by a forest of jury-rigged electricity poles. The few broad streets lined with concrete and brick were trying hard to look urban as pedestrians, push carts, and rickshaws strode, rolled, and pedaled along them in the absence of cars, trams, and trucks. There was no sun—ever, just a fine but steady rain in the humid September air.

The first thing that struck me about the place was that I was invisible to most of the Chinese, rushing through the streets. No deference, no notice at all. And there were hardly any other western faces among the flood tide of passers-by. The other thing that struck me was that these people were at war, not with the Japanese, still less with the Communists, but with one another.

It was the war of each against all, struggling to survive, in an environment where everything was in short supply and everyone knew it. Their truck and barter had none of the veneer of good humor I'd been offered in the Hong Kong market. The margin between misery and sufficiency was thin and stark.

When I mentioned it to Wendy, she glared. "What did you expect, Will, good manners, deference?"

"Well, you don't seem to be at war with the rest of humanity."

Her voice became angrier. "How would you know? Maybe you're the difference between drowning and keeping my head above water?" I was silent, trying to figure out what she wanted me to understand. Then she shook her head. "I didn't mean that. But you've got to understand that this is China. No one here ever has anything handed to them, you have to fight. Even then you don't get much, never enough."

I pulled her towards me. "I don't have enough of you." Wendy knew I'd fallen for her, hard, maybe even from the moment she'd taken charge back in Hong Kong. She'd liked me well enough to stay when we got to Chongqing.

One morning she came back to the hotel room we were sharing with the keys to a nice flat high up in a western bank building in the middle of the peninsula. The building was high enough to see from the window of our hotel room. "Pack up, Will. We're moving."

I liked the sound of 'we.' "How'd you wangle it?"

"Owners are scared of the bombing. They rented it for a song." That was when I realized she was staying in Chongqing, staying with me.

———

I was training a dozen pilots of the 24th Pursuit Squadron of the Chinese Air Force in the niceties of the Polykarpov P-16 fighter plane, the same type I'd flown in Spain. It was a solid, maneuverable platform for guns and cannon, and pretty much ruled the air over Madrid till the German Condor Legion got its Messerschmitts in '38.

By now the Japanese fighter planes had made the P-16 obsolete in China too, but there was no alternative. The Russians had sold the Chinese plenty of them. In fact, the 24th Pursuit Squadron had more planes than pilots. But with no spare parts coming in from the Soviet Union every week the number of planes the mechanics could keep flying got lower.

Once you got a P-16 into the air, it was tricky to fly. Just looking at it showed why. The fuselage was short and fat, the wings were stubby. It was a modern ship all right, all metal, enclosed cockpit, retractable landing gear. But loaded up with a cannon to go along with its machine guns, it was too heavy, and the center of gravity was too far forward. In the air, even when straight and level, you couldn't just let it fly itself. What it could do, at least in the hands of an experienced pilot, was maneuver out of trouble, banking, turning, even spinning its way out of range when faster German fighters bounced it. I was the experienced pilot who'd done that, at least until I'd been shot down. I had to hope I could teach my tricks to the Chinese cadets and that they'd work against Japanese Zero fighters once we began to see them. There was one two-seat dual control ship on the field I could use for training.

I liked my students, all from wealthy families, ones that could have bought them out of service. Even the few who hadn't spent time abroad before the war spoke a fluent colloquial English. I tried to get them to teach me a little Mandarin, so I could talk to the ground crew. These kids were drawn to the glamor as well as the thrill, the feeling you get in the air, of freedom in every direction. But they knew they were probably going to die up there. It wasn't a bitter knowledge, but somehow an expression of what their country meant to them. I couldn't share it.

Meanwhile, the Japanese were bombing Chongqing several times a month. Chiang Kai-shek had moved his capital there from Nanking. It was almost two thirds of the way to Tibet at the western end of China, so he was ceding the coast and most of the great cities to the Japanese. The Japanese army couldn't advance that far west, so the bombing was meant to destroy the government by demoralizing the residents of its political capital. They were killing a lot of people, but all it proved was that bombing civilians just strengthens their resolve to resist. It was a lesson the Germans were to learn over London six months later.

My pilot-cadets were straining to do something. By the autumn of 1940 I figured they could handle their machines well enough. Besides, I hadn't seen any modern Japanese fighters—Zeros or Oscars—accompany their bombers over the city.

———

The Japanese came twice that month, more than a hundred bombers each time. My boys went up. They managed to knock out a half-dozen of the Japs with no losses. Meanwhile all I did was cower in a bomb shelter with Wendy.

It was dark from dust and smoke, one day in the middle of September, 1940, after a long raid, when we emerged, along with a couple hundred others, from the bomb shelter dug down into a hillside. I had to get away from the packed bodies, their smell and the heat, the closeness of strangers' faces breathing at you. When Wendy said she needed a drink, I didn't disagree.

"But not the Bob-a-link." It was a supper club for Europeans and the westernized Chinese on the take from Chiang's regime. Wendy performed there three nights a week. I wondered why she hadn't gone back to Canton to resume her espionage work. I wasn't going to ask. I liked the arrangement too much.

We found something that resembled a bar and took a small table, on which a candle burned in an ashtray advertising Pernod. My Mandarin even got us a couple of passable scotches, or maybe the barman was humoring me. We were almost alone in a space no less dark than the gloom outside the bar's open door.

Wendy lit a cigarette when the drinks came. I could tell she was going to unburden herself. We'd been together continually since that night she'd found me in Hong Kong three months before. It hadn't been easy for either of us. I'd never before shared my life, my bed, my thoughts with anyone. Wendy had probably never treated a European—that's what I was in the East—as anything but a mark. The war had broken down that barrier and now we were a number. She gulped and then spoke. "Will, I never thought I'd care about anyone, not till I met you. It wasn't just that you needed me, counted on me…"

"You mean followed orders?" I smiled and covered her hand.

"Not just that. I know how you feel about me. You haven't hidden it. I feel like we're some kind of a team, us against the world. And I love it." She gulped. "I love you." I didn't feel the need to reply. She knew. "I've refused to go back to Canton. I'm just going to sing for my supper here. I'll pass on what I hear to the *Juntong.*" This was the government's intelligence service. "But I want to have a life…" She reached for the back of my neck, pulling my head close to hers. She was too tough to cry, but the voice was telling me more than words as it cracked slightly. "With you."

"You've got it, lady." I whispered. Even in the gloom of the bar I could see the need for reassurance in her eye. "Not going anywhere, not without you." I thought for a moment. What did this woman I loved really need from me? I was prepared to provide it if I could. "Tell you what, let's get married."

"No. Not here, not yet. When this war is over."

I frowned. "We can't wait that long, Wendy. Besides our side's going to lose."

"No, Will. Japan can't win this war. There are just too many of us, not enough of them, and the country is too big. Somehow… we'll win." She paused. "But I need you to live. I'm worried about your flying." Now I was silent, worried she was going to demand something I couldn't give her. Wendy understood. "I know you have to fly. I'd never take that away from you. But promise me you won't…fight."

I shook my head. "Don't worry."

"I can't help it. I hate them…I wouldn't be able to stop myself if I had the chance to shoot one down. But you can't. Promise me. I couldn't live with the fear of losing you."

"I promise. I'd never…" What would reassure Wendy? "I couldn't. I'm not a combatant. My country isn't at war with Japan. If I started shooting at them it would be…well, murder, maybe even a war-crime."

Wendy's laugh was sardonic. "Who'd prosecute you? Who'd even stop you if they knew? No, Will, but believe me, if you get into this shooting war, I'll leave you, I swear. I've lost too many people already to face losing someone I'm counting on."

There was a determination in that lovely face I couldn't miss. There was only one thing to say. "I promise." There and then, at that moment at least, I meant it. She read my face and smiled.

———

Wendy started teaching me Mandarin. I was eager to learn. Right from the start, it helped me on the airfield.

Through that fall, the Japanese bombers kept coming, hundreds of them, now escorted by small numbers of Zero fighters, just enough to knock off any of my boys who were silly enough to dog fight. I'd made it clear the only strategy that worked with the P-16 was to dive from the sun and keep going down after firing on the bombers. But the young pilots had too much moxie to listen. One-by-one we lost pilots till there were more serviceable planes on the ground than flyers to use them. That's when I started flying missions. I couldn't help myself. It was like slipping into one of the hundred opium dens without anyone noticing. You couldn't do it just once and after the third time you were a goner. How long before Wendy found out? Maybe never if I was careful

And lucky.

The Japanese had been bombing Chongqing several times a month, as weather permitted. The rural country stretching west from the Japanese bases supported a sprinkling of early warning spotters radioing dispatches, giving direction and numbers of bombers. But there was no longer much we could do with the information.

One day in late December, it was the turn of another city of a couple of million people no one outside China had ever heard of, Chengdu.

Our base, a gravel strip on the sand spit in the middle of the Yangtze twelve miles north east of the city, got word that a couple hundred bombers were headed to Chengdu, two hundred miles west and north of us. With four planes and three pilots there wasn't much chance the boys could do more than break up their formations. But at least we could try. We, I realized with a rush of adrenalin, included me. I grabbed my flight helmet, jumped into the last ship, and followed my Chinese students down the runway.

We had to keep the mixture lean just to reach Chengdu and have enough fuel to engage and return to base. The three pilots with me understood and we arrived in good order, but there was no sign of the Japanese bombers and nothing to do but loaf over the city, waiting. My wing-man saw them first, a hundred or so, below and to the east. What we didn't see were the eight Zero fighters flying in the midday sun above.

We waited till the slower two-engine bombers arrived beneath us and then cut through them, firing canon. It was enough to break up a stack of a dozen planes in four Vees. At least one of the planes began to smoke from an engine. We couldn't tell who got him and we were too busy forming up for another go to see whether the damaged ship would recover or go down. Climbing is slower than diving and with our heads turned towards the bomber formation none of us, me included, saw the Jap fighters that now pounced from the sun.

There was the terror again, the bitter bile in my mouth I'd tasted in the Spanish air, turning my chilled skin instantly hot with rancid sweat. It was all I could do to slew the plane into a spin that I hoped would fool my attacker into thinking I was a goner so he could turn to another target. The P-16's best stunt was its tight spin, easy to start, easy to stop. But there was no cloud cover that day, nowhere to hide. I pulled back and straightened out at two hundred feet, over a patched quilt of small cultivated fields. Looking up I could see two of our P-16s plummeting out of the sky, each at the front of a trail of smoke that made it easy to follow them down. I watched both auger into the farm land, billowing yellow fire and grey dust. There were no Zeros or bombers to be seen above. But looking at my fuel gauge it was hopeless trying to head back to Chongqing. I pulled a map onto my lap and tried to find an air field. My finger found something marked Fenghuangshan field, ten miles south of the city. I had to decide whether to head that way, in the direction the Japanese had been heading, or turn back towards Chongqing and dead-stick into as flat a farmer's field as I could find. At my altitude I could see too many stone walls and irrigation ditches between the small fields to fancy the chances of my very nose-heavy craft. I'd have to try for the field.

It was easy to spot the airfield, from the smoke rising and bending into a west wind. At least some of the Jap bombers had decided to make it a target. There were a half-dozen Chinese planes lined up neatly, mainly obsolete American Hawk 75s by the look of them. I banked in for a landing on the grass and dirt field. It was there that my luck ran out, or my stupidity kicked in. I brought the plane down and was rolling easily along the almost flat ground, engine at idle, about to turn for a taxi to the buildings and hangars at the field's edge. Suddenly the ground gave way beneath my gear. I felt the plane shudder as its propeller bent into the earth and twisted the whole plane with it. The left wing dipped, its landing gear buckled and suddenly I realized I'd run right into a bomb crater, one I should have looked for as I came in to land.

By the time I unbuckled, pushed the canopy back and climbed out, there were a couple of ground crew members standing near the broken wing, shaking their heads. They weren't expecting an American to clamber out of a Russian plane flying Republic of China markings. They smiled at my smattering of Mandarin, and began replying at a speed I couldn't handle. All I could do was shrug my shoulders and ask them to slow down. It was then I realized that this P-16's flying days were over. This ship couldn't be repaired and there might be no more at the 24th field on that sand spit in the Yangtze. I'd just crashed my way out of a job.

I was a week getting back to Chongqing and for the first three days Wendy had no idea where I was or even whether I was alive or dead. When I finally reached her by phone she was livid. "So, you're alive." The relief turned icy. "Well, don't expect me to be around when you get back." The line went dead. When I dialed again, there was no answer.

There was no sign of Wendy when I finally got back to our flat in Chongqing. No sign even of her things. Almost immediately I recognized that she'd left, moved out, carried through on her side of our two-sentence phone conversation. I began to look for a letter, a note, some sign from her. Not a trace, not a mark she'd ever been there. Nothing. The bedroom looked as impersonal now as a hotel room. I found myself collapsing into a chair, facing the neatly made bed. *Damn you, Wendy…No, damn you, Will. You knew what the woman you loved was made of.* The emptiness I felt swamped everything. I leaned forward, tasting bile creeping up my throat. The same bile I'd tasted when the Jap planes bounced us above Chengdu.

It was dark when I finally rose from the chair. I thought I knew where I'd find Wendy.

I heard her voice even before I walked into the floor of the supper club that night. It was dark everywhere except the circle of bright spot-light below her shimmering gown. She was finishing a Cole Porter song, "Just One of Those Things," and moved out of the light, but the applause brought her back. She looked around, perhaps sizing up the audience, and began to sing something I'd never heard before. It took only a few lines of the lyric to see why I'd never heard it, not on the radio State-side at least.

When the only sound in the empty street
Is the heavy tread of the heavy feet
That belongs to a lonesome cop
I open shop
When the moon so long has been gazing down
On the wayward ways of this wayward town
That her smile becomes a smirk,
I go to work.

I was beginning to burn as the mournful image washed over me. Could she see me there in the dark? Was she sending me a message? It was all I could do to stand still at the back of the room, waiting for the set to end. The lyrics got worse.

Love for sale, appetizing young love for sale
Love that's fresh and still unspoiled
Love that's only slightly spoiled
Love for sale
Who will buy?
Who would like to sample my supply?
Who's prepared to pay the price
For a trip to paradise?
Love for sale.

Now she faded away in the applause that spent itself in the resignation that there would not be another encore. The spotlight went out and the house lights rose. A maître-d' approached and recognized me as a frequent patron. Before he could say a word, I turned and left.

I was three streets away when I finally decided what to do. I dropped my smoke to the ground, ground it out and went back.

There was no trouble at the stage door. The old man providing a minimal kind of security knew me well and ushered me into the cramped hallway between the performer's door and the club floor. I found my way to Wendy's closet-like dressing room, and saw the line of dim light still visible across the bottom of the closed door. She was still there. I knocked. She knew the knock.

"Go away." Nothing more.

6

I opened the unlocked door. Wendy was at a small dressing table, in her old kimono, unbelted and open in the close heat of the airless space. Staring into a mirror she was removing makeup, she made no effort to cover up but turned in resignation and tilted her head up towards mine.

"May I sit?" I pointed at the stool in the corner. She nodded acquiescence, but offered no other encouragement. I dropped on to the seat. "I'm sorry. I know it was wrong. I broke a promise. But I'm still alive." I waited for a response. None came. "I can't lose you. I'll give it up, I swear." On the inside I meant it. How to convince her?

"Will. I've told you. I'm not hitching my wagon to someone who's going to get killed before we can even start a life."

"I understand, I do…If we stay together I'll quit flying altogether. I'll do whatever it takes to stay alive."

She shook her head slowly. "You didn't need to fly that bombing run to Chengdu. You'd promised me, and that didn't stop you. You didn't do it out of any special loyalty to the Republic of China. You did it because you're addicted, Will." I opened my mouth to speak but she raised a hand. I knew I had to listen. "Flying is the only thing that keeps you going, really. Isn't it? And here, flying is going to mean fighting." She shook her head. "No, Will. I can't trust you. I can't afford it." She was burning bridges so she wouldn't have to hear me plead again. "I didn't want to fall in love with you to begin with. Well, it happened. Flying is too dangerous to build a life on. But against my will I couldn't stop myself…But flying *and* fighting. That's too much."

I heard those words, *I didn't want to fall in love with you.* I grabbed on to them. "So, you do love me."

"It's not enough, not for me. If you'd steered clear of the fighting…" She pulled her kimono around herself. "But you can't help it. There's a war on, and maybe you've taken sides. Our side. I don't know why. But you're going to fight. I know it. Then you'll die. And where'll I be?"

"Well, I'm going to have to stop. There are no more planes to fly. I crashed the last P-16 we've got here at Chengdu."

"You can promise, you can even convince yourself for a minute that you're serious. But you'd just be a drunk, drying out on the wagon, waiting to fall off. You can't stop. I know what's coming and I know you won't resist. That's why I packed up and got out."

"What are you talking about?"

"I hear things…in the club, when I'm making the rounds, drinking with the customers." I waited. She said nothing further.

That was when I made my fatal mistake. Curiosity got the better of me, or was it my addiction? Suddenly I wasn't thinking about Wendy, but about…the war, fighting, flying. "What've you heard?"

She grimaced. "Chennault has gone to the US to bring back a lot of new planes and they'll be looking for Americans to fly them."

I couldn't stop myself from a low whistle as I let my breath out. Chennault was Claire Chennault, a former officer in the US Army Air Corps who was Chiang Kai-shek's most influential foreign military adviser. I couldn't keep excitement out of my voice. I was making things worse, and I knew it. "What exactly have you heard?"

"It's not very nice, what I heard, not for us Chinese. But probably good news for you flyboys." The tone was impersonal. Wendy had really written me off. *How do you just do that to someone you love?* What I should have asked myself is why I cared about this news, if I really loved her, and I did. Of course, she was right. The news was the lure of the opium den getting control of me.

Maybe Wendy thought the more she told me the more likely I was to give up on her, leave her alone. She just kept filling my opium pipe. "The US government is selling a hundred fighter planes to a shell company. One of Chiang's in-laws set it up. These planes are ones the Brits ordered but don't want anymore." I calculated quickly. They had to be Curtiss P-40s, a serious improvement over the Soviet plane I'd been flying, but still too slow to play on the same terms with German fighters. "The shell company will double the price and then sell them on to the Republic of China. It'll be a cool couple of million split between Cash-My-Check, his wife's relations and Chennault."

Wendy had managed to crowd love out of my head with politics. I asked, "And nothing anyone can do about it?"

"Do about it? Whose going to do anything about it? It's the way our government works."

Now my question had admitted it to her, to myself, that Wendy was right about me. I couldn't, wouldn't give up flying. But I still needed her too. Telling her again was all I could think of. "Look, Wendy, I love you. You say you love me." I pleaded. Why can't that be enough right now? Whether I fly and fight or not, we don't know what's coming." I wasn't in control of my face any more. I was crying for the first time since I was seven. "Can't we just stay together as long as possible? Why do we have to give up that happiness before they make us do it?"

She was brushing tears from my eyes as she spoke. "You've got to understand. I love you too much for that. If I know you're going to die, it haunts every minute we're together, no matter what we're doing. You'll be shot out of the sky. And then the rest of my life I'll feel the way I did those first couple of days last week when I thought you were dead. I won't do that to myself." She stood. "Come find me when this war is over, Will. Now get out." The voice was quiet but resolute.

I got up and left. When I went back two nights later she wasn't there. On the small marquee at the entrance her name was covered over. No one in the front of the house seemed to know anything. She'd quit, that's all the manager said. The maître d' knew less and was too busy to talk anyway. I went around to the back alley, where I'd been greeted at the stage door by the elderly Chinese man. When he saw me coming down the dim alley he smiled, held up a hand and nipped into the door. Coming halfway up the alley he held an envelope in his hand, which he passed to me with a formal bow. I tore it open, but the light was too dim for reading. We moved back towards the stage door and the old man held it ajar. I was able to make out the words in the light that shone out.

Will,

I know you won't take no for an answer. So, I've gone back to Canton. Going back to work, just like you're going to. It will be easier for both of us if we can't see each other.

I'll find you after the war.

Wendy

7

The next morning I woke with a sinking feeling. There was nothing keeping me in Chongqing anymore and there wasn't anywhere else to go. I was adrift. The money would stop now that there were no more planes and no more cadets to train them on. I clambered down the hundreds of steps that led to the Yangtze, and found a rickety taxi that would take me across the bridge to the air field. There I cleared my locker and desk—just my flight log and an extra helmet and goggles. The local rep of T.V. Soong's China Development Corporation was already there, waiting for me with a last paycheck. I wanted to marvel out loud that an enterprise so corrupt could be that efficient in cutting losses. But there was no point berating a low level flunky who was just trying to get by. Now the problem was to get out of China.

But when I got to the US Embassy that afternoon everything changed. I'd been checking in on an informal basis with the air attaché, a guy I'd known slightly in flight school. Andy Logan had been a major in costal artillery but by the early '30s knew that was a dead end in this man's army, so he'd transferred to the Air Corps in '34. Now he was a lieutenant colonel itching to get back to the States as its outfits began building up.

Logan's door was open. "Thought I'd be seeing you sooner rather than later." He rose from his desk and held out a hand.

"News travels that fast in Chongqing? Only this morning I was paid off."

"No. The embassy sent you a letter asking you to come in. Didn't you get it?" I shook my head. Living with Wendy I used a post box address and hadn't checked it in days. "Well, glad you stopped by." He pointed to a chair, picked a packet of American cigarettes and offered me one, which I took. We puffed away companionably for a few moments.

"Look, Andy, now I've been paid off, I'd like to go back to the States." He frowned slightly. "No, no…I won't try to get back in the Air Corps. It's just…" I thought of telling him about Wendy but decided it wasn't Andy Logan's business. "I need a change of scene."

"That's too bad. We had other plans for you." Andy pulled at his middle desk drawer and withdrew a manila envelope that he passed to me. "I ought to ask for proof of identity before I do this." He smiled. "Open it." I did as he asked.

January 3, 1941

To: William Thurlow, captain (ret), US Army

From: Chennault, C., Lt. Col. (ret), US Army, Military Advisor to the President of the Republic of China

CONFIDENTIAL

Greetings:

I herewith invite you to join the Central Aircraft Manufacturing Company of China, as a consultant, test pilot, and trainer.

Should you agree to participate, you will be paid $650 per month for a one year term of service, renewable on good behavior and military necessity.

Duties are expected to commence February 1, 1941.

I looked up at Andy. "What's this all about?"

"You don't get it, do you?" I was silent, confirming his judgment. "Chennault's gone to Washington, along with Chang's brother, Soong. They're buying a hundred P-40s the Brits don't want. And they're scrounging for pilots to fly them out here against the Japs."

"Doesn't say anything about that here." I passed my hand over the letter.

Logan grimaced. I was obviously being dense. "'Course not. US is neutral. Roosevelt is conniving with the Chinese behind the back of Congress. There'll be hell to pay with the America First crowd when they find out." America First was the group agitating to keep the US out of the war. Lindbergh was its most famous member. Logan smiled, hoping I'd understand what side he was on. "Lucky bastard! All that dough and the chance to fly P-40s against the Japs, while I get to fly this desk at 135 bucks a month."

If he was right, it was like being back in the Air Corps but on much better terms. "Why do they want me?"

"Should be obvious. To begin with, you're here. You've got a lot of experience. More than guys who've been in the service all the time since West Point. The P-40s not so different from the Russian ships you've been flying. Heavy in a dive, well armored, but a bit too slow straight and level. You know how to take advantage of that kind of plane. Chennault has been developing Russian fighter tactics since he got here. That's where you fit in."

I leaned back and took a breath. "How does Chennault even know about me?"

"Somebody does, Will." He rose, walked around his desk and my chair to close the door. "Almost from the moment I reported to Washington that you were here last year, the War Department has been asking for weekly reports...about you... by name."

"Who's been asking? Why do they want to know?"

"That's the thing. No signature, just G-2, Air Corps Chief of Staff." G-2 was army-language for intelligence. "No reason given. Every week, like clockwork, 'Report status William Thurlow, Captain (ret.), now employed by Chinese Development Corp as flight instructor.' Every week, same request. Always marked 'Secret. Eyes Only.' Somebody up there must like you." He paused. "You didn't hear it from me."

"Still doesn't explain why Chennault would tap me for his new group."

"Will, don't you understand. This project has approval all the way up the chain of command through Hap Arnold to the President." Arnold was the chief of the air staff. "Whoever's doing the leg work was probably aware of those reports on you we've been filing. Hell, they may have been the ones who asked for them. Seems to me you've got a friend in high places."

Why, I wondered, not for the first time, would someone up the chain of command want to keep tabs on me? Was it the same person who wanted to keep me out of the Air Corps? I smiled. "Where do I sign, Andy?"

"Atta boy!" He rose and slapped me on my back. Then he went back to his desk. He handed me a letter already typed.

I herewith accept employment by the Central Aircraft Manufacturing Company to provide testing, training, and instruction in the flight of such airplanes as the company acquires, for a period of one year from date of this letter.

There was a line at the bottom on which my name had already been typed. Andy's fountain pen was in my hand. The paper was an inch away, below it. Suddenly I stopped. *Too fast. Think again, Will.* I heard the voice in my head. "I don't know…"

"What's stopping you?" The tone wasn't urgent or exigent, just inquiring. Andy wasn't going to pressure me.

"I guess I'd like to think about it overnight." I put the pen down and looked at the honest open face before me. "Andy, you and I, we know what's going on here, in Chongqing, in China… The poor peasants are paying the price of the Jap invasion, the people in the cities too, so are millions of soldiers, no rations, no arms, no leadership. Meanwhile the government and Chang's family are all making fortunes off the war, off us too."

"So?"

"I'm not sure I want to be a part of that anymore. They can't win the war that way."

"They don't have to. They just have to outlast the Japanese. They're more worried about the Communists in Yunnan anyway."

"But where does that leave us?"

"Well, everybody knows we're headed for war with Japan. They figure we'll win their war for them by defeating the Japs."

"There's a lot of isolationism back home, Andy. The US will never fight a war this far away."

"There's where you're wrong, Will. They'll stop Roosevelt from fighting in Europe alright. But the army and the navy are gearing up to fight the Japs. They can't wait to get at them. Don't you see that's what's driving this whole project of Chennault's."

I rose. "I'll think about it, Andy. Give me a few days."

He smiled reassuringly. "Take it. The offer isn't going away. It's what you've wanted. A ticket right back into the Air Corps when…if we join the war against the Japs." I knew he was right. But it bothered me. Was the War Department so interested in every last pilot who'd left the service, or was it just me?

8

In the end I decided I had to sign up with Chennault's shell enterprise—the Central Aircraft Manufacturing Company. Wendy had been right. It was a job I wanted.

Two days later I was back in Andy Logan's office. Once I signed the sheet of paper, he reached into his desk and pulled out another slip as well as a thicker manila envelope. He passed the slip to me. "Here's a chit for first month's pay. It'll have to last."

"That's alright. I've still got plenty from my Chinese paymasters. Living here is as cheap as life gets."

Without comment he handed me another envelope. It was open. Apparently Andy had read it already. "Your instructions, Will." I began reading the orders. I had to get myself to Rangoon, Burma, where the planes would arrive from the States in crates, be unloaded and assembled. Then maybe I'd get a chance to fly one. "Rangoon, Burma? How far is that from here?"

"It's about a thousand miles, and you've got plenty of time," I read further as he went on, "The planes won't get to Rangoon for another three months."

"How do I get there?"

"China Air's still flying three times a week. Here to Kunming, then Lashio to Rangoon. DC-3s we sold to their air force but ended up doing something else." He shrugged. The DC-3 was the latest in passenger planes state-side too. "It'll cost you half your first month's pay."

"I got three months to get there. Maybe I'll hitch on the Burma Road." We both laughed. A hundred thousand Chinese coolies had been forced to build a highway through Burma from India to supply Chang's armies. Then the British closed it to pacify the Japanese. They couldn't afford another fight when they had their hands full keeping the Germans at bay.

———

I could have stayed in Rangoon forever…if Wendy had been there. Even without her, living was easy, too easy. Like a drug, it drove away the ambition even to rise from the chaise longue overlooking the broad square between the grand white buildings of the British Raj. The city was nothing like China, not the European part of it any way. Rangoon seemed to have been purpose-built on a neat rectangular grid, at the great bend of a broad river a score of miles from the Indian Ocean. It was peopled by just the sort of loyal Indians and mercenary Chinese required to enable the English to effortlessly rule. Where the Chinese and the natives lived, and exactly how they got on, was not visible from the great open squares before the white man's hotels, banks, counting houses, law courts, and government buildings.

Rangoon was India without the turbulence I'd read about every day in the morning newspapers. After Spain and China, I couldn't begrudge myself the luxury, even as I hated it in principle. I would sit in the shade for hours watching the orderly files of turbaned Sikhs marching through the midday heat going about the business of serving the colonial elite.

The rare times I was up just before nine, I'd see the cabriolets and convertibles, disgorging the merchant bankers, plantation officers, and shipping agents in their dove-grey suits, leaving chauffeurs or carriage drivers to carry their women-folk to the next destination. By late afternoon I'd find myself propping up the hotel's long teak bar, astride the gleaming bamboo parquet, listening to the Sahibs tell each other how well they were doing out of the war. With a million men under arms, and thousands already fighting Germans for their British masters in Egypt, the Indian Army had an insatiable demand for Burma's rice.

Each evening I'd still be in the hotel's terrace bar long after the gleaming brass began to reflect the lamps as they were turned on. No one was rude enough or interested enough to ask me what I was doing in Rangoon. The most I'd hear was "American, eh?" What was I doing most evenings? I was waiting for Wendy to walk in the bar, up the stairs from the open square. Day dreaming, I'd spin out a story of how she'd come in, and on the arm of which Hong Kong merchant banker she'd arrive. I wouldn't care, so long as she was here, safe and ready to give me another chance. Night after night a long, strong drink before dinner made me mournful. In my mind's eye I would dress her… in the half-caste's shimmering gown…, and watch as she stood at the top of the stair, surveyed the room, and finally focused on me. Then the spell would be broken by someone's shoulder jostling me at the bar, or the request for a light, or the barman asking me if I wanted another.

I'd spent the better part of two weeks killing time at the bar. 1941 was well into February when my idyll ended. I was sitting in the hotel lobby, reading a two-day-old newspaper from Calcutta, full of the great British victories over the hapless Italians south and west of Egypt. The Eyeties had apparently become no more formidable since the Spanish Civil War. Suddenly there was a shadow across the page and someone was standing quietly till I noticed him. I looked up. Before me was a slight man with owlish eyes framed by round glasses. He spoke.

"Mr. Thurlow?" I nodded. "I'm Dan Gourlie, from the Central Aircraft Manufacturing Company. I think you work for us?"

I rose from my chair, put out my hand. I hadn't been forgotten after all. "Right."

Gourlie was studious looking with clear-frame glasses on a face without landmarks to remember it, but when we shook hands I could feel the callouses of a working man. He smiled sheepishly. "We're almost ready for you now."

"Ready for me?"

The smile persisted. "We were here about two weeks before you came." I calculated. It meant Gourlie had been in Rangoon a month. "We had word you'd arrived but decided to give you a bit of a break. Didn't really need you anyway."

"And now you do?"

"Yup."

He pointed to the rattan and bamboo lounge chairs across from the bar. It felt like a gentle command to take a seat for a briefing. I complied. This man had a way of making you trust his authority I'd rarely experienced.

"We've set up our assembly hangar, uncrated the planes, and started to put the P-40s together. I've got one test pilot taking them through their paces, but we're going to need you too. And then we'll have to fly them up country."

"Where've you been working? No one in these parts seems to have heard of you."

"We're tucked into a corner of the Rangoon airfield. I've had orders to keep things as quiet as we can. The Brits aren't at war with the Japs and what we're doing could upset them." I nodded. "Still it's a pretty big operation. A hundred ships, well ninety-nine, to put together, with more than a hundred Chinese mechanics on the job. Had to order up a couple trucks just to get the crates off the docks and then rebuild some sheds away from prying eyes at the Rangoon airport."

I couldn't help being impressed with the dimensions of his task along with its invisibility. "And now you're ready to see if they'll fly?"

"Got one test pilot already—Byron Glover. But they're rolling out a couple a day and we'll need all the help we can get. If you'll come out to the field tomorrow, you can familiarize yourself with the work. Ever fly a Tomahawk?" This was the trade name Curtiss had given the P-40, the latest of a line of aircraft called Hawk they'd sold around the world.

"No, I left the Air Corps in '36. But I did fly the P-35 a bunch of times." This was a precursor to the P-40 that had been tested by the Air Corps in 1935.

"It'll have to do, I suppose."

"Been flying Russian models the last few years…tricky planes compared to the P-35 anyway."

He rose and handed me a card. "You'll have time to adjust to the P-40." I looked down at the card. It was his business card. On the back was a small map of where the sheds and hangar were to be found at Rangoon airport. By the time I looked up he was quietly walking away back to the stairs out of the hotel.

By ten the next morning I was being shown around by the other test pilot. Byron Glover wasn't an Air Corps flyer, but he'd been a pilot for the Curtiss company and I was glad he'd be there to get me started and share the testing. We walked through several sheds where engines were being serviced and a large hangar where wing assemblies were joined to fuselages.

Coming around a crate from which a dozen men were slowly pulling out a complete wing, we met another American. "Will, this is Andy Sargent. He's in charge of the Chinese mechanics putting the planes together."

I was impressed. "You speak Mandarin, Andy?" I knew from eight months in Chongqing how hard that was.

"Nope, but I've got about ten guys who speak English—Chinese-Americans trained in the States." He pointed to a card affixed to the wing. "Together we've figured out a check list for each team, and had them written out." He nodded to the workmen swarming over a fuselage. "These guys are great. Smart, hardworking, you only got to show them once!"

Glover, the pilot, nodded. "Seems to work out alright. I've taken six ships up so far and every one has checked out." I was reassured. "Come on, Will, let's get you in one of the planes."

There were two P-40s at the end of the assembly building. I'd only seen pictures before, but they didn't do the plane justice. It was pleasing to look at, especially after months with the pudgy Russian P-16s stubby wings, flat nose, and over-sized tail that screamed out makeshift and jury built. Even on the ground, standing stock still, these two planes just looked fierce, each ready to snort flame from a half-dozen jet black twin exhaust pipes radiating power, behind the rakish conical spinner.

"Come on." Byron clambered up the wing and indicated for me to follow. "Get in."

"Wait a minute, I'm not flying this thing without a chute."

"You're not flying it at all just yet. It's got to taxi about a mile down to the other side of the control tower, and you've got to get a feeling for keeping it from nosing over into the dirt!"

For the next ten minutes Byron walked me through the startup procedure. I hadn't flown a late model American ship in five years. So a lot of it was new. When I had the sequence right he called over to a technician and spoke a few words of Mandarin. I understood them from flying the Russian P-16s. It meant 'pull through'. The Chinese technician walked up to the propeller and pulled on it hard enough to make it spin through one cycle. Then the man stood away.

Byron spoke. "Alright, Will, throttle, battery, carburetor… prime engine…engage starter." Suddenly the propeller moved while the radiator coughed and spit a flame. The propeller began to visibly slow and Byron reached in to make the fuel mixture richer, then he turned the booster pump on. He shouted at me. "You'll get the hang of it. Just a matter of knowing where the controls are." I nodded. The noise had become a deep, satisfying roar. He leaned into the cockpit. "Now put your feet on the brakes and turn up the throttle slowly." Again there was nothing to do but nod. "And remember, I'm standing on your wing, hanging on!" Slowly the aircraft began to move forward.

The view was no different from a Russian P-16. All you could see straight ahead was a big nose. I had to move my head from side to side to keep the ship on the gravel road way. We crawled down to the other end of the airfield, Byron on the wing, telling me how to keep the engine running smooth and warning me when I came too close to the verge. It seemed an eternity but finally we arrived. I'd been so focused I hadn't said a word since the ship had begun to move away from the hangar. At the end of the runway I lined the P-40 up with another one. Now Byron leaned into the cockpit again and went through several steps before cutting the power. I followed most of them well enough, but I was glad to leave it to him.

"Okay. Good job. Let's get back to the hangar and try it again."

It was two days before I'd mastered the checklist—magnetos, oil pressure and coolant, and two dozen other things Byron kept walking me through. I'd started up and taxied three planes down the road to the end of the runway without bending anything. That afternoon Byron handed me a parachute and told me to take it up and around once and land it. Suddenly, I could recall my first solo flight in a Stearman trainer back at March Field in '33.

Once I was in the air, everything was familiar, only more so. In some ways I was flying the same kind of machine I'd gotten used to in Spain and Chongqing. But it was better in every way—faster to climb up from the ground, faster straight and level, faster in a dive, and no less maneuverable than the Russian planes. But it was much steadier, easier to fly, much more forgiving about mistakes and good natured about doing what you asked it to do. I found myself liking this machine very much.

Soon enough we were both taking off in an echelon, my plane tucked behind Byron's as we rose up into the heavy Rangoon air. Once we were at 3000 feet I began mimicking his movements, taking my ship through the same paces as his—bank, roll, loop, stall, spin, and then managing to stay on his tail as he tried to shake me. It was too easy to keep him in my sights. My fellow test pilot hadn't been a combat flier the way I'd been for a couple of years in Spain. We switched places and I managed to lose him so thoroughly that twice I was able to come back behind his plane undetected.

9

It was a week after I'd begun test flying the finished planes that the trouble began. By now there were a half-dozen completed ships parked in a row on the runway, painted with the Chinese insignia—a circle surrounded by triangles to symbolize the sun. Like all days that time of year in Rangoon, it was grey from a high overcast, hot and muggy enough to work up a sweat wearing a flight jacket and a parachute bouncing on my fanny every step I took. I taxied the seventh plane from the sheds to the end of the field, revved my engine and took her down the runway into the air. I'd cool off quickly enough with an open canopy. There were no radios in the P-40s yet so I had to use hand signals getting take-off clearance from the diminutive control tower.

At 2000 feet I circled back and began going through my test checklist. I'd got to the point of pushing the throttle forward and climbing up into the clouds above the field when suddenly my engine oil pressure gauge and the heat gauge began to signal something badly wrong. Even before I could cut the throttle back there was smoke coming out of the cowling, then steady flames visible around the exhaust ports in the nose of the P-40. It was a replay of the time I'd been shot down in Spain three years before.

I cut the engine and watched the propeller slow down to a wash in which each blade became a blurred shape. The plane went into a stall and began to dive. There was enough airspeed to keep it trim and I banked for the field, hoping I had the altitude to reach the runway and dead stick in. After the deep throated roar of the Allison engine the wind-rush silence was eerie. The motor oil smell was strong as viscose liquid continued to seep along the fuselage, spread by the same wind rush. Time crawled slowly so I could think carefully about how to handle the heavy glider my ship had suddenly turned into. The landing gear was rugged enough to take the several bounces I needed to bring it to ground and apply the brakes.

I sat in the plane at the end of the runway, thinking things through, sweating in the humid air, till someone came up in a truck and drove me back to our assembly buildings. It was obvious what had happened. There'd been a break in the lubrication system and all the oil had run out. It was a simple thing to fix and I was glad I'd saved the plane. We had no replacements.

Back at the sheds where the ships were being put together I slung my parachute down at the entrance to Dan Gourlie's office and stood waiting while he shouted down the telephone to someone far away about the need for radios and spare parts. He hung up and saw me. "Well?' as if he'd been waiting for me to speak instead of the reverse.

"Almost lost a ship this afternoon."

He pushed away from his desk. "Almost?"

Once I'd finished my report Dan picked up his phone again, ordering a truck to tow the plane back to the sheds. Then he looked up again. "Take the rest of the day off, Will." I nodded and walked out.

The next morning I was just waking up when there was a knock at my door. It was Andy Sargent, the engineer who managed the Chinese mechanics putting the planes together. He looked the worse for wear, greasy overalls, a day's worth of stubble on his chin, bleary eyed. "Dan wants to talk to you."

"Okay. Just let me get some clothes on."

"Doesn't want to meet at the sheds. He's coming here." He responded to my look of surprise. "We've been working all night. Took apart the plane you tested yesterday."

"No sleep? You look it, Andy." As he came in Dan turned up, no more rested than Andy, who moved from the door to let him in. He pointed Andy to a chair and sat heavily on the unmade bed. I remained standing, leaning against a wall.

I broke the ice. "What's up, gentlemen?"

"Someone did quite a job on that ship you took up yesterday, Will. You were very lucky or pretty sharp bringing it back in one piece or even surviving at all." I wasn't going to tell them I'd had a little experience coping with this sort of failure back in Spain. He pulled out a pack of Chesterfields and passed them around. We all lit up and he began again. "The lines to the oil coolant radiator had been cut halfway through."

"Cut?" my voice was loud, too loud.

"Keep it down. That's not all. The line leading from the coolant radiator was also punctured, pretty close to the engine block."

I lowered my voice. "Close enough to catch the oil on fire when the engine heated up 'cause it wasn't getting enough oil?"

They both nodded. Then Andy spoke. "That's not all. Somebody monkeyed with the hydraulic pumps. One more roll or spin and the electric power would have disconnected. Your flaps would have been shot and the gear would never have come down even if you made it back to the field. You were lucky the oil pressure failed first before the hydraulics had a chance to break down."

All I could say was "Sabotage?"

Dan looked at each of us. Then he started again. "Looks like it. All three ships that were at the end of the runway, ready for test flights. That's not all. You checked the 'chutes, Andy. Tell Will what you found."

"Might be worse than just sabotage, Will. That parachute you dropped at the door of my office yesterday, was it the one you were wearing on the test?"

"Yup. Sorry I didn't mean to just drop it there."

"Whoever packed that chute must have wanted more than just to destroy a couple or three planes. They wanted to kill some pilots too."

"What d'you mean?"

"There was a pretty obvious knot in the ripcord line. You'd have pulled on it and nothing would have happened. Same deal for the other chutes in the pilots' lockers."

Now Andy spoke. "This morning we were short a worker on the engine assembly team. Nobody knows where he went. Just gone with all his kit."

I looked at each of them. "You think he might have been the saboteur?"

"Dunno…we've lost a couple before now…but always with an explanation or apology."

There was a silence that Andy broke. "Trouble is we can't really question the Chinese guys who're putting the planes together. We don't have the language, couldn't really tell if they were lying anyway. Besides, if we spook them we'll never get these crates put together."

I thought for a minute. "How about your Chinese-American guys, did they see anything? Can't they ask some questions?"

"Only ten of them, a couple of hundred Chinese ground crew. Easy for one guy to monkey wrench a plane without anyone else noticing, here or out at the field tuning planes up for test flights."

By this point I couldn't help starting to wonder if the whole shooting match was the target of the sabotage or maybe it was just me. The Japs had been looking for me in Canton. I figured I'd dodged that bullet once I wasn't training Chinese pilots to fly Russian planes. Could they still be looking? Then the paranoia dissipated and reality took hold. *No, you're not that important, Thurlow.* In the silence between us I finally spoke. "So, what are you going to do?"

Dan rose from the bed. "Dunno exactly. Set up sentries in the main hangar. But it doesn't look like your problem anymore, Will."

"How's that?" My tone was more belligerent than I wanted it to be. Were they going to fire me because someone was sabotaging their planes?

"Cool down. You're just changing jobs. You're going to start ferrying the planes up to Taungoo." This was an RAF base a hundred miles north where the American Volunteer Group was to be organized. "Byron will test-fly them. Then you fly them up."

I thought about the plan for a moment. "So, you really do think someone was trying to get me. That why you're taking me off test flying?"

Both of the men shook their heads. "No." Dan went on. "Orders from Chongqing. We talked to Chennault's office about the problem this morning. Then we got a cable an hour ago to reassign you."

The next day I flew one of the P-40s Byron had already checked out up to Taungoo. It was a short flight over what looked like mostly trackless jungle a hundred miles north of Rangoon.

The RAF base was set in a valley between two mountain ranges that hemmed in the town. It looked like the Brits had been there long enough to have taken root. The base had an officer's club and billets to go along with hangars and machine shops at the edge of the grass landing strip. There wasn't much more to the control tower than a wind-sock and raised walkway. The other thing there wasn't much of were planes. I'd expected to see Hawker Hurricanes, but there were only a dozen obsolete American built P-35s. It was obvious that the RAF didn't think there was much risk of the Sino-Japanese war spilling over into Burma. The planes were all parked in a neat row on the small tarmacked surface in front of the hangars, ready to be destroyed on a single pass by a low flying enemy.

Jumping down from my P-40 I was greeted with great warmth by a trio of flight lieutenants and then the CO, a Captain Blythe. Watching their eyes dart to the plane, even as they shook my hand, I could tell these pilots were more interested in my P-40 than they were in me.

"Good to see you…" Blythe was looking for some rank insignia on my collar or shoulder so he'd know how to address me and whether I might even outrank him. There was none.

I put him out of his discomfort. "Name's Thurlow, Will Thurlow…civilian."

"I see. Well Mr. Thurlow, you'll stay the night and join us for dinner?"

"Didn't bring any overnight kit, sir. I was hoping to get a lift back in one of your planes. There are two more P-40s read to deliver today."

Blythe grimaced. "Can't be done, old boy. We've got nothing but these single seat planes…and we can't afford the fuel and maintenance in any case."

I suppressed my incredulity. "No two seaters, no trainers, no support aircraft at all, not even a Lysander?" This was the rugged two seat plane the Brits had plenty of in England. These were used to fly in and out of dirt strips in occupied Europe almost on a schedule.

"They keep us on a tight leash out here." He brightened. "Come and have a drink." I'd noticed the flight lieutenants climb up the wing root of my plane. Blythe noticed. "Don't worry about them. They haven't seen one of those yet."

The sign above the open bamboo veranda said "Out of Bounds to Other Ranks." A teak bar ran the length of the building. Behind it was a short man in a white coat polishing glasses. Reaching the bar Blythe turned to me. "Gin and tonic?" Before I could nod my agreement, he went on. "Only thing we've got actually."

We leaned against the bar, surveying the field in the late afternoon sun. I had to ask, "You can't be happy stuck out here when there's a war on back in Europe."

"It has its consolations. Other than the lack of a good single malt we do all right out here. Much more comfortable than back in Blighty." This man was not very interested in the war raging on two continents. Did the other officers here share his indifference I wondered?

I wasn't about to reprove my host but I couldn't help at least telling him there was another war on not very far from the bar we were propping up. "Certainly is much more agreeable here than what I lived through flying for the Chinese against the Japs the last year or so."

Blythe just wasn't interested, professionally or politically. "Ah, the Japs. Well, we're not worried about 'em. Government will close the Burma road again if it has to keep them on side." This had been Chiang Kai-shek's main supply route for American aid coming up from Rangoon. The British had already closed it once. They couldn't risk a war with Japan while they were losing one to the Germans. No one particularly blamed them. So it was assumed they'd knuckle under again if the Japs put pressure on. Blythe went on. "We won't get any trouble from that quarter." Then he looked at me hard. "Unless your lot attracts too much attention to us."

"I'm afraid we will."

"Yes…I've had my orders." Blythe looked grim. "I've been told you're to have every facility."

"Well, the planes and pilots will only be here long enough to train. Then they'll be headed to Chongqing. Let's hope the Japanese don't get too interested," I said, casting a glance at the neat row of a dozen RAF planes ranged beneath what passed for the control tower. I could see discussing the war was going to wear out my welcome pretty quickly. "Look, Captain, how can I get back to Rangoon if none of your boys can fly me back?"

"No hurry, old boy. There's a train runs down every day in the morning. No first-class, not even a Europeans-only coach. You'll have to ride with the wogs." He shrugged his shoulders and took a belt of his gin and tonic, turned to me with his empty glass. "Your round now, Thurlow. Bartender takes cash."

It was a long day's ride back to Rangoon and not very comfortable for any of the passengers, sitting in open carriages going slowly enough to let me count the vines snaking up each banyan tree we passed. There were about a dozen other passengers, mainly Chinese and a few Malays, all sitting well away from me, averting their eyes in a show of misplaced colonial deference. Riding along, there was time to think a great deal about things I didn't want even to contemplate. The evening in the RAF mess at Taungoo had gone some distance to disabuse me of the picture of valiant British fighter pilots. Five thousand miles from the Battle of Britain the men I'd met, especially the CO, were more than happy to be sitting out a real war, and reluctant to do anything that would jeopardize their comforts.

Maybe that's why they've been posted here in the first place, getting them out of the way. I decided to hope so.

Jostled gently south, the forest canopy and the breeze through the open carriages kept me comfortable enough. I had the luxury to try to figure things out again. Was there any connection between the sabotage at Rangoon airport and the Japanese manhunt Wendy had saved me from, back more than a year before? Half of me wanted to toss the whole idea off as silly egotism. *You're not that important, Thurlow. Who's gonna reach out from Tokyo to kill one lousy American mercenary flyer? And then try it again a year later?* The other half of me wanted to be suspicious, to knit everything that had happened to me into a story, a plot, a conspiracy, something that would connect the dots. I tried, more than once, but every time the train of thought brought me to Wendy. The person I wanted not to think about in the worst way. And not wanting to just made me think about her more—where she was and whether she was alone. I could conjure her too well still, in a cabaret spotlight casting a spell on me, lithe in a casually open kimono, inviting me to her bed. Then I remembered Wendy rushing at me in a rage of fists, demanding I stop endangering myself in ways less dangerous than the ones she insisted on exposing herself to when I had refused. *She's the reason you're here, Thurlow, nothing else holding your loyalty to China, to Cash-My-Check and his crowd…*

10

I didn't know it, riding down to Rangoon that evening in July of '41, but I was going to get what I had wanted back in 1940: my commission in the Army Air Corps, and without much paper work, without explaining my past, groveling to staff flunkies or making nice with anyone. All I had to do was keep ferrying P-40s into Taungoo till I got spotted by Claire Chennault. Once he found me he didn't care too much about my distant past. Besides, that past was too much like his to trouble him overmuch.

Byron found a Piper Cub at Rangoon airport and we began to move planes up to Taungoo as fast as he could bring me back to Rangoon. Sometimes we could do three a day. By September we had thirty-five P-40s on the ground up there.

I was at the bar of the RAF officers' club, after my first trip of the day, scanning the southern horizon for Byron in the Piper Cub to get me back to Rangoon. An American sedan pulled up—painted a military green—and a woman stepped out. Then it pulled away, heading towards the hangars. She sauntered up the steps and moved to the bar. Looked me up and down.

"American? Flyer?" I nodded and smiled. She put out her hand. "Olga Greenlaw, glad to meet you." It wasn't a girlish handshake. She was almost as tall as I was, early 30s I'd say, a brunette with a leathery complexion and a tan that showed she wasn't afraid of the outdoors. Her pants were tight and her blouse was open at the neck just one button too low.

I replied. "Will Thurlow."

"American Volunteer Group?" The unit was still too new for everyone to recognize the short hand, AVG.

"Not sure, exactly. I work for CAMCO. I've been flying these birds up from Rangoon for three or four weeks."

"Harvey will know." Seeing the question on my face she went on. "My husband. He's the air exec for the AVG, reports to Chennault direct. He'll be here in a few minutes."

Harvey Greenlaw was a bear of a man, striding up the steps of the club two at a time. Dressed in the khaki and leather jacket of an American airman. His head fit the large body. It was a coarse face—large, almost outsized features under a buzz hair cut in need of a fresh shave. His flying jacket showed where patches and insignia of rank had been removed. Greenlaw was carrying a clipboard and a side arm, the first I'd seen since leaving Chongqing.

"Harvey." Olga waved him over to us. "This is Will Thurlow. I think he's one of ours, first one to come in."

Greenlaw evidently hadn't been listening. He looked me up and down then in a voice too loud said, "Name?" and turned a page on his clipboard, holding a pencil presumably to check me off.

It was too peremptory. I felt like saying *Who's asking*. But I decided to act smart instead of smart ass. "Will Thurlow. I signed up with the Central Aircraft Manufacturing Company in Chongqing."

"Not on my list." He growled and I shrugged. "Where'd you come in from, Thurlow?"

"Been flying your planes up from Rangoon."

"Before that?"

I gave Greenlaw my details. West Point '32, quit the Air Corps in '36. Spanish Republican Air Force, training the Chinese to fly Russian planes.

"You were flying Soviet equipment in Spain and for the Chinese? I don't like it."

"The Russian planes aren't so different from a P-40." I observed. He let me go on. "Sturdy, heavy, better in a dive than the Jap planes."

"Not what I meant, Ivan." The name was an accusation of disloyalty.

A little belligerence was called for. "Hey, I wasn't flying for the Russians, just flying their planes, Okay?"

"Simmer down, Thurlow. Anyway, the AVG won't be needing you."

"I signed a contract, bud."

He caught the anger in my voice. "Don't worry. You'll be paid, right up to your last delivery. But I got all the fighter pilots I need." Behind him Olga was slowly shaking her head. I didn't understand why.

There was nothing to do but walk away, down the stairs and onto the tarmac where I watched Byron land the Piper Cub. Without cutting the engine he opened the door and I climbed in for the flight back to Rangoon.

———

Every day for the next couple of weeks as I brought in the ships, there were more and more young and not so young men at the bar of the officers' club. All shorn of insignia and rank, all carrying training manuals and complaining. Almost from the start they made me an object of interest and envy. I was actually flying the planes they were only learning about, in ground school. So, I got to know some of their names quickly: Pete, Jack, Oley, Jonny, Bob, Sandy, Red, and one pilot who answered only to Tex. I didn't bother learning the last names attached to them since I wasn't going to get to know any of them well enough to do more than share a drink.

One afternoon, jumping down off the P-40 I'd flown in, I noticed ground crew up on step ladders at the nose and cowling of a plane, paint cans and brushes in their hands, large stencils on the ground beneath the propellers. They were painting what looked like shark teeth on the cowling. I'd seen the same paint-job before, on the twin engine Messerschmitts of the Condor Legion. I walked up to the crew chief standing beneath the man carefully painting white teeth into the shark's mouth. "Whose idea is this?"

Involuntarily he came to attention. "Mr. Greenlaw's." He seemed about to add 'sir' till he remembered that no one here had military rank in any recognized army. "Saw it on a photo of some German fighters. Thought it would look good on our planes." I shrugged, not my business, but not what I would have painted on planes fighting against Germany's allies, the Japanese. Just then another man came up, wearing the coveralls of a ground crew man.

"You Thurlow?" I nodded. "Boss wants to see you."

"Mr. Greenlaw?"

"His office, yeah, but it's General Chennault who's asked for you." He pointed at a building a few hundred feet from the main hangars. "This way, sir." My guide hadn't broken his military habit. I followed him. I'd never met Claire Chennault, but I'd seen him often enough across a café or cabaret floor in Chongqing, usually in the company of hefty Chinese business men in tan colored suits that stood out in the subdued lighting. He'd been in China for years and was Chiang Kai-shek's chief air advisor. Before that, like me, he'd quit the Army Air Corps. The scuttlebutt was lack of discipline, inability to follow orders he didn't like, over-aggressive advocacy of airpower, things that send a career to the graveyard in a peacetime army.

Harvey Greenlaw was sitting behind his desk, a sour look on his face, and Chennault was sitting on a corner of the desk, smoking. He was wearing Army Air Corps green and brown but with Chinese insignia where US Army Air Corps had been. It was my turn to reflexively come to attention and stand before a senior officer waiting to be recognized. Not being in uniform. I didn't salute.

"Take a pew, brother Thurlow." He smiled and stubbed out his cigarette, only to light another and offer me one, which I accepted.

"Greenlaw here says you flew Rooskie ships for the Chinks."

Not for me to quibble with a general's nouns and adjectives. "I did, sir."

Greenlaw added, "And before that for the Commies in Spain."

Chennault smiled. "Me too. Flew Russian ships for the Generalissimo." This was Chiang Kai-shek's honorific title. "Knocked down a few slow Jap bombers. You?"

"No sir." I couldn't help addressing an older man in the uniform of a general that way. "My job in Chongqing was limited to training." I stopped and calculated whether to go on. But Greenlaw had let my Spanish cat out of the bag already. "I did manage to bag some Italian bombers and two Me-109s in Spain."

Chennault's bushy eyebrows rose. "In a Rooskie P-16?" I nodded. "How much time in a P-40 Thurlow?"

"Not much, General. I've been ferrying them up here from Rangoon for a month or so."

He shook his head. "No experience with them in the Air Corps?"

"No. I was separated from the service before we got any. Just flew P-35s and Brewster Buffaloes."

"Well, I've flown them both. A Russian P-16's pretty much like a P-40."

"I wouldn't say that, not exactly, sir."

"What would you say, Thurlow?"

"Every fighter has its good points and its weaknesses. The P-40 has some of the same ones as the Russian plane. Only the P-40 doesn't fight the pilot all the time in straight and level. It's easier to fly and it's faster, more rugged, better armed, and heavier. The Soviet plane has a much lower ceiling than the German planes, just like the P-40, no supercharger, but it can turn tighter than the German planes at lower speed. And its weight makes it drop like a stone when you have the altitude on the enemy. Even the Germans couldn't catch us. That's where the P-40's strength would be too."

"Exactly." Chennault smiled and looked towards Greenlaw who was unmoved. He turned back to me. "I flew one of those ships myself, testing them out before Chiang laid out the dough to buy them. Liked what I flew too."

"Look Thurlow, I've got a problem." He lit another Chesterfield and offered them around. Greenlaw took one. I declined and reached into my shirt pocket for a Lucky Strike. "I got twenty-five flyers here, all quit the US Army to come fly for China against the Japs. Nice pay, some chance of action, get away from pettifogging." He paused. "You know what that is, Thurlow."

"Yup, reason I bailed out of the Air Corps myself." It was a lie, but the truth might have been pettifogging.

He went on. "Trouble is almost none of them have much experience in single seat pursuit planes. Most all of them lied about their experience to get the job. They were multiengine boys—bomber pilots and co-pilots, transport flyers, Navy guys, and a Marine too. Even the ones who did fly fighter planes have never been in combat. They need a lot of schooling. These boys don't like to admit it, but that's a fact." I could see pretty clearly what was coming. I could also see Greenlaw fuming in his seat, making the chair swivel in his pent-up anger. "How would you like to help train these guys." He pointed out past the wall in the direction of the officer's club.

"Sir, would I report to your air exec here?" I looked directly from Chennault to Greenlaw.

"Yes. Look, Thurlow, Greenlaw here doesn't trust you. But he doesn't have a better idea about someone we can lay our hands on that's qualified to train pilots."

I looked at Greenlaw. "Why doesn't he trust me, sir? He doesn't know me. We've only met once, a couple of weeks ago."

Greenlaw was about to speak but Chennault put his hand up. "It's just your politics. But Harvey hasn't been out here long enough to see it'll take all types to fight this war."

I remained silent and Chennault took it as a sign I wasn't going to refuse his offer but was prepared to bargain with him. He was right. "So, Thurlow, you'll have squadron leader pay. We don't have ranks, but it's the top job, $750 a month US. That's the highest pay in the AVG."

"Will I be a member of the AVG, sir? Mr. Greenlaw said you were full up, didn't need any more pilots."

"Sure, you'll be a Flying Tiger." He smiled a gap tooth grin that wrinkled his whole face. "Is it a deal?" *Flying Tigers?* I said the words silently to myself. Suddenly I understood why the ships were getting a paint-job stolen from the German Luftwaffe.

———

So I went back to Rangoon, packed my kit and moved up to Taungoo the next day.

The first week I spent in a hangar converted to a classroom with the initial group of thirty pilots, going over check lists and flying tactics that the years in Spain and China had drilled into me. Teaching the Americans was very different and much harder than teaching the Chinese. Their overconfidence was matched by their contempt for the enemy. It was a toxic mixture, but not one I could correct on the ground. In the next few weeks more and more ex-Army Air Corps pilots came in, and I had to start new ground classes with each group, meanwhile getting the earlier groups into the air, flying the P-40s, low and slow, practicing landings gentle enough to preserve the gear and tires. More than once they were told we'd fight this war against the Japs without spares.

By the end of three weeks I had enough semi-trained pilots to send down to Rangoon for the rest of the planes. By the middle of November 1941 we had all ninety-nine airworthy ships in Taungoo. Only the one I'd tested was permanently out of commission and was being cannibalized for spare parts.

That time of year the sun set early and the bar at the officers' club set up early too. The AVG pilots now far outnumbered the Brits and the supply of liquor had improved as well, with shipments coming down, with General Chennault's complements, from the purchasing mission in Chongqing. I never stayed long. There was too much paperwork and preparation every evening for classes and flight training the next day. Chennault had set a December 20 deadline for three squadrons to be ready to fly to Chongqing.

I was going to show him, and Greenlaw, that I could make that deadline. Killing a lot of time at the bar was out.

It was too early for most of the guys when I stopped at the club for a belt before heading off to my billet in the town. I was nursing a weak whiskey when I heard a woman's voice. "Buy a girl a drink, Mister?" It was Olga Greenlaw who had come up the stairs and across the open veranda to the bar. I turned and smiled. She spoke. "You owe me one, buddy."

"What'll you have?" I replied.

"Same as you." I picked up my glass and motioned to the barman, a RAF sergeant happy to wait on Yanks. Olga was the only woman on the Taungoo RAF station and she was in pretty much the same getup she always wore, the tight pants, the blouse open one button too many and mostly everyone knew why. It was a signal we all could read. With her husband's acquiescence Olga had become the combination den-mother and sexual release for more than one pilot in need of a woman's attentions.

We sipped our drinks. She took one of my Luckies. I watched the smoke come out of her nostrils, like two ghostly shafts of a dragon's breath. "So, Olga, why do I owe you?"

"I got you your job, silly." As she spoke she leaned her cleavage forward and put a hand on my arm. The message was clearer than a Western Union telegram.

Slowly and with as little offense as possible I withdrew my arm. "How's that?"

"I told Chennault all about you, everything you told Harvey. He wasn't going to, but I saw that you were the solution to our problem and cornered Chennault one night when he came down to Rangoon for an inspection." *So, she's slept with the boss too.* The thought flashed through my mind. "Harvey wouldn't have told him anything about you."

"Well, then I do owe you." It came out the wrong way. I had to backtrack. "By the way where is Harvey tonight?"

"Went up to Chongqing yesterday." As air exec officer, Greenlaw was back and forth between Taungoo and the base being readied for the three squadrons back at Chiang Kai-shek's capital. She moved her hand lightly, stroking my forearm to make it certain I'd catch her drift.

"Look, Olga, I appreciate the offer, and I find you mighty attractive, but I can't afford to get on the wrong side of your husband any more than I already am, not if these guys are going to be ready to fight next month."

She drew on the cigarette and drawled under her breath. "Harvey's not around and he won't know anyway…you need the…" she searched for the word, "distraction…and I need some fun too."

Would she get angry? "No sale, honey. Maybe Harvey is broad-minded, or maybe he is, except for guys he's got it in for. And besides, you know there aren't many secrets on a base like this. Anyone suspects, there'll be enough ribbing that Harvey will catch on." She was silent. "Hell, you think it's a secret you're the base *femme fatale*?" She frowned. I had to be sure she wasn't angry enough to make her husband more of my enemy than he already was. "Look, you're pretty irresistible, but I'm carrying a torch. You can understand that." The statement had the virtue of being true.

She withdrew the hand. "Stateside girl?"

"No, Chinese spy…" I let the words hang in the air. Then I went on. "Woman I met in Hong Kong, took me through the Jap lines to Chongqing. Ditched me when I wouldn't quit flying combat. Went back to occupied Canton."

Olga thought for a minute. "Will, I've got time to listen. You don't have to send me a telegram. Start over." So I told her the history of Wendy and Will. As I spoke I found I needed to tell someone, and telling a woman I liked was easier than telling any man I knew.

11

For the moment, with Chennault breathing down his neck to get his air force ready, Harvey Greenlaw couldn't do much without me. I was his chief flight instructor, whether he liked it or not.

Mornings I was giving lessons on cockpit checks that pilots had to memorize, then lecturing on flying tactics I'd learned in Spain and above Chongqing. The ex-Army fliers had their own ideas, mixed up with Air Corps doctrine that bore no relation to reality. Mostly they were eager to under-rate Jap eye sight, intestinal fortitude, and aeronautical design. It was a combination of errors that could get a guy killed fast. I had to dislodge all three ideas over and over.

Afternoons, I'd take three pilots up with me at a time, trying to get them to fly in a loose spread of planes arranged like the fingertips of a right hand, lead pilot where the middle finger was, with the index finger and pinky pilots wing men, weaving behind the leading pair, covering them while scanning the sky behind. It was a secret we'd hit on in Spain that I didn't think anyone had yet. It was only when I got to England that I learned the RAF had been flying that 'finger four' formation for the better part of a year.

It was tough keeping these cowboys even in a loose formation. We didn't have radios yet and signals had to be made by hand. That meant even closer watching and easy excuses for failing to keep in formation. But the pilots got the hang of the P-40 pretty quickly and their eagerness to get the training over and begin mixing it with the Japanese was music to my ears. So was the steady roar of the Allison engine yanking me through the air as we climbed away from the heat and the damp and the insects into the clean blue above the morning rain clouds.

The other three planes would form up on me and then we'd fly some lazy circles, trying to stay together, taking turns as wing man, pretending to watch for fighters about to bounce us. It was too far from anything real to actually prepare flyers for combat. But it was a beginning, and a lot more fun than anything else they could do. After this formation flying, I'd signal pairs to try some mock dog fighting, allowing them to find the rough limits of the P-40's aerobatic envelope. They would have to find the outside of that envelope in real combat, I knew. To survive for long they'd have to know exactly when and how much to exceed it.

I liked them all. I still didn't want to learn their names, but it couldn't be helped, ordering them around up to just the point they wouldn't obey any more. Olson, Sandell, Armstrong, Little, Hill—those are the ones I still remember.

October passed into November, more men came in, we went through the same round of training, being careful enough not to lose any of the ninety-nine ships we had. The ground crews worked through heat and insects, and rain, rain, rain, along with sun so hot you'd burn your hand if you touched an unpainted piece of cowling or a leading edge. Men who'd come in earlier and finished training, spent a lot of time in the hangars, watching the ground crews, learning more about their planes than they would ever need to know. I was glad they were interested, but had to warn more than one crew chief not to let a pilot start to claim ownership of a ship or worse take it up without authorization.

Some of the pilots, especially the older ones, ended up hanging around the bar, drinking too much. You'd pass the open veranda and they'd raise their gin and tonics. "Had your quinine today, Thurlow?" Malaria was a serious problem and mosquito nets were always in short supply. There was no trace of atabrine—the only drug around for malaria.

We were aiming to finish training the AVG by about December 20, 1941. We'd finally received radios from Chongqing and begun trying out the P-40s' machine guns on towed targets. There would be three squadrons, sixteen planes each, twenty-four pilots. But Chennault hadn't gotten around to making assignments, picking squadron leaders or asking for any advice about the matter, when suddenly matters were taken out of his hands.

7:00 AM Honolulu time is 11:30 PM Rangoon time. Don't ask me where the extra half an hour comes from. What it meant was the morning of December 7, when the Japanese attacked Pearl Harbor, no one in Burma would know till they woke up, across the international dateline on Tuesday, December 8, a full day after that fateful Sunday morning.

Nothing much happened at Taungoo over the next few days, while everything changed in the rest of the world. We sat around radios, listening mainly to the BBC service from India. First, we were told that the US Pacific Fleet had been sunk at Honolulu, then that the Japs had invaded the Philippines, catching McArthur's entire air force on the ground at Clark Field. We looked at our planes spread out in a disorderly pattern on the perimeter of the field and breathed a sigh of relief. The next day Roosevelt declared war on Japan and suddenly the AVG became the only group of Americans anywhere ready, or almost ready, to fight the Japanese. We thought that it would be in China as soon as we could get there. We were wrong about that. A lot of us spent the first month of the war fighting in Burma. Once the Germans declared war on the US, the Brits on the base stopped treating us as paying guests. The Japs had invaded the Hong Kong crown colony the day they attacked Pearl Harbor, and they began their drive on Singapore a few days later. So from the start everyone knew we were in the same war.

That afternoon Greenlaw called a meeting of all the "employees" of the AVG at Taungoo, every fighter pilot, ground crew man, mechanic, all the service personnel. There were a couple of hundred now, including the sixty or so pilots.

He raised his arms above the din in the hangar. "The AVG is moving to Kunming right away." This was a Chinese city half way from Burma to Chiang Kai-shek's wartime capital at Chongqing. Greenlaw looked down at his ever-present clipboard and began to give each ground-crew team its departure dates, in rough order of what would be needed to organize a fighting air base. The pilots were growing restive, waiting and knowing that they wouldn't be needed, in fact would be in the way, till everyone else had set the base up. I was standing against the hangar's back wall, watching the pilots drift in and out of the rear of the crowd, which thinned as each group got their marching orders. Finally there were only the pilots left in the hangar.

Greenlaw looked around. "Listen up." The men responded, moving into a couple of concentric circles around him. I joined the outermost one, close enough to hear everything he said. "Alright. If you were listening, you'll know, there'll be three squadrons, twenty-four planes each. We're assigning twenty pilots to each one. He began to call out the assignments, first designating three squadron leaders. Having trained most of these guys I could see he was distributing the best pilots evenly, and also spreading the weaker ones out among the three squadrons. As the names were called there was the usual ragging, cat calls, friendly abuse, expressions of mock horror at assignments to one squadron or the other. When Greenlaw had finished, he looked around, without waiting for questions, he shouted, "That is all," turned and left.

I must have been the only one to have noticed that my name wasn't listed for any of the three squadrons. Most hadn't noticed, absorbed in listening for their own names. More than one of these turned to me and asked "Which squadron, Thurlow?"

"Dunno. Missed hearing my name."

Tex Hill, one of the best pilots I'd checked out, cut in. "Greenlaw didn't call your name. I was listening for it." He smiled. "Wanted to be in the same squadron." He looked at the others. "Only one of us with combat experience." I smiled back and he continued. "You already got another assignment, Will?" I shook my head. But I understood well enough, or thought I did. Greenlaw had never been happy with me. I'd been forced on him by Chennault. Now, with Chennault in Chongqing, he'd be able to get rid of me. The boss would be too busy to notice.

When I was finally left alone I made a bee line for Greenlaw's office, waited while his office flunky checked whether he was in, and then told me to take a seat. Greenlaw was evidently on the phone, probably to Chennault a thousand miles away in Chongqing. Ten minutes of cooling my heels and I was told to go in. Greenlaw was at his desk, scowling as I entered.

"Well?" It was as close as he could come to an invitation to speak.

The AVG didn't have ranks, but I decided to address him at his former US Army rank. Maybe it would conciliate him, maybe it would invite some professional bearing. "Captain Greenlaw, I didn't hear my name when you read out squadron assignments."

Before I could frame a question he replied. "That's right. Didn't call out your name." Immediately he sought to resolve the confusion shown on my face. "You're not assigned to any group. I don't trust you. I don't want you flying for me."

"But sir, I was good enough to train all these guys…" my arm swung around indicating the field behind me.

"Thurlow, that was the General's decision. This one's mine." He threw down the pen he was holding. "I can't have some Commie who quit the Air Corps to fly for the Reds in Spain in my air force. Probably spying for the Russians when you were flying their planes for Chiang Kai-shek."

I didn't know where to start in my reply. Since when was it his air force? Why and when I left the Air Corps was my business. Besides all these flyers had quit too. "Come off it, Greenlaw, I quit the Air Corps a year before I started flying in Spain. I didn't look for that job training Chinese pilots on Russian planes. They came looking for me."

"You're not flying for me, Thurlow. You're under contract to CAMCO. You can hang around here and pick up a paycheck, but you're not going to Kunming."

That was when I lost it. "What's the matter, Greenlaw? Grounding me because I'm the only guy on the base who's turned down your wife?" The man was rising to strike me as I turned and left his office.

Within a week, one of the three squadrons of P-40s had flown to Kunming, preceded by flight after flight of Air China DC-3s, carrying the ground crews, their tools and the spare parts on hand. A few days later the second squadron flew off. Then things changed again.

It was a grey humid day in late December when the air raid sirens began to sound across the field. Every pilot, every crew chief and a lot of the ground personnel on the station began to walk, then jog and finally run, not to bomb shelters or slit trenches—there were none, but to the base of the control tower, or what passed for one. Tex Hill, the 3rd Squadron leader was standing at its base, hands on hips.

When we arrived, each heaving for breath, Hill spoke. "No threat here, guys, but it was the best way to get you all together quickly. Jap bombers are headed towards Rangoon. Flights 1,2,3, and 4, take off, head to Rangoon airport. We'll try to gain enough altitude on the way to bounce the bombers when they reach their targets."

The sixteen flyers in these groups headed quickly to their planes, along with their ground crew chiefs. I didn't envy them their mission, not much. No radios, no good information about the Jap bomber's numbers, altitude, exact location or direction. Still I would rather have been flying with them than hanging around an airfield with nothing to do at all.

Sixteen ships went out and all came back two and a half hours later, now blooded by successful combat. The Japanese bombers were slow, unescorted by fighters and completely surprised by an attack from well above their altitude. Our pilots counted about thirty Jap ships and took down six while effectively breaking up their bombing formation. The Brits at Taungoo had sent every one of their Brewster Buffalos aloft too, but they all came back, pilots complaining that they couldn't even fly fast enough to catch the Jap bombers.

It was the same drill the next three days, as reports came in of the Japanese rapidly gaining ground towards Rangoon from the east. By the end of December Chennault sent word that the 3rd Squadron was to move back down to Rangoon airport, where we'd originally assembled the P-40s. The squadron's mission would be to protect the city from the persistent bombing campaign coordinated with the ground offensive the Japs were mounting against demoralized units of the Indian Army—Britain's only military force in Asia.

I was in my billet when there was a knock on my door. "Come in." It was Hill, the squadron commander. "Orders from Chongqing. You're assigned to me as flying officer. We're taking you to Rangoon, you'll be in the flying rotation from now on."

I raised my eyebrows. "What's up?" I had no idea how much Hill knew about my grounding.

"No idea. Just orders."

"Greenlaw's?"

Hill shook his head. "Or Chennault." He was shaking his head. "Somebody up in Chongqing must like you, Thurlow or hate you…"

"Why's that?"

"Greenlaw told me you were to fly every mission we got."

Had Chennault overruled Greenlaw? Or had Greenlaw decided it was the fastest way to get me killed? Hill was still wondering about his new orders. "Any idea whose pulling strings for you?" I could only shake my head.

Within a few days we were all back where I'd started, at Rangoon airport. But we didn't stay there long. The AVG squadron gave a good account of itself in the air for the first few weeks, knocking off unescorted Japanese bombers. I got two myself, since I was flying every day, sometimes twice a day if there was enough time between raids on Rangoon to refuel and rearm.

But then the Japanese air force began escorting their vulnerable multi-engine bombers with the army version of the Japanese Navy's Zero, the Nakajima Ki-43. All of a sudden it wasn't a turkey shoot for the Rangoon squadron. We started to lose machines, though at first the pilots were mainly bailing out or bringing the ships back for crash landings. The fliers began to ask me to remind them of the lessons I'd tried to teach back at Taungoo—finger four formations, attack only from altitude, once through a formation keep going, never, never try to turn in front of a Japanese fighter—they'd cut across your curve in a cord that gives them a perfect shot at you. The P-40 really was a bigger, badder, tougher Russian P-16, and the lessons I'd learned in Spain and China were the keys to survival. But it wasn't enough. There were too many raids, too many bombers, too many escorts. We began to lose planes and pilots. Worse, the Japanese ground army was unstoppable in its relentless approach to Rangoon.

By the end of January both of the other squadrons of the AVG had returned to Burma from Kunming, all three had moved to the last defensible airbase the Brits had left in Burma, and suddenly we had begun to attract the interest of the American press. The AVG, the Flying Tigers were the only Americans actually fighting this war, from the day it began, dying for our country and taking down a lot more Japs with them. And there I was, Will Thurlow, ace, with three slow Jap "Betty" bombers and two Nakajimas notched on my belt. I declined to have the red meat-balls painted on my plane, not wanting to be a target for enemy pilots eager for revenge. But I couldn't stop the newsmen eager to tell a story that would distract people Stateside from the disasters we were facing everywhere in the world at the beginning of 1942.

12

By the middle of February, wear and tear left only ten serviceable P-40s in Rangoon, facing a couple hundred bombers and dozens of escort fighters pretty much every day. I was flying as much as anyone. It was work, but the Japanese weren't making it hard. Their bombers were slow and their escorts didn't always come along. Even as attrition diminished us to a negligible fighting force, the AVG's ratio of Japs bagged to its losses was keeping us in the broadcasts, headlines, even newsreels back home.

Three things made it hard. One was the lack of sleep, no decent chow, and constant buzz of malarial mosquitos on the ground. The second was the feeling you couldn't suppress as you watched a bomber on fire, a half a dozen men trying to extract themselves. There was often time enough to count the 'chutes. It was different from a *mano a mano* duel with a single pursuit ship, not really kill or be killed. You'd start to hope they'd make it. Then you'd think about being hung up eighty feet above the ground at the top of a jungle tree canopy, trying to choose between dying in the fall or dying in the tree tops. The third thing that constantly bore down on me was the futility of what we were doing. There was no chance we'd staunch the flow in Burma. In fact, sometimes we'd make matters worse.

Four of us were coming back after a sweep to the north when we'd found a long column of infantry coming across open ground. There were a few trucks among them and as we swept down we could see soldiers dragging heavy machine guns along. It was something we'd seen Jap infantry do in the newsreels from China. The flight leader, I don't remember who any more, got on the radio. "Enemy column below. Follow me." Then he dropped his nose and turned to line himself up with the head of the column. We were going to strafe the length of it.

Somehow it didn't look right. To begin with there was no intelligence that Japanese troops were in this part of the country, this close to Rangoon yet. I grabbed my map case and glanced at it. We were west of the Irrawaddy, the great river that ran north and south and divided the country in two. There shouldn't have been any Japanese forces there. Had we come upon a secret offensive operation, another surprise attack? I was tail end Charlie in this flight, so I had the luxury of trying to think this all out as I waited my turn to dive and strafe. But then I dropped the map case, pushed my stick down and hit the air breaks. I felt like I was going to catch up with my bullets as I ran the zipper of my four .50 caliber guns up the long line of soldiers spread along the trail like ants stopped in their tracks by DDT.

The middle of the next morning a British staff car pulled up at our operations building, a small open classroom structure used to brief and debrief the handful of pilots we could still put into the air. A lieutenant-colonel, spit and polished to his cravat and gaiters, even carrying a swagger stick, jumped out of the car, but only after his Indian driver had scurried around to open his door. It looked like the Americans hanging around the building were going to start ribbing him, until they saw the red-faced glare. He glared at us with contempt. "Who's your commanding officer?"

One of the pilots volunteered, "Atkinson's in charge of this squadron. I'll get him."

A few minutes later our squadron commander shambled up, looking the worse for having been woken up. He looked the British officer up and down, but not wearing a hat, decided not to salute. "What can I do for you, sir." The tone was sincere, I'll give him that much.

"Do you know that four of your planes strafed an Indian army column in retreat yesterday?"

This got Atkinson's attention. "The hell you say?"

"I can repeat it, but I dare say you understood me perfectly well."

Atkinson began pushing his shirt-tail in and hitching up his trousers, as his face reddened. He looked at the man's shoulder boards, gaging his rank. "Please explain, Colonel."

"Four monoplanes, all marked with your shark's teeth…" He gestured his riding-crop towards the planes on the tarmac. "Came down on the 8th Battalion, Indian army, in an orderly retreat west of the Irrawaddy. There are no Japanese units west of that river." Someone in the crowd around the colonel and Atkinson said the word 'yet' into the silence at the end of the officer's statement. He glared around. "You gung ho fly-boys killed and wounded a hundred soldiers, our soldiers, your 'allies.'" The last word was spat out. "Whoever you were, you were flying low enough to see the color of their skins. They were Indians, not Japs." There was a slight reduction in the look of consternation that had spread across most of the men gathered round. The colonel raised his swagger stick as if to strike the nearest man. "So, it's not quite so serious if the dead soldiers are wogs?"

This was too much for one of the pilots, I think it was Red Probst. "Seems like that's what your officers think, the way you treat them Indian soldiers."

I didn't like the direction this conversation was headed. So I spoke up. "The way the Japs are closing in on Rangoon, everybody's a bit trigger happy." He turned towards me. Was he expecting an apology? "My ship was one of the four that attacked your column. But it was an honest mistake. Your men were on the west side of the big river, and heading west too."

The Brit turned to me. "What's the point…?" He was looking for rank on my shoulder, but there was none.

"Well, no Japanese reported in the area, right? So, it was either a unit abandoning its position or a surprise attack coming. We decided it was an attack and tried to stop it. We were wrong." I stopped. "Colonel, your unit was retreating. Was that retreat ordered?"

The officer looked around once more and decided there was no point continuing to exercise his high dudgeon. "Very well. I'll take this matter up with your superiors." He about faced and swept his arm at the car door, where the Indian driver was still standing. We never heard about the matter again.

But a few days later I had reason to be grateful to some of the same Indian Army soldiers we had mistakenly attacked.

By this time the Japanese were close enough to Rangoon to have taken out most of the early warning sites giving us advanced warning of bombing raids. So we had almost no time to get from the ground to an altitude high enough to drop down on the formation of the two-engine bombers—Bettys, we called them—coming at us. It was mid-February and we had only a half-dozen ships left.

I was to fly wingman to the lead ship, piloted by Probst. We took off through the heavy humid air and piled on as much throttle as we could to reach the incoming bombers' altitude. We knew that once we got through the formation, we'd be bounced by the Jap fighters coming down from above the planes they were there to protect. Couldn't be helped.

The stream of Betty bombers came at Rangoon in staggered arrowhead formations, each group three Vees of three planes each. There were six groups, fifty-four bombers in all. We could figure their heading because we knew the fields they were flying from in northern Thailand. Within five or six minutes we could see them above us, making contrails in the wet air.

Probst came on to the radio. "Two o'clock high. Let's go."

We were already at full throttle and climbing so it was just a matter of heading right for the lead group. They were flying low, beneath a thunder cloud that we knew had to be hiding their pursuit escort. Probst picked out the lead bomber and began firing from a couple thousand feet. At that range his machine gun bullets couldn't do much but he was trying to break up the formation. As we got close enough to do some real damage I veered off his wing just enough to pump some .50 caliber lead into the bomber to the left of the leader. The bomb bay doors were open and I must have hit something because the plane suddenly fireballed and it was all I could do to jink around him, avoiding debris coming off in every direction. There were no 'chutes. I raced through the formation, and glanced down to see that our four planes had managed to force much of the stream of bombers to spread out in disarray. I gained enough height to look down on the bombers and decided which one to go after next.

Looking down was a luxury I couldn't afford. The Oscar that came out of the clouds firing at me from point blank range must have been watching and waiting. He just knew I was going to dive, using the P-40's weight and power to escape. I knew it too, but looking past the bombers I decided there wouldn't be enough space below to outrun him, so I whipped the stick back and clawed my way to the nearest cloud in as steep a rolling climb as I could make the plane deliver. It gave the Japanese pilot a fair shot, at me at least for five or six seconds. Since he could cut the arc of my turn, he'd pump bullets into my entire profile till I made it into the cloud. Then I had three seconds grace before he twigged to my strategy and was back on my tail firing steadily as we went into the cloud. I could stay in the cotton candy long enough to lose him, but I knew that the other three guys I was flying with needed me down there inside the bomber formations, so I dropped out of the grey cloaking me and began to head back to the bombers. I hadn't reckoned on the Jap being smart enough to play my game of chess. There he was, just under the layer of grey, waiting for me to come down. If I had dived from above him, I'd have been a lot safer. But I was holding altitude just below the cloud to locate the bomber stream. Once I saw him I couldn't try the same trick I'd used before. The thunder head was too far away now. It would be a dog fight of the kind I'd experienced before, back in Spain…and there was a good chance I'd lose.

Snap rolls, a slip S, nothing shook the pilot loose, but he wasn't firing, not yet. I suspected he was worried about running out of ammunition, so he wanted to line up a really clean shot. I had some distance on him and in level flight the P-40 wasn't much slower than the Oscar. I made a wide turn to the west and headed for the Irrawaddy River. Would he follow or stay with the bombers? He decided that taking me out was the order of the day.

We both headed west, the Oscar slowly creeping up on me until finally he was in range and began to fire. There really was nothing to do but hope he'd run out of ammunition before he hit something vital. We crossed the big river. I almost made it. It must have been his last few rounds that hit a fuel line. My propeller began to slow and feather. Now he could catch up and put an end to me. To my surprise the pilot came up to fly at my wing. I could see two dozen or so kills painted below his cockpit, all of them Chinese circles. I'd been taken out by an ace. He shrugged his shoulders, waggled his wings, gave me a salute and flew off. I had to bail out before losing too much more altitude. At least I'd be jumping into territory the Brits still controlled. I unclipped from the seat, pushed the canopy back and turned the ship over.

Relaxing my body I dropped out, and pulled the rip cord. It was lovely—warm, silent but for the wind-rush, and my pendulum swing beneath the white silk mushroom sixty feet above me would have put me to sleep if the rainforest canopy below me hadn't been so disquieting. I watched the P-40 spiral slowly toward the ground and break through the trees with an explosion that might draw some attention.

At five-hundred feet from the ground I could see a track through the jungle and began to pull on my 'chute straps to approach it. As I came through the high trees my parachute snagged on the upper branches and I was hanging twenty-five feet from the ground, contemplating roots, puddles, dried coconut shells, and sharp palm fronds littering the jungle floor. They were hiding stumps and rocks or worse, snakes, poisonous insects, or other figments of an imagination fed by the experiences of other pilots who'd been forced to bail out.

When the Indian Army infantry squad found me I had been dangling for several hours, working up the courage to press the release on my harness and drop the twenty-five feet, risking a broken leg or worse. I had also been listening for the sound of a P-40 out looking for me. My wreckage was probably smoking not more than a few miles away and the white silk of the parachute above me would have been clearly visible against the green of the forest canopy. Anyone looking for me would have seen it. By twilight I'd just about decided to risk the drop when I heard the rustle of men moving beneath me.

One of the soldiers expertly climbed the tree, a stout rope attached to his belt. He threw me the rope and indicated that I was to tie it round my waist. Then he climbed down. Three men grasped the rope and I pushed down the release on my chute. The rope took my weight as they lowered me to the jungle floor. I hugged each of them, took out my wallet and began trying to pass around the Burmese currency I carried. All declined with stern faces. None spoke any English, but they pointed north and led me away. It was not more than a half hour's walk to their company command post where I met an English-speaking non-com. He came to attention and saluted smartly, "Ahamed, sir, Sergeant major." Though hatless, I returned the salute as a mark of respect. He stood at ease and then invited me to sit on a camp stool. Each of us lit up our own cigarettes and fell silent, expecting the other to speak first.

Finally I broke the silence. "Your English is excellent, Sergeant Ahamed."

"T'ank you, sir."

"But none of your men seem to speak it."

"That is why I must. The officers are all English, and don't speak our tongue."

How could an army fight if its officers couldn't speak to their soldiers? "None of them speak…Indian?"

"Hindi, sir, or Urdu…" He looked almost wistful. "I met one who could, once…"

"But what about the Indian officers in the Indian Army?" I was surprised.

"There are none in our brigade, sir." He shook his head firmly. I looked around. A company needed at least a captain and a couple of lieutenants. I saw no officers at all. "Where are your officers then?"

"It's the weekend, sir. They've gone up to the officer's club at Magway." This was a town about eighty miles north.

I didn't understand. "Weekend? It's Friday, not the weekend. Besides, does the war stop for the week end?"

He was too well disciplined a non-com to reply. I decided to be impertinent. "Sergeant, what is this unit doing west of the Irrawaddy? The Japanese are still on the other side, nowhere near here, and they're heading south, away from you."

"Regimental orders, sir."

So, someone had taken an entire regiment out of the line of battle...for the officer's convenience, I suspected. Sergeant Ahamed decided to change the subject.

"You'll be wanting to get back to Rangoon, sir. It will take a few days. We won't be having any transport till officers return… on Monday." He responded to the frown on my face. "We can get you to the river. There you'll be finding a boat down to Rangoon. It will take less time than waiting for transport to return." It would be enough time to figure out why my Flying Tiger squadron had ended up strafing a friendly unit going the wrong way.

————

In the end it took a week to get back to base, and when I got there I found everyone packing up. Chennault had sent the two squadrons from Kunming to help stave off the bombing, but it had done no good. The Japs were rapidly approaching Rangoon and all three squadrons along with what was left of the RAF were moving north.

"Where to?" I asked Probst when I finally tracked him down supervising the ground crews packing the few spares in the hangars.

"Magway…it's a town three-hundred miles north."

"Well, at least it has an officer's club." I smiled, thinking of the Indian troops who'd saved me and sent me back.

"How do you know, Will?" Before I could answer, he spoke. "Say, I'm sorry we couldn't send anyone out looking for you. Orders."

"The other guys saw you flying west with that Oscar on your tail. You were credited with the Betty destroyed. We reported the loss, but before we could organize a sweep that way word came down from Kunming, no search. Not enough fuel, no planes to spare, they said."

"I told them you were probably out there. Made them check with Chongqing, no deal. No search. Probably Greenlaw's orders. He must really hate you."

"Yeah that must be it."

13

Every British and American plane in Burma wound up at Megway, all thirty-eight of them, including eight P-40s and twice that number of RAF Hurricanes. We were still picking off more than our share of Jap bombers and fighters. But by the middle of March their entire air force in Burma had nothing to do but bomb out our little field. Every pilot still in one piece was becoming an ace, but that was because sixteen of us were sharing the planes, each flying every day, being smart—slashing through the bomber formations, avoiding the escorting fighters and diving away. It didn't make much difference, hundreds of bombers, a few dozen of us. But it kept the few newsmen busy sending out upbeat stories. By the end of January we had four planes left. It was time to leave Burma. The planes were flown to Loiwing, across the border in China, and everyone else went over land through treacherous passes and rickety bridges.

Within another few days we were all back in Chongqing, the whole AVG, bloodied but pretty proud of the record we'd amassed against the Japs. With the Americans and the Brits in retreat everywhere else in the east, the Flying Tigers were the only thing America could boast about. Things continued to get worse right through the spring and summer of '42 for everyone but us. Hong Kong fell within the first two weeks of the year, the Dutch East Indies by March, Singapore in April. Then before long Manila, Bataan, Corregidor, and The Philippines were all Japanese.

But now that the US was in the war, the flow of spare parts, and even a few new model P-40s, began to make a difference to what the AVG could do. Still it wasn't going to win the war, and all of a sudden almost everyone in the outfit was beginning to try to figure out how they could get back into the US Army or Navy. We all knew the AVG would be replaced by real American units in China. Almost no one wanted to end up in one of these units. I was one of the handful who wanted to stay.

No one knew what kept the five or six others, whether it was loyalty to Chennault, their botched service records back in the Army Air Corps, hatred of the Japs? No one had anything good to say for Cash My Check or his government, and contempt for the Chinese people was axiomatic in the AVG.

Me, I had a reason to stay. I was hoping to find Wendy back on our side of the lines. Once we got back to Chongqing it was worse. Fighting and flying were the only things that kept her out of my thoughts. But I wasn't sleeping much. We all had to spend too many nights in the bomb shelters. When I awoke on any morning, I'd actually managed a night's sleep, I knew I'd been dreaming about her, and it was a different dream every time. Days I was grounded, walking through Chongqing I couldn't stop seeing her standing at a market stall and then slipping away from me into a seething wave of people. Sometimes I would speed up my pace, work my way through the crowd, pushing people aside, only to have the woman turn around and reveal she was someone else entirely. Why did I even think Wendy might be back in Chongqing?

I was flying three days a week, sharing a plane with George McMillan. Mainly we were trying to break up bomber formations before they hit targets in Chongqing. Targets? That was a joke. The Japanese were just plastering the city, trying out what the Germans had been doing ever since they hit Guernica in Spain.

Just like in London, it wasn't working to break resistance. But the Japs were doing it anyway. Why? Because they had the bombers and the bombs, so they might as well use them. That was the only explanation we could think of. Breaking up the bomber formations was more a matter of keeping moral up for the Chinese who paid any attention at all—the government, the foreign educated, the rich. Everyone else was stoical, no panic, not much more emotion than annoyance. Most of Chongqing was just interested in taking shelter when they had to and going about the business of surviving the rest of the time.

Coming out of shelter I'd watch people looking around, checking to see what had been hit, whether they could go about the business that the raid had interrupted, then turning their heads to the pavement as they moved off, trying not to see the dead and wounded, the weeping children, husbands or wives. The thousand personal tragedies arrayed before them didn't have the power to deflect them. Was this outward inhumanity just a way of fighting back? I hoped so. I saw it over and over, day after day, when I wasn't in the air. The experience in those shelters and the streets after raids would turn out to be more important to me than the time I spent trying to break up the bomber formations above Chongqing.

———

I was alone at a bar nursing a bad Asian whiskey one night when Olga Greenlaw came in, looked around and came straight towards me. Seduction was not in her gait, nor on her mind if her glance revealed anything. In fact she looked worn-out, too tired for caring about anything but the bar stool she pulled out. I lifted my glass in greeting, and signaled to the bar tender for another drink. She drank the shot down before speaking. "I've been volunteering in the Government Hospital. Met someone who knows you. In fact she's asking for you." I knew before she spoke again, but I found no words. Olga nodded. "It's Wendy, that woman you told me about back in Burma." I rose from my seat, but before I could move further Olga grabbed my wrist. "Listen, before you see her, you've got to know some things."

"Where is she, exactly?" I glared at Olga.

"I'll tell you. Give me a chance. But you can't go now. She's out…heavily sedated for the night. Go in the morning. First thing. They said she'll be able to talk to you then."

I looked at my watch, gauging how long I'd have to wait. She was still grasping my wrist.

"What is it I've got to know?" I tried to shake her hand off my wrist, but she grabbed it with the other hand, pulling me back hard. Olga was a strong woman. "She's not doing well, and she's been through hell."

"What do you mean?" I stopped pulling away and she relaxed her grip.

She swallowed. "Listen, I didn't get this from her. It was a nurse who told me, and only after she knew I could find you." I waited. "She was in Hong Kong when the Japs took it. There was a Canadian unit there, on the mainland side."

I didn't need the history lesson. "Yeah, two-thousand guys from Manitoba sent by the Brits to frighten off the whole Jap army."

"Anyway, after the surrender, the Japs called for volunteers to translate prisoner interrogations. Wendy came forward to do it."

I understood immediately. Did Olga? "You know why?"

"Not exactly…to help the Canadians?"

I explained. "She's an agent, or was one, for the Chinese, for us. Translating would be a chance to get some intelligence. So, what happened?"

The difficulty of what she was about to tell me showed on her face. "There were atrocities, Will, ones she saw, and ones she was subjected to."

"Nurse said she saw them…" Olga was hesitating. She spat it out, "beheading escapees." She watched my eyes widen. "it got worse." I waited. "When they finished the interrogations, she was taken away…and sent to an Army…brothel."

Why was she watching my reaction so carefully, to see how much she could tell me before I couldn't take any more? "Go on." It was all I could say.

"She was there for weeks. They think the place was for officers."

"Why?"

"Just what the nurses were told when she was brought in.

"But you said she's in a bad way, what happened?"

"She was wounded escaping. She managed to get away, but got no treatment, or at least none soon enough. It's peritonitis. She won't make it. The surgeons tried to stop the infection, but now they've given up."

"Given up…What are they doing?"

"Morphine…That's all." She fell silent. "The pain is terrible. She knows…She's going to need lots more very soon. I guess that's why she wants to see you first thing in the morning…" Olga must have known I'd want to be alone with my thoughts. She rose and leaned towards me in an embrace of comradeship. Then she was gone and I was alone with those thoughts.

———

Of course I didn't want to sleep, not even after several more belts. In fact, I never turned in at all. I left the bar in an alcoholic daze but knowing I was headed for the Government Hospital, repeatedly asking myself what Wendy wanted to tell me. I knew well enough what I wanted to tell her. The night's darkness was dotted by naked incandescent bulbs flickering every few hundred feet. Beneath each sat a clutch of homeless men and women, some drunk, others stupefied by opium, none of them the slightest threat to a large European. Nearing the hospital I found myself in a rubble field. It was surrounded by broken and blackened hulks. I began passing catafalques of reusable brick, piled up at intervals, bricks scavenged from the ruins to begin the rebuilding. Trudging along I could see no reason to rebuild or to do much of anything at all, not if Wendy was gone.

Finally I was there, in front of the hospital, dark and closed, not even a casualty ward open. It was about 2:45 in the morning. First I stood, then I leaned at the doorway. Finally I just slid down to the pavement, drained and overcome by sleep.

An orderly came out and shook me awake at dawn. When I asked the duty nurse for Wen Anying, she picked up a phone and spoke in Chinese. A few minutes later a small woman of middle age approached me. Her physician's coat had a name embroidered in English, Dr. Wang. "Mr Thurlow, please follow me."

"Thank you." I forced myself to ask, "What can you tell me about her condition, doctor?"

She turned to me. "What do you want to know?"

"Whatever you can tell me."

"I suppose I better. She's been asking for you steadily since she was brought in four days ago." She looked at me, waiting for me to tell her why Wendy wanted me.

The only words I could have said would have been bathetic. I stammered, "We were…lovers."

"Well, I have to tell you, Mr. Thurlow, she will die soon. The peritonitis had set in well before she arrived. Caused by a gunshot wound, military caliber. The bullet was still lodged in her intestine when we began treatment. There were other injuries…severe, that must have been…inflicted…" she saw me wince. "Do you want to hear it, Mr. Thurlow, or not."

"I'm sorry, please continue."

"She'd been…assaulted…many times. Do you understand?" I nodded. "There were marks from beatings as well…and scars on her ankle from what must have been a metal ring." Her clinical tone broke down. "I'm afraid we seen it before. The Japanese army are…monsters."

"Doctor, how did she get here?"

"Military intelligence brought her in. She'd escaped and made contact. That's what they told me. I don't know how long they debriefed her before getting her here. But once they got her here they left."

The reason seemed obvious to me. "Probably they'd already gotten everything they thought they could."

"I suppose so, but if we'd seen her earlier…" There seemed nothing more to say. She turned and I continued to follow her.

Dr. Wang led me into a ward where the beds that hadn't been screened off were unoccupied. And then I was beside Wendy's bed. She was awake. There was an attempt at a wan smile. The look in her eyes told me she'd been waiting to see me. Suddenly I felt glad. I could still recognize her, in spite of the wounds on her face, the shorn hair on one side of her head, the bandages reaching across her shoulders and up to her neck. Wendy patted the bed twice. I understood the signal to sit. I pulled the chair up and sat down close to her head. Then I took her hand, leaned over, and kissed her cheek.

I was about to begin to talk when she raised her hand to stop me.

"Listen, Will. I don't have much time. It's painful to keep a head clear enough." It was a hoarse whisper. I nodded. "You did what you had to do, Will. So did I. Don't regret it now…try not to…I thought of you every day after I left you…" I was about to speak. "No, let me talk, please." Wendy grimaced at what must have been a stab of pain, then she reached out for my hand. "They sent me to a…" She hesitated. I wanted to help. But I couldn't do it. "…a military brothel…when they'd finished using me to translate. But I'd found out something, something you need to know…"

She fell silent, eyes closed. For a moment I thought she'd lost consciousness, but she squeezed my hand, taking a breath and speaking again.

"It's why I had to try to escape. They caught me the first time…They thought they'd beaten me enough not to do it again."

Anguish was all I felt, watching as each slight movement of her body brought a grimace to her face. Her eyes seemed focused on the ceiling. Did she even know I was there? I leaned over the bed. Wendy reached up to my face. She spoke my name. "Will." Then she moved her hand to cover my mouth. She needed to speak.

"It wasn't the Japs who were looking for you when we were stopped on the Pearl River back last year. It was a Chinese underworld syndicate—the Triad. Ever hear of them?" I shook my head. This wasn't what I needed her to say to me. But she was not to be silenced. "Triads been around forever. Lots of connections to Kuomintang." This was Chiang Kai-shek's corrupt ruling party.

It was our last few minutes together. I had to stop her talking and tell her what she meant to me, how much I loved her. How much I now regretted. I tried to interrupt, "Wendy…"

Her hand came over my mouth again. Her voice was commanding. "No, Will, listen. It's your life I'm talking about." She began again. "The captain of the patrol craft that stopped us, when he found out I was back in Canton he reeled me in. He wanted more of the opium I was trafficking. I got him connected to my supply." Suddenly she winced, but then began again. "He told me the Canton Triad thugs knew you were due to come through. They'd been paid to find you and…kill you." Now she pushed herself up from the bed, almost a signal she was finished speaking. "He didn't know who was paying or why. But he knew your name, Will."

It was only much later that my thoughts tracked back to what Wendy was telling me. But sitting at Wendy's bed I wasn't interested in any of it.

"No one's tried to kill me except Jap pilots." I knew what I had to tell her. "And I'm not going to let them do it. I'm going to stop flying. I promise. If you'll take me back." I reached for the hand still on my cheek. I wanted to say it a hundred times but I spoke the words only once. "I love you."

She smiled one last time. "Maybe you do, Will." Then she shook her head slowly. "But you've been trying to get yourself killed since the moment you got to China, flying those Russian planes and now…" Her arm slid down to stroke the leather sleeve of my AVG flying jacket." I tried to smile back at her. "That's why I had to leave you, Will. I didn't want to be the one holding the bag at the end." She dropped the arm to the bed and leaned back, sighing. "Guess I managed to do that." There were no more words to be said between us. Another spasm came over her. "Will, ask the nurse to come. I need that morphine badly."

Evidently a nurse had been lurking behind the curtain around Wendy's bed. She came through the opening with a tray and a syringe already in her hands. A moment later Wendy's face settled into the vacant gaze of the pain-free. Then she slept.

"How long before she's awake again, sister?"

The woman shrugged her shoulders. "The question is how long can she bear the pain when the morphine wears off. She was in agony, and hiding it from you very well." The woman looked at me hard. "If you care for her, don't make her endure more."

I couldn't have even if I'd wanted to. She never woke. I was still there, in a chair against the wall of the ward, next to her bed when Wendy died that afternoon. It was the death of the only person I'd ever loved, and I'd brought it about, I might as well have killed her, when I broke my promise, when I had decided I had to fly. *You fool, you fool. You could have had a life. She could have had one. Instead both of you got a death sentence. And I was going to pass that sentence on myself. Very well, Thurlow, your punishment is to fly, to fight, to keep at it till you are dead.*

14

By the end of April, the Flying Tigers had pretty much run out of airplanes. We all knew that with the US now in the war, soon there'd be a real American air force in China. Before that could happen, the brass hats began to try to take things over from Chennault.

One day towards the end of the month, all the pilots and ground crew still in Chongqing were called together in an empty hangar. An officer replete in Sam Browne belt over a faultless tunic, two rows of service ribbons, and a tight-lipped smile mounted a platform that had been set in the middle of the hangar and moved to a lectern. There he stood, assuming that his general's star was enough to quiet the hundred or so men before him. When it didn't work, he cleared his throat several times, to no avail. Finally he called over a sergeant-major wearing a pre-war regulation wide-brimmed cavalry hat. The man had been standing at rigid attention on the back of the platform. After a moment's consultation, the sergeant faced front and bellowed.

"Attention!"

Several of the men looked up and the din died away just enough for everyone to hear someone shout. "We're not in your army anymore, sarge!"

Now the officer spoke, making himself heard above the continuing din. "My name is Bissell, General Bissell. I'm here to offer you re-induction into the Army Air Corps." A general groan spread across the body of men. "You've all been living pretty well here, getting three times army pay…"

A voice interrupted, "And a bounty for every Jap confirmed down." There was a round of appreciative laughter.

Bissell frowned. "Well, that's over now." He pointed to a table at the side of the hangar wall. "Form a line at the table for your re-enlistment paper work." No one moved. "That's an order."

"Hell, Bissell, we're not in your army and we don't take orders from anyone but Claire Chennault." This riposte was echoed by a cheer.

"Don't sign up and you'll regret it. Go back home and you'll be drafted into the infantry."

The threat provoked even more hostility from the men standing around the platform. I could hear the murmured oaths from men beside me. Bissell was oblivious. He looked down at a document and then continued. "Every pilot who signs up to stay will receive the rank of first lieutenant and be assigned to the 10th Air Force."

The muttering that greeted this bit of bureaucracy increased. Bissell tried to regain their attention. "It'll be commanded by Brigadier-General Claire Chennault." The mention of this name had little effect. Seeing he'd lost his audience, Bissell executed a smart about face and left the platform, followed by his top sergeant. The men who had gathered now dissipated. About twenty of the crew members began to saunter over to the recruiting table, looking rather sheepish. None of the pilots were among them.

I knew why. Most of them had left the army and the navy with higher ranks and blotted copy-books. That's why they'd been prepared to join the AVG. It had been a way of escaping a dead-end in their military careers. Now they'd have a chance to rejoin their old units, get their ranks back, from commanding officers who'd have every reason to ignore their records of insubordination, flying infractions, and general hell-raising. They were all about to become the most experienced combat flyers in the entire US military. These men would be able to write their own tickets, they didn't need Bissell, the 10th Air Force or a shooting war in China for that matter.

I wasn't in their shoes. That was for sure. I needed a way to get back into the Air Corps if I was going to stay in China. It was what I wanted to do, the way I was going to pass that death sentence I'd imposed the day Wendy died.

As the mob of disaffected pilots and ground crew left the hangar I sauntered over to the enlistment table. There were only a couple of men in front of me when General Bissell came up to me. I wasn't in a real uniform—just khakis—and held no rank. Nevertheless I drew myself to the semblance of attention. Bissell looked me over and then spoke. "Are you Thurlow?"

I was surprised he knew my name. "Yes sir."

"Don't bother filling out the paperwork. My offer didn't include you." Before I could speak he turned and walked away.

I followed him, ordering myself to remain temperate. "Sir, can you tell me why…" He just kept walking. "General, I've had more experience than all these guys…" His stride didn't slacken. "I've shot down seven Jap planes. Doesn't that entitle me to a reason why I can't sign up?"

Bissell turned around. "Alright, maybe I owe you an explanation, Thurlow. I've looked at your personal file and you just don't smell right to me. You quit the Air Corps, flew for the Commies in Spain, then took over for the Soviets training the Chinks to fly Russian planes. All that and I don't even think you're a US citizen anymore." He turned.

I reached for his arm to hold him. It was a military mistake. I realized immediately and let go. As he straightened out the sleeve I spoke. "General I was just doing what Claire Chennault was doing before we got the P-40s. He flew those Red P-16s for the Chinese too."

Bissell's next words came with spittle and hatred. "Yeah, you and Chennault, two of the same kind of guys. Just can't play for the team. Think you're different, better…" And with a look of pure contempt, he marched away.

————

A buzzer on the secretary's desk sounded. "The General will see you now." The middle-aged Chinese woman spoke state-side English. I rose, went through the swinging gate and knocked on the translucent pebbled glass.

The raspy voice said "Come!" and then I was enveloped in Claire Chennault's cigarette smoke. He was leaning back in a swivel chair, tunic over the back, sleeves rolled up and ink on his fingers from a leaky fountain pen. His desk was strewn and the ashtray overflowing. Chennault's craggy face wrinkled into a smile of recognition, or was it just relief from facing the paperwork before him. "You're Thurlow, right?"

It was said that Chennault knew all his pilots by name, but I was pleased. "Yes sir."

"What can I do for you?"

"Well, General, I hate to go over an officer's head, but your new adjutant, General Bissell, he won't…"

Chennault interrupted. "Got it wrong son. Bissell's my superior." A grim smile came over Chennault's face. "He's one day ahead of me on the promotions list…arranged it that way with Stillwell." Vinegar Joe Stillwell was the acid-tongued man who commanded all US forces in China.

"I see. Sorry to trouble you." I began to leave.

Chennault beckoned me to a chair, offered me a smoke and even lit it for me. "Look, Thurlow. You've shown a lot of moxie for a long time here. Tell me why you came to see me, now you're not going over a superior officer's head anymore."

I explained. Just setting the scene for Chennault took several minutes and by the time I'd finished he knew how badly Bissell had offended Chennault's men and how they'd reacted.

When I finished Chennault nodded. "Hell with the paperwork. Let's see what I can do."

"But what about Bissell, sir?"

"Leave it to me. I still got some friends in the War Department. You're too good a man to lose. Now get out of here." He dismissed me with the wave of a hand as he reached for the phone. "Get me Stillwell."

Was it to impress me? Was he going right to the top in Chongqing? Was it other, more important business? I wasn't going to stay to find out. I rose and though still not in any uniform, saluted. Chennault made a gesture of saluting back. Then I left.

———

With hardly any planes, too many pilots, and the transformation of the AVG into another cog in the bureaucracy of the American war effort, there was not much flying for anyone in the next few weeks and none for me. Other pilots were exchanging news about the invitations they'd received to join Stateside units, at their former ranks or even promotions. Aces, like Boyington and Howard, were in high demand, probably as a result of the newspaper articles that had been written about them. I didn't expect the same treatment from anyone back in the States. The Flying Tigers would cease operations completely by the end of June. Maybe my war was over just as I began to have a taste for killing Japs.

Almost two weeks later I was lying, fully dressed on my unmade bunk, reading some trash, maybe *God's Little Acre*, when mail call started in the lounge. The doors to each pilots' quarters were paper thin, so you could hear pretty well right through them. But I wasn't paying attention, when suddenly I heard my name. You know how it is, your own name breaks through even when you're not listening. Who was writing to me? I rose from the bunk and came out into the large room. The clerk was reading recipients off the addresses. He didn't stop as he handed me one he'd been left holding as others reached out for theirs. It was unaccountably thick, buff-colored, and without a stamp or return address. I took it back into my room, sat down and began to read,

Department of the Army, Army Air Corps
War Department
Washington DC

TO: Captain (retired) William Thurlow

You have been accepted for service in the US Army (Reserve), at the rank of first lieutenant, with effect from July, 1 1942 until six months after the duration of hostilities on the orders of the secretary of war.

You will immediately make your way by available means to the command, Eighth Air Group, Grosvenor Square, London, United Kingdom, and report for duty as assigned by the commanding officer. Travel via the United States is not authorized.

Attached: travel orders and vouchers

Beware what you wish for, Will Thurlow. I said it to myself again, aloud. I wanted back in the army, but I wanted in only to fight here, in China, to kill the monsters who had destroyed the woman I'd loved. I had to get these orders changed.

The next day I was back in Chennault's office. I'd been sitting for an hour and a half, while Chennault's secretary pretended he wasn't behind the pebbled glass and I pretended to wait until he came in. The only approach I could think of was playing on his vanity, expressing personal loyalty, beseeching him, imploring him to let me fly and fight for him. By 4:30 I must have called his bluff. Chennault's door opened and he was trying to rush through the outer office. I rose and followed him, holding out my travel orders. "General…general, can you spare me a minute, please, sir." Chennault didn't stop until we were out in the street. By the time we'd gotten there I'd said everything I could about wanting to stay and fly for him. Chennault didn't turn once. His driver saw him come out of the building and jumped out to open the staff car door. Only then did Chennault stop. After glancing in each direction he turned to me and spoke quietly. "Look, mister, I couldn't get anywhere for you." He hesitated and then actually whispered. "Someone pretty high up' in the war department told me to butt out."

"Is it politics, sir, same as Bissell?"

He shook his head. "Nope. Since Pearl Harbor the Army's not making any more trouble for 'premature antifascists.'" That was the polite name for fellow-travelers. "I don't know what it was, but I sent three telexes about you back to Personnel at the War Department. None of them was answered. Then I got a call…all the way from Washington. I won't say who from, but it wasn't anyone you want to get mad at you, not if you want a job in this man's Army Air Corps." Again, he paused, weighing whether to say more. "I was told to drop the request and stay out of the matter completely."

Now I was completely confused. "You mean you didn't procure these orders for me?" I held out the envelope.

"What orders? Let me see them." He rifled through the pages. "If that don't beat all…Look, Thurlow, I don't understand it, but it looks like you got what you want without my help, or in spite of it." He would listen to no more. Chennault got into his car and nearly shouted at his driver. "Let's go. Stillwell's headquarters. We're late."

———

Suddenly I needed the dark and quiet of an uncrowded bar. I had a lot to think through, including, for the first time I realized, what Wendy had told me that last morning in the Government Hospital. It was the middle of the day and the club where Wendy used to sing was not far away. But that wasn't the right place to ponder things coolly. I knew the Chinese pictograph for bar well enough. It was three symbols but the only one you really needed to know was the last one—a pitched roof over the wrinkled brow of a worried face. So I wandered into one of the alleys that came off the broad street of western office buildings, looking for the sign. Where I ended up might have been as much opium den as bar. But in the middle of the day the tables were empty and so was the counter along the left side of the place.

I put the shot of rot-gut rye down and looked at the envelope with my orders in it. Why had I received it? Why had this happened? It wasn't because I had to keep flying till I bought the bullet I deserved for the way I'd treated Wendy. The world didn't work that way, giving you what you wanted without asking. Still, nothing was adding up, any way I did the sums.

First the Army Air Corps turns you down, and the same week the Chinese come after you to help fight the Japs. Coincidence? *Coincidence? Could be. Or they knew the US army would turn you down before you did.* They would have known if they had a friend high up in the War Department. *Then someone comes looking for you on the Pearl River before you even get started. And if Wendy was right, it wasn't the Japs.* Someone was sending me to China, and someone else was trying to stop me from getting there? What came next? *Ah, yes. Wendy leaves, the Chinese pay me off. But then the American air attaché gets me into the AVG and sends me to Rangoon.* It was adding up to more than coincidence. *Had someone in Washington been keeping track of me?* Why couldn't it have just been dumb luck at that point? *Maybe it was.* But then there was the sabotage of the P-40s I was testing in Rangoon. *Just to kill me? Come on, Thurlow, think you're so important? The Japanese weren't gunning for you. They'd have good reason to knock out the AVG before it got started.* Destroying the planes before they got to China would have been smart. *And if someone had gone to a certain amount of effort to get you killed in Burma, who was it? Someone in Chongqing, or someone in Washington, sending me to Burma to be killed? Or had they found me there?*

Once the American shooting war started Harvey Greenlaw wanted nothing to do with me, wouldn't let me near his fighter planes. *But then he just changes his mind completely—fly every mission! Or else it was someone back in Chongqing who got me off the ground. Had to be Chennault, no?* No. *Why would Claire Chennault overrule Greenlaw just to get some guy he didn't know into this fight?* It didn't add up. *And now?* I looked down at the orders. I'd gotten what I'd wanted—back into the Air Corps, and I hadn't gotten what I wanted—to stay put in China. Again, why, who? *Who cares about an ex-captain in the middle of a world war?* Was someone keeping tabs on me? Were they trying to get me what they thought I wanted? *Then why do those orders say you can't travel via the US? If you've got a guardian angel, what's he scared of?* No answer came.

At least you're still fighting for the good guys, or at least the better ones. At least this time they'll win. And there was still what I owed to the memory of Wendy.

15

I had plenty of time to figure things out and no success doing so over the next month or so. That's how long it took me, in that summer of '42 to find a path from landlocked western China to London.

Didn't take long to pack and there were plenty of tailors in Chongqing ready to kit you out in Army Air Corps khakis, gold collar bars and service ribbons if you wanted them. The other things I'd need were as many cartons of American cigarettes as I could cram in my duffle. The only way I'd get to London was by making friends with Limey transport officers along the way.

I figured the first couple of legs would be hard but fast. The Army Air Corps had just begun flying over "the hump," the Himalayan mountains between India and China. The only way the US could supply Cash My Check's army (and his relatives) was by air, once the Japs had taken Burma. Delivering everything that could be loaded onto planes, the transports were flying back over the hump almost empty. Seats were not in short supply. It was a long, cold flight, to Chabua in Assam and then across India to Karachi, bumping along in the canvas slung from chair frames that passed for seating on the cargo C-47.

In Karachi things turned out to be not much more difficult, at least if I wanted to get to Cairo. The British army in Egypt was in headlong leaderless retreat from Rommel, and the panic in the desert had seeped into headquarters in Cairo. It was bad enough to send the red tab staff colonels who'd been wallowing in Egyptian fleshpots back to India for "essential consultations." Every RAF transport going back to Cairo had empty seats. All it took to wangle a seat were a couple of cartons. It was the right direction. I just didn't know what the next move would be from there. The Mediterranean was a German/Italian lake at that point in the war and Gibraltar was out of reach, at least from Cairo.

Coming out of the blistering tarmac heat and blinding sun and into the terminal door I looked around and said to no one in particular, "Where am I?" The lethargy surrounding me was palpable. It came with a strong odor of defeat. Officers with briefcases were nervously pacing, and the "other ranks" looked like they were waiting to surrender to Rommel's advancing army, still four-hundred miles away in Libya.

At the door was an RAF quartermaster's corps corporal with a clipboard in his hand. "You're at RAF Fayed, Yank."

I smiled. "Corporal, What's the next transport out of here?"

"Just loading one for Karachi, sir."

"Anything heading the other way?"

"Only down to Khartoum, in the Sudan, sir. Be a little time yet." He looked at the envelope in my hand. "Orders, sir?" I handed him the envelope, and pulled a carton of Luckies out of my bag. "Can you get me on that flight, corporal?"

He looked at me, back at his clipboard. "That'll make you first alternate, sir." He took the carton and dropped it to a shelf hidden beneath his counter. I passed him another carton. He nodded. "I'll see what I can do." Now there was nothing to do but sit motionless on the benches against the back wall of the open hall, hoping no one would come along from the Air Corps bomber squadron looking for spare pilots.

An hour after I'd begun sitting still, alone on the bench, but perspiring profusely even in the shade, when a whistle split the hum of voices. It was the corporal, bidding me back to him with a hand motion. As I stood before him he spoke, loud enough for others to hear, if anyone cared. "Sir, just take that bag out to the navigator on the Dakota about to take off. They'll need it." Dakota was what the Brits called a C-47.

I picked up the bag, walked out onto the baking tarmac, where the two engines of a converted RAF Douglas DC-3 were howling up a sandstorm. The corporal with the clipboard was right behind me. We headed to the open passenger door near the tail. I walked rapidly towards it, slung my bag in and then hauled myself through the door. There were perhaps a half-dozen British Army officers spread across the seats. Real seats, I smiled. None of the other passengers turned around. They hadn't even heard me climb aboard. Just as I dropped into a seat the door was closed. I looked down to see the duty corporal walking away. Then the plane taxied away.

It was seven slow hours to Khartoum. Once past the pyramids there was nothing to look at but the ribbon of the Nile snaking down the featureless desert. Soon enough the sun set and the need for sleep caught up with me. I hadn't spent a night in bed since leaving Chongqing four days before. I pulled out my flying jacket and covered my shoulders and chest, pushed my hat down over my eyes and let the roar of the engines wash over me.

It was still dark when I awoke. Someone was leaning back from another chair, pulling at my arm. He smiled and passed back a sandwich wrapped in wax paper and then a flask of tea, but no cup to pour it into. I shrugged, took a swig and handed it back across the empty seats. "Any idea how far to Khartoum?"

The RAF officer looked at his watch. Then he shouted over the din. "Ought to be there at dawn." That was another three hours I figured and closed my eyes again. Sleep didn't come. Instead I lurched forward and dropped into the seat next to the RAF officer who'd handed me the sandwich and the tea. He looked at me, smiled and then leaned his head close enough to my ear that he didn't have to shout. "Seems like we've got something in common, leftenant." *Leftenant?* It wasn't a lisp. Had to be British pronunciation.

"What's that?" I replied, thinking we had a lot in common along with everyone else trying to get away from Cairo.

"Tomahawks." He replied.

"Don't follow?" I hadn't understood.

"What you Yanks call P-40s…we call them Tomahawks." He pointed to the paintwork on my leather jacket. "You and I have both been flying them for a while now, haven't we?"

"Thought you guys flew Spitfires and Hurricanes…I saw a few Hurricanes in Burma anyway."

"Not enough of those planes to go round. We took every Tomahawk you would sell before your lot joined the war. Better than our ships out here anyway. Stronger, rugged, good at low altitude."

I knew what he was talking about. "Yup. I helped put them together out of the crates, back in Burma, worked for something call Central Aircraft Manufacturing Company before it turned into the Flying Tigers." He nodded. "Trouble is it can't catch up with a Jap Zero, or a Messerschmitt at altitude…But drops like a rock if you have to outrun one."

"Have you tangled with Messerschmitts then, Yank? How could you have done?"

Should you tell him? Just gets you in trouble Stateside. "Flew against the Nazi Condor Legion in Spain back in '38."

The broad smile surprised me. Then he leaned over and grasped my right hand, pumping it hard. "Good show. I say. Good show!" He stopped suddenly, looking a bit sheepish. "I'm Gibbs, Pilot Officer. Call me Bobby."

"Will Thurlow." I put out my hand and he grasped it again. I wasn't going to say *leftenant*.

"You know, we painted that tiger shark mouth on our Tomahawks before your lot did, last year, when we first got hold of them. Why'd you copy us then?"

"That's funny. First I saw the tiger mouth it was on a German Messerschmitt 110, the two engine fighter, back in Spain. Never liked the damn insignia after that."

Gibbs settled back into his seat and fell silent for a moment. "Wouldn't take it seriously, old man. Just pilots, not politics."

I wanted no argument. "I suppose you're right."

It seemed as if he was trying to decide whether to put the question fighter pilots always seem to ask each other. The words "how many" came out of his mouth and then he fell silent.

"How many? Between flying Russian P-16s in Spain and China, I had about six. Then I got two bombers over Chongqing in a P-40." I smiled. "Shot down twice for my trouble." Courtesy required me to ask. "You?"

"Three. A Vichy French fighter over Syria and two Italians last winter in the desert."

That matter out of the way the ice seemed to have broken. "Where you headed, Leftenant Thurlow?"

"Will, please…London. That's where I'm headed.

"Me too."

If Gibbs had a route, he might be able to help me. "How are you getting to England?"

He reached into his tunic and withdrew a sheaf of travel orders, looked at them and then spoke. "Lagos, Accra, Bathurst, Gibraltar, London."

"Haven't heard of most of those places, Bobby."

"Three places along the west African coast. RAF bases. But just names to me too."

I frowned. "Don't have travel orders for any of them, not ones your people have to honor anyway."

We could feel the descent now, as the Dakota came down along the Nile widening as it approached the Khartoum airfield. I was surprised to see a half-dozen paddle wheel steamers, the sort you'd see along levees on the Mississippi, all tied up along a shore of two story warehouses. There was a real town down there. Bobby watched them for a moment. Then he spoke. "Look, stick close to me and these other blokes. We'll just take you along all the way to London, or as far as they'll let us."

"How'll you do that?"

"Well, to begin with, you've just become the Central Aircraft Manufacturing Company rep for the Desert Airforce's Curtiss P-40 Tomahawks!"

And that's how I got to London, hardly any questions asked all along the way.

16

It was a dark, blustery winter day in July, raining sheets into a somber morning twilight all the way from RAF Northolt to the Grosvenor Square headquarters of US forces. When we got there the double decker London bus couldn't get any closer than the far side of the green space in front of the big red brick building. So, everyone was soaked by the time we'd managed to show a salute, a pass, and reason to be in from out of the wet. Smelling like mildewed bed clothes, twelve officers, not one of us field grade, found ourselves looking at a very temporary directory on a trellis to the left of the entry way. The sign pointed me to a room on the second floor, *Army Air Corps Headquarters (annex)*.

The sign on the door said "Don't knock," so I entered, to find half a dozen soldiers behind the same number of desks, all wearing Tech Corporal chevrons, all busy on the same number of typewriters. There was a telex machine in the corner and no officer in sight. The man at the first desk on the right wordlessly put out his hand. I gave him my now well dog-eared orders. He looked them over briefly, picked up a telephone receiver and was shortly communicating my details to someone on the other end. Then he hung up and, pointing to a hard wooden bench, said, "Sit, Lieutenant." A quarter of an hour later his phone rang. The clerk said nothing but nodded his head several times. Then he pulled a form from his desk rolled it and two carbons into his typewriter and began typing very quickly. Five minutes later he looked up and with a forefinger drew me towards him. "New orders, sir."

I took them. I was assigned to the 304th Bombardment Squadron of the 97th Bombardment Group at RAF Polebrook, wherever that was. I looked from the orders to the corporal and back once more. Then I spoke, immediately appreciating I was talking to the wrong man. "But I'm a fighter pilot. There's got to be some mistake, corporal. Please call back and check."

"No mistake sir, orders from General Eaker's chief of staff."

"Eaker?" I knew that name. He'd commanded my fighter wing, back in '36 at March Field California, just before I quit. A hard man, demanding on everyone including himself.

"Commander, Eighth Air Group, sir." There it was again, someone's malign hand or a benign one. Why would my assignment matter to the general officer commanding? "Train from Victoria Station, out at Peterborough. There'll be a bus, every hour, to the field." He handed me the directions, on a mimeographed sheet.

I was alone on the platform at Victoria Station, alone again in the compartment, alone finally with my thoughts, as the sky brightened into an English summer's day. I found myself overwhelmed by the colors of the countryside, green hedge borders framing tawny fields of wheat, dotted occasionally with farm workers, all of them women in blue coveralls, kerchiefs wrapping their heads, walking in pairs down tracks under elms that divided the countryside into pasture and field. Every few miles there were villages, rows of small, warm yellow sandstone structures. The ones my train passed through looked welcoming and untouched by what was now almost three years of war. It made me want to feel at home, even with myself.

The feeling stayed with me off the train, into the small local bus that rattled out from Peterborough down narrow roads through the same fields and a few patches of woodland. Then my pastoral reverie was broken by another kind of visual harmony. By the side of the road I saw my first B-17 Flying Fortress, then a second, a third, and finally a dozen or more, all seeming to graze across a greensward like so many thoroughbreds out to pasture. Their gleaming transparent noses rearing up above a wavy line separating the sky blue camouflage of their undersides from the tawny tan above their wings. Each high tail-plane traced a graceful curve down towards the cock-pit blister above the glass of the nose. There was a symmetry to these machines that would make men treat them like beautiful but temperamental women, painting their undraped portraits on their upturned noses.

The little bus turned a corner and ran along a wood on one side of the road, the airfield on the other, then stopped at the base entrance. Suddenly I was back in America, for the first time in three years. The guard looked at my orders, saluted smartly and pointed. "Headquarters down the main road five-hundred feet. 307th in a Quonset on the left. Report to Major Tibbets." I returned the salute.

When he rose from his desk Tibbets was a man of middle height, in his late twenties, a widow's peak of dark curly hair, a cleft in the chin of a broad face, unsmiling and stubbled with five o'clock shadow. He was in khakis under a leather flight jacket much newer than mine and without the paint work. I saluted as smartly as I could, eager to explain the mistake that had sent me to a bombardment group.

He took my orders, scanned them, then he picked up a telex lying on his desk, and looked at me again, hard. *What's he looking for?* Then he scrawled something on a slip of paper and handed it to me. "Thurlow, you're assigned co-pilot of 121482." He read out the numbers two by two. "She's on a hard stand out there.

Find her and report to the pilot, Captain Fredrickson." He was expecting a salute and about face. I stood there. "Well?"

"There's been a mistake, sir. I'm a fighter pilot. Can't fly a B-17. I should never have been assigned to this unit."

Tibbets glared at me. "Report to Captain Fredrickson, lieutenant. Start learning how to fly a bomber. You don't have much time." The frost in his voice chilled me.

It was about 6:00 in the evening, but the sun showed no sign of setting that summer night, when I found my billet—more like a narrow corridor with a door at one end, a blank wall at the other, with a cot between. I dropped my bag and decided to find my plane, my big beautiful B-17, the one I'd belong to, instead of the single engine pursuit ship that belonged to me. I was going to need to feel that way if I was going to keep my spirits high enough to survive.

At the edge of the tarmac a dozen half-ton trucks were stopping and starting, dropping off ground crew and picking them up. I hailed one. The driver brought it to a stop.

"I'm looking for a plane," glancing at the number on the scrap of paper Tibbets had given me. "12 14 82…Captain Fredrickson's ship."

"Hop in."

He pointed to the open back of the truck. Five minutes later I could read the number on the tail as the truck came to a stop under the wing. There were three men working on an engine from which the cowling had been removed. I climbed out of the truck and it moved away. The men working were too absorbed to notice. Coming out from under the wing I saw the nose art. It was Veronica Lake, her signature blond tress covering the right side of her face, a nightgown fallen below her left breast. Beneath it the words read *I Wanted Wings*. I looked around, no one was paying me the slightest attention. So I came under the nose and hoisted myself into the plane. I spent a few minutes slowly wandering down to the waist gunner's ports on each side and found the tail gunner's hatch. Then I turned around and climbed back to the cockpit, where I sat down on the right side, the co-pilot's seat. The angle to the ground was so high there was nothing to see through the windscreen but early evening sky and a pale white crescent moon. So I climbed down into the nose, passed the navigator's desk and sat down at the bombardier's glass nose. From there I could count sixteen other ships, each a camouflaged patchwork above a sky-blue underside that couldn't disguise the plane's pleasing symmetry.

There was a noise behind me. I turned to see a head in the hatchway. "Hey you, come outa there!" I rose and moved towards the hatch and jumped out. When the man saw the gold bar on my collar he brought himself to something resembling attention. His eyes moved down towards the painted tiger on my leather jacket. "Where'd you get that paint job, Lieutenant?"

"Earned it, Sergeant." I wanted no more questions, not immediately. I had my own. "This Fredrickson's ship?"

"Yup" He watched me, tight lipped. Would I demand a 'Yes sir?' No. He relaxed slightly. Then he went on. "Actually it's mine, sir. I just let Fredrickson fly it. Sergeant O'Hara. Everyone calls me John. Crew chief.

"I'm Thurlow, new co-pilot. What happened to the last one?"

"Eye infection…they said." What did he mean 'they said'? I wasn't going to ask. But O'Hara volunteered. "…and he was getting out of his flight suit to use the comfort tube every half hour, the crew told me. There was a mess to clean up after every flight." We both nodded in mutual understanding. The guy had caught the clap. "Anyway, I'll introduce you to some of the ground crew, Lieutenant Thurlow."

There were handshakes all around as O'Hara introduced three other men in fatigues and forage caps. Then he spoke to the others. "Looks like Lieutenant Thurlow's seen some action out east."

I shrugged my shoulders. "Some." I wouldn't be drawn out. "Look, Sergeant, I'm gonna need some help. I've never flown multi-engine types and I don't think there'll be much time to learn."

O'Hara nodded. He looked at the others. "Back to that oil pump, guys." Then he turned back to the fuselage. "Let's get a start Lieutenant." Two minutes later I was beginning to memorize the instrument panel.

We stopped when it got too dark to see much in the cockpit. Finally, walking to a jeep about a hundred yards away from *I Wanted Wings* I had to ask, "Where can I find Captain Fredrickson, sarge?"

He looked at his watch. "Right now, sir?" I nodded. "No idea, sir." He said nothing more. We walked in silence to the jeep. "Better hit the sack, sir. Squadron training flight tomorrow morning."

There was plenty of daylight the next morning at 4:45. I knew because I'd already been up for a quarter of an hour and was headed out the door to the officer's mess three-hundred feet away. I sat alone and no one joined me, gulping a cup of coffee to wash the powdered eggs out of my mouth. At 5:30 every man in the place seemed to rise from the long tables in unison, and we headed for the rank of jeeps taking us to the flight line. I looked for O'Hara and found him standing at a jeep with two officers in the back. He must have been watching for me and now he was urgently signaling. I hopped into the seat next to him and the jeep lurched forward.

O'Hara spoke over the noise, "Todd, Mack, this is Lieutenant Thurlow, new co-pilot."

I noticed the non-com was on a first name basis with these two officers.

I leaned over to O'Hara, "Call me Will."

He smiled. "Todd Sawyer, navigator, Mack Weil, bombardier." I turned to the back seat, put my hand out and we shook. They were very young, so young they looked like they didn't really need the shaves that had nicked each of their faces in a different place.

The rest of the crew, six men, were standing in a line abreast under the wing when we pulled up. Each had a parachute before him. I leaned over to O'Hara. "Why are they lined up, John?"

"Captain Fredrickson likes it that way…parade ground formation. Better get in line,…" He was trying to decide between 'sir' and 'Will.'

At that moment Fredrickson drove up, the only passenger in a jeep driven by one of the ground crew. Everyone else drew himself to attention, so I followed suit. The plane's commanding officer walked down the short line like an inspector general. He was a large man, sporting a black Clark Gable mustache under a stiff officer's cap so low on his brow you couldn't make out his features. No leather jacket like the rest of us, he wore a regulation tunic over a shirt knotted with a tie. I noticed the razor edged crease in his unwrinkled trousers. It was 6:00 in the morning but this man was dressed for a decoration ceremony. He stopped before me in silence.

O'Hara volunteered, "Lieutenant Thurlow, new co-pilot, sir."

Fredrickson looked me over. He seemed to be waiting for a salute. So I gave him one. He returned it with a smirk and climbed into flight coveralls. *Are we getting off on the wrong foot?*

O'Hara handed me a parachute, goggles and a leather flight helmet. Then I followed Fredrickson into the airplane, sat down in the co-pilots seat, buckled in and turned to him. "Sir, I've never flown a B-17. Single engine only."

"On the job training, lieutenant." He pulled on his head set and I did the same. I picked up the clipboard on my control wheel and followed along as he went through the start procedure. I found myself shuddering as the inboard engines came to life.

Then I heard the voice through the intercom. "Stand on those brake pedals, Thurlow." The deep roar of the four rotary engines was a world apart from the high-pitched scream of a P-40's Allison. Slowly we moved into the line of planes heading for the runways. It must have been ten minutes later that his next command came. We were now third in line for takeoff.

"When I give you the order, full throttle on all four engines." He pointed at the four levers between us. "Then pull up the gear." He pointed to another toggle switch. I nodded.

The bomber's nose blocked any view of the ground in front of us. We snaked along the runway a few dozen yards as Fredrickson made certain there was no one in front of us. Then he signaled for the throttle. We lurched forward and began picking up speed. A long time later we were in the air and he was ordering the gear up. As I eased my hand onto the control wheel to follow Fredrickson's movements I realized that unlike a fighter, the pilot didn't fly this plane, it flew him, or at least fought him for control every minute.

I could hear the voice of the squadron commander, Tibbets, "309th, form up into Vees. Heading ninety degrees." I knew this was straight at the European continent only about forty-five minutes away. *Is he leading us into a combat zone on a training run, without bombs or armed machine guns?* It was really a stupid notion and I was reddening with embarrassment to have thought it.

There were twelve planes in two groups of six, in a line of three-plane Vees. We were at the back. Keeping position was hard work, continually adjusting throttles and flaps to hold speed and altitude constant. It took concentration. Fredrickson must have figured Tibbets couldn't see him because he relaxed and began allowing our ship to slip further and further away from its position in the rear echelon V.

Suddenly the intercom crackled with Tibbet's voice. "What's the matter with you Fredrickson, Get your ship back in formation."

The pilot put his hand to the throat mike. "Sorry sir, I was letting my new co-pilot get the hang of the airplane." He turned to me with a look of menace. It was enough to tell me what sort of an officer I was dealing with. Tibbets was still talking, now to the whole squadron. "You've heard me say it a hundred times. If we don't fly in a tight formation, we'll get picked off one by one."

We were walking back to the ready room for debrief after the training flight when the bombardier, Weil, caught up with me. "That's what the boss is like, Will. Don't turn your back on him or he'll walk over you." I looked at him quizzically. *How did he know?* He answered my unspoken question. "I was standing behind you in the cockpit for a while. I could see he was flying the airplane when Tibbets squawked."

"Drop it, Mack. We're a team and we've got to support each other. I didn't mind getting Fredrickson off the hook."

17

Fredrickson didn't make himself easy to like, or even admire much. But the crew was another story.

The captain put a lot of distance between himself and the rest of us. His demand for respect due to his rank was unvarying as was his insistence on a spit and polish—down to neckties and polished boots—demands that most every other officer, including Tibbets, had surrendered to the war. He put one of the waist gunners on report for making fun of his Clark Gable mustache. What I noticed was his style in the officer's club. He'd come in, look around and stay only if officers of higher rank were drinking. Then he'd join a group of them and buy a round. Twice he came in, saw me sitting alone at a table and left immediately.

It secured for him an unvoiced disdain that was both a cement and a lubricant for the rest of the crew, right down to the armorers, mechanics, sheet metal guys, and electricians that serviced *I Wanted Wings*.

The crew were all kids, drawn to the Air Corps by its glamor, the extra pay, and a dread of infantry life. Everyone had started out wanting to be a pilot and then found his niche elsewhere in the plane or around it. It didn't take long to learn their stories once I found out where the crew, non-coms, and the two young officers—Sawyer and Weil—spent their time.

When they could they'd hop a bus or commandeer a jeep, or leg it into Oundle, the village two miles away from base, where the *Ship Inn* welcomed Yanks as though they'd been coming since the pub was first opened four-hundred years before, something the publican was pleased to tell you nightly. Even in the twilight, the yellow sandstone of the building was still warm to the touch and the din from the open windows comforting. It was often so crowded with locals and Americans, they'd come outside with their pints, lean against the still warm stone and watch the sky slowly darken.

The second night I came into the pub and out the back door I was waved over to a half-dozen ground and flight crew of *I Wanted Wings*. When I bought a round, the men began to relax.

"Kinda old for a lieutenant, aren't you, Will?" O'Hara was the only man on the team—ground crew or air crew—old enough himself to make the observation. "You wear that Flying Tiger jacket, but you never talk about it. Did you buy it off some guy Stateside?"

I smiled and shook my head. "Haven't been Stateside since 1940."

"Scuttlebutt says you went to West Point. Only a single bar on your collar to show for it? What gives?"

"You really interested, John?" He nodded as did the two or three others leaning against the wall surveying the back garden's picnic tables crowded with GIs. "Wasted life, gents. Yes, I was at West Point. Quit the service in '36. Flew in Spain. Then I went to China."

Todd Sawyer, the navigator whistled. "So that's why you never flew multiengine. You're a pursuit pilot."

"Was. Now I'm riding shotgun on your stage coach."

Victor Stemkowski, one of the waist gunners, spoke. "You were shooting down bombers bombing cities in China. Now you're going to drop'em on German towns. Feel strange, Lieutenant?"

"Hope we're not going to be bombing places people live, Vic." I replied.

The other waist gunner spoke. I hadn't yet learned his name. "Why not? Squeamish,…sir?"

I looked at him hard. The challenge coupled with the 'sir' was meant to test, to provoke.

"Maybe I am a bit, sergeant. But the people in the shelters in Chongqing didn't react to bombing any different than the people in London. They didn't panic. Morale stayed high. They didn't stop resisting. If bombing civilians didn't work here or in China, I don't think it'll work in Germany."

Weil spoke. "Well, we're here to bomb military bases and war production, not people." Everyone nodded in agreement and downed their pints.

We'd been flying training missions for five weeks before the 97th Bombardment Group got its first real mission. I was glad to have the time. I'd taken the B-17 flight manual away from its slot at the co-pilot's side the night after that first flight. Between memorizing starting checks, landing procedures, and anything else I could learn from a book I was learning as fast as I could. Along with all the training flights Tibbets imposed on the squadron I was just beginning to feel comfortable in the co-pilot's seat.

———

I was sitting next to Captain Fredrickson in the middle of a briefing hall the size of a school assembly room. We were expecting another training flight. It was early morning but cigarette smoke was already a thick blue haze beneath the concave corrugated barrel roof of the biggest Quonset hut on the base. The group commander, Armstrong entered, followed by Tibbets. The officers rose, stamped out smokes and came to attention as the two men passed each row. They vaulted onto the stage where Armstrong stopped and Tibbets moved to the curtain on the back wall. In the past it had framed a large map of the Western European coast line. Now the curtain was drawn over the map. As we sat, Fredrickson handed me his clipboard. "Take notes, Lieutenant." That meant I'd have to listen for two slightly different sets of instructions. Sitting next to me, Weil and I exchanged brief glances.

"No training flight today." Armstrong's announcement produced a wave of noticeable relaxation moving back through the room. Then his voice grew louder. "Today we've got our first mission." Every head in the room snapped to attention as Tibbets pulled back the curtain. "Rail road marshaling yards at Rouen."

Our route from Polebrook was marked due south by a red ribbon that crossed the Channel and stopped about fifty miles inland.

"The rail lines will be easy to find. It's going to be clear all the way to the target. They'll be visible along the Seine River just west of some docks." Tibbets pointed to an insert mapping the streets of Rouen. "There'll be maps in the bombardier's packs. Stay away from the cathedral. You can't miss it. Middle of town, nowhere near the marshaling yards"

It was what later we'd start calling a milk run. But not for *I Wanted Wings*. Our flying fort never got much beyond the coast at Hastings.

We were the twelfth and last ship in line for takeoff. By the time our turn came I could see the Vees forming up on Tibbet's lead ship circling above the runway. Pretty soon I was watching our shadow moving and diminishing along the grass beneath us.

Fredrickson was calling out each step in getting the plane airborne, trimmed, with the right throttle and mixture, checking on waist and tail gunners, ordering the navigator to confirm the heading and route, even as he could see the entire formation in front and above him. It wasn't like Fredrickson to be so scrupulous or so communicative. I was watching small craft in the Channel below when Fredrickson's voice came through the intercom.

"Thurlow, check the indicators starboard outboard engine."

This was the engine farthest from me. I looked across my instruments and the pilot's dials too. Nothing seemed amiss. I got his eye and shook my head. Fredrickson was leaning over his control wheel, flicking switches, tapping gages, turning his head from place to place on the instrument panel.

"Don't you hear it? Port outboard is misfiring."

Looking above his glaring eyes I saw drops of perspiration on his brow below his flying helmet. "Check your oil pressure gages, Thurlow." There was a tremolo in his voice.

I had just glanced at them but I looked again. "All normal sir."

He reached over and tapped each of the four gauges in front of me. "Don't you hear that, lieutenant?"

I didn't want the crew to hear me contradict him. I shook my head again. He turned back to his side of the instrument panel and held his throat mike to his neck. Then he announced, "Hydraulic lights flashing too. We're going to abort this mission. Bombardier, open bomb doors, release bomb load when clear below."

Weil's voice came onto the intercom. "Do you want to wait a bit, captain. Hydraulics might clear up?"

"That's an order, lieutenant." Fredrickson was peremptory. But everyone knew that he had funked it. Hydraulics only worked the landing gear brakes and the engine cowling. They wouldn't jeopardize the mission, just make the landing dicey. We could hear the bomb doors crank open and then feel the lift as the load was lightened by four-thousand pounds. Again Fredrickson broke the silence on the intercom: "Navigator, plot course back to base." The plane wheeled around even before Todd Sawyer could call out the compass heading.

The mission continued in preternatural silence. The pall over the whole crew did not abate as we emerged from the plane, slung our gear in the truck that came to meet us, and jumped into the two jeeps headed to debriefing in the vast hall where we'd begun the day. There was not a word of small talk as we slunk in. It was as if we were a group of boys filing in for corporal punishment by the headmaster. But much more serious. We entered to see tables in place of the rows of chairs, where debriefing non-coms were still setting up their typewriters, forms and pencils. The base adjutant pointed us to a table in the back. We slumped into the seats around it.

At the table sat a major, an older man, pencil poised over a clipboard. He was bald with a paunch under his tunic and two rows of First World War service ribbons. He looked at each of us and then Fredrickson. "Ship?" He wrote down the particulars. Then looked at Fredrickson once more. All he said was "Well?"

Once Fredrickson finished his brief explanation the major looked at me. "Anything to add?"

I'd been thinking carefully what I would say and was rapidly coming to realize that contradicting the captain would be a mistake, and lying along with him would be catastrophic. The ground crew would check the plane and shortly gainsay everything Fredrickson had claimed. The trouble was none of us had said a word even as everyone knew what was happening. Well, none of us but Mack, who had tentatively suggested temporizing before following the order to jettison the bombs. Were we all to be tarred as cowards by the brush of Fredrickson's actions? Speaking out now, when it was too late, would just mark me out in ways I didn't need. Silence was the only course. The major's patience ended.

"Do you want to say anything, co-pilot?" I didn't even shake my head no. His eyes moved along the table. "Rest of you?" Nothing. Very well. He closed the file before him. "Dismissed."

We never saw Fredrickson again. A year later I heard his name. He'd become a supply officer on some base back in Idaho or Montana, and was the butt of some practical jokes still being enjoyed by a couple of officers five-thousand miles east of Boise. But Fredrickson had left me a parting gift, or so I thought. All of a sudden I was going to come to a lot more attention than I ever wanted.

The other eleven planes in the squadron came back in the early afternoon, all of them, and without a scratch. The crews were cock-a-hoop and certain they were going to win the war all by themselves and in a matter of days. Despite the briefing's details about German fighters there hadn't been any, and almost no flak either. The last bomber had reported smoke and flames rising from the tracks. Everyone was satisfied. It was only weeks later that we learned the Germans had gotten the train marshalling yard back in running order only two hours after the raid.

Two days later came our second mission. I'd been waiting for orders to assume the pilot's seat, but none came. Meanwhile O'Hara confirmed that there were no mechanical problems with *I Wanted Wings*.

It was even earlier in the morning of August 19 that Weil, Sawyer, and I arrived at the briefing room still in the dark about who would fly our airplane. This time Tibbets was already there on the raised stage with the group commander, Colonel Armstrong. Once the seventy or so officers in the room had settled down, the colonel began.

"We've got an important job today, men." He looked at his watch. "This morning the British and Canadians began a division strength raid on the French coast." He looked down at his notes, "at Dieppe." He looked back up. "We're going to try to keep the Luftwaffe off their backs by bombing local fighter fields…" Armstrong glanced towards Tibbets, who pulled back the curtain. "Abbeville."

He began to brief and I took down the pilot's notes while Sawyer and Weil wrote down what they'd need to know. Sheets with radio frequency, weather and wind, and schematic maps were passed back from the front of the room. Then, just as Tibbets finished, Armstrong came forward. He looked around the room.

"Aircraft 12-14-82 crew remain here." It was our number.

Everyone else filed out. The three of us—Weil, Sawyer and I—remained, standing in a row in the middle of the hall. The group commander motioned us forward. When we were at the foot of the stage. He looked down.

"I'll be flying with you today." Then he picked up his clipboard. "Names?"

Each of us stood at attention and stated our names, rank first. Everyone knew Armstrong had flown the first mission as Tibbets' co-pilot. We didn't know why. Now he was flying ours as pilot. We didn't know why either. Each of us saluted and executed an about turn. As we walked away Armstrong spoke.

"Lieutenant Thurlow, spare me a moment."

I turned and he was reaching for a packet of Camels. He offered me one. I took it and he began to walk me slowly out the door, enough that the others were soon out of earshot.

"I pulled your jacket, Thurlow." This was the Army personnel record I'd brought along from China and submitted on arrival. I was silent. "Pretty thin for a guy your age…West Point class of '32, March Field, California, 17th pursuit group…those stubby little Boeing Pea Shooters?"

I nodded and smiled, recalling how they prepared me for the Russian P-16s. But I wasn't going to bring that up.

"Then a big blank till you started working for the Chinese Central Air Manufacturing Company." It wasn't a question, so I remained silent. "You're credited with two Jap bombers flying for Chennault. Why are you just a first lieutenant, Thurlow?"

"That's what General Chennault was able to get for me when the AVG folded up."

"And a transfer from China all the way to the ETO?" This was what we had begun calling the war against Germany, the European Theater of Operations.

"General Bissell, officer commanding, didn't want me, sir. No one ever told me why." Had Armstrong seen my travel l orders too, the ones that forbade transit through the USA?

We were about to clamber on to Armstrong's waiting jeep. "Well, Thurlow, ready to fly *I Wanted Wings* in the pilot's seat?"

"Thought you were going to do that sir."

"No, I'm not checked out as a B-17 pilot yet. Not enough hours. But you've had enough."

18

With plenty of fighter cover from the RAF it was another milk run. Twenty-two B-17s took off. Two ships had to turn back due to real mechanical problems. The trip wasn't any longer than the run to Rouen, weather clear, target easy to spot, everyone made it back, a little less euphoric than after the first mission, but still the men were altogether too pleased with themselves. This time our crew had been infected too. I had managed to keep the airplane's place tightly in the formation, there and back, with no instructions or injunctions from Tibbets in the lead ship. It was still like driving a truck that wanted to go its own way, hard work, constant adjustment against shearing gusts, sudden tail winds, keeping the trim as the fuel feed shifted from tank to tank. There were only a few moments where it felt like flying. We'd salvoed on the target right behind our lead. I began to feel really good when Armstrong cut the engines, looked at me from the co-pilot's seat, pulled off his helmet and earphones, and spoke into the sudden silence.

"Nice flying, lieutenant."

Two days later there was a rap on the side of my open door. I was lying across my bunk reading the Armed Services edition of James Thurber I'd found in the officer's club. I looked up. It was a clerk typist. "Colonel Armstrong wants to see you, Lieutenant. Sixteen-hundred hours." I looked at my watch. That was another hour or so. I nodded and returned to my book.

There was no waiting. Armstrong was ready for me when I got to his office in the one and only brick and mortar building from Polebrook's time as an RAF base. "Go on in, Lieutenant." It was the same clerk typist who'd come looking for me. He was frowning as he pointed to the door behind his desk. It was as though he knew what I was in store for. The thought came to me, *Probably does know, since he types all the colonel's paperwork.*

I came to attention and saluted. Took my hat off and waited. Armstrong returned it, dropped the pen he was scribbling with, and lit up again. "Take a pew, Thurlow. Smoke if you want," He touched his shirt pockets and shrugged. "I'm all out just now." I sat in the chair facing his desk, trying hard to look innocent of whatever he was going to accuse me of. "It's like this, Lieutenant. After the run to Abbeville I decided to make you the pilot of *I Wanted Wings,* along with a promotion to captain.

"Thank you sir."

He waved my thanks away. "But I can't, Lieutenant." I wanted to ask, but I knew he'd tell me if I needed to know. "Sent a routine promotion request up to Pinetree." This was Eaker's Eighth Air Group command headquarters. "Word came back in less than a day. No dice." He was silent for a moment. "How come, soldier? What gives? Does Eaker have something against a low-down over-age first lieutenant?"

The last thing I was going to do was confide in a superior officer. "Can't think of anything, sir. We barely knew each other at March when he commanded the 17th pursuit group. He'd just arrived when I quit. Signed my discharge orders is all."

But now I was asking myself who would care enough to countermand Armstrong's decision? Maybe someone in Washington, but surely not anyone up the road at Pinetree. I thought back to my interview at the War Department in the fall of '39 when I had tried to return to the Air Corps. I tried to remember the officer's name, the one who had rejected me. It came back, *Rankin.* Might he be serving in England now? But back then he was just carrying water for someone more important, surely? Whoever had stopped me rejoining in '40 hadn't been able to stop me in '42. Then another thought came: *Or maybe hadn't wanted to stop you this time?* I remembered how Chennault reacted when I had confronted him about my orders to England. He'd said he'd been warned off my case by someone much too high up in the War Department. All this flashed through my thoughts as I sat there, trying to keep my face immobile, open, innocent.

"Very well." Armstrong picked up his pen. "Dismissed." I saluted, turned, and left.

Two days later the 97th flew three-hundred miles to attack an aircraft factory at Meaulte, one hundred and fifty of those miles right through swarms of German Messerschmitt 109 and 110 interceptors.

With no regular pilot assigned to *I Wanted Wings* the team assumed, rightly it turned out, that Armstrong would be flying with us again. I took pilot's notes, and co-pilot's, at the briefing. Tibbets laid out the details, take off time, formation altitude, weather—tail winds out, head winds back, time over target, and then he came to expected resistance.

"We're going right over Abbeville again, the main Luftwaffe FW-190 base. Both ways." There was a slight groan among the officers in the hall. Tibbets waited it out. "Plus flak…there are 88s just north of the factory on our trajectory." German 88mm cannon sent up a twenty-pound shell set to explode at the bomber's altitude, sending shrapnel in every direction. "Tight formations, there and back, if you want to survive. And don't look for help from Spitfires from the RAF. We'll be flying out of their range."

Armstrong climbed aboard only a few minutes before *I Wanted Wings* was called into the line of a dozen planes the 305th was able to put up. Everything checked out and, very gingerly, I released the brakes and we began to roll out from the apron onto the taxi-way. Armstrong was kicking the tail back and forth in a regular rhythm so I'd be able to see what was in front of us. We stood at line, every pilot waiting for a flare from the ground control officer standing on a cat-walk outside the control tower. When it came, the takeoff ritual began.

When we reached the runway Armstrong gunned each engine for me as I watched the RPM and heat gauges. Our number called, we began to roll. Once the rear wheel came up it was time to nose the big bird into the air. We both pulled back on our control columns. Even before I shouted "Wheels up" he had his hands on the hydraulic switch and at my signal they folded in, giving us an appreciable boost in air speed. Everything below got smaller very quickly and for a moment I was flying, not driving a truck. I watched our shadow moving across the still deeply green pastures and the very yellow wheat fields that surrounded Polebrooke. Then it was back to work, constant adjustment as we strained to catch up to the planes impatiently waiting for the formation to be completed. At ten-thousand feet we leveled off and went on to oxygen.

I didn't feel good about the formation we were flying—a line of three plane elements, each element in a Vee. I'd seen its weaknesses from the other side, the pursuit pilot's point of view, shooting down bombers in China. Now I was on the other side of the equation I'd been solving in China, in the bomber instead of the fighter. That day I got a good taste of the problems that come with flying a bombing mission in a line of three plane Vees. When we got back that day it set me to thinking. Knowing what I knew as a pursuit pilot shooting down bombers, what was the best way to defend bombers against fighters. The first thing I realized was that Vee-formation didn't take advantage the B-17's dozen machine guns to provide mutual protection. It was a problem that would intrude every time I tried to get some rest over the next few weeks. But just at that moment I was too busy flying *I Wanted Wings*.

The tail winds pushed us across the Channel quickly, too quickly. I had just authorized the test firing of guns as we crossed the French coast south of Calais. Suddenly the starboard waist gunner began squawking. "Twenty bandits at one o'clock high."

I looked in the direction he'd indicated. Armstrong was on the intercom. "Distance, waist gunner, distance."

He was right. I should have demanded it. Our RAF escort had just turned back. This was the limit of their range, and the Germans knew it. Armstrong's voice continued, with preternatural calm.

"Wait until they're in range, then short bursts."

I heard the squawk from other planes stacked above us, that had also spotted the fighters.

"FWs at three o'clock level."

I looked right to see another dozen or so aircraft. Then it started. Each group of German planes seemed to line up on one bomber and come in, fire, peel off, and dive away. They came in very close and each let loose round after round of 20mm canon, a projectile that punched holes into fuselages visible from where I was sitting in *I Wanted Wings*. When they struck engines or fuel lines the flying fort would start streaming black smoke and shudder. We were beginning to lose airplanes. I watched two fall from the first echelon and begin wide spirals downward. Then it was our turn to start taking the canon fire. It was coming in from the starboard side, Armstrong's side. I felt the shock waves come at me as the pattern of canon shell hits crept along the fuselage towards the cockpit.

Armstrong was looking down out the side wind screen. Was he watching debris fall from our wing or the plane's body? A moment later I suddenly felt the plane resisting me much more strongly, as though my co-pilot had taken his hands off the controls. Armstrong wasn't just looking down. His body was leaning over, slumped against his shoulder harness. I reached out and shook him. No response. Then I saw the ice crystals around his oxygen mask. I reached over to the breathing tube. Even with my gloved hand I felt the stiffness, rigidity of a frozen tube. How long had he been out? It couldn't have been very long.

"Pilot to navigator. Grab a walk-around O2 cylinder and bring up to cockpit. Fast!" A moment later Weil was standing over Armstrong, replacing his oxygen tube with one from the small cylinder under his arm. We waited, but there was no change. Suddenly I realized the mask was blocked by ice too. I reached over, pulled it off the unconscious Armstrong and showed the blockage to Weil. He pulled out a pocket-knife and quickly chipped the crystals out of the mask. Then he replaced it on Armstrong's face. Within a few minutes the bladder below the mask began to inflate and deflate slowly, sufficiently to show the man was breathing. But he was still unconscious.

I didn't have time to think about it. Up ahead of us there was a wall of flak. The Luftwaffe fighters had all disappeared. Then the buffeting began, first the shock waves, then the crunch and snap, the ripping sound as shrapnel began to pepper the aluminum skin of the airplane. Tibbets was back on the intercoms. "Target in sight. Salvo on my drop."

I was about to open the bomb bay doors and give the plane to the bombardier when there was a roar on my left and the outboard engine began smoking and then flaming. I reached over the still unconscious Armstrong and feathered the prop, cut the engine, and increased throttle on all the others. We had to keep up. The engine roar increased. Now ahead and above I could see the bombs dropping in 'sticks' from the bombers ahead of us. I pushed the bomb bay door button, hoping we weren't too late.

"Bombardier, the plane is yours." The control stick moved under my hands as the navigator made the small adjustments while peering through his site to center our load on the explosions below. There was no way of telling whether Tibbets' bombardier had found the target, but that wasn't our job. As the B-17 lifted away, lightened by three tons or so, I turned towards Armstrong. His eyes were open and blinked occasionally but he still wasn't moving.

The formation banked left away from the target. At first we were able to keep up, but when our heading turned west into the fierce tail-winds that had brought us east across the Channel so quickly, they became head winds. I watched the ground below pass behind my line of sight with agonizing slowness. With only three engines pulling, we soon found ourselves losing the squadron speed and altitude, just as we re-entered the flak field. Flying below the rest of the squadron I figured the flak would pass us by. But some of the gunners below were definitely laying for us. We were an easier target after all. The bursts started again and the ting made by the shrapnel hitting us was audible to everyone, punctuating the engine noise.

"Pilot to crew. Expect the attention of the Abbeville gang." These were the Focke-Wolfs that had hammered us on the way in. Now alone at four-thousand feet and two-hundred-forty miles an hour we'd be easier pickings.

I was just able to see the waters of the Channel when my starboard waist gunner alerted us. "Twelve bandits four o'clock low, coming up fast." And then the ball turret, the top turret, and the port waist gun were all sending five lines of tracer at the oncoming FWs, undeterred by our .50 caliber machine guns. The fighters were smart. They'd noticed the feathered port engine on the way in, so they were all aiming at our starboard engines. Getting one of those could finish us before we could make it back to a Channel rescue from the RAF speedboats.

We didn't manage to hit any of the fighters but we seemed to have fought them off by the time we'd overflown Calais. I was beginning to fancy our chances when the outside starboard engine began smoking and losing power. I feathered and then cut the engine. The plane began to feel like lead in my hands and even without the nose going down it was definitely losing altitude we couldn't spare. I had a choice, restart one of the engines or trust our luck to rescue. *No, there was no choice really.* With a comatose Armstrong, I wasn't going to ditch anyway. I restarted the feathered engine again. The smoke from the cowling told me it was trying. I held my breath and watched the prop begin to spin. I ran the mix up richer and richer till she was pushing air behind us and we had stopped losing altitude. Could we pick up any speed? *Don't chance it, Will.* We'd make the coast and look for somewhere to put down.

"Navigator. Pull out a map, find me the closest airfield"

Within a minute Weil was on the intercom. "RAF Hawkinge, fighter base. Grass runway it looks like. Too short."

"Compass heading?"

He hesitated. "Skipper, it's not long enough for a 17."

"Next one along?"

"Couple along the coast. All the same."

"Hawkinge it is. Heading?"

"Current heading. You'll see it on your starboard beam."

I brought the gear down early to give us even more drag as I lined up the longest run on the grass field, hoping it hadn't rained for a while. A B-17 would sink in up to the pilots' elbows on a soft grass field, then the nose would come down and everyone forward of the waist gunners would go splat. But the ground held.

As I taxied back to the small control tower, I saw ground crew scurrying around to vacate the base's only concrete slab for us and turned the ship towards it. It was clear from the grimace on the non-com that guided me on to the hard stand that we weren't particularly welcome.

I Wanted Wings wasn't going to fly off from RAF Hawkinge, ever. And the crew would probably be there overnight, waiting for ground transport back to Polebrooke. After reconciling themselves to the unwanted guests, most of the base personnel became pretty accommodating. We were directed to a vacant Quonset hut and told how to find our way to the pub in the nearby town. Most of the air-crew left, taking several RAF ground crew with them.

19

Colonel Armstrong and I were sitting companionably at a small coal stove, glowing in the gloom of the unlit hut. We were both drinking from mugs of strong, sweet tea, and surprised to find ourselves warming to it.

He'd been the last man out of the plane, last before me that is. I had watched his labored rise from the co-pilot's seat. I was afraid he'd drop from the hatch behind the bomber's chin turret like a sack of soft vegetables. He managed to control the fall and then walked with measured tread to the base of the control tower.

"Some pretty swell flying today, Thurlow." He waved away my reply before I could speak it. "I'm promoting you…"

I interrupted. "Thought they'd told you at Pinetree that you couldn't, Colonel."

"Let me finish…*acting* captain. Battle field promotion. They can't stop me doing that. You deserve it. You'll get your own ship when a replacement comes in."

I smiled. "Thank you, sir."

Armstrong leaned back in his chair, took a sip of his tea. Then in a quiet voice he spoke again. "There'll be a debrief when we get back to base." I nodded. "No need to say anything about my blackout…Captain." The promotion he'd tacked on now sounded blatant.

"What do you mean, sir?"

"Exactly what I said." He wouldn't elaborate.

"Look sir, it's got to be reported…by you, or…someone. If it happens again you could die, and your crew would be in danger. You may have had an embolism, or even a stroke, mild heart attack…I don't know. But you've got to get it checked out anyway. Besides Weil knows. He's the one who gave you the supplementary oxygen, cleared your mask, and all. What if he mentions it at debriefing.

"You'll order him not to."

"I can't give an illegal order. I can't tell a subordinate to lie."

"You can ask him to do you a favor." I was silent. "Just like I'm asking you to do me the favor, Will." He smiled, suddenly reversing the relationship between us, becoming the supplicant. "Will, I know what the problem is. In one way it's not serious. In another way it's very serious."

"What do you mean, sir?"

He looked at me hard. "Will, scuttlebutt is that when you were at West Point, you went out of your way to make friends with Ben Davis, the colored cadet everyone was giving the silent treatment to. Is that true?" I noticed he used the word 'colored.' Most people I knew in the Air Corps, especially men with southern drawls like Armstrong, would have used the word 'nigger.'

"Yup. Got me started on a slippery slope I've been trying to climb back up for a while now. What's it got to do with your breathing problem, Colonel?"

"I'm from a small town in North Carolina, Will. Mainly colored folks and poor white farmers. In my town there were folks whose kids died young, generation after generation I was told, from a sort of anemia. Then there were kids, I knew some of them, who sometimes had trouble breathing, especially if they had to run or swim a long way." He stopped, and looked like he was beginning to regret speaking about this. I didn't have any idea where the story was headed. "Seems like I've had this same problem once or twice. It hits me sometimes at altitude, especially if something isn't exactly right with my oxygen supply." I was still silent. "Never happened when I was flying pursuit ships. But then we never flew above ten-thousand feet and that high only for a short time."

"I'm sorry sir. I don't understand why you need to be quiet about this."

"I guess I'll have to spell it out for you, Will. Only colored people have this problem. It's called sickle cell anemia. Comes in two forms, fatal—kids die young, and another form that almost never flares up. Anyway, it seems I've got the milder form. Now you see why it needs to be kept secret?"

I put my foot on the skirt of the little coal stove and pushed back my chair. If Frank Armstrong wasn't passing, he was at least afraid of falling victim to the "One-drop" rule. If it came out he was part negro his career in the air force would be over. And a simple blood test might be enough to unmask him.

I rose, walked over to my bunk and picked up a pack of smokes from my cot, lit one, and then offered the pack to Armstrong. I hoped he would understand the sign of understanding and acceptance. It was almost superfluous but I said it anyway.

"Your secret is safe with me, Colonel."

I was surprised by the sudden grip of his hand on my arm. His look had changed too. Suddenly it wasn't the same man any more, the first commander I'd come to admire. There was fear in his face. His voice was trembling as he spoke.

"It better, Thurlow, or you're a dead man." Why was he suddenly worried? I wasn't going to say anything to anyone? Then the voice in my head spoke. *Armstrong, if you want to kill me get to the back of the line.*

––––––––

Despite the threat, or because of it, it looked like Armstrong was going to trust me with his secret. I got to wear the two bars of a captain for a few weeks. But then a lot of things changed for the 97th, for Armstrong, for me, and for the bars on my collar. Not that I much cared about the rank. I did get a pilot's seat for real, along with a co-pilot in one of the replacement B-17s that came in as the 305th Squadron and the whole 97th Group began to lose planes.

Once that began to happen I decided I had to speak up about flying some other formation instead of Vees. That changed things for me too.

We were debriefing after our toughest mission yet, low level against the German submarine base at Lorient. The 97th had sent up fifteen planes, lost three, with six badly damaged, thirty men dead, and several wounded crew men. My ship had managed to scrape through with only a couple hundred little holes in the skin. We were dogged all the way across the Brittany peninsula by fighters. And when the squadron got there the bombs, the biggest load we'd carried so far, just bounced off the concrete of the submarine pens like ping-pong balls.

We waited quite some time outside the assembly building. When our turn at the debriefing table came up, I recognized the face sitting next to Tibbets across from me. It was the Eighth Air Group commander, Ira Eaker, who'd briefly commanded my pursuit squadron at March Field six or so years back. Would he recognize me?

I handed over the clipboard I'd filled out identifying our ship and logging the flight data, target results, and damage. The unit intelligence officer was an older man, a retired New York attorney skilled at cross examination, name of Barrow. He invited the crew to sit while he looked over the form. "Anything to add?"

It was at this point that Eaker began looking at me hard. He took the clipboard from Barrow. Was there a scowl on his face when he spoke? "Do we know each other, captain?" Would he remember telling Armstrong he couldn't promote me?

"I don't think we've met, sir. My name is Thurlow, I was regular Army till 1936, served in the 17th Pursuit Squadron at March in California. You were commanding officer my last few weeks in the unit. We never spoke."

Eaker pushed his cap back. "Then what?" I did not speak. "Well, Captain? What'd you do then? Were you a hobo? Did you ride the rails?"

I knew better than to mention Spain and flying Russian fighters in China. "I flew P-40s in the AVG till we were disbanded last spring."

"So, why are you just an acting captain flying bombers, Thurlow?"

It was not a question I could answer. And evidently Eaker couldn't either. So he certainly wasn't the officer at Pinetree who'd countermanded my promotion. Well, there were plenty of other desk jockeys who could have.

"I'm just fine with what I'm doing, sir."

This was my chance to make a difference. I'd been thinking about bomber formations from the point of view of a fighter pilot for a month. I'd even doodled some ideas.

"Sir, I was a pursuit pilot in China, shooting down Jap bombers. I learned something about what makes a bomber squadron vulnerable to fighters, and to flak. I think we're doing things wrong, sir."

Barrow, the intelligence officer, emitted an expression of exasperation. "As you were, Captain." He turned to the group of men behind us and shouted "Next plane." But Eaker's look silenced him.

"Spill it, Thurlow. What's the problem?" He pulled a pipe from a side pocket and filled it, a sign he was willing to listen.

"To begin with, sir. We're all flying at one altitude, Vees in line astern." I used my hands, one in front of the other. Then before Eaker could interrupt with a question I lifted one hand, putting it above and close behind and on one side of the other. "If we flew like this and bombed this way too, we'd have better, much better gun coverage, our planes wouldn't all be at the same altitude for flak gunners to set their fuses to." Eaker was nodding an invitation to say more if I had anything to add. "And this way, close together, the squadron would also drop at exactly the same time, raising the odds of hitting the same spot." I got up, worried I'd outworn Eaker's patience, stood to attention and saluted. The intelligence officer spoke sharply. "Dismissed."

As we shuffled off stage left, Sawyer, our bombardier, muttered. "What's with that retired major. Doesn't he see you were trying to help?"

"I broke the rules, Todd. Didn't go through channels. I'll pay for it."

I really should not have been surprised by what happened next, or at least I shouldn't have been surprised by all of it. Three days after the Lorient mission, there was an officer's only assembly for all three squadrons of the 97th Bombardment Group. The target curtain was drawn back when we entered, so there was no mission being announced. About one-hundred-forty lieutenants, captains, even a few majors were cooling their heels in the briefing hall, speculating about the reasons for this meeting.

Finally, there was a loud crash of the door slamming. Colonel Armstrong strode up to the front, as each row of officers rose.

Tibbets, his deputy and my squadron commander, was just behind him as they leapt onto the platform.

"Gentlemen. No notes. This briefing is top secret." This quieted down the remaining undercurrent of japes, jokes and other wisecracks. "In a matter of weeks, the US Army will launch an invasion of western North Africa. The 97th has been reassigned to the 12th Airforce. You will prepare to fly to Gibraltar for deployment in support of that invasion. The 305th will leave next week, followed by the 304th and then the 309th." He turned to his deputy. "Tibbets."

The major began to itemize the steps each airplane commander had to begin taking to ready his plane, air crew, ground crew, and their equipment for the move. The assembled men listened, trying to hold in mind a large number of steps they had been forbidden from writing down. The consternation on the faces looking up at Tibbets and the murmurings finally penetrated. Tibbets looked up from his clipboard. "You'll each be getting sealed orders with these instructions." Sitting in the middle of the hall I could hear one or two officers behind me whisper to no one in particular, "Why didn't you say so."

The sealed instructions came a day later. The pilots of the 305th were crowding around Barrow, the intelligence major who'd had so little patience for my out-of-line observations to General Eaker. He spoke each name and handed them an envelope. My name was last. I should have known something was afoot when I looked at the name on the envelope. I was back to First Lieutenant Thurlow. Everyone else had already walked away from Barrow by the time he handed me my envelope. His face looked blank. Either he'd forgotten my transgression or it no longer mattered to him. Walking away I opened my envelope.

To: Thurlow, William, First Lieutenant

From: Headquarters, Eighth Air Group

With immediate effect you are hereby reassigned from 305th Squadron, 97th Bombardment Group to Eighth Air Group Headquarters. Report to Colonel Hull, A-2 at Pinetree, Wycombe Abbey School, High Wycombe

I didn't know the name Hull but A-2 was intelligence. Then it struck me. Armstrong was getting rid of a guy who knew his secret.

I was packing my gear when there was a knock on the hollow core pine door of my billet. Not bothering to wait for an invitation, Weil and Sawyer entered and closed the door behind them. They looked at my half-filled duffle. Quietly Weil spoke. "Scuttlebutt is we're moving out, Captain. Headed for North Africa." So much for top secrecy I thought. I shrugged my shoulders and remained silent.

Sawyer raised his voice slightly. "Come on, Will, what gives? We got a right to know, don't we?"

I moved the duffle off the cot and motioned them to sit. I pulled out a packet of smokes and we all lit up. "Look, fellas, I don't know exactly what's happening to you. The unit is flying to Gibraltar. Not me though. I'm not going anywhere but Eighth Air Group headquarters the other side of London. They'll assign another pilot or move up Hawkins." This was the fresh faced co-pilot who'd flown two missions with the new, still unnamed B-17 that had replaced *I Wanted Wings*.

Weil drew a breath. "Headquarters, eh?" Then he brightened. "Eaker's pulling you upstairs. He probably liked your idea about a new formation. You're moving up, Will."

I handed him the orders I'd gotten from Barrow. "Moving down actually." He glanced at the words on the buff colored envelope. "I'm back to first lieutenant, Sandy. Somebody up there doesn't like me, even if they want me…"

Sawyer opined, "Well, there's the right way, the wrong way and…" He didn't need to finish the line, we all knew how it ended, 'the army way.' He stood up, came to something like attention and put out his hand. "It's been fine flying with you, Captain Thurlow." Weil did the same and they left my cubicle.

There wasn't really anyone else to take leave of, except O'Hara, the ground crew chief. He found a jeep, pulled the canopy up against the intermittent autumn showers, and took me to the railway station at Peterborough. The rain was coming down hard when we arrived. I stood in the wet trying to express my thanks for his work.

"Get out of the rain, Thurlow!" He smiled and drove away.

There was a train for King's Cross London standing at the platform as I came out on to it. Midday Friday the London train was still pretty empty. Late afternoon on the underground from King's Cross to Marylebone station was another matter. The second class smoking car was crowded with hardened faces in shabby clothes that needed washing as much as the men and women who wore them. These people all looked like they were fighting a war and were determined to win. No wonder, now in early November of 1942 the war news from Russia and Egypt had been turning favorable after more than three years of reverses.

From Marylebone, it was another train ride, increasingly empty that Friday afternoon to High Wycombe.

20

I wasn't met at the station. Didn't expect it, but didn't expect the half-dozen US AAF staff cars parked on the street across from the station either. It was grey and cool as I walked down from the suburban station to the Wycombe Abbey School. I was glad of the chill. My duffle was heavy on my shoulder and I didn't want to arrive in a lather of perspiration.

A few streets of undetached houses beyond the station I was confronted by a long wall, stretching in both directions as befitted a girl's school. It was pierced by a surprisingly small single car track and a single sentry box. Its occupant, in class A uniform and white spats came forward as I walked up and put his hand out. I handed him my orders. He looked at them briefly. "No one here today, sir. Everyone's gone into London for the week end."

I pushed my hat up in wonder. "War stops for the weekend around here, soldier?"

He ignored the remark. "Go through, sir. Billets around the building to the left, sir. Might be an orderly who can find you a bunk, sir." He returned to his station.

Beyond the gate was a three-storey building in impressive stone, ending in a large coffered chapel which must have borne stained glass windows before the war. As I turned to its back side, the cladding turned to stucco, worse for the wear of hard times and three years of war. On one side of the building some of the grass had been trampled into muddy footpaths, though the deep green spread away from the house in what had to have been pre-war field hockey grounds. Away from the building, along a lane of large trees heavily in leaf, there was a body of water, long and narrow but too slow and smooth to be a river.

There was indeed a sergeant sitting on a crate in a guard shack around the back of the building, smoking and reading *Stars and Stripes*, the Army newspaper. He didn't rise or offer any military courtesies, and I didn't require them. He looked at my duffle and spoke. "You'll need a place to stow that before you head out?"

"Head out?" I asked.

"To the flesh pots." I still looked quizzical. He clarified. "Piccadilly, the VD infection zone…"

"I do need a billet, Sarg, but I wasn't planning on any fun this weekend. Got some work to do I think."

A quarter of an hour later I was wandering through the unguarded, empty hall of the Abbey, opening doors and trying to find someone, anyone I could report to. At the end of a long corridor I found a pebbled glass door with a paper sign G-2/A-2 taped to it. I tried the door. It was unlocked. The large space was empty and dim in the late afternoon light. There was work on most of the desks but the typewriters were covered in plastic. At the side of the room was a mimeograph machine, a stack of stencils and some reams of paper. I wanted to make myself useful. No, more than that. I wanted to make a difference for this man's war, contribute something that could get noticed, that could work, to drop more bombs more accurately, spare more aircrew lives, or both, and maybe civilian bystanders too.

So I found a desk beneath a window, pulled out a legal pad and began to write out my proposal for B-17 bomber formations. By the time I'd filled five pages with text and descriptions, the afternoon had darkened into a gloomy early evening. I only really noticed when suddenly dim street lights came on above the walls that surrounded the grounds of the Abbey School.

I was on a roll, and didn't want to stop. There was a desk lamp and I turned it on. When I had finished, I reread the document. Then I went over to the mimeograph stand and pulled out several eight by fourteen-inch stencils, rolled one into the typewriter, and began carefully to peck at the keys with my index fingers. I hadn't finished by twenty-two-hundred hours that evening, so I left the fifth stencil in the typewriter and turned in.

Next morning after coffee and biscuits at the non-com's canteen, I returned to the desk I'd been working on, finished the last stencil and began fiddling with the mimeograph machine. By noon I had a dozen copies of my memorandum. I put one in the office out-tray, marked for Eaker, and left the rest in a stack at the in-tray of the A-2/G-2 commanding officer, Colonel Hull.

Now I was ready for a day and maybe even a night in London. There was no way to tell when I'd get another chance since I figured I'd shortly be under the thumb of a staff-officer.

I returned the sentry's salute as I walked out of Wycombe Abbey, back the way I had come, to the railway station, wondering exactly what I wanted to see and do in London. It occurred to me that I hadn't spent any time in a large city since leaving Chongqing almost six weeks before. I'd hardly walked above ground the day before, when I'd changed trains and taken the subway—the Tube they'd called it. I decided that most of all I needed to walk some of the streets, see how different a bombed London and a bombed Chongqing felt to me. One thing I knew already. Bombing people in their cities didn't have much of an effect on their morale. It hadn't worked in Spain or Chongqing, or here in London for that matter.

A few streets below Marylebone Station I found myself at a little park, Montagu Square, faced on each side by neat rows of three and four-storey houses, with gaps like a kid's missing front teeth, where incendiaries had burned a building into an urban fire break. The structures were almost all the same, red brick above stone, streaked by coal soot, four steps up to a front door and short stairway down to a below-level entrance, that must have been for servants before the war conscripted every valet and most of the chamber-maids in the country. As I walked down the long, narrow square of large trees over thick, green foliage, none of it was any longer protected by the wrought iron fences I'd seen before the war. *Of course. They've all been taken for war production.*

Then, against the greenery, I noticed a gaggle of men and women, about a half-dozen, all of them the worse for years of clothes rationing. They were surrounding a woman sitting on the raised stone base that had held the pre-war wrought iron rail. Looking rather posh by comparison in a belted and buttoned trench coat, she sat behind a cardboard box. As I walked along the pavement across from the square I could see what was afoot. It gave me a pang I didn't want to feel. The woman was dealing three card monte, and taking in small sums, by the look of the bedraggled players and the coins they were placing before her. The only other woman I'd ever seen do this was Wendy, at home one night in Chongqing, showing me how she used to do it as a girl in Canton.

I crossed the road and stood watching, trying to identify which were the shills—her confederates who would lay bets and win to encourage the marks. But every one of the men were betting and losing. If she had no shills, she was living dangerously. There'd be no one to signal if a policeman happened on the square, or to protect her from a poor loser. From the by-play I could tell at least one player was already expressing aggravation at his losses. The woman dealing the cards was giving him as good as she got in the same accent, bereft of 'h's and 'g's. The accent was incongruous with her horsey face and fine long hair, under a pert little hat.

Suddenly the mark reached for her in a threatening way. "You was droppin' a different card. I saw…" The others nodded as he took hold of her lapel. For no reason I could think of I intervened, easily pulling the small man back.

"Steady on." I tried to say it in a good-natured way, with a smile. But it wasn't going down with the mark or the others. None looked sturdy enough to pick a fight with me, but they were prepared to make threatening gestures. As we squared off the woman calmly but quickly rose and walked away, leaving cards and money. When they noticed, the men began squabbling over the cards on the box, each asserting he'd lost the most. I took the opportunity to beat a retreat myself.

A few minutes later I found a pub, *The Carpenter's Arms,* halfway between Montagu Square and Marble Arch. I was nursing a pint and lighting up a smoke when the same woman, trench coat now buttoned and belted, came into the bar. We nodded companionably and she took a position a friendly distance from me, pulled out a packet, and then looked to me for a light. I obliged. She said "Ta," but didn't presume further on our acquaintance.

She couldn't know that I wouldn't judge her. I'd already once fallen deeply for a woman who made a living singing "love for sale." The stab I felt, thinking of Wendy, must have spread out across my face, because suddenly she looked concerned, raised an arm, but again thought better of it. I decided to allay any concern with some bonhomie.

"I'm Will, Will Thurlow." She seemed surprised I'd put out my hand.

The accent was not what I expected when she replied, "Do you really need to know my name?" the voice belonged in Kensington.

"State secret?" I smiled.

"Rather. Weekdays I'm a cog in the Ministry of Home Security."

I resisted the urge to ask how low the pay was to make her moonlight in midday. In fact, I felt the need to put her at ease. "You're actually the second woman I've ever seen dealing three card monte."

"You're very broad-minded, Will. My name is Ellen." She put out her hand and I took it the way I figured one would shake the hand of a lady in waiting to the Queen. She liked that.

"Broadminded?"

"Shaking hands with someone who works in Home Security…" We both laughed. She looked at my almost drained glass. "My round?" Then before I could reply she caught the attention of the girl behind the bar. "Two whiskies." The girl's jaw dropped, as though she'd never seen a lady buy a drink for a gent. But Ellen affected not to notice. Instead she looked towards me, "Neat or watered?" She put a ten shilling note on the bar.

"I'll have it your way."

"Neat."

She looked at the wings on my tunic. "Flyboy? Fighters or bombers?"

"Used to fly pursuit ships, now it's the four engine jobs."

"Hope you can do better than the Luftwaffe. All they did in London was open a lot of new space for builders."

"I know what you mean. Saw it in China. Bombing civilians doesn't work. But we're not gonna target cities at all. It's daylight precision bombing."

"You may be aiming at military targets, but that's not what you'll hit." I felt like saying 'What would a grifter know about it?' But she beat me to it. "How would I know? It's my job. Not this." She shrugged in her trench coat. "We've been looking at bomb damage for two years, in England, and in mission-photographs over Europe the RAF gives us. No one can seem to get more than twenty percent of their bombs within two miles of their targets. RAF's no better than Jerry."

I said nothing but smiled, thinking about our Norden bombsights that computed altitude, velocity, wind speed. We'd been told repeatedly they could drop a pickle in a barrel. It was the Army Air Corp's most closely guarded secret. Ellen took another belt of her whiskey and responded to my smile. "Think your Norden bomb site will make a difference? Well, you're welcome to try."

"Say, what do you know about it, sister?" Who was I talking to, not a German spy, but a loose lipped British one? Ridiculous. I wasn't going to take this bait, if that's what it was. But I wasn't going to cut bait either. She might be a card sharp, but she was holding my attention like no other woman since Wendy.

"I'm sorry…" She searched for my name and found it, "Will?" I nodded. "If we're going to be friends," there was an emphasis on friends that I thought I understood and approved, "I should explain…a little. I do work in the Ministry of Home Security…bloody dull statistical work. But it's important and I'm good at it, trained to do it at the university before the war."

I had to interrupt. "And the three card monte in broad daylight?" I shrugged in imitation of her own gesture.

She took a pair of glasses out of her purse, tortoise shell, and put them on. Suddenly she looked like a bluestocking instead of a grifter.

Then she turned away and stared at the mirror behind the bar. It felt like she was going to make an impersonal confession and I was her confessor. "Did it for the thrill. First time actually, but I'd practiced a bit."

"Don't you know you can be beaten up running that grift alone?"

"Grift?" It was a question. She looked puzzled too.

"Con-game, trickery, fraud. Not what they teach at the university. Why take the risk?"

"Part of the fun, Will, most of the fun, like flying." I let her go on. "I've always needed to take some risks and just lately they've been hard to find."

"Wouldn't have been very hard to find a year ago. You could have just taken a walk anywhere in London."

She nodded. "When the Blitz started I spent every night in the street watching the flames, listening to the buildings fall. Even got a ARP arm band and a helmet so the police wouldn't stop me. After a while the rush wore off, and then the Blitz ended anyway. They won't let me fly a bomber with two engines out. Before the war I did lots of stunts, just to keep boredom at bay."

I looked at my watch. I didn't want another drink and I had forgotten to eat all day. Dinner was a meal I never liked facing alone. Suddenly I found myself blurting. "Will you have dinner with me, Miss Ellen…?" I waited for her to supply her surname.

"Ashcroft-Metcalf…Double barreled I'm afraid. I'd love to dine with you Lieutenant Thurlow." She said *Leftenant* in a way that I decided I'd get used to. "But it's much too early for… grifters."

"I can wait. What's the best restaurant near here?"

"The Grill at the Dorchester…it's bomb proof."

"I'll meet you there in an hour."

When she got there, only ten minutes late, Ellen was wearing a stole over a pre-war cocktail dress that did a good deal of justice to her double barreled name—Ashcroft-Metcalf. She caught her breath as she took a seat too quickly for me to rise or the maître d' hurrying over to pull it out for her. She shrugged out of the wrap with an audible sigh and sat, looked up at the waiter and spoke.

"An American martini, twist, please." She hadn't noticed this was what I had before me. Then she looked. "Beat me to it, Will." I smiled and she continued. "Shall we begin again?"

I took her meaning. "My name's Will, Will Thurlow."

"Just so. And what is it you do for a living, *Leftanant* Thurlow?"

I still wasn't expecting that pronunciation, but I let it pass. "Well, I used to try to shoot airplanes down, first in Spain, then China. But now I'm driving a bomber mainly over the French coast."

She didn't ask which side in Spain and immediately I liked her more. "And the story of your life, Miss Ashcroft-Metcalf?"

Ellen looked at me in mock dudgeon. "If you must be formal, it's Lady Ellen, very impoverished very minor nobility on father's side. Shall we order before I start?" She glanced at the menu before her and dropped it. She'd evidently been here before. When the waiter took her order I simply added, "Same for me."

I wasn't going to let her forget her promise. "Can you get back to that story you stopped so we could order?"

"I suppose I must. Went to that damn girls' school where your air force is based right now."

"Wycombe Abbey?"

"Yes. Then Girton, where I read economics." She saw the frown on my face. "Girton? Woman's college in Cambridge. Didn't wait to be conscripted. Found a place suited to my talents in the Ministry of Home Security, statistical section."
"Conscription? Do they draft women in England?"

"Every woman under 30. Began a year ago. Anyway I work for a very smart man in the Ministry trying to make sense of the Blitz."

"What have you learned, besides it doesn't work?"

"Mainly that soldiers and politicians don't listen to scientists."

"Convince me we should?"

"Here's one example. Convoys. For a year we couldn't convince the Admiralty that it's just as hard for a German submarine to find a whole convoy in the vast Atlantic as to find a single ship in it. And a whole convoy can be protected. The Americans still don't believe us." The obviousness of the observation floored me. She must have noticed my jaw drop. "Shall I go on."

"There's a war on. And I need to stop thinking about it for at least one evening."

I was deciding whether to take her hand across the table when she covered mine. Our meals came, adhering impressively in their composition to the rationing, but departing from them at least in appearance, parsley on the boiled potatoes, slivers of almond on the sautéed cod. It was almost like eating food. But sitting across from Lady Ellen Ashcroft-Metcalf I had no reason to regret the square meals I could have had at Wycombe Abbey officers' mess.

We were smoking companionably over two coffees at the end of our meal. We'd avoided current events all through the meal and both felt pretty good about it. Ellen exhaled and spoke. "Can I bring up another war?" I nodded. "Spanish…did you say you flew in Spain? For the Republic?"

"Do I look like a Luftwaffe pilot?" I smiled as I said it. She needed to know that I didn't really take offence at the question. "In fact, I was shot down by one." I shivered recalling the experience more vividly than I had expected.

Ellen didn't notice. She was sharing the experience of Spain. "I was there too. Went out with a Scottish ambulance two summers when I was at Cambridge."

"Funny, you don't strike me as a Communist." We laughed together.

We were there another hour, telling stories about Spain, remembering the hardships, and the solidarity, the wine, the songs, the dangers too. It felt good. Suddenly it was late and the grill was closing. We rose from our chairs. "I hope you'll let me see you again, Ellen."

"Perhaps." It was better than a flat no.

21

There was a great deal of bustle in the Air Intelligence office when I turned up on Monday morning in a class A uniform, and presented my orders to the clerk. He took them and went into the inner office. He came back three or four minutes later.

"Take a seat, lieutenant. Colonel Hull will see you when he has a moment." The corporal returned to his typing.

I sat there most of the morning, with two breaks while I went outside to smoke. It was after 11:30 when the clerk called my name. "Lieutenant Thurlow? Colonel Hull wants to know if this is yours?" He was holding the stack of mimeographs I'd made on Saturday morning.

"Yes, Corporal."

"Then, you're to go in right now, sir."

A moment later I was saluting Hull. "Thurlow, Lieutenant. Reporting, sir."

Hull was holding a copy of my report, the one I'd left in the in-tray of his clerk's desk. "What's this, Thurlow?"

"It's a recommendation about mission formation, sir. I talked about it with General Eaker. When I was ordered up here I assumed he wanted me to put it down on paper. Figured that was why I was sent here when my unit was shipped out to Africa?"

Hull dropped the copy he was holding into the trash. "Don't know anything about that, Thurlow. We got an order from the War Department to keep you flying B-17s right here in the Eighth. You were ordered here to be reassigned. That's all. Cool your heels in the officer's club till we find you a new unit. Dismissed."

There it was again. Why did someone in the War Department care where I was or what I was doing. And why were they pulling the strings through military intelligence instead of personnel?

It didn't take long to find a B-17 unit that needed more pilots and co-pilots. They all did. Two days later I had my new orders. The 360th Squadron of the 303rd Bombardment Group, at Molesworth, not ten miles north of where I'd started, Polebrooke. Just another bomber base an hour's train-ride back up towards Peterborough. Seen one bomber base in East Anglia, seen 'em all. The country side was just as bucolic, the permanent buildings of the RAF base just as small and sparse, and the vast American GI infrastructure surrounding it pretty much laid out exactly the same way as Polebrooke.

The air exec looked down at my orders, then back up at me. "Well, Thurlow, you're way ahead of us. Six missions. Don't know how soon you'll get any more. We're still training in this unit."

I smiled. "No hurry about getting back into combat, sir."

He leafed through my paperwork. "Six missions, eh…Maybe you can help."

———

It rained all day, every day for the first week of November. The intermittent sheet of cold water in midday gloom, cutting into clothes, spraying between tent-flaps, gusting through hangar doors, made the hours of mere rain seem like a brightening summer's day. There was no point trying to fly formations. Airplanes, everyone knew, would simply knock one another out of the sky. Yet, everyone also knew, at least from hearsay, that staying in formation was the only way to survive.

One late afternoon, a sign went up in the officer's club. *High Pressure Front Coming in. Squadron will fly tomorrow.* I was nursing a beer when the clerk came in to post the notice. A moment later the squadron CO was standing next to me.

"Name is Robinson, Major Robinson." I was about to move to attention and snap a salute when he took my arm. "As you were, Lieutenant. We're off duty. Can we talk?"

"Yes sir." He took my pint and carried it along with his to a table.

"We're going to work on formation flying tomorrow, Will." He hadn't asked to call me that. He'd just done it. Perhaps it was because we were the same age, a half-dozen years older than the other pilots in the 305th. "Any advice."

"Quite a lot, sir. But don't know if you'd be allowed to follow it."

"Why not? Unorthodox, unapproved. This group is too green not to use all the good advice we can get."

"All right, major. Two things. First, the formations we fly, half the guns can't be used half the time because they're pointed at our own planes. Second, the Luftwaffe has figured out the B-17's weakest point is the front of the plane. They line up and come in at us twelve o'clock high, one after the other. That's because the plane has only a couple of .30 calibers in the nose, not the .50 calibers everywhere else on the fuselage."

"Not much we can do about that, is there?"

He hadn't seen. "Look, major, the problems are related. Just because one airplane can't get its guns trained on an enemy right in front of it doesn't mean others can't. If we fly in a vertical echelon, like the treads in a staircase, then planes below the target plane can use their upper ball-turret guns to protect the ship under attack. And the ships above can use their lower ball turret."

His eyes opened. I had his attention. "I get you."

"Not just that. Flying like that, the bombs will all go out at almost the same time and cluster closer together. If the lead bombardier is on target, everyone else will be too."

"Did you fly this formation with your old group, Thurlow?"

"No, sir. I'd just started working on the idea when the group was transferred to North Africa."

"Why didn't you go with it?"

I wasn't about to start explaining or speculating. "Don't know, sir."

The major took a small notebook out of his leather jacket and a mechanical pencil. He opened the book to two blank pages, passed it to me along with the pen. "Okay, Will, sketch it out for me."

I tried to reconstruct the figures in the memo I'd mimeographed back at Wycombe Abbey. *Why didn't you save a copy?* I passed my diagrams over to Robinson, and explained how the staircase staggering of Vees solved both problems.

"We'll try it tomorrow, Thurlow." He rose and put a hand on my shoulder to stop me getting up. "As you were." He reminded me we were off duty.

The next morning, an orderly shook me awake in the dark. I'd packed my flight gear the night before. It was a habit I'd gotten into after forgetting a glove liner and suffering the beginnings of frostbite on a previous mission. No one spoke at breakfast. Although it was a practice mission, these pilots, navigators, and bombardiers were green enough to worry.

They were early to the briefing hall too. I came in just before Robinson swept down the middle isle and jumped onto the podium. He pulled forward a blackboard on wheels and spoke.

"Listen up. We're going to fly a new formation today, see if we can do it and if we like it. It's got some advantages if we can figure out how to fly it." Then he drew the formation I had drawn, but better. He sketched a top view with six Vees of three planes each in a bigger Vee, then a front view in which the top group was on the right and the bottom group on the left of the middle group, and finally a side view, a staircase in which each Vee flew above and a step behind the Vee below it. He began to explain. "Look, this way every plane can fire all its guns to protect itself and every other plane, not hit our own ships, and train a lot of guns twelve o'clock high, where the Messerschmitts and the Focke Wolfs come in." I smiled. He'd understood and he'd figured out a way to sell it even better than I had.

When the plane assignments were handed out my ship was riding shotgun on the tail-end Charlie of the bottom squadron, the most vulnerable plane, the one that benefited least from the formation I'd figured out. And it was the hardest position to fly in the formation. *Your reward for coming up with the idea, Thurlow.* I laughed out loud. It was the Army way.

Just getting twelve planes to fly in the general vicinity of one another is hard enough. It was harder once you added cloud-cover and the prop-wash of other planes, plus gusts of wind, that made a plane jig and jag even while one held the controls steady. Robinson spent the better part of the three hours we were in the air nagging at pilots up and down his stair-staggered formation and back and forth across the fanned out Vees. By the end of the run, most of the pilots had gotten the hang of the formation. I knew they wouldn't like the amount of extra work it took, monitoring the lead ship in each Vee and constantly adjusting for the turbulence of close flying. But they were just about able to manage it and from the way the gunners in their turrets were playing at firing I could see that they understood the benefits of the formation.

Robinson's plane was the last to land. It was still midafternoon, but the sun was making a rare golden hue on the western horizon, something one never saw that autumn in East Anglia. Somehow it fit my mood. For a change things seemed to be going a little better. The major's ship taxied right up to the squat two-storey building and he was the first to tumble out of the B-17's nose hatch. I was waiting at the base of the control tower, hoping to bask in the glow of my initiative, and to ask why I'd been relegated to a co-pilot's seat.

Well before he reached even hailing distance a staff car drove up at speed, screeched to a stop. Even before the driver could open the door, an officer—a lieutenant-colonel by the eagles on his collar—was thrusting himself out of the back seat and striding towards Robinson. He didn't mind who could hear him as he began to abuse the 303rd Group's commander.

"Major, just what the hell were you doing up there?" He gave the target of his abuse no chance to reply. "There's regulations about formation flying. They're meant to prevent clowns like you doing stupid stuff." The colonel stopped, his rage momentarily spent. By now Robinson was standing at attention, trying hard to look contrite if not shamefaced.

"Colonel Le May, I'm sorry. I was…experimenting with something. If it worked I was going to bring it to you."

"You'll bring it to me alright, Robinson. Your office, now!" He turned and almost stomped into the control tower, followed by his driver and an adjutant. Robinson followed, but shot a glance of anger my way as he entered the building.

I turned to another pilot, one who'd been in the 303rd since the squadron had been formed Stateside. "Who was that?"

"Who, the iron-ass bird colonel?" This was a reference to eagles of a lieutenant-colonel's rank on the officer's shoulder boards. "Le May, commander of the 305th, Deputy Head of the Bombardment Group. Stay out of his way." Then the man turned and walked away, as though it had been dangerous even to identify him.

The next time I saw Le May it was at the briefing for our first mission, a week later, a week spent flying the old way, the regulation way.

It was still cold and black at 7:30 in the morning. Flight crews had been up for two hours but ground crews had been working all night. In the gloom you could see the glow of lights under the planes as we walked to the briefing hut. No one spoke. It was nerves for the other officers, and a sort of fatalism for me.

Le May pulled back the curtain to show the mission. I breathed a sigh unnoticed by the others. It wasn't exactly a milk run, but it could have been worse. Our primary was La Pallice, a seaboard sub-base, with Lorient, the bigger base a hundred miles closer, as the secondary target. But then Le May continued.

"There's going to be flak, lots of it. But once we hit the initial point and start our bomb run, there's to be no evasive action. Straight and level. Any pilot that disobeys, you'll be up before a discipline board before you can get your flight gear off." He paused and looking like a snarling boxer dog, added one last line. "Get it?" Then he stepped off the podium and walked out of the briefing hut.

There were three squadrons on the mission, but the group couldn't get more than twenty-six planes in the air. It took almost an hour after the 10:00 take-off time to form up in a line of Vees behind the lead ship with Le May flying. The flak started over Nantes, and the formation began to loosen as the big planes tried to avoid the small bursts in front of them. Within minutes despite the chill at ten-thousand feet I was awash with sweat, trying to move my ship around and away from explosions. Once we were through the flak, German fighters took over.

Le May was in the lead ship and saw them first. Over the intercom came the orders, "Tighten up…stay with me."

My arms were flaccid from the workout. I pushed the co-pilot's arm. It broke his spell. Indicating the control column, I put my hand to the throat mic.

"Take over, will you. I need a break." He tried. We were the tail end Charlie of the last Vee in the formation, drifting further and further back. I knew once the Focke Wolfs got past the formation in their head-on run they'd start picking us off one by one. And with the fewest guns from other ships to protect us, we'd be picked off first. I took the plane back from the co-pilot, and pushed all the throttles forward. It lurched forward into the prop wash of the Vee ahead of us.

It was then all three squadrons in the group began to lose airplanes. I could see one in the second Vee and another in the first, attacked head on. Both were hit in two engines, it looked like. One suddenly lost a wing. They fell out of formation and began spiraling slowly towards the ground.

Over the intercom I could hear one of our gunners. "See any chutes?" There was no reply. Instead, the noise of machine-gun fire filled the plane. The top turret and the waist gunners were taking on the same German fighter coming in at three o'clock level.

I watched the fighter come in steadily, refusing to be turned away by the line of tracers that streaked towards it. Suddenly the thought came to me. *You used to be on the other end of this encounter. How does it feel to be taking instead of dishing out?* I could remember the feeling of invisible, invulnerable, pleasure, glee, joy, shooting bombers out of the sky, only later thinking that there had been human beings inside them, fighting for their own lives. *And now it's all you can think of.* Why are they doing this, killing flesh and blood people without a second's hesitation or compunction? On neither side did the combat feel like a *kill or be killed* duel. To the fighter pilots taking aim it was just a matter of destroying large, slow, inanimate objects. To the bomber crews it was the feeling of being hunted—victims of ruthless but entirely mechanical killers.

The navigator interrupted my reverie. "Lieutenant Thurlow, we're way off course. The group's been doing a slow 270 turn and we're headed back to the coast. I think the lead navigator is lost."

I pulled out a map, trying to orient, but the cloud cover was sixty percent and we weren't near enough to the coast to match any landfall to the shore line traced on the chart.

"Thanks, navigator. Group leader must know something we don't know."

As we came back to the coast, the fighters peeled off, having taken down four ships, and the flak began again. Now the navigator came on the intercom. "Lieutenant Thurlow, that's Lorient head on the coast below. Big sub base."

I knew the base from previous missions. It wasn't our secondary, but evidently Le May had decided it was to be our target for the day. The ten 500 pound bombs in each of the fourteen B-17s left would have no effect on the fifteen meter concrete roofs of the U-boat pens, even if we managed direct hits.

Le May's lead plane stopped jiggling and juking as it passed the initial point and flew straight and level through the thickest of the flak, dropping its load accurately enough, it looked like, on the U-boat pens. The other planes followed suit. The bombs came out of the ship ahead and I watched them till they faded into small dots above the landscape, knowing they would literally bounce off the concrete and explode harmlessly above it.

The group continued out to sea and then wheeled right, keeping far enough from shore to feel safe from flak and fighters as we returned to base.

22

I flew another three missions in the next ten days. The railroad marshalling yards at Rouen, where I'd been once before, La Pallice, our primary on the 303rd's first mission, and Rotterdam, a run that cost the group a third of its strength, eight planes lost to fighters and flak. Then the weather turned from grim to awful and we were stood down for almost a week. Crews that had made the missions, without turning back for mechanical "breakdowns," got passes.

It was a Saturday morning at the end of the stand-down week, still dark between the wan roadway lights as the jeep I was in drove away from the base. At the Peterborough railway station I had a brain wave and went to the post-office across the street and asked for the London phone directory. There was one and only one listing for an E. Ashcroft-Metcalf, no address. I rang, four rings, five, six. I wasn't going to hang up. Brits didn't jump to the phone like an American.

Now it was on eight or nine, and suddenly a languorous "Yes?"

"Ellen, it's Will, Will Thurlow."

"Will?" There was a little more interest in the voice now. "Still alive, then?"

"I've got a fourty-eight hour pass. Coming into London. Can I see you?"

"I'm working all afternoon."

"On a Saturday?"

"People worked here Saturdays even before the war." The observation was monotone. Then in a more inviting voice she continued. "Meet me at the Dorchester Grill again, 7:30." There was another pause. "Don't bother trying to get a hotel room. I can put you up."

"In that case you'll have to give me your address."

"Sorry, no. I'll guide you home from the Dorchester myself."

"What'll I do till then?" I began to hum the words, *A rainy day in London town…*

"National Gallery, Victoria and Albert, British Museum? A man who is tired of London is tired of life." It sounded like wisdom, but whose I wondered? Before I could ask she'd rung off, hung up, left me looking at the receiver.

Just to be contrary I went to the Tate instead. Methodically lavishing attention on each picture, I managed to pass an agreeable afternoon, along with a half-dozen other US Army non-coms. At least four sergeants saluted me as they passed through the galleries. Not a single officer. Why non-coms only? I began to worry that the Tate was *off-limits* to US personnel lieutenant or above. *Ridiculous!*

I stood for a longtime before Leighton's *Bath of Psyche*, risking arrest, hoping to be joined by one of my cultured fellow countrymen. They must have treated my interest as prurient, for I was left alone in my contemplation.

Ellen was already one American martini ahead of me when I arrived at the Dorchester Grill. She raised the cocktail as I approached, shaking rain off my trench coat. The *maître'd* looked from Ellen's raised glass to me and I nodded. Before she could speak, I asked, "What did you mean by that question, on the phone, *still alive?* As though you expected otherwise?"

She frowned. "Well, what is it now, ten, eleven missions?"

"Twelve actually."

"So, if the figures we're getting from your headquarters are right, there's more than a sixty-five percent chance that you're already dead."

It was my turn to frown. "Let's see, we've got to fly twenty-five missions to complete a tour of duty, so I've got well over a one-hundred percent chance of buying it."

"Well, let's hope the loss rate stays as low as five perent. A lot of the RAF bombing missions, it's eight or nine percent. And they're all night-time."

"This conversation is making me hungry." I smiled and picked up my menu as my martini arrived.

The only way to avoid shop talk was to lie some more to each other about our lives before the war. So we did. Not exactly lying, but picking and choosing from the past, with shadings and elisions to make ourselves look interesting, if not always good.

I told her about China, but didn't tell her about Wendy. Ellen told me her stories, escaping from Cambridge, coming back to London from Spain, a free agent for the first time in her life. I was sure she was keeping as much from me as I was from her. Once the stories brought us forward far enough we couldn't avoid the war and our parts in it.

Ellen pushed her plate back. "My masters can't understand it. It's been six months since your lot came in. There are fifty-thousand air crew, ground crew, and staff here now. But the Eighth Air Group can't seem to get more than one-hundred-forty planes into the air at any one time. Our lot have been sending eight-hundred planes a night over Germany, every plane carrying twice the bomb load of your Flying Fortresses."

"With what sort of results?" I made the tone earnest, not skeptical. It was the professional bomber pilot in me asking.

"Nothing to speak of so far." She shook her head. "It's my business to know." She leaned back, drew out a silver cigarette case, took one and handed the case to me. The fags were oval. I hadn't seen that before. Then she continued. "Not quite nothing. Two ways to look at it, maybe three. The best way is this. The real damage we're doing to the German war effort is to keep about a million soldiers, five-hundred fighters, and a hundred-thousand 88mm flak cannons in Germany. Otherwise they'd be pounding the Russians even worse."

I had to grant the point. "For all we know it's the difference that's kept the Russians from defeat" There had now been two successive years of German advance in Russian, each time brought to a halt as much by weather as resistance. "So, what are the other two ways to look at it."

"Bomber Harris's way. Kill as many German civilians as you can. Break their morale." Bomber Harris—Air Marshall Arthur Harris—head of Bomber Command since the beginning of 1942. Everyone had seen his pronouncements of biblical retribution on the newsreels.

We shared a grimace. I spoke. "Won't work. I've seen it. You've seen it. Hell, Harris has seen it. Right here in London." She nodded. "You said there were three ways to look at it. What's the third?"

"Well, we've got to do something to convince the Russians we're serious about the war. This is the only thing we can do, even if it has no military value."

"Don't tell the guys flying our planes that. They don't even want to be here. All they want to do is shoot down Japs."

She reached out a hand and covered mine. "You've got to find a way to stop flying, Will. Twenty-five missions is a death sentence." We were both silent for a long moment. Then the small dance band began to play and we rose to move slowly around the floor, hoping the shared arousal might obliterate the conversation.

Afterward Ellen led me back to her flat. We walked slowly through the dead quiet of the blacked-out streets, in a light drizzle. She held my arm under the umbrella, guiding me as we were passed occasionally by a cab or car, its headlamps emitting the slit of light allowed, shimmering a few yards of glistening pavement ahead of us. We must have walked a quarter of an hour, with only a turn or two before we found ourselves at an open square and a terrace of houses broken by an occasional vacant space of cratered rubble. It was only the next morning I was able to see it was Montagu Square, where I'd first seen Ellen, brazenly tempting gamblers.

She led me down the stair to the service flat, reaching into her purse for the latch key. "Looks intact, neat façade, but every story above this one is burned out. Incendiary, winter of '41." She flicked the switch on a lamp and then reached for the electric heater in the fireplace. "We'll get cold pretty quickly if we don't get into bed." She smiled, pointing to the only bed in the room, a bare double. "Bathroom's over there. You first." She handed me a rather nice man's dressing gown. There was still a Selfridges' tag on it. Pricey at eight quid. Looked like I'd be the first to use it. I came out of the loo and Ellen went in. So I sat down in the only lounge chair there was, under the lamp, smoking and waiting. Ellen came out in a dark silk robe silhouetted against a bright bathroom light. For a moment I saw Wendy standing there in the gloom of a Canton tenement.

———

When Ellen shook me awake that Sunday morning, it was bright. "Rise and shine, lieutenant." I began to protest that I didn't attend church. She was shaking her head. "Not divine service. Breakfast with my boss. You'll like him, Will." She rose from the bed, undraped and unabashed. I pulled her back, but she resisted. "Time for that when we return."

It was a tube ride to Leicester Square and then a short walk down Coventry Street to a very crowded Lyon's Corner House, filled with people who had just gotten off night shift. As we entered, a hand came up out of the sea of heads bent to their breakfasts. Its owner rose and waved us towards him. He was short, with curly hair, dimples and a jovial smile, wearing a suit that had been slept in.

"Hallo Ellen." He spoke with finality and sat back in his chair. "So this is your flyer?"

She nodded as a waitress in black and a small lace cap approached.

Our host announced, "Three full breakfasts," and handed her a wad of coupons. Then he turned to me. "Zuckerman. Most people just call me Solly. I hope you will."

Ellen now spoke. "Will, I wanted you to meet Solly. He's the head of the research department at the Ministry.

"Home Security?"

"It's one of the places I work. More like a general dog's body for the government. Wherever they seem to think a bit of statistical analysis will help."

"Can I ask where, or would that be…" I searched for the right word, then found one the Brit's would use. "Indelicate."

Zuckerman looked at me hard. "That would depend."

I didn't know how to continue but Ellen broke the silence between us. "I wanted Solly to tell you what we've learned about the effects of bombing, at least so far, here in Britain."

Zuckerman's brow knit. Then he began to speak. His words sounded more like a ministry briefing than a conversation. "Ellen and I designed a questionnaire and administered it, in Hull, on the east coast, second most bombed town in the country."

"After London." Ellen spoke quietly, not wanting to staunch his flow.

"We did a study of productivity in the munitions plants round the town. What we found was surprising. Luftwaffe bombing raids had no effect on morale. We couldn't find any measurable psychological effects, at all. Just anger."

Ellen couldn't restrain herself. "Production actually went up after bombing raids."

"Yes. Even in plants that were hit by bombs. Machine tools don't seem to be harmed. The workers just pulled lath and plaster off and wiped away the dust. That's what they told us."

Zuckerman nodded. "And the data bear them out."

"What you are telling me is…bombing doesn't work? I guess I knew that already from China, and before that in Madrid."

"Actually, there's one kind that does. The German dive bombers, the Stukas, the single engine planes with the fixed landing gear. They fly slow enough and low enough and they aim their bombs by diving the plane at their targets. They worked well, in France and even during the Battle of Britain, attacking shipping in the Channel."

I shook my head. "But they're too slow to protect themselves against fighters. We managed to shoot them down in Spain, flying Russian P-16s."

"Look, Lieutenant Thurlow, I've been asked to start examining data on the RAF's strategic offensive against Germany. Gauge effectiveness, help on target selection, reduce the loss rate. Trouble is we can't get much cooperation. Bomber Harris isn't interested in whether the campaign will work or not. Just wants more and more planes to order about."

Well, I thought, he's no different from any other brass hat. "How do I figure in this?" It came out a little more aggressive than I wanted it to. Zuckerman was taken aback.

Ellen spoke. "We'd like to compare data from your daylight bombing with our nighttime missions if we can get any."

"Is Harris sharing information about night time bombing with your lot?"

"He's been ordered to. Whether he will remains to be seen. But we're getting some info from people on his staff."

"I'm nowhere near anybody's staff, Mr. Zuckerman."

"They show you pilots the strike photos, don't they?"

"Sometimes. We're not much interested."

Ellen spoke. "Do you think you can get your hands on any?"

I nodded. "Wouldn't be difficult. They get left around the debriefing rooms."

By this time our breakfasts had arrived, powdered eggs and sizzling spam.

———

Usually sitting alone, looking at a landscape becoming more and more two-toned in the late autumnal twilight, my thoughts would turn to Wendy. That night I noticed that without any volition on my part, they just kept turning to Ellen Ashcroft-Metcalf. I could tell she wasn't making me forget the pain of losing Wendy. I still felt it even as Ellen's voice, smell, look, kept gently forcing their way into my conscious vision of the fields giving way to pastures and to fens, etched in a sort of dry point across the compartment window.

———

When I got back to Molesworth that Sunday evening there was a note on the hollow core door of my quarters. *See adjutant* was all it said. Too late that night to find out what it was about, I turned in. No mission the next morning so I was awakened late, only about 7:00, by the sound of a reveille bugle on the PA system.

Handing the note from my door to the adjutant's clerk, I asked "What's this about?"

He took the piece of paper. "Name?"

"Thurlow, William." I pointed to the rank on my collar tabs. "Need the serial number?"

"Nope." He pulled a file from beneath others on his desk. "Transferred. 401st Squadron, 91st Bombardment Group, Bassingbourn. Effect: immediately." He pulled a sheet from the file and handed it to me.

I began to protest, to no one in particular. "But I just got here. I hardly know the names of my crew." They weren't going to let me get settled down anywhere, gain a crew's confidence, let alone train one. It was a recipe for killing a bomber pilot quickly. I should have seen it.

The clerk looked at me, then back at his file. "Orders of Lieutenant-Colonel Le May." He lowered his voice. "Personally." At least this time I knew who to blame.

As I walked back to my bunk I saw a groups of pilots, co-pilots, and other officers heading to the briefing hut. It was too late in the morning for a mission. I stopped one of the pilots. "What's on?"

"Whole group's meeting, all three squadrons. Le May's been promoted, taken over the group and he's ordered us to assemble. Don't know why." He turned and I decided to follow.

I walked in and found some standing room at the back of the briefing hut, a pall of cigarette haze obscuring the sightline between the back of the Quonset hut and the podium. There, on the podium, was Le May. Unusually, he was waiting for us, instead of arriving after the officers had taken their places. On the trestle table before him was a stack of papers.

He whistled, with two fingers between his teeth, a sharp, shrill sound, to silence the unruly officers, who may not have realized he was already in front of them, but also to gain the attention of a couple of men in the first row, who came forward, took the stack of paper and began distributing it.

Soon enough the hubbub subsided, as the men began glancing at the document being handed out. There were not enough to go around, and the last couple of rows did without. A few raised their hands in plaintive demand for more copies.

Le May surveyed the crowd. He spoke. "There'll be more mimeographed." He pulled a blackboard on wheels forward. From where I stood I couldn't make it out. Then he looked down at his copy of the paper, picked up a pointer and began talking. "Men, from now on the 93rd Bombardment Group is going to fly a new formation. One I've designed to improve our defensive fire-power against Kraut fighters and to tighten up our bombing pattern. The paper you've got explains it in detail, but I've made a couple of drawings here on the blackboard."

I left my place at the back of the hut, cut to the far left side of the rows of chairs and walked down far enough till I reached someone sitting next to an empty chair at the end of an aisle. He had the copy of Le May's paper in his hands.

"Can I look on with you, buddy?"

"Sure." He smiled a tight smile and lifted the cover sheet back. "New mandatory bombing formation. Drafted by Lieutenant Colonel Curtis Le May, USAAF." Then I looked at the first page of text. He hadn't even had my stencils retyped! There it was, all eight pages of my proposal, my argument, my diagrams. Where had he found it? At least now I thought I knew why he'd had me transferred. He didn't need me around when he took credit for these ideas, did he? *Should have waited a day, Le May, long enough to see me gone.* I got up and sauntered slowly down the aisle till I was standing by the wall at the front row, hoping he'd notice me.

He didn't. Efficiently enough he went through the missions we'd flown, my reasoning about the head on attacks by German fighters and the advantages of an echeloned stagger and spread. The officers in the room were nodding by the time he'd walked them through it. "Won't be easy but we're going to practice this formation till we get it right, starting tomorrow. So, study it. Dismissed."

I stood there on the left side of the hut, as he came down the podium and walked back along the middle isle. He hadn't noticed me. *You probably think it really is your idea anyway, Le May.* I walked back to my billet and packed my duffle again.

23

My new squadron was a hard luck outfit, the 401st Squadron in the 91st Bombardment Group. Things were going to get worse for the 401st and the whole bomb group. By the time I was shot down over Schweinfurt in August, the Eighth Air Group had to replace half its air crews. The half we lost never made it past their fifth mission that spring and summer. Getting though that many in one piece was mainly dumb luck. That's what I thought, anyway.

The base was plush by the standards of East Anglia. Bassingbourn was an established pre-war RAF station ten miles south of Cambridge. The 91st Group had simply commandeered the field when its commander discovered the place was vacant. Occupy and ask questions later. And it worked. There were real barracks, and a parade ground square, long runways and four dispersal areas, in front of a small control tower and hangars too small for the flying forts dispersed around the field on hard stands. Like my two previous air fields this one had spread out paving over a lot of farmland. The runways cut through hedgerow-framed fields. These were still tawny in winter from the wheat stubble, when the sun deigned to shine. That was only in the few minutes it took to rise from the horizon to the low bank of cloud that would so effectively hide it till it dropped down from them to the horizon again that night. But I was often awake early enough to enjoy the brief glimpse of bucolic England in its moment of sun glow.

The field was a few miles north of a town on the London-Cambridge rail line, Royston. Untouched by bombing, still quaint in the fourth year of Britain's war, a high street jumble of brick and plaster two-storey buildings—bank, pub, corner newsagent/tobacconist, a butcher's resolutely displaying scrawny but feathered fowl in his window. There was a withered food shop with unrationed cabbage and other root vegetables displayed on untended stands anyone could steal from. I never saw one bought or stolen. The high street rose gently on rolling ground towards fine old trees, starting from a crossroads where a lively jumble sale was being conducted the Saturday morning I arrived.

By the time I got there just before Christmas in December of '42, the 401ˢᵗ's hard luck reputation had gotten around. Like I said, it was going to get a lot harder. They had already lost a couple of commanding officers to enemy action. As the train rattled up the line from King's Cross in London I decided I wasn't even going to try to make friends. I'd lose them soon enough to enemy action, or they'd lose me. Either way, it wouldn't be worth it. But of course you can't just decide things like that. You get to know someone, you like them or hate them, their lives start to matter to you pretty fast. It happened that way to me, especially watching the guys on my ship—cool and calculating, efficient killing machines, unflinching at their .50 calibers, even as German tracer rounds came through their gun ports, then hours later quivering as they dropped out on to the grass, holding heads in their hands as we drove to debriefing, finding peace only in sleep if they could get any.

I was standing before the squadron commander. His name plate said "Edward P. Myers, captain." The man looked haggard, his shirt collar too large, even when knotted by a regulation tie tucked in below the 3d button. He glanced from me to my papers in his hand, put them down, picked up a pencil and began tapping his desk. He was sizing me up, squaring what he saw before him with the documents. Didn't seem to me there was much to think about. Was there something else he was factoring into the equation I didn't know about?

"Okay, Lieutenant Thurlow, you're too old and too experienced for your rank. You've also got more missions behind you than most of the guys in this bomb group." I nodded. Was there any point mentioning my temporary promotion to captain? Not to this officer, not now, I decided. "You're co-pilot rank. I don't need co-pilots. Got too many of them. Besides, you're too old." I nodded. "So, you're going to be a pilot." He was silent for another moment. "In fact you're going to be the squadron's new-crew qualifier. Every new co-pilot, bombardier, navigator who comes to this squadron is going to be in your ship first."

I managed to control my voice. "Permission to speak, sir?"

Myers seemed to be bracing himself. "Go on."

"Sir, if you do that I'll have no chance to train a crew to survive the mission requirement." Silence. "I'll be doing all the work on every bomb run, just to keep the crew alive long enough to fly another mission." Still nothing. What I wanted to say was *Were you ordered to do this? Who put you up to it. Do you want me to desert? Why not just shoot me?* "Colonel Le May, did he order you to do this?" *He must have wanted to kill me along with stealing my idea.*

Myers stood up. "Dismissed." There was nothing to do but salute and turn. Before I reached the door, he spoke. "Soldier, I'm not in Le May's chain of command." The thought came to me quickly enough. *Not now, maybe, but you'll be wanting to lick Le May's ass soon enough. Why not start now by getting me rubbed out as quick as you can?*

I walked out into the grey December morning contemplating my death sentence. German fighters, 88mm ack-ack, radar jamming, navigator error, pilot fatigue—there was no chance of surviving three missions on this assignment, not at current casualty rates. The Japs hadn't managed it. Harvey Greenlaw had missed his chance. Colonel Armstrong would have been glad to do it. Now Le May had motive, means, and opportunity. And he was the kind of guy who didn't even need it.

———

My reprieve arrived a week later, the day of my first mission with the 401st. It turned out to be Captain Myer's last. He was killed in action that day over Brest. It was one U-boat base I hadn't yet visited, but the 401st had been there a dozen times already. It was certainly ready for us.

I had a new B-17, and a crew fresh from the replacement pool. They were willing and, more important, willing to listen. My co-pilot. Wainwright, was a captain, which made it a bit difficult. He'd been pulled out of fighters against his will because of the shortage of bomber pilots, but once he found out I was a retread pursuit pilot we got on famously. We were still flying the old formation, the line of Vees, in spite of the success of Le May's group flying the staggered echelon of Vees—he called it a box. But at least the idea had spread to other bomber groups and we'd been ordered to try it out the next time we stood down from missions. Too late for Myers. And I was able to keep the crew of transfers and recruits they'd put together for me to train.

The thing I'd had my crew practice on our one and only training flight was juking to avoid flack. Everyone on board had to know the maneuver was coming, so they could brace themselves. Otherwise broken bones were the least they could expect. It saved us. The group lost seven planes out of thirty that day.

There'd been some passes that Christmas week and a couple of my guys were gulping oxygen right from the start of the mission to cure their hangovers. I turned a blind eye, wanting them awake when we got across the Channel. We were in the squadron's second Vee, with a clear view of Myers' ship at the front. Our tail gunner was watching the last Vee and reporting their distance behind us and formation keeping.

The FWs from Abbeville, their yellow spinners visible from far off, came up as we crossed the coast, heading south southeast, cutting across the Cherbourg peninsula towards Brittany. When they saw we had some fighter cover—P-38s and Spits—they decided to hang back and wait. Our little friends would have to turn away once past the isle of Jersey off the Normandy coast. That would give them about forty-five minutes and a couple hundred miles before the flak guns around Brest would take over annoying us.

We only lost one ship to the German fighters. Maybe they'd spent Christmas in Paris and were not in the best shape themselves. The FWs and the Messerschmitts certainly wanted no part of the flak and peeled off just as the sky beneath us began to show the pock marks of smoke from bursting 88 shells. Every guy in every plane knew perfectly well that our bombs wouldn't do any good against sub pens even at one-thousand feet, let alone seventy-five-hundred feet, even flying straight and level through the flak.

I wasn't going to do it. I knew I could get back into the bombing run even if I juked enough to confuse the ground radars directing the 88s. I turned to my co-pilot.

"Wainwright, I'm going to need your help on the control stick. Just push and pull in the same direction I do. We'll dodge some of this flak." I'd seen enough patterns to suspect that flying right into a spent puff of ack-ack would keep the plane away from a shell in the next salvo. But that meant treating the big ship like an aerobatic pursuit plane.

"Pilot to crew. Safety harnesses now." I knew I was going to have to explain myself to Myers, why I'd broken formation on the run up to the initial point. If I was back in place after that it shouldn't matter. We started to break, first right, then left, up a little and then back down, dancing to the tune of the German 88s.

The navigator cut in. "Initial point." That meant we were ten miles out, about three minutes away from the target.

"She's all yours." I spoke to the bombardier as I settled the plane back into the Vee. Then I continued. "Crew hang on some more. When we drop, I'm going to take her down in a hurry, down, not up."

Everyone, including the Germans, knew that a bomber freed from its cargo quickly rose hundreds of feet. The flak pattern always adjusted for it. So I was going to take the B-17 down and to the left, hard and out of harm's way in the few minutes we turned out to sea and began forming up again on the leader.

Just as the bombs released and I pushed the control yoke forward as hard as I could, another plane seemed to be making the same maneuver. When I looked again, there was a hole a yard wide in the plane's port wing and smoke streaming from all four engines. The next moment the whole ship was gone, a fireball and no 'chutes. I didn't know then but it was Myers, the squadron commander.

There was a flying officers' meeting the next afternoon. The 401st had been in combat less than seven months and was about to welcome its fourth commanding officer, a lieutenant-colonel named Gillespie. He was going to outlast me anyway.

The first thing Gillespie did was introduce Le May's new formation. So, he was probably a protégé of *Iron Ass*—it was what the whole Eighth Air Group was calling Le May. But if the new squadron commander knew anything about the death sentence assignment Myers had given me, he didn't try to enforce it. I stuck with Wainwright and the crew he'd brought along, as co-pilot, so everyone else thought anyway. The air crew knew I was on the left side in the pilot's seat. Wainwright and the rest of them seemed to want it that way. Lucky charm? Or else my antics in the air were keeping us flying through that winter while the 401st racked up an almost complete turn-over of planes and crewmembers. But in April of '43 there was exactly one B-17 in the whole group, the *Memphis Belle*, that looked like it was going to survive to twenty-five missions.

Right through January we continued to fly missions over France at low altitudes—eight times. That suited me. I knew how cold it would be at ten or twenty-thousand feet. The Air Corps had begun introducing electrically heated flight suits, a sort of blue onesie pajama you wore under your leather clothing and plugged into the plane's electric system. They were dangerous, often shorting out when they worked, and were provided only to the waist and tail gunners anyway. Once we started to bomb Germany from altitude, I warned the crew they had to make sure they took off with everything they'd need to avoid frost bite.

That first trip, to Hamm, a town in the Ruhr, made a permanent impression on the crew. The town wasn't very big or even very far away. But it was astride the largest marshalling yard in Europe, dozens of lines fanning out into hundreds of sidings and switching tracks in four different areas surrounding the main station, all surrounded by the town. That's what it looked like on the large photo pinned up next to the route map when, at 5:00 in the morning, the curtain was pulled back by the 91st's new operations officer, Myers' replacement,

Lieutenant-Colonel Lawrence. As he drew a pointer along a red ribbon stretching from East Anglia across Holland to Germany, Lawrence elicited a range of noises, from an expression of awe at the thought of finally bombing Germany to wolf whistles and deep sighs from pilots who'd been over the German coast, in the summer of '42. Then the group commander, Colonel Wray, spoke. "Target Hamm, top of the Ruhr, where they make all their steel. Secondary, Rotterdam, but don't even think about it. If we can't hit Hamm, they'll cut the Eighth Air Group out of the war." He paused. "We're in the lead. Four other groups behind us, eighty ships in all."

He turned to the weather officer, Atwell, who knew the pilots would be too distracted for detail. "Clear for assembly, getting worse as you cross the Channel, better inland and very clear right across Germany." A groan from those who immediately understood it would make things easier for the German fighters.

Then it was intelligence. The man was listened to attentively. "You'll be too far north for the Abbeville crowd." This was the fighter unit with the Focke-Wolves and the yellow prop spinners. "But we expect upwards of two hundred fighters before you hit the flak. The concentration of 88s will be about as heavy as you'll find anywhere in Europe." He looked over the assembled pilots silently absorbing his word. "Well, it's Germany."

If my gut was anything to go by, there was now a knot in every stomach in the briefing hall. Lawrence came forward.

"That is all. Dismissed." Everyone rose at attention and then began to cluster in groups.

Wainwright turned to me. "Been there before?"

"No. We bombed the German coast a few times last fall. This is going to be much more serious."

We ambled out slowly, in no hurry to experience the darkness and wind whipping down the fens. Waiting for a second round of Jeep runs to our revetment we were joined by several others in our crew.

Each looked at me and then Wainwright. "Where to, sir?" They greeted the answer with silence.

24

The crew chief, Bill Egan, was waiting when we pulled up at the chin of our ship, *Nike of Samothrace*. The name had been chosen when orders came down from Pinetree to get rid of the nudie nose art proliferating in the Eighth Air Group. A wise guy had suggested it to allow us to paint a naked woman with the angel wings.

"Everything checks out, sir." Egan addressed me. On the flight line there was no pretense about who was flying the ship.

"Did you double check the electric circuits for the flight suits?" I needed the crew to be warm enough to fight. "Can't have any shorts today. We'll be at altitude in winter over Germany today, Bill."

"I'm gonna check 'em again right now, Capt…" he corrected himself, "…Lieutenant." He turned and the crew stopped stowing gear and ammo long enough to let him lift himself into the nose.

The navigator, Goldstein, stopped me. "Navigator's briefing sir, they said twenty-two-thousand feet going over. That'll be temperatures of thirty below or worse, I think."

I turned to the crew still passing equipment hand over hand into the fuselage. "Everyone got your warm stuff on? Gunners, check out your heating suit plugs before we take off."

By the time we'd assembled, the 91st had already lost two ships and were down to sixteen planes. We were on the top and port side of the echelon, looking down on the rest of the group. We came out of the clouds over the Rhine, only about a half an hour from Hamm.

I spoke. "Co-pilot to tail gunner. How many airplanes behind us?" I knew there were supposed to be four groups on the mission—eighty planes.

Silence. Then he spoke. "Don't see any sir."

I put my hand to my throat mike and my hand on Wainwright's arm. "The other two groups are gone. Better tell 91st leader." Then I spoke to the navigator. "Position check."

The voice came back. "On course for Hamm, sir."

Wainwright picked up his communication mike and spoke. "*Nike* to squadron leader. 91st Group is alone. The other three squadrons aren't visible behind us."

Alone, cold and getting colder. Sixteen ships, not eighty, heading for two-hundred fighters and the biggest concentration of flak guns in Europe. Suddenly there was ice hanging over my eyes. It was frozen sweat. I was perspiring into the cold, pumping out the heat of fear into my fur-lined leather flight suit, my stomach cramping as though I'd been denied a toilet for a week. The ice crystals woven into my eyebrows melted salty drops that stung my eyes. *Well, you knew you weren't going to make the mission requirement. It's just like Ellen told you.* The voice in my head was shaking me by the lapels, hard. *Stop it, Thurlow, Get a grip. You're not dead yet.*

That's when Wainwright saw the bogies. "Twenty-one bandits nine o'clock level. Waist gunners check your guns for ice." He was taking over.

Good. About time. The flight of twin engine Ju-88 night fighters were clawing their way past us to come in from head on. We were so close to Hamm now they'd only be able to get off one full attack before we hit the flak alley.

The group leader's voice came through. "Make your rounds count. We'll have to deal with these guys on the way back out."

A few minutes later they were coming at us. The odds looked like they were two to one. Each brace of German fighters had chosen one of the sixteen bombers to concentrate on. We knew their aim was to break up the formation. Then they'd be able to pick off single planes.

The stagger of our three Vees allowed every nose and top turret to fire forward without worrying about hitting another B-17. We stayed together and just after the Ju-88 interceptors came through, the sky all around us began to pock mark with smudges, as the sound of hail-stone showers swept along the fuselage and the smell of cordite twitched the nostril. I took the control stick and went into my juking and swerving, by now matched with only the slightest delay by Wainwright. Other planes were doing it too. Now the sound of hail-stones was submerged in louder hammering and then the clatter of shorn sheet metal, twisting and beating in the wind-stream. We'd taken damage somewhere.

"Co-pilot to crew. Damage?"

The port gunner reported. "Port wing root superficial damage."

Then another voice, the tail gunner. "Port horizontal stabilizer, half gone, sir."

I hadn't noticed any change in our flight characteristics. So I kept up the dance around the flak pattern and we avoided several more bursts. Two other B-17s weren't so lucky. We watched one take a direct hit, collapse out of formation in a stall and then begin a rapid corkscrew. Everyone watching knew the Gees would be too strong for anyone to jump. Then another ship lost its wing at the inboard starboard engine and fell like a stone. Silently I counted the 'chutes coming out of the gun ports: one, two, three, four, five…no more. Then we were at the aiming point, each plane—by now we were only twelve—releasing a salvo on the squadron leader's drop. I pushed the stick forward, banked right to get below the flak that was still coming at us, and began looking for other planes to form up with. It was then I realized that from the moment the Luftwaffe fighters appeared I'd stopped feeling scared, stopped sweating into my suit, stopped thinking about anything but mechanically doing my job to keep the crew alive. And now, turning around, going back through what we'd already been through once, I was getting scared again.

The fighters were waiting. This time it was single engine FWs firing 20mm canons along with the Ju-88s firing rockets whose contrails you could see as they bore in on other planes. Coming straight at you their cross section was too small, the speed was too great.

The waist gunners began to talk. "Comin' in port side." "Starboard too."

The plane shook as the .50 caliber machine guns fired and shell casings started clattering along the gangway. There were three or four fighters buzzing around us, uncoordinated, not going for any one piece of the plane, or we would have had it. A 20mm canon round cut right through the fuselage, without hitting anything vital.

Then we heard an audible groan on the intercom, followed by "Charlie's been hit." It was one waist gunner reporting on another.

I spoke. "Stay on your gun, Stoneman, keep firing. Bombardier, go back there with a first aid kit." The action ended as suddenly as it had started.

"Co-pilot to crew, report position of squadron. See any other planes?" There was silence on the intercom. I turned to Wainwright, put my hand to the throat mike again. "Let's get down to the deck and see if we can fly home without getting noticed?" He nodded and we dove the last four-thousand feet till we were tree topping on a compass heading for East Anglia.

Somewhere between Rotterdam and the Hague as we neared the Dutch coast, the fighters found us again. Four Messerschmitts came at us from the sun, firing deflection shots. We watched the tracer rounds ahead of our nose coming closer. Suddenly my windscreen was pinging from shards of plexiglass pulled into the slipstream as the machine gun fire broke into the bombardier's nose. The lucky guy wasn't there. He was back at the waist gunner's window, manning a .50 caliber. By then the German pursuit ships were at our level without any space to maneuver but coming straight at us. They kept at us until their magazines gave out as we left Holland and found ourselves over the North Sea. Again I used the intercom.

"Damage report?"

One reply came back. "Just a lot of holes in the sheet metal." By then I knew we'd make it. I looked at Wainwright and took my hands off the controls.

Egan, the crew chief was there to meet us as we dropped ourselves out of the hatch, welcoming the solid ground beneath us. He was shaking his head in mock displeasure.

"Look what you guys did to my airplane." He slapped each man on the back as we crowded around.

Debriefing was rough. We'd lost a quarter of the squadron, and the crews that came back didn't see many parachutes from the planes that went down. There were no strike photos. All the planes equipped to take them had bought it. And we learned what had happened to the other three groups. Once they lost the lead squadron—us—they'd all decided to head for Rotterdam, the secondary. They all came home with nothing more than some flak damage and 20mm canon holes from a few FWs who found them in the cloud cover. They had photos, showing damage to civilian housing, but nothing of military value.

The next day the 401st Squadron commander who led the group, Fishburne, was crucified for taking sixteen planes unescorted into Germany, and coming back without any evidence to show for it. Then a newspaper photographer turned up with some pictures of the marshalling yards we had aimed for, showing significant damage. Fishburne and the rest of us who'd flown with him suddenly became heroes. In fact, every officer and crew member on every one of the twelve planes that came back got weekend passes to London.

I'd need to be discrete once I got Ellen on the phone. Army intelligence was probably listening on our end, MI5—British counter-espionage—listening in on hers. It took several tries over a few days and it was only well into the evening middle of the week that I reached her.

It must have rung five times before I heard the pickup. It was her voice, officious, I thought. "Kensington 4821."

"Ellen, Will here. Coming into town next week end. I'll have some nice stuff from the PX for you." I hoped she'd understand. She'd made something of a show of rejecting American luxuries more than once. I hoped she'd understand.

At first there was annoyance in her voice. "I've told you…" Then she understood. "what I need, just some coffee."

"I'll bring enough to keep you awake all weekend."

She hesitated again and then spoke. "Would you like to see a play, that actress you like, Sally Sugarman is in something good in the West End." Now it took me a minute, to realize she was talking in code too. It was Solly Zuckerman, the government statistician, she was asking me to meet."

"I'd love that."

———

I spent the next two days discretely plucking strike photos off of bulletin boards, collecting discarded bomb bay pictures from under coffee mugs and even beer mats in the officers' club. By the time Friday afternoon rolled around I had pictures from almost every one of the dozen sorties the group had made since Christmas. I even had a few from other groups, shared around to help identify targets we hadn't visited yet.

Ellen and I had seen each other exactly once since my weekend pass to London back before Christmas. It had been at the end of January. Ellen had found an excuse to come up to Cambridge for an event at Girton. She'd got the use of a fellow's digs outside college. The university town was only a dozen miles up the line from Royston and I was able to leave a phone number with Bill Egan, the crew chief. He'd know if there was going to be a mission before anyone else in the crew. When I got there it was a thatched roof cottage across from the college a couple of miles from town. That suited me. I hadn't come for the sightseeing.

Ellen and I didn't leave the cottage for thirty-six hours, not till her train back down to London Sunday afternoon. Somehow she knew…she never brought up the war, flying, the past or the future. She was just focused on now, the delicious minutes and hours. Mutual insatiability made food and drink and sleep entirely superfluous. When finally on Sunday morning we had to stop for nourishment, I pulled my overnight case from the cold larder, planted it on the kitchen table, and brought out some real eggs, a slab of bacon, American white bread, and peach jam, along with a tin of coffee, all courtesy of the base PX.

Now, six weeks later, rattling along on the last down train to King's Cross, I began to worry about what I could bring Ellen for an encore besides those strike photos. I knew that another weekend couldn't be as transcendent, as untethered from reality, as oblivious to the world as that weekend in Cambridge. We wouldn't even try to recreate it. After nine in the evening there was still a little twilight in wartime double British summer time when I came out of the Underground at Baker Street. It wasn't until I turned into Dorset street that I realized the figure in the dark ahead of me was Ellen. I quickened my tread but worried about frightening her in the blackout, I called out. She turned, stopped and gave a smile visible even in the dim light left in the sky. She slipped her arm into mine and we walked on companionably.

Down the stair into her flat we still had said nothing. As she flipped on a lamp I broke the silence.

"Working?"

She nodded. Then she unbelted her trench coat and without taking it off slumped into a chair. Before she could find the fags in her pockets, I took out a pack and we continued to sit in silence, smoking and smiling at each other. I could see the pleasure in her face must have mirrored my own. Crushing out my cigarette, I pulled a manila envelope from my map case. Ellen knew what it was.

"Not tonight, Will. Let's just go to bed." I dropped the envelope to the floor.

I had assumed we were both too jaded and too old for arousal to trump deep fatigue. I was wrong.

25

When I woke the next morning, Ellen was sitting at the small round table that divided the kitchenette from the rest of the bedsit. A cup of tea was getting cold next to her elbow and a fag already hanging from a dry lower lip as she studied the strike-pictures. She held up a photo from the latest mission.

"Hamm. Where's Hamm. It's the only one that shows damage to anything but housing blocks."

I levered myself up and challenged her. "What about Brest and Lorient?" She shook her head still holding the one picture. "That's Hamm, marshalling yards. Too big to miss."

Ellen didn't argue. She picked up another photo. "Also Hamm?" I came over, glanced and nodded. "Well, your lot also took out a good deal of housing nowhere near the train tracks there."

Knowing I didn't drink tea, Ellen rose and went into the kitchenette to make me some coffee. She put the American percolator together, filled it with water and put out her hand. She knew I'd come supplied with ground coffee. I reached into the case where the pictures had been.

"Here."

"I want to get these pictures to Solly right away. The Eighth Air Group hasn't given us anything for weeks." I frowned. But I knew she was right. "Will, you've got to come too. Solly'll have questions." She took a few steps to the cupboard, took out a plain grey civilian suit. "Can you wear this, please?" I didn't protest but I didn't much like being treated like a spy. She handed me a pass, made out in my name, but leaving out my rank. "Just show this at the Senate House security check point." Senate House was a vast modern all-concrete building at the university. Hard to destroy, it was in fact unscathed so far in the war.

There was a lift at the Tottenham Court Road tube stop. We waited in an orderly queue that made me feel very British. What, I wondered, could I tell Zuckerman that the strike photos couldn't? Ellen stood slightly away from me and made no eye contact. Did she think we were being observed, watched, followed? Was I in trouble? At the pavement we crossed and walked north towards the British Museum and the vast Senate House of the university. This is where Zuckerman's ministry offices were. More lifts but no wait on a Saturday morning. Soon enough we were on the eighth floor walking towards the only open door, wafting clouds of smoke and the distinctive aroma of Balkan Sobranie pipe tobacco.

It was a large room, bright above the low London gloom, with unshaded windows. Zuckerman was alone, standing at a large table covered with glossy aerial photographs. He removed the pipe and motioned us towards him. Ellen slapped down the manila envelope of my strike photos. Zuckerman ignored them. He pushed the glossy in his hand towards us.

"Look at this." He smiled broadly. "Hit the target, the entire squadron it looks like."

This was unexpectedly good news I thought. Looking down at the photo I could see immediately it was from a night time raid, the explosions were close together on what looked like a refinery or a chemical distillation plant. I looked up at him, pleasure on my face.

"Well, maybe we're getting somewhere after all?"

Zuckerman frowned. "Thurlow, how many sheets are spread out on this table?" I looked down its length. He continued. "About four-hundred-fifty, two months' worth. And that…" his pipe was pointing at the picture in his hand, "…is the only one." I remained silent. "Low level Mosquito raid." I understood immediately. The Mosquito was a two-engine bomber, the fastest in the RAF, made almost entirely of plywood, and so with a very small radar signature compared to the four engine RAF Lancasters, and our Superforts and Liberator B-24s the RAF and the Eighth Air Group were flying. It didn't have much of a payload so couldn't do much damage but it could get past intercepting fighters, fly below anti-aircraft flak and locate targets visually.

Zuckerman picked up my envelope of strike photos. He led us to a trio of worn leather chairs under a chalkboard across from which there were enough Greek sigmas and Roman lower case p's to show they were statistical equations. He reverted to my first name.

"Thanks for those, Will. Must have been tricky purloining them."

"Not particularly. Once the flight crews give them a once-over, they just get left around. Not really considered hush-hush, not on base at least."

"Well, we can't winkle them out of your staff for love or money." He riffled through the twenty or so I had brought him. "Can't say for certain, but these don't look any different from the ones we get behind Bomber Harris's back." Harris was still head of RAF Bomber Command, famous now for insisting that his bombers could win the war without help from anyone else, including the Russians. "I suppose Ellen has told you what our latest studies show?"

She spoke before I could. "Actually, no sir." It sounded an official voice, all business, one suited to the surroundings I thought. "I thought it better you do so, not knowing exactly what's…" she hesitated. "…confidential."

He nodded. "You were right, Miss Ashcroft." Why had he left off the second barrel of her name, Metcalf? Was this some bit of English etiquette I needed to learn? "Anyway, shouldn't tell a bomber pilot something he'd regret knowing if he were shot down and interrogated." He looked at me seriously for a moment. "How many missions is it now, leftanant?"

It was not a number I needed to calculate. Every pilot knew how many he'd flown, how many he'd still have to fly. "Eighteen."

"So, the odds against anyone doing eighteen missions are about ninety-six percent. Any explanation of your success?"

"Just dumb luck. You know that." I pointed to the formulae on the chalk board.

"Your modesty is becoming, Will. I won't press you." He paused, looked over to the photos on the table. "Look, I won't keep you, but I've a few questions you may be able to answer in spite of your modesty."

I looked from him to Ellen and back. "Shoot."

"Have you heard anything about a new mission for the Eighth Air Group and RAF Bomber Command? Code name *Point blank*?

"No."

"Not a word?" I shook my head. He smiled. "Perhaps secrecy is being maintained for once. Look here." He was poking me with his pipe. I pushed it away. "Beg your pardon. Has there been any change in target selection in the last month."

"No. We keep going back to the U-boat pens on the French coast. We went to the German coast twice to hit U-boat pens there, well beyond fighter cover, and got a bloody nose for our trouble."

"Look, Will, I've got to put you on the spot. This new mission, *Point blank* is a direct order from joint chiefs of staff, your president and our prime minister, to switch to targeting fighter aircraft factories in Germany. Now you know something you shouldn't. But I've got to know has there been any operational change to take on that mission?"

"Nothing I can see, Dr. Zuckerman. But I'm awful low in the organizational table."

"It looks as though the air staff are just ignoring the directive. Do you think there is any way you can find out anything, Thurlow?"

"All I'd ever hear is scuttlebutt, rumors, coming down through a dozen layers from *Pinetree*—that's headquarters."

Zuckerman waved his pipe. "Yes, I know. High Wycombe… But this is madness, dropping bombs all over the continent, never hitting anything of military value, and losing planes every night. Why won't they do what they're told?"

"Look, sir, maybe they can't. We don't have enough planes yet, the fighters can't cover us very far into Europe. Do they even know where the factories are?"

He wasn't listening. Zuckerman was on to something else. He rose and went to the table, where he briefly studied some of the pictures and then picked up two.

"One thing has changed, for your lot at least. Since early January at any rate. Your formations still don't manage to hit their targets, but your bomb-pattern has become much tighter, damage is greater and more confined. Any idea why?"

My smile tipped him off. He leaned back on the desk and waited. "I think I do."

"Don't keep us in suspense, boy."

He wasn't that much older than me, and looked younger anyway, but I let it pass. "New formation since December." I explained the change from a line of Vees to the staggered echelon spread. Zuckerman understood the effect on bomb patterns immediately. But I had to explain how it also improved protection against German fighters too.

He nodded in appreciation. "Well I hope whoever dreamed that up got himself a promotion. The idea would be worth a knighthood if it could be combined with target-accuracy." I didn't want to ruin my reputation for modesty so I said nothing.

"Two more questions, Will. When you can't reach primary target and head for secondary ones, how much target information do you have."

"Not much, just a general location…the city's coordinates, and then something like 'On the river, south of the city,' or 'cluster of large smoke stacks surrounded by steel superstructure,' that sort of thing." He was silent. "Your other question, sir?"

"Yes, thanks. How would you compare target selection, bomb aiming, care about hitting exactly the right target when you are diverted to a secondary?"

"Well, it's pretty obvious I'm afraid. When you've already bailed on the primary—bad weather, headwinds, too many fighters, pilots just want to unload and go home…" My words hung in the air between us.

Zuckerman drew on his pipe. Finding it cold, he tapped it in the ashtray standing next to the lounge chair and rose, muttering something like "Just as I supposed…"

———

I hadn't liked what I had to say in answer to Zuckerman's questions and I didn't like the look of all those strike photos on his work table. It all hit me harder than ever that morning, on the tube going back to Montagu Square. From time to time Ellen had something to say. But I could barely reply. I couldn't even look her in the face. The pointlessness of wasting so much and so many lives left me in despondency that was threatening to give way to tears. I couldn't let her see.

The people around me on the tube, they weren't so different from the people in Rotterdam or Hamm for that matter. People like them were getting killed, I was going to get killed, and it wasn't going to make a damn bit of difference to winning the war.

We were standing, hands touching at a steel post in the underground carriage, a smoking car heavy with the waft of Woodbines. The fug was I hoped, enough to explain away the glint of tears in my eye. But Ellen saw through it clearly enough. She pulled me around so her mouth was close enough to my ear for me to understand everything she said. Looking up, her eyes found mine. There was a deep sadness in them. "I know…I know." She grabbed the lapel of my coat. "But maybe Solly can do something about it." She understood the grimace that crossed my face. "He's got the ear of the minister. They're trying to get him to brief Churchill."

The thought did nothing to lighten the hopelessness I was feeling. Once we were up the stairs in the thin sunlight above the Marylebone tube stop, I spoke.

"We're not fighting the war, Ellen. We're just killing people—Germans and us—to prove to the Russians that we're on their side."

"No, Will. You know better. Every time you fly, you know how many German fighters and flak cannons we're keeping away from the Eastern Front." She stopped. "You can see the build up here. Sometime next year there'll be a second front too."

"Ellen, can it. You're sounding like an Army morale officer."

There was anger in her voice. "We have to do it, Will. We have to do something. You weren't here in '40 or '41 when they were bombing London every night."

"I was in Madrid in '38, Rangoon in '41, Chongqing in '42, Ellen. You were here in '41. Killing people in their houses or bomb shelters doesn't work."

The exasperation left her voice. She was calm. "That's why we're trying to change things, Will." She squeezed my hand. "Can you just try to live long enough to see it?"

Did she understand that trying to survive as a bomber pilot had nothing to do with actually surviving? More like trying to win the Irish Sweepstakes lottery…when even buying a ticket was against the law.

We were walking back to Ellen's place, both dreading the long afternoon and evening we'd have to face, unavoidably returning to the melancholy subject fixed in our minds. Suddenly she grabbed my arm.

"Will, take me to the cinema. I want to see the new Vera Lynn, *Rhythm Serenade*." She forcibly turned me away from Montagu Square and down towards Oxford Street. "It's on at the Regal at Marble Arch."

It worked a charm. Within a few minutes I wasn't feeling sorry for myself and the world any more. It was the terrible film making me feel sorry for Vera Lynn—the *Forces' Sweet Heart*. Ellen and I chortled and whispered our way through the film so persistently patrons began to shush us and the matron came to admonish. Keeping a straight face was difficult as we murmured our apologies and left half way through.

Heads cleared, we were ready to find real oblivion in Ellen's bed. We kept at it until hunger and thirst forced us out of it at midday on Sunday.

We were having a companionable breakfast that Sunday afternoon when Ellen spoke. "Will, tell me about Wendy."

"Who?" I'd heard perfectly well, but Wendy was not a subject I'd ever brought up with Ellen.

"It's a name I've heard you murmur when you're sleeping. More than once, actually." She reached out to my hand, and gave me a searching look.

She didn't need to know, but suddenly looking at Ellen I needed to tell her, pass along some of my suffering to someone who looked like she wanted to share a little of it.

"Someone I knew in China. She died about a year ago, just before I left." There was the reassuring warmth of Ellen's hand again, covering mine, inviting me to go on. The way I told it, it took a long time, without interruption or questions from Ellen, but long pauses while I tried to recall the detail. It was Wendy I was remembering, savoring images, incidents, conversations, that made me go on. I wasn't thinking, not once, what effect my narrative was having on Ellen. I wasn't even looking at her, but gazing into the darkness of the bedsit behind her. When I finished I felt both spent and unburdened. Only then did it come to me how long I'd talked and how much I had dredged up, for the first time since leaving China. Ellen rose from her chair, came round to my side of the small table and pulled me to my feet. We stood and embraced, swaying slightly, for a long moment.

Ellen and I were waiting at the barrier for the train for Cambridge to pull in. Leaning on the rail, smoking companionably, sending puffs into the gloom of the darkened station beneath its double line of glass skylights. We were looking down the track, hoping not to see a train come in at all. Ellen's voice was hesitant.

"Will, I couldn't have done what Wendy did." I looked at her, wondering if I wanted her to go on. "I couldn't have left you the way she did. I can see it. Refusing to pin your own happiness on a flyer you know is going to get killed." She was shaking her head. "But I couldn't do it." She grabbed the lapels of my trench coat and tears glistened in her eyes. "I can't do it."

I had to pull her to me and hold her close. "I'm glad. I love you too selfishly to want you to do it, Ellen."

She pulled a handkerchief from a pocket and blew her nose. Then her voice turned cool and analytical for the first time since the morning with Zuckerman. "The last thing that Wendy told you…before she…"

I supplied the word, just to make her go on. "Died."

Ellen gulped. "Yes…you believed her, didn't you?"

We were looking at each other now. Where was she going? This wasn't idle chatter waiting for a train. "Sure."

"Well, I think whoever was after you a year ago in China still is. Only they don't want to kill you themselves any more. They want to get the Germans to do it for them. That's why you keep getting posted to units with the biggest losses, never promoted like every other pilot who's kept themselves alive. You should have been a squadron commander, even a group leader, a left…" she corrected herself to the American, "…a lieutenant-colonel by now," She stopped. "Who's got it in for you, Will Thurlow, sending you on one death-mission after another?"

"What do you mean exactly?" I knew what she meant. I'd been thinking the same thing for months. I needed to hear it from someone else to prove I wasn't paranoid enough to think someone had arranged the whole Eighth Air Group combat mission just to kill me.

"Here's what I think. Someone, somewhere in the US War Department wants you dead. But he doesn't want your blood on his hands, or is frightened that actually having you killed could be found out…or else just wants the Germans to pull the trigger for them.”

These were all thoughts I'd been obsessively running over in my head for months. Now Ellen was thinking them through for me. It was my turn to be silent, letting her go on.

“So, they sent you here from China in order to be chewed up by too many missions to survive. That way everyone is in the clear.” She smiled at me dryly. “Trouble is, you've got nine lives. Or maybe eighteen?” Now we saw the switching engine bringing the carriages down to the end of the platform. “Will, I won't leave you, ever. But please, find a way to stop flying missions.”

26

My number came up the day the most numbers in the 91ˢᵗ Bombardment Group came up, August 17, 1943. I learned later that the bomb group lost ten ships that day, but mine was about the first to go down.

It was my twenty-fifth mission, and I was back in the co-pilot's seat. Wainwright was long gone from *Nike of Samothrace*, first to his own plane and then to a fire-ball explosion in a flak-filled sky over Bremen. The squadron lost another four planes that day. When the squadron commander tried to give me the plane officially, someone at Pinetree told the group second in command, Colonel Lawrence, to remind 401ˢᵗ Squadron that I was co-pilot material only. It wouldn't do to have a first lieutenant order around a captain or a major, even on a flight deck. The squadron commander, Gillespie, was nice enough to tell me himself, and to tell me the order had come down from staff headquarters. He thought I might have an idea why. All I could say was "Damned if I know, sir."

The night before my last mission every pilot, co-pilot, bombardier, and navigator on the base was crowded into the briefing hall, wondering what was on the map behind the curtain. The din of a couple of hundred young men, cat-calling, whistling, and signaling to one another died away from the back of the structure as Wurzbach, the group commander swept down the rows of folding chairs to the podium, followed by his deputy and the operations officer.

He stood at the lectern, feet apart, and unfolded a sheet of paper. There was momentary silence as he spoke. "As you were." Then the scraping of chairs as the officers took their seats. "Message from Eighth Bomber Command." He began to read. "To all leaders and bomb crew. Today's mission is the most important air operation yet conducted in this war. The target must be destroyed. It is of vital importance to the enemy."

Would he tell us something new? Had Solly Zuckerman finally got their attention at Pinetree and RAF Bomber Command? Wurzbach continued reading but still we learned nothing new. He read the last line.

"Your friends and comrades who have been lost, and those who will be lost today, are depending on you. Their sacrifices must not be in vain. Good luck, good shooting, good bombing."

Someone brave enough to challenge the exhortation shouted from the middle of the room. "Good bye." Most of the men couldn't help laughing nervously.

Wurzbach pretended not to hear any of this. He folded up the sheet he'd been reading, cleared his throat and spoke again.

"Gentlemen, maximum effort tomorrow. Not just us. There will be three combat wings flying tomorrow, about four-hundred-fifty planes. Two missions. One is diversionary. Ours is the main mission. 91st is the lead group."

He turned to the map, watched avidly by everyone in the room. The groan came up as the officer's eyes traveled the red ribbon from East Anglia into the middle of Germany. There it divided, one ribbon heading south till it disappeared from the map in the middle of the Mediterranean. The other went north and returned to England. There was an arc drawn across the ribbon just past the coast. Everyone knew this was the limit of fighter escort.

When the groans subsided Wurzbach began again. "Three wings, about one-hundred-fifty planes are going to start out ahead of us, they'll turn south here." His pointer touched the map where the ribbon divided. "They'll take the German fighters with them, bomb Regensburg and fly on to North Africa. We'll be coming in behind this task group. With the Luftwaffe cleared out, chasing the first group, we'll turn north and hit Schweinfurt." He stopped. "What's in Schweinfurt?"

He reached into his tunic pocket and pulled out something small and shiny. Then he held it up in the light between thumb and forefinger.

"Ball bearings." He paused to see if he needed to explain. "Practically two thirds of the entire German supply is made in Schweinfurt." He didn't need to say more, everyone there who'd ever tinkered with a hot-rod or a roller skate for that matter, knew that without ball bearings no motor could move anything, on the ground or in the air.

So, Solly must have talked some sense into the air staffs. *Operation Point Blank after all.*

Suddenly you could feel a surge pass along the rows of seats. Men began to sit straighter, some looked to see the reactions on either side, others staring intently at the map. No one spoke. Did they share my thought? *This is a target that might be worth dying for?* Then I looked again and suddenly I realized the Germans somehow had to know we were coming. For the previous three days, we'd had reports of redeployments of Luftwaffe fighter *staffels*, their squadrons, hundreds of fighters, back from the French coasts to the very corridor the ribbon was running through. The white faces around me showed that I wasn't the only one who'd twigged to the chance there'd been a leak.

Wurzbach handed his pointer to the operations officer, Alford, turned to the audience and said, "We'll all be flying tomorrow." Then he pulled a clipboard from beneath the lectern to take notes and sat down in Alford's chair.

The next morning, any optimism I had about the mission dissipated into the heavy morning fog. I kept looking at my watch tracing the minutes we were falling behind the diversionary group headed towards Regensburg. By the time we took off, an hour and a half late, we all knew that the German fighters were going to get enough time to take on the first group and reload for us. It was the end of any tactical surprise. The voice in my head was begging for the brass to scrap the whole mission.

No chance.

We lost another half an hour forming up in the clouds over East Anglia. As the lead group, the 91st didn't have to find the others, but we had to fly slow and steady enough for the other groups to form up on our position. After that it wouldn't take long to break through the Channel clouds into clear skies over Holland. At thirty-thousand feet it wasn't quite winter temperatures but when we lost the P-47 Thunderbolt escorts over Aachen, everyone got colder. We knew what was coming, and it didn't take long.

My new pilot, Hibbert was doing a pretty good job. Keeping a cool head as the FWs and Me-109s came at us from dead ahead and behind. The fighters were disciplined. They came at us in line, one at a time, firing cannon and breaking off for the next fighter behind. Our ship, *Nike*, was at the bottom of the echelon, as usual, the most vulnerable position for flak but a less tempting target for the fighters bent on breaking up the formation. Hibbert and I were calling out the incoming attacks on the intercom and the gunners were confirming as they fired. We'd managed to fend off about five onslaughts when up ahead the sky seemed filled with dots. Hibbert pointed forward and then held his throat mike to his neck.

"Are we catching up to the lead division?"

I was about to reply that they should be diverging south when I realized he was pointing to a flak field, the thickest I'd ever seen, not a bomber force. I spoke.

"Hang on, crew. Heavy flak coming."

By silent agreement Hibbert gave up the control column and I began to take the airplane through its gyrations towards the last flak burst, and we hoped, away from the next.

We managed to fly through a couple of bursts of shrapnel before *Nike* took two hits, shuddered and broke apart. The first explosion took the cockpit and nose from the rest of the fuselage. I looked back and saw the sky spread out behind me as the sheet metal fell away and the control lines snapped. Gravity had not yet overcome momentum and the two parts of *Nike* were flying together for a last second. The second hit must have penetrated the bomb bay and triggered at least one of the five-hundred-pound bombs, because the rest of the fuselage simply disappeared into shards and the two wings snapped off at the root and began to fall.

Beneath me the bombardier's nose and the chin turret were gone. I looked towards Hibbert and then didn't look again. There was a torso and some severed limbs where he had had been sitting. There was no point I knew, but instinctively I put my hand to the throat mike.

"Crew, abandon ship. Bail out."

There was no sound in my helmet headphone and I knew I was the only one left alive. Now what was left of the cockpit was falling. I unsnapped, rose from my seat, and just walked off the flight deck into the sky.

I was high above what looked like open pasture farm land, dotted with hamlets. Different crops divided the landscape into rectangles and triangles, punctuated by small wood lots. A river meandered to the west, cutting through a town standing on each bank and some small islands midstream. Soon enough a tracery of roads divided the landscape. I hadn't been counting and now began to wonder when I needed to pull the rip-cord. It was tantalizing in the even whistle of wind rush to drop further, but too soon was going to be better than too late. I guessed it was ten-thousand feet, maybe less when I decided to pull. Once I felt the upward jerk of the 'chute lines I began really to give up to the limbo of floating away from the war for what was going to be several minutes. I was actually enjoying the difference from the last time I'd had to do this, above the jungles of Burma a life time and eighteen months ago.

The wheat field, or was it a field of hops, came up to me slowly enough to realize that I was fulfilling Ellen's wish for me. I'd found a way out of the mincemeat maker of relentless missions over Europe. I thought about the other nine guys who'd certainly died in *Nike*, fellows I'd tried not to get to know. Was I numb to their deaths? Well, their fate wasn't preoccupying me. I knew they'd died quickly. That was enough consolation for the moment.

The ripe harvest and the soft even ground beneath it cushioned my landing and a gentle wind pulled me slowly towards a stone fence where the field boarded a country lane. I was trying to fold my chute when two teenagers pedaled up to the stone barrier and unslung their elderly carbines, made a show of throwing the bolts and took aim at me. I dropped the chute and raised my hands. Somehow I couldn't take their threats seriously. It was a beautiful summer day, a brilliant sun warming the land, the blue sky dotted with small clean white clouds. I just couldn't turn these boys and their bolt action single shot rifles into much of a threat.

I understood the German they used well enough, and had enough to respond. "Hände hoch." I put up my hands, then tried out my German.

"Can I pick up…der…" I didn't know the word in German or whether it was a der instead of a 'die,' "…the parachute?" I pointed at the yards of cloth on the ground. Maybe I could trade the silk for a little lenient treatment. One of the boys nodded and I managed to bundle it up and throw it over the fence.

By this time, I could see a small sedan approaching from the town to the west. When it stopped I could read the word *Polizei* stenciled in white on the door. An elderly man in a Wehrmacht uniform stepped out, took his side arm—a luger—from his belt and spoke rapidly to the boys, a bit too rapidly for my German. They retired with ill grace. The man pointed the luger at the 'chute and indicated I was to stuff it into the trunk of his car. I did so and then he ordered me to turn around and snapped a pair handcuffs on my wrists. He opened the door to the back seat and pushed me in.

There didn't seem an excess of force, or much malevolence in his treatment. But there was rather more in the faces of the bystanders, when he opened the backdoor of the car in the town square of Villach, at least that's what the sign called it as we entered the town. The square was centered on a small fountain and framed by gingerbread and Bavarian timbered architecture. In front of us was a stuccoed two-storey building with twin stairs mounting to a balcony over the main entry way. It could have passed for a Lehar operetta stage.

The car had attracted a crowd, and as I stood, a half-dozen men and woman, mostly elderly, approached with menacing gestures, two carrying crofting implements. They began speaking loudly to the policeman, and pushing their long implements past him and at me. I was fending them off by turning my body when a loud order, *Achtung*, came from a door that had been thrown open.

A man stood there, hands on hips, looking every inch the German army officer, except for the funny shako on his head. The crowd immediately relented, the policeman came to attention and saluted. The superior officer spoke a few words to my elderly guard and I was frog-marched inside.

Inside, the officer looked me over, demanded the handcuff keys from his subordinate, and removed them.

"Sprechen Sie Deutsch?" The other man retired to the door, but remained facing us with his hand on the holstered luger.

I replied, "Nur ein bisschen." It had been the language I chose to study back at West Point. Now two years of it was gathering dust in the further reaches of my memory.

He indicated his pockets and said "Tasche öffnen, bitte." I pulled my trouser pockets out to show they were completely empty. We'd been told to take nothing with us but our dog-tags and escape kits. Mine was now a million little pieces floating down over the German countryside.

When he said "Setzen Sie," I decided it was dumb to speak any more German. If they thought I didn't understand anything they might say something I could use. I stood there till he pointed me at a bench along the wall behind me. Then the officer sat down, looked in a ledger and picked up the telephone in front of him.

It looked and felt like he'd been through the drill of dealing with downed bomber crew before. Soon he was nodding his head and repeatedly saying 'Ja' and 'Sicher' and 'Genau' in answer to questions. Then he put down the receiver, opened the door on the roomy cell with a grill of vertical bars and invited me to enter.

I rose, felt for my smokes, found them, put one in my mouth, and held out the packet offering him one. He shook his head, and pointed at the door. Glancing briefly at the other man still barring the entry, hand on sidearm, I entered.

27

An hour later I heard the sound of a truck coming to a halt. It was late afternoon. The door was opened by someone with enough braid on his Luftwaffe blue shoulder-boards to show he was a sergeant. The noncom was followed by an officer, also in blue, who spoke in rapid German to the police chief. He had risen immediately on seeing the officer and given the required 'German greeting,' as they called the "Heil Hitler."

The cell was opened and the Luftwaffe officer spoke, in English. "Follow me. No speaking."

At the back of the tarpaulin covered truck, the tailgate was open and two soldiers armed with submachine guns stood, one on either side. Looking up I saw the truck had three air American crew in it already, all officers by the look of them. One raised his hand, at which the German snarled, "Silence. No talking."

I climbed in and the others made room for me. The truck rattled out of town, over a river bridge and headed west. By now it was too dark even to read the names of the towns as we passed beyond them. None of us was prepared to defy the guards sitting next to us along the benches on each side of the truck.

We were cold, hungry, tired, and in need of a toilet three hours later when the truck came to a stop at the entry to what had to be a POW camp. We'd passed through a large city I later learned was Frankfurt.

Off the truck, we were allowed to relieve ourselves in a trench at the edge of a barbed wire fence about eight feet high. Above it we were invited to contemplate a watch tower with a heavy machine gun silhouetted in the glare of a search light. Then we entered a long building and were each unceremoniously thrust through a separate door.

Mine opened to a cubicle of rough wood, a plain table with a chair under a single strong light that swagged from the ceiling. On the table was a piece of oak tag paper about fourteen inches long, a nib pen, and open ink well.

I sat and scanned the writing on the oak tag, *International Red Cross Prisoner of War Information Form.* Besides name, rank, and serial number the form had blanks for the prisoner's home address, next of kin, education, and service record—place of induction, basic training, advanced training, flight specialties, units to which the officer had been assigned, and then base locations in England. I smiled as I read through this list. It was transparently not a real Red Cross form. I carefully filled out only the first three items, as required by the Geneva Convention of POWs. Did they expect me to do more, I wondered?

Putting the pen down, I leaned back in my chair and lit a smoke. It was my first mistake in captivity. The door was opened. An officer not in Luftwaffe blue but in SS black came in, holding a luger, reached around me and pulled my cigarette from my mouth.

He snarled in a Hollywood German accent, "Fill out ze form!"

Proffering it to him over my shoulder I said quietly, "I did."

He looked at me with a glare, made a show of shifting the safety on his weapon and placing it at my neck, and then repeated the words. They'd briefed us enough back in England for me to think this was a bluff. Still, I could feel the cold steel against my skin. Slowly I rose and handed him the form, looking him in the eye. He lowered the luger, and walked out of the room. A moment later I heard the sound of the door being locked and then the light went out in the windowless room. I was in the dark. How long I would remain there was something they probably weren't going to tell me. I felt my way to a corner and curled up, glad of my leather flight jacket, folded under my head as a pillow.

When the light came on next, it might have been morning—my watch had stopped. I noticed a covered slop bucket in the corner and made use of it. Then I hammered on the door. I needed water, food. There was no response. I sat at the chair for a while, then tried to curl up on the table. It was too small. So, I folded my leather jacket into a cushion again and slid down the wall to the floor.

You need to pass the time, Will. Let's walk back your life. How much detail can you recall. I began the experiment, focused first on picturing the room I grew up in, trying to identify the posters and the model airplanes I carved, all the balsa wings I stretched tissue over, doped, and hung from fine fishing line from the slanted ceiling of my dormer window. The details came—a Spad, like Frank Luke's, a Sopwith Camel like Billy Bishop's. Then smoothly I was in the air, seated in the front cockpit of a barnstormer's DH-4 Jenny realizing for the first time that flying was the only thing that really made me happy. No, not any more. It wasn't flying. There was Wendy's face in my mind's eye, and then, I realized, Ellen's face, somehow diminishing the freedom of flying into something smaller, something more venal, less important than love. On the floor of that cell, leaning against a cold wall, I began to be afraid to die, or better, I began to have something to live for, someone to live for.

The next morning, that thought was the last thing I could remember thinking about, and it was still with me.

When the door was finally opened, it was by an officer in Luftwaffe blue. He smiled as he reached out a hand to pull me off the floor.

"I am Hauptman Schiller, assigned to your case." He looked around, smelled the slop bucket, leaned over for my jacket, handed it to me as he spoke. "Let's get out of here. My office is a little more comfortable." He led me out of the building and into an afternoon light.

There was a tray at his desk. "Take a pew. Have some grub." The tone was as colloquial as the words. I sat and smeared some margarine and a rather thin kind of preserve on a slab of black bread. Then took a healthy bite. I smiled inwardly. It was just me suddenly wanting to live. *Better late than never.* The voice in my head was sardonic.

He spoke while I ate. "Sorry about your reception last night. SS demands *le droit de seigneur*, so we let them play their little game. But this place is run by Luftwaffe and we're not going to let them come between us and guys who are no different."

Still, I didn't speak, shoveling the dark bread into my mouth. It was only when I started gulping the hot liquid in the cup before me that I realized I wasn't in an American mess any more. Schiller caught my grimace. "Know what you mean there. Haven't had a decent cup of java practically since this war began."

Finally I spoke. "Where you from, Schiller…in the States I mean?"

"Detroit, Michigan. That's where I was raised. Born in Stuttgart, taken to the States when I was a little kid just after the Great War, in 1921. Came back for a visit in '39. Got drafted. Here I am…pretty much against my will, like most of you guys."

He looked at me. "Try me out if you don't believe me. Hell, my favorite player growing up was Hank Greenberg. Say, what's he doing now?"

"Don't know the name. Haven't been Stateside myself since 1938." As I finished the words, the thought came. Fool, you've just blurted out information to the enemy. It's too easy just to talk.

Schiller understood immediately. "Yah, I know…I'm probably better at proving I'm a Yank than you are."

I decided to play along. Maybe I could get something out of him. "What do you mean, Schiller?"

"Call me Herm. It's Hermann here, but back home everyone called me Herm. What I meant was you don't have to prove who you are to us. We've got a file on you, Will…can I call you that?" I nodded. "West Point '36. Then you quit, flew in Spain. That's where we picked up your name first. Then China, the Flying Tigers, before you got here."

"Didn't know I was so famous, Herm." I smiled.

He grimaced slightly. "You're not. We know most of the stuff we need to know about every guy here, even before they get here."

"How's that?"

"Let's just say the aircraft carrier is a leaky ship." Just using the expression showed he was in the know.

The 'aircraft carrier' was local slang that had sprung up among Eighth Air Group crew for the spread of American airfields across East Anglia. By now I'd finished eating. Schiller pushed the tray aside. Then he looked down at a piece of paper. It was the oak tag form I hadn't fully filled out the night they'd brought me in. He pushed it towards me.

"You gotta fill this in, Will."

"No can do, Herm." I needed to use his nickname back at him. "Besides, I thought you just said you already know everything."

"Look, this is just to get word to your family Stateside quicker. By now they've gotten the missing in action telegram. Don't you want to relieve them?"

"I guess you don't know everything, Hauptman Schiller. No family to inform." I pushed the paper back at him. "Besides, you're asking for a lot more information here."

"Lieutenant Thurlow…" We were back to surnames, I noticed. "You're making things difficult for me, and for you. If you don't fill out the form, that guy in the black uniform you met last night will make me put you back in solitary." He paused. "And you'll stay there till you fill it out."

I rose. "Better get started then."

He misunderstood. "Good. Here, use this." He proffered a nice looking fountain pen.

"No. I meant better get me back to that cell."

I was in solitary for four days. Twice a day bread and water, each morning the form, an ink-well, and fountain pen placed on the desk along with the 'breakfast.' It was removed when the evening ration came in. Then the light went off. At least they hadn't taken my leather flight jacket.

The main problem with having that much time on my hands was the fear that kept intruding on the excavation of my memory. I'd find a seam in my past, something I hadn't thought of for years, often inconsequential but still interesting. I'd begin working through it only to be distracted by my immediate future, more interrogation, compulsion, torture, then years in a POW camp. I kept telling myself it couldn't be as scary as flying through flak bursts, being targeted by German fighters firing cannon shells, still less than being in a dog-fight, bounced by a fighter plane coming down at me from the sun. But alone in that cell, with nothing to distract me but those fleeting memories, I found myself overwhelmed by the unknown future. I was probably too dehydrated to cry, because the tears didn't come, but several times I found myself shaking with fear, and then slightly glad there was no one who could see me curled up on the floor of a black space.

I've got to admit that a hundred hours of solitary, half of it in complete darkness, was reaching into my resolve, telling me that what they wanted was of no military value.

Hard to sleep when you don't need much. Nothing to do when the light is on but wait for it to go off. I told myself that was exactly what they were counting on. I thought of using my dog tags to scratch a message on the walls, and that immediately began my search for any messages others might already have left. But the walls were pretty freshly painted and then when I tried to scratch anything into them the lines stood out like welts from a hickory stick. They'd be noticed and effaced before the next inmate arrived.

The fourth day—I think it was anyway, I was still awake about an hour after the lamp was turned off, when the door opened slowly, spilling hallway light into my room. It was dim enough not to cause me to squint, and it shadowed a man in a leather trench coat with his finger to his mouth, murmuring me to silence. He entered, closed the door quietly, and turned on a flashlight. In a German's English he spoke.

"Don't talk. You're getting out of here…" I nodded. "Turn around." He held up a pair of handcuffs. I looked at him puzzled. "It needs to look like a prisoner transport for further interrogation."

I rose, put my flight jacket on and put my hands behind me. He closed the cuffs on my wrists. With infinite slowness the man opened the door, then he peered both ways, and then led me out into the corridor, down to the entrance. We passed the guard table. There was a glass tea cup, still steeping and steaming on the table but no one behind it. I looked at my liberator. He smiled and rubbed a finger against his thumb. I understood the gesture to mean a bribe had absented the guard. Now I was much more curious. What subversive force was reaching into a Luftwaffe POW interrogation center?

Outside he stopped. "Now, we will walk to the camp entrance. It's not far. When we get there, you will make a show of the handcuffs, complain they are painful, unnecessary… anything, just so the guards at the gate notice you are wearing them. Understand?"

"Yup. I can play along. I'll pretty much do anything for someone who got me out of that cell."

"Don't overdo it. My papers are not foolproof." He touched the pocket of his leather coat. "We could both be shot."

We approached the main gate, guarded by three Luftwaffe non-coms, two holding tight to leashed German Shepard dogs straining in our direction as we approached. I began to complain loudly about the handcuffs, and was reproved in stern German. Then my new friend pulled several sheets folded together from his outside pocket and handed them over to the guards, volunteering his flashlight. After only a cursory examination, the sergeant drew himself up, clicked a heel and indicated to his men that the gate was to be opened.

28

There was a small car parked beyond the camp gate. As we approached, a driver came out and opened the rear door. The German pulled off his leather coat to reveal a blue naval officer's uniform.

"Too hot, that coat, but you have to look the part for those fellows." He jerked his head back to the gate.

We got in the car, the driver slid behind the wheel, and we took off. Sitting in the back seat together I observed him withdraw the handcuff key and turned my back to let him take them off. Soon I was freed from the shackles and watching the night streak pass the window of the car. The dim headlamps in the blackout kept the town we drove through unnamed, but soon enough we were driving past distance markers to Frankfurt. That must have been the city we'd been trucked through on the way to the POW interrogation camp, I thought. Meanwhile the naval officer said nothing. When we got clear of the city and found ourselves on the new autobahn signposted to Berlin, 508 kilometers away, he turned to me and spoke.

"Admirable self-restraint you are showing, Lieutenant Thurlow. Not asking me any questions. Well, I am authorized to make a statement to you and to say nothing else."

"You've got my full attention…" I looked at him, wishing I had a name to attach to my liberator.

He was reading my expression well. "Can't tell you my name. For your sake as well as mine. So…" He paused. His 'so' was more like 'zo.' "You are being taken to Berlin. No harm will come to you…unless we are apprehended by the Gestapo. Everything you need to know will be explained when you get there. Now, settle back it's a long ride."

He leaned back and closed his eyes. After four days of sensory deprivation, I couldn't do the same. I stayed awake and watched the early dawn of an August summer day. The sun rose up in front of the windscreen and made me squint.

It was late morning when we passed road markers for Leipzig and Halle, surrounded by suburban ruins and bomb craters. I knew the RAF was beginning to reach this far into Germany. It was the only damage I could see all the way to Berlin. Much of the countryside was neat and a great deal of it in wheat, some already being harvested by combines drawn behind eight or a dozen stout horses. Finally, the warmth and the smoothness of the autobahn lulled me into sleep.

We were driving along a leafy city street by the side of a canal when I finally awoke. The imposing buildings on my left were draped not in Nazi flags but flew the Iron Cross insignia. Here, my companion held up the hand cuffs and I turned around to have them reinstalled.

"Thank you," was all he said.

We passed what looked like the main entrance and turned into a narrow lane that evidently went around the back of the building.

The door was opened by a soldier in Wehrmacht field grey, not someone in Luftwaffe blue. We entered, prisoner ahead of jailer and walked down a narrow corridor into an imposing vestibule, then up a broad set of marble stairs, passed a handful of officers coming downstairs at a clip. Then we turned right along a wide corridor. I could see the open quadrangle at the interior of the building as we walked down the hall and finally entered a wood-paneled office, where a woman in a naval uniform sat behind a desk with three telephones. My handcuffs were removed. Then the officer turned to the woman.

"The package from Oberdorf that Admiral Canaris is expecting." He bowed slightly, nodded to me and left.

The woman buzzed an intercom and spoke my name. The German came back. "Herein." To which she replied "Sofort." Then she rose and opened the door behind her. "Eintreten, bitte." It was the polite imperative for a change, not the one you use with servants. I hadn't heard it since I'd hit the silk, and that must have been a week before.

I was standing before a short man with a long face and white hair, wearing a naval uniform. His office was large and had a view through gauze curtains down into the quad. He put his finger to his lips and then turned. Behind him was a large polished wooden cabinet with the words *Grundig* in black letters across the top. He opened the doors, revealing a radio, which he turned on. As the tubes warmed up, he continued to indicate silence. Once the classical music was blaring he ushered me to a brace of chairs in the corner, indicated one and took another. He pointed at the walls and ceiling. I understood. This officer was anxious that he was being bugged. Then he began speaking at me, quietly, in the unaccented English of an upper-class Brit, better even than the subordinate naval officer who had brought me to him.

"I am Admiral Wilhelm Canaris, director of the Reich military intelligence. I have an important task for you, Lieutenant Thurlow, one that only you can carry out. It must be accomplished with utmost secrecy, for the sake of the speedier end of this war, and for the sake of millions of innocent German lives." He stopped. "I cannot emphasize how grave a task I am charging you with. It is a dangerous one, both for you and for me. If there were another way to accomplish it, I would certainly make use of it."

"A few days after you were shot down, Lieutenant, the RAF visited Berlin. About seven-hundred Lancasters. Each carrying twice as much as your B-17s. We managed to destroy about fifty of them. Their bombs wrecked nothing of military value whatever. But they killed nine-hundred civilians. This of course was their mission, Your ally's RAF bomber command leader, Harris, calls this 'dehousing.' Your Eighth Air Group may try to destroy targets of military value but all you actually do is more of the dehousing of German civilians." I was about to agree, but Canaris must have thought I was going to disagree. He waved his hand. "Of course you know about the week long bombing of Hamburg last spring." His tone turned interrogatory. "Perhaps you even participated?"

"No, sir."

"But you know what happened. Your friend Solly Zuckerman could have told you if your own air staff didn't."

Now I understood why I was sitting here in Berlin, or at least that it was my acquaintance with Zuckerman that had spung me from *Luftwaffe* interrogation. But why? Canaris was continuing.

"A week of RAF and Eighth Air Group bombing, a firestorm that destroyed the entire old town of Hamburg. Do you know what a firestorm is, Lieutenant?" He didn't wait for a response before going on. "A three-hundred-meter-high fire, reaching temperatures of eight-hundred degrees, killing fourty-thousand civilians. There was no significant military production damage done at all." He stopped. "The port was only closed for a day or so." Now he raised his voice slightly. "Your people did it again twice more this spring and summer. seven-hundred bombers, thousands dead, no impact on the war. Our civilians are no more cowed by terror bombing than the British."

I interrupted. "Or the Spanish by your bombing and the Chinese by the Jap bombers."

"Just so, Lieutenant." He rose and walked to his desk, picked up a portfolio and brought it back to the low circular table before the two lounge chairs. "Your Professor Zuckerman knows what we know—that your bomber offensive has no impact on our war production, not even killing munitions workers, just killing thousands of women, children, and elderly people."

Keeping my voice down I spoke as coldly as I could. "I've had about enough lecturing about this from a Nazi."

Canaris gave me a hard look. "You have no reason to know, Lieutenant, but I am not a Nazi, never have been. You'll have reason to believe me perhaps, in a moment." He opened the portfolio. "This is a list of German munitions factories all over the Reich, with individual maps, latitude and longitude, and aerial photographs taken in clear weather. The ones that were in large towns have been moved to locations in the country side. They have been camouflaged as well. The portfolio comes from the Reich armaments ministry itself." He passed the portfolio to me. "You may examine it if you wish."

"I'm no expert, Admiral. It won't mean much to me."

"Yes, yes. But I need you to get this file to Professor Zuckerman. He'll be able to persuade your high command to target these locations. It will win the war for you by cutting our production of airplanes, tanks, artillery, and at the same time it will save thousands of civilian lives."

"Why do you think the Brits and Americans will believe you, Admiral? Why wouldn't this just be a ruse to get our bombers to drop explosives in wheat fields?"

"You may not believe that I am anti-Nazi, but your intelligence services know the truth. I have been dealing with them at risk to myself for years. They have no question about my *bona fides*."

"So, why use me, then?"

"This material has to get to Zuckerman. I have to be sure he gets it. If I give it to the OSS in Switzerland, it may languish for months. Even if it gets to England, there will be those who want to keep bombing German civilians…*Rache*." It was a German word, but I knew its meaning well enough—revenge. "Only you can get it into his hands for sure."

"How do you know I'm acquainted with Zuckerman?"

"Come, come, Lieutenant. I'm the director of the most powerful intelligence network in the world. Your name has been in our files since you were shot down by a Condor Legion Messerschmitt in Spain in 1938. When our man at the Durchlag passed us your name, it was like a gift from heaven."

I was beginning to believe Canaris. "I'm flattered, Admiral. But how am I ever going to smuggle a portfolio this size back to Britain?"

"You continue to underestimate us. You'll get this entire file as a set of microdots you can swallow if need be and still carry out of Germany…You speak Spanish no doubt?" I nodded. "Well, in an hour or so you will be a Spanish diplomat on his way back to Madrid. The only trouble is we won't be able to protect you. You'll be on your own as soon as you walk out of this building."

I understood only too well. "Kitted out with civilian clothes and false identity, liable to be shot as a spy if I'm caught."

Canaris nodded. "There is a risk." He buzzed the intercom and I realized he hadn't even asked me if I was willing to undertake his mission. Somehow he knew he didn't need to.

I was ushered out of Abwehr headquarters well within Canaris' one hour time-table. I'd been kitted out in a civilian suit of a radical cut I could only assume was fashionable in Madrid, then photographed for a passport. I was briefed one last time. The functionary was young, English speaking and dressed in civilian clothes.

"Lieutenant Thurlow. This is for you." I was handed a small envelope. "Rice paper. Edible, contains two microdots. Spanish diplomatic passport. It is genuine, a Spanish diplomatic passport in the name of one Jorge Santilla y Tendosa, diplomatic officer, but your identity is not genuine. So do not present it at a Spanish consulate." The passport looked suitably used. I leafed through it, noticing the stamps of countries I'd never visited myself. None of them were German speaking. He continued. "Exit visa from the Reich, railway ticket, first class to Paris. There is no sleeper." He handed me a wallet. "Enough Reichsmarks to purchase a first class sleeper to Madrid." Then he picked up a small valise. "Toiletries, fresh linen, change of clothes. A book, in Spanish. You read Spanish, yes?" I nodded, wondering what German intelligence thought I'd like to read. He handed me the valise. "Follow me."

We went down to the street level on a back staircase, and then wended our way through service corridors till we came to an exit door. It was guarded and locked, but the man at the entry simply rose and opened it. Outside there was a taxi-cab. We both stood in the hidden car park where I'd been dropped off.

"Admiral's apologies. Your visit has been a well-kept secret. The cab will take you to the Anhalter Bahnhof." He looked at his watch. "Your train leaves in an hour."

I dropped into the back of the cab, and it moved off without a command. Suddenly I realized I hadn't slept for days, except perhaps an hour in the back of the car bringing me to Berlin. My head ached and my eyelids wanted to close. But I had to watch Berlin go past, the canal, then a vast green space, a glittering golden column, and the Brandenburg Gate looming up until the cab abruptly turned right and joined the traffic flowing towards the terminal.

The impression I got was order and dispatch. Everyone on the pavement had somewhere to go, quickly it seemed, both civilians and men in uniform. I watched arms go up at every building entrance, but along this route no cafes or shops, or even many women. The taxis all seemed to be powered by the wood burning gasogenes, but there were plenty of gleaming black Mercedes shouldering the smaller cars aside. And there were trucks, closed or tarpaulin covered, invariably a couple of soldiers sitting at the tail gate.

Suddenly we were in the queue of taxis waiting to disgorge their passengers at the station entrance. When it was my turn I began looking for the taximeter to see what my fare was. The driver turned and shook his head, resetting the meter to zero. Then spoke in English.

"Good luck."

I replied. "Thanks."

He leaned towards me, grabbed my arm and growled fiercely in accented but colloquial English. "Oldest trick in the book, mate. You're a goner even before you step out of the cab." He could see I didn't follow. "It's simple. Gestapo checking *Ausweis*—identity, gives yours a glance and hands it back. Says 'Good luck,' you automatically reply 'Thanks,' like you just did, and your cover is blown." My face turned red. He spoke once more. "Viel Glück" and leant across to open my door. I replied in Spanish.

29

I was on the overnight Berlin-Paris express of the *Deutsche Reichsbahn.* No sleepers but half the cars were first class, almost every seat taken by a youngish officer, all cashing in the Führer's promise that every Wehrmacht soldier would have at least one furlough in Paris. Most of them were behaving as though they'd already arrived, and the conductors were not enforcing the decorum demanded by the disgruntled looks the one or two civilians in each compartment silently cast upon the merry making. Reading my Spanish book—the plays of Lope de Vega, which held little interest, I was left unmolested by the four lieutenants, briefly detached from an Army Group serving on the Eastern Front, who shared my compartment.

Even in uniform, bemedaled, and slightly inebriated, these officers were subject to the same repeated identity check imposed on the Spanish diplomat wordlessly sharing their compartment. None of the police inspectors, all in black Gestapo uniforms, tried the puerile "Good luck" trick on me, but at least twice a Spanish speaking agent was called upon to vet me, and each time I was required to pull down my valise from the baggage rack above my head and disgorge its contents.

At about four o'clock in the morning the train stopped. The Gestapo came through the cars, poking heads in each compartment to announce *Grenzkontrollen*—border checks. The Wehrmacht officers and the civilians all roused themselves, pulled down their kits and shuffled sleepily down the narrow corridor and out onto a platform. There, despite the fact their country was completely occupied, French police were standing hard by Germans, the one checking exit visas and the other pretending to examine German soldier's leave documents along with the few civilian passports.

The Gestapo officer looked my passport over with distain and handed it to a French gendarme. He addressed me in French.

"So, diplomat…" He tapped the document against his palm. "Where?"

"Bucharest, *señor*," I replied, hoping he'd never been there himself.

"How long?"

"Three years, Monsieur."

My diplomatic passport was four years old. That made me a creature of Generalissimo Franco, and should have secured some good will from a servant of Vichy. Instead he snarled "Falangiste." This was Franco's fascist party. Was it an accusation or a question? I stood silently, prepared to plead guilty to the charge if needs be. His look took my silence for a cowardly admission and he waived me on. But he wasn't returning the passport.

I asked for it, "Por favor, el pasaporte…" holding out my hand. Shaking his head the man called to another uniformed police officer, handing him the passport.

"Suivez-moi, s'il vous plaît." *If you please, my foot!* He might as well have said *Raus!* in German. There was something about me they didn't like. At a customs inspection table I was required to empty out the few items in my valise, and allow every seam of the extra underwear and shirt to be felt. But the valise itself was not examined and I was not required to empty my pockets. I had begun to worry for the envelope in the breast pocket of my jacket. But they really didn't seem interested in anything but harassing me.

Everyone else was already on board when I was allowed to entrain again myself. My German compartment mates asked in German whether I had been smuggling German wine into France, but I decided not to understand the German cognate, *schmuggeln*.

We were all still asleep when the train stopped suddenly in an open field just before the city of Rheims. The sun was up and we could see a formation of bombers—they looked like American B-24s coming from the west and banking back towards England. They'd obviously just bombed the city. *Champagne warehouses?* The men around me woke and began to grumble at the delay, eating into their furloughs. One rose and left the compartment. When he returned he announced a several hour delay…damage to the marshalling yard. In the end it was only about two hours before we began again, and no destruction visible as we rolled through the switching yards before the station itself, or after it for that matter.

It was nearing eleven o'clock when we finally pulled into the *Gare de l'est*. If I'd been eager to see Paris again, it took only a few minutes to make me realize I'd want to forget this trip. It wasn't the Paris I'd left in the early spring of 1940. The gothic *Fraktur* of the signage was jarring, directing disembarking soldiers to the Army Headquarters, the SS and Gestapo, the Luftwaffe and the *Kriegsmarine* commands, even giving the distances in kilometers to Berlin, Rome, and to Moscow, this one visibly defaced. I passed a kiosk, bereft of anything but German language newspapers, including one for Wehrmacht tourists. At the tabac, Germans were buying cigarette cartons with French francs, but no ration tickets, while the French in the same queue were limited to a pack or two.

I knew Paris well enough. Down the metro at *Gare de l'est*, *correspondence*—change—at *Châtelet*. In twenty-five minutes I was at the ticket window, displaying my diplomatic passport and requiring a sleeper to Madrid. The man behind the ticket window looked at me strangely.

"What planet do you come from? No *Wagons-Lits* in France since the Germans began their Russian war."

I settled for first class with a seat reservation. Ticket in hand, I began to wonder how to spend an afternoon in Paris. I found the left-luggage and passed in my small valise against a ticket. Soon enough I was walking along the left bank of the Seine towards the Ile de Saint Louis, watching Notre Dame enlarge to dominate my view as I approached. Suddenly I knew where I was headed. It was an old restaurant near the Luxembourg Gardens, one of the few that catered to an unrefined taste like mine. But just being in Paris so unexpectedly, so free, feeling invulnerable in my diplomatic status. I suppose I should have felt the eyes on me, steadily cast by a couple of cheminots—railway workers, kitted out in very blackened *bleus de travail*—the sail cloth blue uniform of French manual labor. It wasn't the fashion in the student quarter I'd entered once I crossed the Austerlitz bridge to the Left Bank. But I hadn't even given a thought to the chance I was being followed.

Standing in front of the *Crèmerie Polydor* trying to make out the menu, just as I had a half-dozen years before, on my way to Spain, it dawned on me that I had no ration tickets. *Maybe they'll take Reichsmarks?*

As I stepped to the door, a gun barrel pushing against my ribs, and a whisper in Spanish. "Come along with us, señor." It was the two railway workers I should have spotted following me from the *Gare de Lyon*, one grey and wizened, the other younger and looking uncertain. I was about to put my hands up, when the older of the two spoke.

"Don't do that. Just act natural."

I complied, and felt myself pushed in the direction of the large open space in front of the Théâtre d'Odéon a block away. Once there, the two pushed me past the columned front and around to the covered passageway at the side of the building that led up towards the Luxembourg Gardens. The columns along the long walkway kept it dark, damp, chilled, and deserted in the bright sun shine. Half way up the side they stopped me. The older one spoke, still in Spanish.

"Dirty Falangiste swine. Give me that passport."

Suddenly I understood. These two were Spanish Republican refugees. They were out to kill one of Franco's henchmen. Slowly I reached into my suitcoat pocket for the document. What should I say? Did I blow my cover? How could I prove to them who I really was, anyway? I had to try.

"Do you speak English?" It was a stab in the dark and pointless anyway. I switched back to Spanish. "Look, I'm not Spanish. I'm an American flyer, trying to escape back to England."

The older one eyed me and then waived the passport. "What's this then? General Franco helping Americans?"

I lied. "It's fake…" They were silent. I plunged forward. "I speak Spanish because I flew for the Republic." Then I raised my hand in the Loyalist salute, arm up, fist closed, and spoke "Viva la Republica, viva le Frente Popular."

They smiled slightly and replied. "Viva el Partido Comunista." The older man lowered his weapon slightly in a mark of détente. "So, where did you get the passport?"

"I told you, it's false."

He shook his head. "I've been in the resistance for two years, we don't make anything that good, certainly not for flyers we're helping."

I saw the man coming down the passage behind them, he was tall, thin, and dressed in a black full-length coat, too heavy for the warm fall afternoon. His snap brim hat pulled down over his face. He had a hand in his pocket and was making his steps clearly audible as he came. My two assailants turned. Before the old man could raise his revolver, the man withdrew a luger and fired twice. A silencer muffled the sounds so well I could only be sure he'd shot because both men crumpled to the ground. He came up beside me, turned and administered a *coup de grâce* to their foreheads, bent down and pulled the passport from the hand of the older one, handed it to me and wordlessly walked away. I was too shaken to follow, to call after him, to do anything except walk briskly away down towards the Boulevard Saint Germain, pretending I knew nothing of two dead men in the passageway behind me.

I had to get off the streets. I couldn't afford another encounter like the one I'd just had. I'd just been the cause of two deaths. I had no idea how or why I'd put these men at risk. If the *Abwehr* had assigned someone to protect me, how many more people was he going to kill? If German security forces caught up with me, was the *Abwehr* going to keep protecting their secret? There was only one way to get off the streets in the middle of the day without having to file a hotel police report.

I needed a movie theater and I remembered one three or four blocks away, up from the Sorbonne. It was playing a film by Pagnol. Though I sat there through three screenings, I was too preoccupied to follow the plot. Middle of the afternoon on a sunny day, there was almost no one in the theater to help me by laughing at Fernandel, a comic I knew well from before the war.

Towards the end of the third sitting a young woman walked up the isle to my seat and sat down. She offered me a smoke and spoke one word. in English.

"Flyer?" I nodded. She switched to French. "Thought so, you fellows always sit through more than one showing…want your money's worth I suppose. Don't know why the Germans haven't gotten wind." I glanced at her slight smile just visible in the darkened theater. "Let's get out of here." She rose and I followed. I didn't feel I had much choice.

She led me down into the Latin Quarter and stopped before a Tunisian bakery.

"Sandwich?" It was said in French.

"S'il vous plait." I replied.

A moment later she was back with two large rolls, filled with little beyond lettuce but seriously laced with a lemon dressing that made it delicious to someone who hadn't eaten for the better part of a day.

We sat down on the stone bench in front of the vast fountain at Place Saint-Michel. Our perch looked and felt far too conspicuous to me. She let me chew for a few minutes and then began to speak.

"I'm Citrine. Copyist at the Louvre, when I'm not scouting out downed Allied airmen."

I said nothing, suddenly realizing I had trusted her from the moment she'd spoken in the darkened theater, without even thinking about it. *A mistake, Will.* She looked me up and down.

"You're not kitted out like any Allied airman I know. Where did you get those *duds*?" The last word was in English.

I'd probably have to tell her a great deal, or nothing at all. I knew I couldn't tell her everything, not even if she was entirely trustworthy. A brutal interrogation would extract everything a person knows and then some.

"I escaped from a POW interrogation center three days ago." Was it only three days now? "Somebody gave me this suit, a Spanish diplomatic passport and put me on a train to Paris."

"Let's see." She held out her hand. I pulled it out and handed it to her. One look at the picture was enough for her. "Someone just gave this to you…Well, if you say so…" The English spoken in an undertone was laced with sarcasm.

"Something the matter with it?"

"No. That's the trouble. It's perfect. It's genuine. They even had you pose for your passport picture three days ago. Are you a German agent, Will. Is it Wilhelm?" She was reaching into her purse. I grabbed her hand.

"It's not like that. I swear." She took her hand from the purse but remained silent. "Citrine, I can't tell you anything about it. But you've got to trust me. I need to get to Spain and back to England as quick as I can." Still she said nothing, looking me in the eye unblinkingly. I had to go on. "I've got a ticket on the sleeper to Madrid, but two Spanish railroad workers have already tried to kill me." Now I was in even deeper. How could I tell her what happened to them?

"What happened? How did you escape?"

"I don't know. Someone came along and just shot them both, used a silencer, right there in the street, or rather a passageway behind the Odeon Theatre. Then he just walked away before I realized what had happened."

She smiled briefly. "Very well, I believe you, Will. One of our people saw everything, just as you described. I was waiting for you to make something up. You didn't. You told the truth."

"But why were they after me?"

"I can't be sure, but I think I know. A lot of the guys in the Resistance are veterans from the Civil War, communists who fought for the Republic. Anybody know about your Spanish diplomatic passport?"

"A couple of gendarmes at the border. They weren't particularly deferential. Then I showed it at the *Gare de Lyon* when I got my sleeper ticket to Madrid this morning."

"That probably explains it. Railway is honey-combed with former Spanish Republicans, almost all of them members of the Spanish Communist Party, or French Communists. They're as ready to kill Franco's people as they are Germans. More ready to kill Spaniards, since the risk of reprisal is nil."

"What do you think I should I do, Citrine?" It was weird, needing someone to tell me what to do for a change.

"I don't know. If you use your ticket you might be in Madrid by noon tomorrow. Or you might be dead." She looked at me. "We're used to not being told secrets, Will. But can you tell me anything? I'll be able to figure things out better."

"'Fraid not."

"Can you say who the guy was that rubbed your Spanish Republicans out?"

"No idea." I had an idea, but I couldn't tell her that it was Germans that had my back.

"If you let us try to get you out, it'll take a few weeks. We try to bring flyers out more than one at a time."

I shook my head. "What I've got can't wait."

"Can we give you a revolver, something to protect yourself?"

"I'd rather have a cyanide pill."

"We'll get you one of those too." She rose and I followed her.

30

Was I really going to kill someone if they tried to stop me again? I'd convinced myself that what I carried was important enough to make me do it if I had to. But I knew that conviction wasn't enough to pull a trigger. *No trouble shooting planes out of the sky, Will. What's stopping you on the ground?* I could feel the small snub-nosed revolver rubbing against my thigh in the deep pocket of my trousers.

What I realized I really wanted was the company of whoever it was that had already been my guardian angel once. He wasn't there now. Nothing but two middle-aged women and an elderly man facing me in the first class compartment. There was no small talk even between the three people who evidently knew each other. They sat and took in the harvested fields and bare grape vines of the Loire, just as I did. The swaying of the train did its best to lull us into sleep, but no one succumbed.

There was still a dining car on the run from Paris to Madrid. Even alone with my thoughts and looking over my shoulder for threats, it was nice to be served by a waiter happy to accept Reichsmarks without the need to present ration coupons. When I returned to my compartment the ladies and their male companion were closing a hamper, glad they didn't have to share anything with the stranger in their compartment. When I offered a packet of the fags I'd bought in Paris they were more than happy each to accept and light up.

Soon we were companionable enough in the blue haze of smoke visible as lighting on the track illuminated the unlit compartment. Running dark through the night in compliance with black out would make reading impossible, so we all settled back to sleep as well as we could slouching on the banquettes, arm rests upraised. Only as I closed my eyes did I realize how many days it had been since I'd slept in a bed—seven if my count was right.

It was well past dawn when I awoke. My traveling companions of the night before were no longer in the compartment. Instead there was a single person facing me, dressed in black all the way down to a knee length coat, the kind we used to call a duster back in Iowa. Instantly, I knew this was the man who'd killed the two railway workers that had threatened me in Paris. Reaching for the small revolver in my pocket was a reflex that he reached out and stopped, putting a powerful hand on my arm. He smiled as he did so, and just as quickly I relaxed, realizing that he'd already saved my life once and could have put an end to it easily while I slept. I smiled sheepishly and relaxed in my seat.

"*Sprechen sie Deutsche?*"

I nodded and replied in my limited German. "*Ja*, if you speak slowly."

"*Sehr gut*. We are coming to the border. I will get down from the train. When the train arrives in Madrid, one of your people will meet you." Suddenly it was clear. I'd been under Canaris' *Abwehr* protection since I'd left Berlin. *Or maybe it was Abwehr observation?* Being found in that movie theater by Citrine, maybe that wasn't a lucky break or the resistance reaching out, just more wire-pulling from Berlin, watching, perhaps testing.

He continued in a smooth, quiet, and confident tone. "Better give me the side arm." I handed it to him, and then reached for the matchbox with the cyanide capsule. He smiled.

"Toss it. Just a fake to keep you calm." Alright, this guy knew everything. And now I knew Citrine was a German plant too. Wish I'd been smart enough to have seen it. Then he rose, and spoke once more, in English. "Good luck."

I blinked and replied, "*Bitte*?" It was what a German said when they didn't understand you.

My companion smiled. "Sehr gut." Then he left without a glance back.

Now the train was slowing to a stop. I watched the words *Hendaye* slide past the window and then saw a group of German border control police in their black SS uniforms waiting to clamber aboard. Soon enough one was in the compartment. I sat, with my diplomatic passport proffered. He examined it page by page, handed it back and clicked his heels. It was then I realized the real test was coming just across the border in *Irun*, where I'd have to masquerade as Spanish for the Spanish border inspection.

————

The *Guardia Civil* in his patent leather *tricornio* cap clicked his heels with no less formality than the German across the border. Perhaps it was a competition? When I handed him the passport he immediately raised himself to a more formal stature.

"*Su excelencia.*" His examination was cursory and he handed it back with a flourish, saluted and left me to enjoy my honorific status.

I was breathing great gulps of what felt like the breath of freedom, or at least my release from danger as I walked down the quay under the vast roof of the Atocha station. It was a place I'd never expected to see again and I wondered vaguely whether they kept records about those who'd flown for the Republic. Coming from the first class carriage at the back end of the train, I was among the last passengers to reach the barrier where tickets were checked one last time. There standing beyond the gate was a man in well-cut tweeds and a trench coat. He was waving and, as there was no one behind me when I turned, it had to be me he wanted. When I reached him, he held out a hand.

"Lieutenant Thurlow?" I nodded. "I'm Osgood, British embassy." He flashed his diplomatic passport, as if I could verify its authenticity. "We've been told to expect you. Please come this way."

My confusion expressed itself immediately. "British Embassy. Why you guys? And how did you know I was coming? I need to get to the American embassy." I smiled at him, hoping to get him onside. "I'm US government property anyway."

Osgood was reassuring. "Of course, Lieutenant." It was actually 'leftenant', but by now I was used to it. "It's just we can get you to London much faster. We've been running this service for downed flyers from Paris for a long time now."

I replied "Is there a rush?" He shot me a look that told me a great deal. This Osgood was in the know, but how much and from whom? When he didn't reply to my question I persisted. "How are you getting me to Gibraltar?" This I knew was the route back to England.

"We're not, old boy. Overland to Lisbon. Then the London flight."

"Not the one that was attacked in June?" The German downing of the BOAC Dakota with the great film star, Leslie Howard, aboard had been headline news everywhere.

"Can't be helped. Not a big risk. They've only ever done it the once. Surprised it would worry you, bomber pilot yourself." His tone was jocular.

My tone wasn't. "I'd rather go via Gibraltar."

"Sorry, orders." Was he going to enforce them? He took a blue document from his jacket. "Here. Better give me the Spanish one…" Was he mind reading? I handed it over, only then realizing the British passport effectively put me in his power. On the other hand, in Spain the one I had could earn me a one way trip to one of Franco's prison farms.

An embassy Daimler was parked at the vast station entrance. I wasn't exactly bundled in but my new friend was close behind as I stepped up to the running board. We settled in on cracked leather seats that sank beneath us and he offered a smoke. I took it with thanks and sat back to watch streets go by that I'd known well six years before.

Madrid was still suffering and by the look of the Madrilenos we passed, so were they. Men and women in work clothes and shabby, shiny suits, patched in places, fewer ties than shirt collars, and those grey with age. Standing at intersections I watched men shuffle across streets while women bore burdens in both hands. There were large potholes still to steer around and hoardings over building fronts and vacant lots. It was another bombed out city, but one destroyed by its own homegrown monsters.

But we weren't heading into the diplomatic quarter and I was beginning to wonder if Franco had moved the embassies elsewhere. The car turned out of streets lined with multi-storey office blocks into residential quarters, then into suburban and finally rural roads, on which our car crossed paths mainly with old trucks and market carts raising dust in the still strong autumnal afternoon heat.

"Say, where'd they move the embassy?" My tone made it clear that I now knew it was not our destination.

"Righteeo, old man. Heading straight for Lisbon. You're too precious a cargo to risk the Spanish finding out about you. The name Will Thurlow still means something to the *Falange*. They hold grudges against Republican flyboys."

"How would they know?" More to the point, how did he know I'd flown for the Loyalists in the Civil War? These people weren't embassy flacks. They were British intelligence. *At least I hope they are*, was the thought that kept coming to me.

Osgood, if that was his real name, answered the question. "You'd have to tell Franco's people, or your embassy would have to, don't you know. American pilot, trying to get back to London?"

I shrugged. Maybe he had a point. "How long's the drive?" At least it was daytime and I'd see more than on my cross-country car ride from Frankfurt to Berlin.

"We're going to drive in shifts, get you to Lisbon by tomorrow night. It's about five-hundred miles but the roads are rough. Settle back."

He leaned forward and brought a straw hamper back from the front seat, sandwiches of salty, stringy Spanish ham, and a flask. *Does he think he's taking me by force, acting in my best interests, protecting me?* Somehow it didn't feel like it. I wasn't in danger from these courteous but very reticent Englishmen. There was almost no small talk all the way to Portugal, even between Osgood and his partner, except to decide when to switch drivers.

Driving west from Madrid the landscape of abandoned farms and uprooted olive groves gave way to the desiccated ridges and scrub forests of Estremadura. Lulled by the soft springs of the Daimler on narrow but straight roads, I slept my way at least intermittently to the Spanish frontier. There, Osgood, in the driver's seat, flashed something at the Spanish *Guardia Civil* and then the Portuguese police—something that didn't look like a diplomatic passport, but made our passage easy—no visas, no customs check, no currency questions, just *By your leave* and some snappy salutes.

Now I was awake, watching a large river—it must have been the Tagus—grow wider as the car glided along its banks, evidently down to Lisbon and the sea. We swept into Lisbon.

Osgood and his friend knew where we were going. It still wasn't a British embassy. The car drew up before an imposing hotel, clean sandstone, brass plate, and golden revolving doors to match, liveried attendant at the door. Walking across the lobby to the registration desk I felt *The Rivoli* wearing its five stars with quiet assurance. Osgood spoke to the man in a swallow tailed morning coat behind the desk in Portuguese. It sounded enough like Spanish for me to make out *Reservation for Thurlow*. The fellow turned, took a key from a pigeon hole and smiled as he handed it across the counter.

The man operating the cage elevator made every gesture with a flourish, and landed us on the eighth floor with suddenness and precision, opening the door even as the lift was still decelerating. We all smiled at his bravura display. Osgood and his partner were still behind me at each shoulder as we walked down the thickly carpeted hallway. Now I felt rather as if I was being frog marched. At the door, Osgood turned.

"It's open. Please go in."

Then he and his friend both turned and headed back down the hall to the still waiting elevator attendant.

That was when everything that had happened since I had left Berlin took on a quite different character.

The room was dark; a curtain drawn against a strong late afternoon sun, but there was a table lamp lit and beneath it, at a comfortable lounge chair, smoking a cigarette giving off the inimitable aroma of an English Virginia, was Admiral Wilhelm Canaris, head of the German *Abwehr*, the very man who'd sent me here from Berlin. He pointed me at the straight back chair facing him. His English was still excellent.

"No need to speak, Lieutenant. I will explain." In his lap was the portfolio he'd shown me in Berlin, at least it looked the same.

"It was very important that there be no finger prints on you from the moment you left *Abwehr* headquarters. If we'd simply flown you here, as I came, well…we couldn't do that without a lot of…what do the Brits call them? 'Chits' and a certain amount of observation, maybe introductions, courtesies, you can well imagine? But we did take some steps, shall we say, to safeguard you." I wanted to speak but he raised his palm. "Still we couldn't be absolutely certain that our brethren in the Gestapo wouldn't exercise their well-known penchant for arbitrary and intrusive enquiry. They'd have found microdots if you had actually been carrying any…" He smiled and nodded. "Then the game would have been up, Mine as well as yours, *Leutnant* Thurlow."

"You're telling me that everyone I met on the way here, including the Brits from the Madrid embassy were actually your people." He nodded slowly. "And that I wasn't carrying your portfolio in microfilm?" He nodded. "Then what the devil was going on, Admiral?"

"Did you expect me to trust that you were who they told me you were, 'William Thurlow' whom we knew had flown in Spain against us, and was a friend of Solly Zuckerman? It was too convenient, your falling into the Luftwaffe's hands. You were almost the only one that could get this material…" He touched the portfolio again, "…to the right person in England. I wasn't going to trust you with anything that could destroy the *Abwehr*. I had to know you were who they told us you were, not some allied pilot they'd turned or one of the Gestapo's people back from America."

"And now you're sure?"

He nodded. "You've passed all the tests I could contrive." He picked up the portfolio and proffered it. "Now take this. The MI5 agent at the Lisbon embassy will be here shortly. His name is Kimberly. He'll see you on to the London flight."

He rose to leave. But I put up my hand. "One moment, Admiral. If you're in contact with British intelligence, and cooperating nicely enough, why do you need me to be your delivery boy? Just pass the stuff along to them, why don't you?"

"We have discussed that option. My contacts in Allied intelligence think that the information will be unwelcome to your air force and to RAF Bomber Command. There is in every military, a chain of command, as you know, *Leutnant* Thurlow."

"Unwelcome?" You're telling me that the people running our bomber offensive don't want to win the war?"

"I'm telling you they think the way to win the war is to kill civilians." He paused. "Just as our side thought. It's not working. And our war production is going up."

I held out the portfolio, shaking my head. "And this stuff is supposed to change their minds?"

"Not theirs. But your friend Zuckerman has direct access to the Allied Chiefs of Staff. He doesn't have to deal with the chain of command. Perhaps he can get Brooke and Marshall to make Harris and Arnold change their targeting. You know these names?" I nodded. Field Marshall Brooke and 5-star General Marshall, everyone knew, were the top British and American military chiefs. 'Bomber' Harris and 'Hap' Arnold were the generals every RAF and army bomber crew saluted. But they reported to Marshall and Brooke.

31

Dressed in a different suit, slightly the worse for wear, but recognizably from Saville Row, armed with another diplomatic passport, this time very British, I left Lisbon that evening on a full flight.

No one said a word, not to their neighbor or even the cabin attendant. It was more reticence than I suspected. Every one of us was anxious. Everyone was bringing home some kind of secret. There was certainly time for me to think, but not about what I was carrying back.

The portfolio was high strategy. My worry was low level tactics. What was I going to do, once I got back? I knew there would be inconvenient questions about how a flyer shot down over Germany made it back to England in a fortnight. That was unheard of. And if I ever got out from under suspicion, what was going to happen to me anyway? There was no chance Le May would want to see my face, not after he stole my formation plan. *What do you care where they send you?* I knew I still wanted to fight a good fight, and be on the winning side for once. But I also knew that someone on the winning side had been trying to kill me, and had come so close to succeeding that he might even think I was dead. *And now you're going to turn up and disappoint him?*

It was a long slow flight in the dark all the way to landfall. Enough time to walk my way through everything that had happened since Spain in '38, still trying to put the pieces of the puzzle together in ways that didn't deform them. The one thing I knew I could exclude was paranoid delusion.

It was the usual overcast late fall morning when I deplaned from the BOAC Dakota at Biggin Hill, the big RAF fighter base and was discretely and politely bundled into another Daimler by a trim looking middle-aged fellow. He'd shaken my hand and mumbled his name as I emerged from the passport control desk, carrying a grip with the portfolio from Canaris.

All he ever said was "Follow me please Mr. Thurlow." He didn't get in himself, but leaned into the driver and spoke. "Senate House, quick as you can."

I was being taken directly to Solly's place. And now I began to worry about how I was going to slip into the returned escapee pipeline that the Eighth Air Group ran. My doings on the continent and my arrival in England were certainly going to have to be covered up. To begin with, I'd need the right costume. A grey English wool suit was not going to cut it as an escape disguise organized by the French resistance. *One worry at a time, Will.*

I knocked on the pebbled glass of Solly's door. It was answered, as I had hoped, by Ellen, who grabbed me as though I was a lost child brought home by the police. Her mouth was so close the whisper roared in my ear.

"My god. We'd never any hope to give up, but here you are." I wasn't going to pry her off me. It felt too good. In fact it was the moment I pretty much decided never to let her go. It was only once she felt the tears on her cheek she decided to let go of me and re-don the sardonic armor she was more comfortable with. "Twelve days? What took you so long?" We both smiled, holding each other at arm's length, surveying the welcome sights.

"Flesh-pots—Berlin, Paris, Madrid, Lisbon…"

Solly approached. "Sorry to interrupt, Will. Glad to see you." He took my hand warmly. "MI6 told me you had something important. Eyes-only."

So, German intelligence hand in glove with British counterintelligence. *It figures.* He pointed me at one of the two chairs. Ellen leaned against the table. We were still staring at each other, sending signals of carnal desire. Solly had to stamp his foot to break the spell.

"What have you got for me, Will?"

I pulled the portfolio out of my case, pulled the ribboned bow and handed it to him. He didn't open it immediately. "What am I going to discover here?"

"You want the whole story, or just the happy ending?"

Zuckerman cast an inviting hand towards me. "Tell me everything." He didn't interrupt. When I'd finished, he spoke.

"There's been some rumbling about contacts with *Abwehr*, but nothing to suggest Canaris is opposed to the regime. Intelligence services always talk to each other, even across the trenches." He reached out his hand. "Let's see."

He opened the portfolio and began quietly mouthing the words in German as he read. Neither Ellen nor I disturbed him for several long minutes. Then he looked at Ellen, "How's your German?"

"Passable if it's mathematics."

He handed her the portfolio. "Look at the third sheet…the map…Everything we need."

"If it's reliable."

"Our friends at MI6 can help. They'll know if Canaris is on the up and up. They'll have agents on the ground in Germany who can locate some of these plants." He looked back at me and then Ellen. "But that's not our biggest problem. Assuming this stuff is accurate, the problem will be convincing the bomber forces to use it."

"That's what Canaris was afraid of. Why he wanted you to have it. Said you could go around them."

"Oh, I can get this stuff certified, and get it into the right hands. But Harris and Arnold will still fight back, they'll stonewall."

Ellen spoke. "Why? We're all on the same side?"

"Yes, but their real loyalty is to their own future, their power. They want to win the war from the air, by themselves, as soon as possible. They may think they can't cut German production even with this stuff," He nodded towards the file in Ellen's hands. "Not fast enough anyway to show that airpower works all by itself. Only dehousing will do that. That's what Bomber Harris thinks anyway." He rose. "Anyway, dealing with this is our job. Will is going to forget he ever saw it, if he knows what's good for him in this man's air force." He looked me up and down. "Ellen, go out and buy our friend one set of khakis, leftenant's bars and pilots wings. Take him home, wash them and let them wrinkle." He looked at me. "Best if you can sleep in them and drop some soup down the shirt front."

I smiled. "Not a problem."

He looked back at Ellen. "Then drive him to Grimsby docks…Rest is up to you, Will. Tell them a story about a fishing trawler when you get to Escapee Debriefing. They won't challenge it much." He bent to a safe behind him, opened it and took a fist full of pound notes from a petty cash box.

We left Solly, smiling at the thought of another weekend together.

———

My escape debriefing was much easier than the interrogation at the Luftwaffe *Durchlag* outside Frankfurt. But there were too many questions I just didn't have good enough answers to. Fortunately for me they were looking for answers to questions that would help other escapees, not answers that would unmask a string of lies.

At the Grimsby trawler docks someone pointed us to the RAF/Royal Navy air/sea rescue slip, where several fast patrol boats were moored, ready to move out into the North Sea at a moment's notice to rescue a flyer before he froze to death in the chill waters or died serving as target practice for a German fighter plane. I presented myself to a sentry.

"Sailor, I'm a US Eighth Air Group flyer, escaped after being shot down. Just came off a trawler. Can you get me to Debriefing?"

He picked up a telephone receiver. Five minutes later I was being driven back the way I'd come, back to London and across it to High Wycombe. It was there that the Eighth Air Group maintained escapee debriefing quarters.

I was surprised that my debriefing was conducted by a sergeant at a typewriter. He asked questions and typed my answers into a form with at least three carbons in it. After giving my name, rank, and serial number, I had to list my missions, all of them, right up to Schweinfurt. That wasn't too hard. Then he asked for the plane's identification number and my fellow crew members on the mission. That was a little harder, given the constant rotation through my B-17. Finally, I had to begin to lie my way through questions about my escape route—Frankfurt to somewhere on the Dutch boarder, from there to Rotterdam docks, and a transfer at sea across a hawser line to an English trawler. He sighed at my ignorance of the names of the people who helped me, the border crossing point or even the names of the Dutch and British trawlers.

"Don't you know anything about the folks who saved your life, Lieutenant?" I shook my head.

I began to suspect he'd end up asking me when the Boston Braves had beaten the Chicago Cubs in the World Series. But he just typed away, recording my useless answers and then passed me the sheet and its carbons.

"Please sign, Lieutenant." I scanned the form, expecting that I was going to have to swear to all the lies I'd told. No, instead above the signature line was an oath I'd have no trouble keeping.

Information about your escape or your evasion from capture would be useful to the enemy and a danger to your friends. It is therefore SECRET. I hereby confirm I will not divulge any of the information I have here provided to any unauthorized person.

Once I'd signed it, the sergeant pointed to a row of chairs behind him. "Please wait over there. I'll get an officer to complete your interview."

The officer, a retread major looked from me to the form I'd filled out and back to me.

"You're the first escapee who's gotten back from the Schweinfurt mission. Lost a lot of guys, 'bout five-hundred missing in action. We didn't expect anyone back for months. Not like getting shot down over France." He tapped the paper with his pencil. I tried to look unworried. "Seems you were very lucky. Trouble is luck's not much help to us, Lieutenant. Can't tell crew to be lucky if they have to bail out over Germany."

Did he expect a reply? "No, sir. I guess not."

He sighed. "Well. Thurlow, that's it, then." He smiled grimly. "*Für Sie der Krieg ist vorbei.*"

His German shocked me. "Huh?"

"It's what the Germans say to downed airmen they catch. *War's over for you, buddy.*" He let it sink in. "Well, goes for you too. It's regs. Once aircrew make it back, they're not allowed to fly again. What you guys tell us about how you escaped comes in handy for other downed crew. Then there are the names of the people who protected Allied airmen, the escape routes and networks that guided them down to Spain. You guys know too much."

All I could do was nod. The major went on, evidently not expecting a response.

"It's the strictest rule in the books. Never seen it waived. Couple of fighter pilots have tried to get back into the air. No can do." Then he looked at my sheet again. "Doesn't matter in your case, Thurlow. If this checks out you were shot down on your twenty-fifth mission. You really are finished flying." He rose. The interview was over. He handed me a chit. "Take this to the quartermaster. They'll kit you out and assign you a billet till your orders come through. Dismissed." I saluted and he did too.

Maybe it was because I was at the Eighth Air Group headquarters, Pinetree, but suddenly the gears of the military bureaucracy were moving with dispatch. For Will Thurlow, it wasn't going to be hurry up and wait. By late that very afternoon an orderly appeared at my door, handing me orders. My eye ran through them with increasing surprise. I was headed back to the 401st Squadron of the 91st Group.

It was a personnel order, "with immediate effect." Someone wanted me gone from Pinetree ASAP. I suspected it was Le May, still eager to bury the guy who dreamed up his bomber formation. I tried to call Ellen. No answer at home. I was dialing Zuckerman's office when I realized that every phone at headquarters was sure to be tapped for counterespionage. Nothing for it but to pack up the little gear I'd been handed—toothbrush, razor, towel, and head back to Bassingbourn.

I didn't expect the corporal at group headquarters to recognize me. But the name must have rung a bell.

"We had a telex to expect you, Lieutenant." He rose from his desk and indicated I was to follow him. "Commanding officer wants to see you right away."

"At ease. Take a seat, Thurlow." Wurzbach was a colonel, but other than a perfunctory salute in response to mine, he was not spit and polish._"I've got orders to restrict you to base, no contacts off-base, no passes." What were they worried about? Was I a security risk now I knew about Canaris? *No. They don't know about Canaris, do they?* "Sounds like close arrest, Thurlow. What am I gonna do with you?"

"Don't know, sir." I thought for a moment. "There's nothing in those orders to stop me flying, is there?"

"Thurlow, I don't know who cut those orders or why. But I can't let you fly anymore. Not if I am going to run this group. If any of those guys..." He pointed through the window at the buildings and runways in the twilight. "If just one of them latches onto the idea that they could be ordered to fly more than twenty-five missions, I'd have a major uprising. You've flown the limit. Besides, everybody is going to find out you went down over Schweinfurt and made it back. Can't keep that quiet. They all know a successful escape is a one-way ticket out of combat." He paused. "No way I'm going to let you fly." As for the base restriction, maybe he'd been told not to ask me why they'd been imposed. I wouldn't have been able to explain anyway.

32

I'd been a glorified filing clerk for over a week, doing everything a corporal could have handled except the typing, which was something I couldn't do. The 91st was gearing up for another Schweinfurt raid. I'd never seen the paperwork avalanche big missions sent down the mountainside from Pinetree, or the requisitions in triplicate every supply bureau demanded to give us the gear we needed to get into the air with the bombs. It wasn't until the meteorology team at the base stumbled on to the presence of a junior-grade officer with combat experience and no particular assignment that I was able to be of any real use.

The two non-coms manning the station—two small rooms on the ground level of the Bassingbourn control tower had a half-dozen gauges and meters whose readings required recording hourly. They were also responsible for pulling weather reports off a teletype from Pinetree. But they had lost their second lieutenant to a transfer and needed someone to carry these reports to officer briefings. Five minutes after I'd poked my nose in their door, the two technical sergeants had assigned me a job I could actually do and begun trying to train me to read their meters.

And that's how I met the UPI newsman assigned to the Eighth Air Group. I was at the desk I shared with the two NCOs when Colonel Alford, the 91st's operations officer, stuck his head in the door.

"Lieutenant, you're not doing much. I got a reporter out here we've been ordered to entertain. I've got a mission to plan." He pointed his thumb behind him out the door. "You do it."

I came out the door and there before me stood a guy of slightly above average height. He looked well fed but rumpled in officer's kit with a big C where his unit shoulder flash would be, no service ribbons, his tie loser than most senior officers would allow, and a mustache—something forbidden across the air service.

As I advanced, Alford moved up the stairs to the control tower. The reporter smiled rather sheepishly. "Sorry to take you away from duty, Lieutenant. Not my idea." He put out his hand. "Cronkite, Walt, United Press International."

An hour later we were sitting in a half empty officer's club. Cronkite brought over two beer glasses. I raised one in thanks. He drank off half his pint and then spoke.

"You know, Lieutenant Thurlow, I didn't need that tour. I've been here before. Flew a mission out of Bassingbourn, end of February, went to Wilhelmshaven."

"Say, I was on that mission too." We smiled at the bond suddenly created. I looked at him. "They didn't allow you to fly that mission with a mustache, did they?" I knew it would have prevented an oxygen mask from working.

"Made me shave it off. Grew it back once I found out Eaker wouldn't let us fly any more. We lost a correspondent—*New York Times* guy—Post was his name."

"So, why'd you come down, Mr. Cronkite?"

"Call me Walt, will you?" He looked like he was looking for comradeship.

"Sure. Same question, Walt, and you can call me Will."

"You really want to know…Will? I know the 91st is going back to Schweinfurt. Last August didn't do the trick." He was right but I said nothing. "I want to find a way onto the mission." He stared at me, gauging my reaction. Could he trust me with this knowledge, could I help?

"Walt, you're looking at the wrong guy. I couldn't get myself on that mission, even if I wanted to go."

He looked me up and down. "I don't follow." He pointed at my wings. "You're a pilot." Then he looked down at my hat. "That twenty mission crushed officer's cap. I know they're scraping the barrel for extra pilots for this one. What gives, Will?"

"Off the record, Walt?" I needed to talk to someone. He wanted to listen. Then I realized, I needed someone to talk to Ellen, tell her why she hadn't heard from me. Cronkite might be able to.

"Off the record, Will." He smiled.

"First off, I've flown the limit. Twenty-five missions. I could fly more. I would fly more. But I flew the first Schweinfurt mission back in August. I was shot down, I escaped and got back. Escapees aren't allowed back into combat. It's a hard rule."

"But escapees aren't sent back to their groups either, Will. Why'd they send you back here?"

This Cronkite knew too much. I didn't have an answer. Not one I wanted to give, even off the record. "Dunno. Maybe it's just a SNAFU. You know the Air Corps."

His head was shaking and he wasn't buying. "I don't get it, Will. You should be back home selling war bonds. What's the story?"

"No story, Walt."

Cronkite was silent for a minute. "Alright, Will, if that's how you want to play it. But if you change your mind…"

I needed to cut this conversation short but keep Cronkite friendly. I rose from the table. "My round?" He nodded. I came back to the table with two more pints. "Look, Walt, can you do something for me?"

"Sure, if it doesn't get me into much trouble." His smile was conspiratorial.

"Don't know about that, but I have a girl in London. Can you look her up for me?"

"You sure you want to set me up? I'm single, you know." He smiled.

"I'll risk it." I grabbed his reporter's note pad and wrote down Ellen's phone number. "Just tell her I'd love to see her down here Saturday or Sunday." I knew this was digging me a deeper hole with Cronkite. He'd have to ask himself why I couldn't just call her, or wangle a weekend pass to London. He didn't.

———

On October 14, the second Schweinfurt raid, was a maximum effort. Every available plane and pilot except me. By the time the last ships came limping back the Eighth had lost sixty of two-hundred-ninety-one ships. That was six-hundred crew. Another hundred-forty had sustained battle damage. Bassingbourn and the 91st had sent up almost forty B-17s and all three squadrons came back so busted up, by nightfall there was no heart to debrief beyond counting the number of crewmen's 'chutes guys had counted.

Turnover since the first Schweinfurt mission had been so great I didn't know any of the guys we'd lost the second time and hardly more than the names of the men who climbed out of the big planes with the gaping shrapnel wounds along their sides. With everyone drained by the mission and mourning their friends, there'd be a lot of AWOL that weekend and the MPs would be lenient anyway.

It wouldn't be hard to get to the cottage in Cambridge where I'd asked Cronkite to tell Ellen I'd try to meet her. I hoped she'd understand the message. Friday evening I found a lift to the B-17 hard stand closest to the road up to Royston. I sauntered across over to where the country lane crossed the runway and began to walk along it. It wasn't hard for an American officer in uniform to hitch the ten miles or so into Cambridge.

No lights in the cottage. I sauntered around back to where Ellen had shown me the hiding place for the latch key and let myself in. In the twilight silence the sitting room carried the cold and damp of its surrounding fields and fens. I found myself shuddering with a chill as I checked the blackout curtains and then turned on a table lamp. The words came out of a still dark corner.

"Been waiting some time. What kept you?"

There was Ellen, blanketed and cozy in a lounge chair, smiling up at me, waiting for my audible gasp of surprise. She rose, opening the blanket, and we spent a long time wrapped closely together, before ardor took over and toppled us on to the chesterfield where we began pulling at one another's trench coats, suit coats, shirts. Finally the number of buttons we were going to have to rip out overwhelmed our passion and we each withdrew to give the other space in which to undress. Wrestling, from chesterfield to the carpeted floor, then making use of a stout wooden chair, we didn't notice the cold for a long time.

Later, head-to-head in the narrow bed, lights off, and curtains open to a harvest moon, smoking companionably in the dark, watching the dust motes iridescent in the tobacco haze, we waited for our passion to rise again. Ellen moved her thigh over my leg.

"How long can you stay?"

"I'm AWOL, like half the guys off the Schweinfurt mission."

"Does that mean you'll be here till they catch you or that you're going back before you're caught?"

I leaned over her. "Depends on you." We began again.

We didn't get around to business till breakfast the next morning. There were powdered eggs and HP sauce, some potatoes from the cold larder with a little life left in them, and some margarine that had kept along with a sack of coffee from our last tryst in the high English summer.

"I'd almost given up on you, Will. Why didn't you get in touch, come down to London?"

I told her what had happened since she'd left me at Grimsby docks.

"Every phone line out of Bassingbourn is tapped by G-2." This was US Army intelligence. "Whoever's out to get me, I didn't want them making trouble for you and Zuckerman."

"Well, someone's making trouble for Solly anyway." He can't make any headway with the stuff you brought back from Canaris."

I couldn't stop myself whistling in surprise. "What do you mean?"

"Just what I said. He's been showing the portfolio to the Air Staffs—yours and ours—and getting stonewalled."

"Stonewalled? Don't they want to win the war?"

"Sure, they do. Their own way. All by themselves, by killing German civilians till they scream stop. Not by cutting off the flow of equipment to the Wehrmacht and Luftwaffe." Ellen's exasperation was showing. She'd been through this with me before. I let her go on. "If the RAF and your Army Air Corps can get the Jerries to say uncle before a ground invasion, they'll win their own war with the rest of the military."

"So, all the statistics Solly throws at them about killing civilians without reducing the German war effort is still pointless, even after they see Canaris's files?" Ellen nodded her head. "Doesn't Zuckerman report to a minister, a politician, someone in Churchill's government?"

"Yes, but it just doesn't work that way. Solly reports to the minister of home security. That's nowhere near the war cabinet or any service ministry. Besides, you know even service ministers won't try to interfere with military strategy."

I laughed. "Except Churchill." Everyone knew he was constantly being overruled by military chiefs of staff. "So, what's Solly going to do."

"Don't know. He's stymied."

"Well, we just lost another six-hundred men bombing Schweinfurt again."

Ellen grimaced. "And nothing to show for it, I'll warrant. The stuff Canaris gave you says that the Germans have enough ball bearings to last a year and where they are storing them. It's not Schweinfurt."

I thought for a minute, then it came to me. "Ellen, Solly has got to get the info to people in the chain of command above Harris and Eaker." She knew these names well enough.

"So."

"Who's gonna command the ground invasion next year?"

"Not decided yet, but there's a good guess it'll be Eisenhower, commanding in North Africa and Sicily. He's coming back to London any day now."

"Okay. You know that guy who carried my message to you—Walt Cronkite. Did you meet him?"

She shook her head. "Just a phone call."

"Well, he's UPI, a reporter. Must be pretty important. Got picked to fly a mission with Eighth Air Group last winter."

She was quick on the uptake. "And you want me…or Solly to brief him on what we've got."

"You'd have to give him enough background on damage surveys and the Canaris file to convince Eisenhower."

"Convince him of what?"

"That the air chiefs are stonewalling and it could wreck the invasion's chances."

"How?"

"It's obvious. Killing civilians won't weaken the Wehrmacht. Wrecking their supplies and their supply lines to wherever the invasion's gonna take place, will."

"Can Cronkite get himself an off the record chat with Eisenhower?"

"It's worth a try." I looked at Ellen. "Can you convince Solly to break a lot of rules?"

"I think so, but you're a dead cert to be dragged in…Solly will have to tell Cronkite where he got this stuff."

"Can't be helped. Besides, he already suspects I'm being hush-hush about something big."

———

One night a week later I was nursing a beer in the officer's club, alone as usual. Sitting at a table, I saw Cronkite enter and go up to the bar. He ordered a shot of something, turned around, looked at me, then slowly shook his head. I understood. He downed the drink and walked out. I looked down at my watch and waited a full five sweeps of the second hand before finishing my beer and sauntering out into the dark.

I saw the glow of Cronkite's cigarette before I made out his shape. He fell in beside me and we walked into the enveloping dark of a runway.

He spoke first. "So, why'd you think Canaris plucked you out of a Stalag and handed you on a plate to Zuckerman?"

"Don't know exactly. Looks like the Krauts've known about me one way and another since I flew against them in Spain."

"Yeh, but how'd they know you were acquainted with Zuckerman? That's what I want to know."

"Been thinking about that myself. There's got to be a spy involved, or more than one. Could be I'm a spy for the Germans. But that would mean I've been covering my tracks in Spain, China, and Burma since 1936. Or there's a spy in Zuckerman's outfit—Ellen maybe?" Cronkite flicked away his butt, still said nothing. "Here's what I think. MI6—that's British intelligence--has been in contact with Canaris for a long time."

"Why'd you think so?"

"He didn't seem to have any troubled arranging to get me back here once I arrived in Portugal. I suspect he's anti-Nazi and has been working with MI6 since before the war."

"Okay. But then MI6 had to know about you and Zuckerman before you were shot down."

"That's easy. MI5—their counterespionage—would certainly be monitoring a shop like Zuckerman's for leaks. MI5 and MI6 are practically Siamese twins by now. One way or another Canaris knew about me and…"

Cronkite interrupted, "And about Ellen Ashcroft-Metcalf?"

"I was going to say Solly Zuckerman." He chuckled. I went on. "Maybe once German Intelligence had my name, someone began looking in Luftwaffe files, and found me."

"Alright, thanks. Look, I'm going to try to use what you and Ellen have given me. I'll keep your name out of it if I can. But no guarantees, understood?"

"What'll they do to me, Walt? Send me on more missions over Germany?"

33

By the middle of February I'd been in the meteorology unit for three months or so and had gotten used to it. By this time Eisenhower had been appointed commander of the cross-channel invasion and the Eighth had pretty much stopped flying missions over Germany.

I was far too low on the pecking order to know why. In fact, so was everyone else at Bassingbourn. No one could figure it out. Why weren't we flying? It wasn't weather, it wasn't readiness, or replacement problems. If anything, the 91st was in the best shape ever. The fighter escorts had finally been fitted with drop tanks and were now able to cover the bombers all the way to target and back. Bomber crews began to think they had a fighting chance to complete twenty-five missions. So of course the minimum number of missions required went up, first to thirty then to thirty-five. But no one really complained. The replacements were itching to fly.

Then the missions started to come in again. As senior weather flunky I had to attend briefings just to pass out charts with sunrise, cloud cover, service ceiling, temperature, and air pressure.

The first mission was the kind of thing even rookies could treat as a milk run—the marshalling yards at Rouen, France, that we'd hit in '42 when we were just getting started.

Then, after a couple of more months it became clear. As far as we could see the Eighth, and the RAF had been completely retargeted against the rail network in northern France and the bridges from the Seine west to the English Channel. In debrief, our crew even described how, with no Luftwaffe opposition, the fighters would peel off and strafe ground targets.

And that's when my charmed but boring life in the Eighth Air Group ended. I knew it couldn't last. I was beginning to want to fly again, though I said so to no one. That month the Eighth Air Group became the Eighth Air Force and got a new commander. Jimmy Doolittle was famous for bombing Tokyo off a Navy carrier in '42. He arrived in England with a whole new set of ideas about the air war.

Doolittle had taken command in early February after we lost Alford, the operations officer who'd assigned me to meteorology. We were pretty sure he made it out of his ship and was a POW. I was surprised when a clerk came into the weather room and told me the new operations officer, Major Lee, had sent for me. The perplexity remained on his face as he took my salute.

"At ease, Lieutenant."

He didn't ask me to sit. There were several pieces of paper on his desk. He picked up one and handed it to me.

"Read it, Thurlow."

TO: Operations Officer, 91st Bomber Group

FROM: Doolittle, Officer Commanding, Eighth Air Force

SUBJECT: Thurlow, William, 1st Lieutenant, serial number 08426880

This officer is separated from Eighth Air Force with immediate effect.

Officer is transferred to

475ᵗʰ Fighter Group

V Fighter Command, 5th Air Force

Dobodura Airfield, New Guinea

Officer will transit via Gibraltar, Cairo, Karachi, Colombo, Perth, Darwin.

"You see who sent that, Thurlow? Jimmy Doolittle. His first day on the job as Eighth Air Force commander. What did you do to get his nose out of joint, Thurlow?"

"Beats me, sir." Doolittle was more famous than Chennault, an icon in the Army Air Corps since before the war, and a hero since it had started. Much too important to care about one William Thurlow, Lieutenant, USAAF. And the last thing one of his group commanders would want was a direct order from the top of Pinetree.

"I want you off this base by tomorrow morning. Take the telex to transport. Dismissed."

I saluted. He didn't. There was a lot in those marching orders to think about. But almost no time to do so, if I was going to get off the base in sixteen hours or so. Almost out loud I muttered "*deja vu* all over again" as I walked out of the base headquarters building.

At least they couldn't stop me traveling through London. With the travel orders I had I'd get a chance to hang around London long enough to see Ellen once more. Watching the rain drops run down the window glass of a train making the milk run from East Anglia, the explanation for what had happened became fixed in my head. *This is all because you talked to the UPI reporter, Cronkite.*

———

My last night with Ellen pretty much settled any doubts about what had happened. Neither of us were in much of a mood when I got to her flat late that evening. She must have been pretty sure she'd never see me again. I needed her to believe that she would. She knew well enough that I loved her. But there wasn't any way to convince Ellen I was bullet-proof.

She must have expected something even before I reached her from a coin box phone on the High Street in Royston to tell her I was coming down.

"Where are they sending you, Will?"

"To the Pacific, to fly P-38s." These were long range fighters that hadn't worked well enough against faster Luftwaffe Focke-Wolfs, but whose twin engines reassured pilots they could fly the distances required by the Pacific campaign. "Look, I'll tell you everything tonight. Okay?"

There wasn't much more for me to tell. I showed her my travel orders. It was Ellen who had the real dope. "I see." She frowned. "Our fault, Solly's and mine."

"What'd you mean?" But I knew.

"Well, we talked to Cronkite, your reporter friend. Funny, when I called him he thought it was going to be a date." We smiled conspiratorially, but I let her go on. "What he told us just knocked Solly over. Cronkite told us what he'd been hearing at SHAEF headquarters." This was Supreme Headquarters Allied Expeditionary Force. "It was early January. Leaks from Eisenhower's chief of staff, Biddle-Smith. When Eisenhower was appointed commander he asked for control of the bomber forces to target the railroads and bridge to the French coast."

"I know. 91st Bomber Group has just begun bombing them along with the rest of the Eighth."

"It's a new directive from Eisenhower. Called *The Transportation Plan*. What you don't know is that Bomber Command and Eighth

Air Force refused to do it, or give up any control. You won't believe what they said when he told them what he needed. 'Can't bomb those targets. Would kill too many civilians.'"

"You're right, Ellen" She looked puzzled. I clarified. "I don't believe it."

"Too brazen, what! When Solly heard this he unloaded. Gave Cronkite everything we had on bomber effectiveness and dehousing." It was the word I'd heard from Canaris too, the tactic of bombing German labor out of the cities where they worked. "Anyway, Eisenhower had been threatening to resign if he couldn't get tactical control of the bombers. Threat didn't work. Marshall wouldn't over-rule his Air Force chief, Arnold." Marshall was George Marshall, US Chief of Staff, superior to Hap Arnold, Ira Eaker, Jimmy Doolittle and every other Air Force officer in the US military.

"Told you. That's how the army works."

"But then Cronkite handed Eisenhower Solly's studies and the stuff from Canaris. That did the trick. Eisenhower was able to show the Joint Chiefs that strategic bombing wasn't working, that the bomber commanders weren't even trying to do anything but kill civilians."

I whistled. "That explains a lot."

"Don't know if it was the hypocrisy of the Air Force or the fact their killing German civilians wasn't working, that did the trick." Ellen shook her head slowly. "But you paid the price, Will. Cronkite had to tell Eisenhower's man, Biddle-Smith, how he got ahold of the stuff from Canaris."

"What do you mean, I paid the price?"

"Well, Cronkite wasn't going to get in trouble for passing that stuff on. Once they got your name, Air Force command back in Washington tried to discredit him. Said you were dead. Shot down, no 'chutes seen leaving your ship, missing in action, no POW report from International Red Cross. So your stuff was a plant."

"Then what?"

"To save his skin Cronkite had to tell them where to find you if they didn't believe him."

"Well, they didn't come looking."

"Didn't have to…All they needed to do was check with Pinetree. And Cronkite did it for them! Eighth Air Force escapee debriefing files were sitting there at High Wycombe. Cronkite went looking and found your file. That was enough for Eisenhower."

We didn't have to speak. We both knew that the Air Corps couldn't sideline Cronkite. But it was getting back at me, sending me to the Pacific.

That last night was my education in the meaning of 'like there's no tomorrow'. But in the morning Ellen didn't make a scene. All she said was "See you after the war." I could only nod.

34

From Cairo to Columbo, Perth to Darwin, nothing prepared me for the smell of food rot and latrine gas heavy on the drip of condensation coming off every surface the first time I landed at Nadzab. It was a field cut out of the jungle at the top of the finger of New Guinea—the fifth largest island in the world—just north of Australia, pointing east.

Now, for the fourth time I swung my gear down from the brand new P-38 I'd ferried from Darwin. The 431st Squadron was going back into action and I was the only replacement the squadron commander could get.

I was surprised 5th Air Force had even let me off ferry service. I was the only pilot they could rely on to cover the 980 miles up to the 475th Fighter Group once it moved from Dobodura at the southern end of New Guinea. When the 5th's commander's chief of staff found out I'd flown B-17s for more than a year, he'd asked how far I could nurse the two Allison engines on a P-38. I told him what I'd been able to get out of the Wright Cyclone engine on a B-17. He didn't believe it, but he told me he was willing to risk one to see if we could really resupply the 475th that quickly.

Lots of pilots had trouble with the Lightning's two engines. Not for me after handling four. I took a P-38 up, set the throttle at lean and dropped the RPM's to sixteen-hundred. The plane purred and when I brought it down after an hour I hadn't used more than a dozen gallons. I never should have bragged. A thousand miles at low revs in a P-38 is seven or eight hours sitting on a parachute and life raft. The first few times the ground crew had to pry me out of the cockpit.

But now I was directed out of the 431st command hut to my billet, a twelve-by-twelve tent on a square platform lifted eight inches above the jungle ooze. The mildewed canvas top had its side walls rolled up to allow unimpeded access to whatever breeze might reach into our rain forest from the coast a dozen miles away.

I dropped my gear on the only empty cot and looked around. In the cot at the back corner a man of middle height in a tee-shirt and shorts looked up from a thin paper back. In repose his face was a frown. For a moment we both stared at each other's faces, trying to place it. He got there first.

"Thurlow?"

"That's me. Do we know each other?"

"We were at the Point together. Then we met…it was back in '40 at the War Department. I'm Rankin, John Rankin, Quartermaster Corps now. I was a major, in personnel back then." Bitterness edged the tone as he muttered under his breath, "Still a major…You were trying to get back into the Air Corps, right?"

"Yup, that was me."

He rose from the cot, put his hand out. "Glad you made it after all." I hesitated and then decided I had no choice but to grab the hand. He saw the hesitation. "No hard feelings, Thurlow. I was just carrying the can." There was no point reminding him of the glee in his voice sitting behind a desk in the War Department, accusing me of being a commie and a traitor. I nodded and gave his hand another pull before letting go.

"How'd you get out here, Rankin?"

"Supply officer. I do the logistics paperwork for chow, laundry, construction material. Everything but the stuff you guys need to kill Japs." He looked at my wings. "You are here to kill Japs, aren't you Thurlow?"

"Haven't seen any yet." I sat down at the card table in the middle of the tent, and invited Rankin to do the same.

"You might not for a while. Hollandia is their nearest base and our fighters can't get there." I said nothing. But Rankin wanted to keep me talking, just to be sure I didn't bear a grudge. "Surprised I recognized you? It was only a twenty-minute chat four years ago." I nodded. "Well, in the next couple of years, your file kept coming across my desk. Maybe it still is, whoever's got my desk now."

"Why was that?" This was a question I suddenly needed to get answered.

"Let's see. What I recall was a lot of folderol, first about getting you into the AVG. Someone in the War Department needed your file to get Chennault to take you on."

"Yeh, well, I was the only guy in the outfit who didn't come right out of the Air Corps or Navy."

"That's right…and then three months later, once we got into the war, there was a fuss about getting you back into the Army after all the other guys in the unit were re-enlisted. First there was a directive from Stimson's office forbidding it." Stimson was the Secretary of War, a powerful figure in Roosevelt's cabinet. "Then, that was countermanded, but with an order sending you to England as a bomber pilot. How come, Thurlow?"

"I have no idea." I wasn't going to speculate for Rankin's entertainment. Whatever I said would sound like paranoid delusion, grandiose expressions of self-importance.

Rankin began to smile, looking almost like he had an answer to his own question. "Last time I saw your file, before they shipped me to Australia, there was a letter in it, letterhead of some bank." There was a question in his tone. "J.P. Morgan?" I didn't react. "Said something like 'Henry, Thurlow again. This little problem won't go away and can't be allowed to come back. Can you do something else?' There were initials on it, not a signature. *O.R.* Mean anything to you?" He still hadn't jogged my mind. "I only remember because the 'Henry' had to be Secretary Stimson and a note like that had no business in a Service record. What gives, Thurlow, spill it."

O.R. meant nothing to me. But now I recalled something General Chennault had said to me back in '42 after he'd gone to bat to try to get me back in the service, something about opposition from a place high enough to scare everyone off the idea of helping me. And then, all of a sudden with the wave of an unseen wand, I'd been re-enlisted and sent to England. So, it was Henry Stimson, Secretary of War, who'd concerning himself with the fate of a permanent first lieutenant so far away from the new Pentagon building in D.C. that he might as well be invisible.

"Can't help you, Rankin." I rose from the table, dropped my duffle on my cot. "Say, where are the showers?

————

The next day I began teaching the pilots in 431st Squadron how to extend the range of their P-38s by five-hundred miles or so, enough to reach Hollandia, the big Jap base on the other side of New Guinea. Even the gnarled veterans among them, captains and majors, were kids ten years younger than me. Thin from poor chow and sallow with malaria, they'd been teenagers when the war began—frat boys, hot-rodders, high school grid iron heroes, guys who just had to have wings, had to get back at the

Japs, but now, after living the war instead of just imagining it, wanted to survive.

I didn't want to make friends with men I'd have to mourn, but I couldn't help it. They were almost all very hard not to like. There were a couple of first lieutenants in my tent—Dave Hutchins and Chet Parshall. We played a lot of cards—mainly poker—with Rankin after chow in the evening. Between hands the first night we played, they asked the usual casual questions. Soon enough we got past home towns, favorite teams, and sexual exploits, into personal histories. I admitted to flying bombers in England. It made sense of the talks I was giving about how to stretch out fuel consumption and navigate by dead reckoning. Before the first time I had to begin seriously dissimulating my past Rankin interrupted. I was grateful.

"Look, fellas, Will here is regular army, West Point. Then he was air attaché in Spain and France. Did a lot of hush-hush stuff. Can't talk about it, can you, Will?"

I nodded hoping they wouldn't ask Rankin how he knew. Before they could say anything, he rose.

"Time to take the atabrine, guys." This was the disgusting concoction everyone was on to ward off malaria. But they must have remembered and believed what Rankin said about me, and passed the word along. No one ever asked me anything personal after that.

It wasn't easy convincing crew chiefs who mothered their airplanes that the engines could operate at such lean mixtures, low engine manifolds, and revs, even after they began to take the Lockheed manuals seriously. But by the end of March 1944 every pilot in the 431st was stretching out the range of his P-38 to over a thousand miles. They were complaining about the discomfort of sitting motionless for eight hours but looking forward to getting back into the war now they'd found how to do it.

There were no Jap air bases closer than Hollandia and nothing much to do besides patrol the east side of New Guinea till they could reach this large base. By that time a couple of the other squadrons in the 475th Group had received new P-38s with bigger fuel tanks and longer ranges. Now planning for escort missions accompanying 5th Air Force bombers to Hollandia became realistic.

My talks generated a certain amount of notoriety among the twenty or so pilots in the 431st, a little admiration and some friendly teasing. That my popularity was genuine showed itself in the way pilots would tell me how many gallons of gas they had left after a long training flight or patrol. It didn't occur to me that the following of a very over-aged very junior first lieutenant would get up the nose of an operations officer who practically ran the squadron. But it did. Captain O'Brien would forget or mangle my name when he had to use it, leave me off of flight duty as much as he could, and assigned me tail end wing man when he had to let me fly.

Word of a mission to Hollandia spread. Everyone knew. Security wasn't an issue on an airstrip linked only by radio to headquarters in Australia. The 431st hadn't received new planes yet, but Major Jett, the 431st Squadron commander and Captain O'Brien, the operations officer, went to the group commander, Colonel MacDonald, offering to prove the 431st could fly this mission with the older planes. They returned to the squadron looking pleased but mum about their meeting with the group commander.

On the morning of March 30, the squadron was assembled, was given a bit of a pep talk by Macdonald—a talk no one needed—and a briefing by O'Brien. He passed out maps of New Guinea, and then turned to a larger one on a tripod easel.

"MacArthur is starting his Hollandia campaign. He's going to need air superiority right from the start. Today's mission, 432nd and 433rd are going to escort B-24s bombing the airbase there."

A groan reflected the shared inference that the 421st was not going. MacDonald held up both hands, and O'Brien overrode the noise.

"Listen up. We're assigned to provide escort for the '24s on the way back. We're supposed to pick 'em up over Tadji." This was a smaller Jap airbase halfway to Hollandia. "Well, we're going to pick 'em up a little west of there." He moved his pointer left across the map till it rested on Hollandia." There was some laugher and low wolf whistling. When it subsided O'Brian continued. "And no objection if some of the boys in the other two squadrons notice you're there." Then he read off the list of pilots who'd fly the mission. I wasn't surprised not to hear my name. My tentmates, Hutchins and Parshall, were on the list, and I got a few jealous back slaps from others, like me, not going along.

Everyone noticed our mission and questions came down from group about how the 431st's planes managed to provide such long-range escort support. I'd learned enough not to want to take any credit. I didn't need the grief from O'Brien or the notice from anyone higher up. I'd had quite enough of that in Europe, and Rankin's story about people paying attention to my fate back in the War Department was still ringing in my ears. The impression MacDonald and O'Brien gave group was that 431st flyers had been experimenting with fuel saving settings on the P-38 that they were willing to share. None of the other squadrons took us up on the offer. New P-38s were good enough for them.

April came and MacArthur's offensive moved into higher gears. We flew a good deal, mainly top cover for bombers hitting airfields and harbors on the north coast of the island. The range was always a stretch but few Jap planes came up to attack the bombers or tangle with the fighters. For aces like MacDonald, the 475th Group's commander, and McGuire in my squadron, it was a dry spell they had a hard time coping with. It would go on till Hollandia was captured and we were flying missions against the Japs in the Philippines.

The worst thing that happened to the 475th wasn't enemy action but weather, and I had to admit it brought out the best in Captain O'Brien. A mission had been laid on for all three squadrons. Coming back we were hit by what we thought would be thunder heads over Hollandia, but it was something much bigger. A typhoon that came out of nowhere and scattered the whole wing of fourty-eight planes. O'Brien managed to keep 431st Squadron tight, sensed the direction out of the storm and, over open water, figured out the heading that would get us back to base. Luck or skill, we lost no one. But the group lost eight P-38s and six pilots, the worst day of the war for the 475th. O'Brien still didn't like me, but I couldn't help starting to admire him for his leadership.

MacArthur's ground and naval forces took Hollandia by the beginning of May, and by the middle of the month the 475th was flying from the base we'd been attacking for the previous month or so. And that was when the war on Will Thurlow finally ended. Afterward I wondered why I had been too stupid to see what it had really been all about.

35

By this time in the war Japanese opposition in the air was so little and so far between, that the entire group had become adept at dive-bombing, machine-gun strafing, and ground support. It wasn't romantic, like racking up enough kills to become an ace, but it was fun punctuated only by the small risk of being brought down by small arms fire and an occasional antiaircraft gun. The chances of being shot out of the sky were nothing like what I'd experienced back in Europe, or China for that matter. Things would heat up again when MacArthur attacked the Philippines, where most of the Japanese air force was stationed—a thousand planes and pilots waiting to tangle with us.

Hollandia was a collection of big runways, paved first by the Japanese and then by the Seabees. That allowed the three squadrons to spread out and reduced the risk that a Jap plane's getting through would do much damage before someone could shoot it down. But also meant that pilots and ground crew were dispersed.

It took a day or so for the news to arrive at 431ˢᵗ Squadron that the group had a rather famous visitor. In fact, few believed O'Brien when he came back from group headquarters on June 15 and announced at a chow line that Charles A. Lindbergh had just arrived on the base.

O'Brien was speaking to anyone in the chow line who would listen, and that was pretty much every officer in the squadron. Lindbergh had spent several months on Guadalcanal representing the Chance-Vought aircraft company, working with Marine Corps pilots flying the gull-winged navy plane, the Corsair. Everyone knew he'd asked for reinstatement of his commission in the Air Corps after Pearl Harbor. President Roosevelt had refused to allow it. Revenge, most military officers thought, for Lindbergh's opposition to rearmament and favoritism to the Allies before the US had been forced to enter the war by the Japanese attack and the German declaration of war.

Someone asked, "What's he doin' here?"

"Sounds like Colonel Lindbergh is fighting his own private war." The rank O'Brien accorded him showed what side of this argument between the President and the Lone Eagle he had chosen. "Guy's been flying ground support for a few months. Now he's come here to try out two-engine fighters."

Someone in the line added. "Fine by me. Maybe he wants to bag a Jap." Another voice added in mock annoyance, "If we can find any."

"Listen up, everyone." O'Brien was now making a general announcement. "Colonel MacDonald has called a meeting of all pilots in the group for tonight at nine o'clock. Going to introduce Lindy and tell us why he's come."

Standing at the back in the shade, along with a couple of the other flyers in the 431ˢᵗ, I was far from the bright lights under the palm-leaf-thatch of the briefing shelter. Standing next to the commander, MacDonald, there he was wearing khakis bereft of insignia of rank, service ribbons, or unit. He was balding, and stooped in a way that accentuated his six-foot-four height. But as I looked at him, there was something familiar. Among the other officers, I was close enough to look him in the eye. In fact, I caught his eye, and he stared back at me, deep, clear blue eyes searching my face just slightly longer than I found comfortable. Looking away, I knew I'd seen that hard look before. But where?

Don't be silly, Thurlow. That's the most famous face in the world or used to be. I gulped, shook my head, walked away. And then it came back, with a hammer's blow. I had seen this man before, twice before. First when those cold blue eyes fixed me like a prey animal at the side of a barnstormer's biplane in an Iowa corn field twenty years ago. And then again, six years ago, in Spain, on the Fascist side of the Ebro, gloating over his "kill," my Russian P-16.

The group adjutant put two fingers in his mouth and emitting a loud shrill whistle that brought everyone to silence. Then MacDonald came forward with Lindbergh looming tall behind him.

"Men, this is Mr. Charles A. Lindbergh." The tall balding man came forward with a dimpled smile. MacDonald repeated the civilian title, "Mr. Lindbergh is here as a representative of a couple of airplane manufacturers, including Lockheed. He's going to fly with us for a few weeks, give us some advice about how to get the most out of our P-38s, and take back our complaints and suggestions for improvements to the planes." The pilots were in awe, too much even to ask questions.

Over the next few weeks Lindbergh flew mainly with the headquarters' flight, on missions led by Colonel MacDonald. Mainly, the group was escorting medium bombers, two engine B-25 Mitchells, attacking a dozen small Japanese air fields across the great bays on the west of New Guinea. Rarely did we see any opposition in the air and the long flights were tedious to most of the pilots. The three squadrons flew these flights in formations small enough to entice a response, but it never came. I wondered if Lindbergh was getting bored, but he continued to fly with the 475th. As missions became longer and longer MacDonald decided to organize talks by Lindbergh to each of the three fighter squadrons about what he'd learned flying the P-38.

I wasn't looking forward to the night Lindbergh was scheduled to brief 431st Squadron. Even hanging in the back it would be hard to remain invisible. *There's no chance he'd recognize you,* I told myself several times that day. *And what if he does?* The rhetorical question didn't provoke a lot of threatening answers, but left me feeling very uneasy. I began to wonder about those negatives I'd left with Robert Capa four years ago in Paris. I'd never heard from him, and my copies of the pictures he'd developed had been confiscated by customs when I got back to the US in 1940. That afternoon, before chow and Lindbergh's briefing, I wrote a letter to Capa, addressed to the hotel he'd stayed at in 1940, figuring that he was with the Allied Armies fighting their way from Normandy. He'd get the letter once he arrived in Paris.

> *Dear Robert,*
>
> *Hope you are well and happy to be back in Paris. I need to know if you or your publicist still has those negatives I passed on to you just before the phony war ended and the Germans marched into Paris. If they survived the occupation, please hang on to them and if anything happens to me, please see to it that they are published.*
>
> *Best,*
>
> *Will Thurlow*

It was only after I put the letter into the censor's box that I began to have second thoughts. What would the officer who read all the outgoing mail make of the letter? Wasn't I being ridiculous assuming that Robert Capa would remember or care about an off-hand promise he'd made four years before. *Besides, there's no chance Lindbergh will notice you, or remember what happened back in '38.* He certainly would never bring it up. I thought about trying to get the letter back. But that would draw attention to it, unwanted attention. I never got a reply from Capa anyway. Turned out I didn't need it.

That evening, after dark, every pilot in the squadron showed up at the briefing hut. It was too small for everyone and a few of us found ourselves in the dark penumbra where the palm-thatch overhung the roof. McGuire and O'Brien introduced Lindbergh, who looked around the space and nodded.

He didn't seem to want introductions or be seeking out familiar faces. Once he began speaking his eyes seemed to be looking up and over us, ensuring that he wouldn't make eye contact with any individual. It was the look of a very shy or very self-contained man. What he said about how to get the most mileage out of a P-38—throttle at auto-lean, engine revs at sixteen-hundred, engine manifold setting slightly higher than normal, wasn't new to anyone in the unit. We'd been flying this way since before we finally received the newer long range P-38s the other squadrons flew. But no one said anything and the attention was respectful. Afterwards, there was silence for a long moment.

"Any questions, gentlemen?"

Lindbergh was expecting some opposition to what he was proposing. He was surprised not to hear any.

Breaking the silence, he said "Pilots in the other squadrons had some questions—effects of low fuel to air mixture on spark plugs, excessive wear on engines pulling the big plane at low revs." He began to answer these questions he'd raised himself. But he could see some restlessness in the row of men standing before him. Finally, O'Brien intervened.

"Colonel…" he stopped himself. "Mr. Lindbergh, our squadron has been flying this way for a couple of months, so there'll be no argument with your suggestions." The pilots in the hut were nodding their heads. "But you had a lot of experience doing low level support with Marine Corps Corsairs at Guadalcanal. Maybe you can give us some tips on dive bombing with five-hundred-pounders. It's not something we've done and I think we're going to have to learn. Lindbergh thought a minute.

"Those Navy ships are very different from a P-38…" and then began to describe his experiences with the plane.

Some of the men at the back of the group began to drift away and neither McGuire nor O'Brien made any attempt to stop them. I decided to slip out as well, just because in a smaller group Lindbergh might have more of chance to recognize me. As it turns out, I didn't have to worry. He'd noticed me. A few minutes after I got to my bunk one of the clerks from the squadron command poked his head under the canopy.

"Lieutenant Thurlow?" I looked up. "Colonel McGuire wants you to meet Mr. Lindbergh. Said to come get you."

We walked back through the heavy, close night air, punctuated by fireflies' glow, to the command tent. When I entered, McGuire and Lindbergh were chatting quietly. Both looked up at me. The squadron commander introduced me.

"Mr. Lindbergh, this is Lieutenant Thurlow. He's the one who brought the fuel-saving ideas to 431st Squadron." I was relieved to see that Lindbergh was treating me like a perfect stranger. There was certainly no sign in his eyes that we'd ever met. He spoke as one technician to another.

"How'd you come up with these ideas, Lieutenant?" I explained my experience keeping B-17s in formation for long hours waiting while other planes joined, nursing planes with a couple of engines out back from long missions. He nodded.

Encouraged that we were strangers to each other, I talked about flying for the Chinese Nationalists, saving precious fuel over long distances. That seemed to be enough. When neither man said anything I asked permission to go, which was granted. *See? Nothing to worry about!* I moseyed back to my bunk feeling the apprehension I'd felt going to the Colonel's billet lifting.

———

That was the only time I saw Lindbergh face to face until August. Early on I was assigned to fly a bomber escort mission to hit the Jap airfield on Amboina Island. It was going to be delicate because the runways had been built by British and Dutch POWs kept under terrible conditions in a compound next to the base, maybe even as protection against raids. It was also one of those rare occasions that O'Brien assigned me to his flight of four P-38s as a wing man. Lindbergh was going to tag along. But he was going to come up from the headquarters area, not the strip we flew off from. We were given his airplane tail letters to identify him, and told to give him all the protection we could if we ran into any bogies.

I was strapped into my cockpit with the canopy open, one engine idling, running through preflight cockpit check. My crew chief was still on the starboard wing when O'Brien loomed into my face. He shouted over the drone of my port-side engine.

"Get out. I'm taking this plane." He glared at the crew chief who immediately leaned in, opened my seat belt and began pulling me out of the seat by the parachute straps. O'Brien yelled again, "Get out, man." I felt myself forcibly lifted out of the cockpit by each man and unceremoniously allowed to slide down the starboard wing root to the ground. O'Brien got the other engine going and I scrambled away along with the crew chief. He began rolling the P-38 towards the runway.

I turned to the driver of the jeep that had brought O'Brien to my plane. "What gives?"

"Captain O'Brien's' plane wouldn't fire up. He ordered me to get him to the closest one that was ready to go." He looked at O'Brien's plane three-hundred feet away.

I motioned to my crew chief, Kaufman. "Okay, Sam, Take us back to his plane."

We hopped in and he had us there in a few seconds. We climbed up to the cockpit and began the checklist. In a few seconds we diagnosed the problem. Someone, probably O'Brien himself, hadn't switched on the magneto. Once corrected, we got both engines humming and my crew chief jumped off. I got clearance and rolled down the runway chasing the three planes that had already taken off.

I didn't really catch up till the squadron was almost over the target. The B-25 bombers had left and 431st Squadron was engaged in free-lance strafing along the air strip. I came late to the party and was high enough to see at least two Zeros make it off the ground and into the air.

As I closed in, I found O'Brien, flying my ship with a wingman whose plane I didn't recognize. It had to have been Lindbergh's. They'd been circling, waiting for others to finish their work. Like me, O'Brien had seen the Japanese fighters and was circling back into a position from which he could bounce them. As O'Brien dove, his wingman slewed behind him, not a position from which one fighter could protect another. It had to be Lindbergh, who lacked experience dog-fighting.

Once the Jap pilot saw O'Brien diving at him, he pulled up hard. Experience told me, as it told any fighter pilot who survived long in combat, what he was going to do—either try a loop to come back on O'Brien's tail or, more likely, climb into the low cloud and escape in the opposite direction. O'Brien knew too, pulled out of his dive, slowed, and headed upward for a deflection shot at the Jap. At that moment Lindbergh began firing, but he was firing at O'Brien's P-38. *No, he was firing at my P-38, thinking I was flying it.* Lindbergh's tracer rounds were boxing the target's cock pit, and he kept firing as he came closer and closer until just before his P-38 would have started chopping off O-Brien's twin tails, the plane blew into a star burst of shards and splinters I hadn't seen since my last B-17 mission over Germany. O'Brien was gone. Lindbergh climbed quickly into the clouds and I lost sight of his plane.

36

The flight back to Hollandia was long enough to figure everything out, even to decide what to do about it.

My best guess made sense of everything. Lindbergh had played his last few cards well, probably as well as anyone could. But he'd had a long streak of bad luck, as least as far as I was concerned, and it had continued right up to this very day.

Somehow he'd known who I was, or at least that I was a threat to him, as far back as 1940. He'd known who he'd shot down in Spain, if not right away, then later. Capa's agent must have shopped my pictures around widely enough that Lindbergh had found out. Flying a German plane in combat, that was a lot worse than accepting a medal from Hermann Goering. Those photos were going to wreck Lindbergh's life once the US went to war with Germany at the end of 1941.

But Lindbergh knew everyone in US aviation—civilian and military. Hell, his wife's family were millionaires tied into every board room and every smoke-filled politician's room in the country. Lindbergh's people had a pipeline through Wall Street to Henry Stimson, the secretary of war, even if Roosevelt had vetoed his reentry into the Air Corps. And Lindbergh knew every general in the Air Corps from Hap Arnold to Jimmy Doolittle, who'd taken command of the Eighth Air Force only days before my transfer to the Pacific. They'd worked together before the war.

I recalled reading the technical articles about their collaboration on high altitude flying right through the '30s.

Was it Lindbergh who got the War Department to turn me down in 1940, got me sent to China? Far enough away not to be a threat, into harm's way, hoping the Japs would solve his problem over Chongqing, or solve it in the Pearl River even before I got to Chongqing?

The image of Wendy came back to me, for the first time in a year or more, telling me it wasn't the Japs who were after me, but Chinese gangsters in someone else's pay. Was it his friends who roped me into the Flying Tigers when I stubbornly refused to die flying for Cash-my-Check's Chinese Republic? Did he pay a Chinese aircraft fitter to sabotage the P-40 I tested in Rangoon?

What I knew for certain was that strings were moving me back into the Air Corps and then yanking me out of China and into the most dangerous place for a pilot to be—bombing Germany in the daylight. These strings were being twitched in Washington. They went so far up the chain of command that they frightened general officers like Claire Chennault.

I'd been the shuttlecock between a person or persons who wanted me dead and at least a couple of others who were willing to allow the enemy to murder me. That's why I was kept in the line of fire so long, hoping that the Germans would do the job Lindbergh needed doing. But I wouldn't play ball, I wouldn't go down. I was a cat with nine lives and someone in the War Department had tried to use them all up before Lindbergh had to take a hand himself.

Below my wings, the afternoon had given way to the endless twilight of the Pacific summer evening, as I thought out and over this sequence of events a dozen times, knowing there was no direct evidence for any of it, but that Lindbergh's going after my P-38 stitched it together as tightly as a Hollywood mystery.

So, Will, what happens next? You land, Lindbergh twigs to his error. Of course, now he needs to kill you again, in fact needs to kill you at least twice as much as he needed to kill you the first time.

But why did he need to kill me? What kind of a threat could I pose to him by publishing those pictures? That's obvious! Lindbergh is still a young man, forty-two years old. He's already become a public figure, all those speeches against US entry in the war. Everyone pretty much knew when he took his stand against Roosevelt. Republicans are already pushing MacArthur to run, why not MacArthur and Lindbergh in '44 or Lindbergh in '48? Because my pictures would sink him without a trace.

Suddenly there was the green canopy of New Guinea slipping by as I reached land and flew treetop towards Hollandia. The time for thinking things through was been rapidly used up. What are you gonna do when you land, Thurlow? How are you going to stop him killing you on the ground? Kill him first? Not a chance. I could shoot a faceless pilot out of the sky by concentrating on the machine he was flying. I couldn't kill anyone standing in front of me. Confront Lindbergh? Who's going to believe you, take your side, stop him from trying to kill you? No one is going to take your word over that of the Lone Eagle, not in this man's air force.

I knew what I had to do, to save my skin, and stop Lindbergh dead in whatever track he was heading. All I had to do was get the gun camera from his plane. It shouldn't be hard. He won't ask for the film to be developed. That would convict him in 35mm celluloid, of shooting down a P-38, maybe even mine, if the tail plane numbers came visible. Unless he asked for it to be developed, the canister will just be set aside to be reloaded and the film tossed away. You need to get that canister!

I was almost the last man back from the mission. I pulled up to my hard stand, just by habit, even though it was O'Brien's plane and should have gone across the strip to where the squadron operations tent was set up. I cut the engines and my crew chief climbed up the wing to pry me out of the cockpit. As he pulled the canopy back, he spoke.

"Did you see O'Brien, flying your ship?" I shook my head. "He's the only one not back yet."

I couldn't spare a moment, not if I was going to survive. "Look, chief, I need a big favor. I'll give you a hundred bucks if you can get ahold of the gun camera canister from Lindbergh's plane?"

The man didn't ask why. He just replied, "What am I gonna do with a c-note out here, Lieutenant?"

He was right. "Okay, a hundred bucks plus two cartons of Camels and a bottle of Johnnie Walker." It would clean me out. "But Lindbergh can't find out you want it."

"Our little secret?" He looked at me quizzically.

All I could say was "Get to it, now, before they ditch the film cartridge. Just walk into the service bay and put it in a haversack. I'll get myself out of this cockpit." I rose and unclipped my parachute.

By the time my crew chief got back with the gun film cartridge, news of O'Brien's failure to return had reached up to 475th Group headquarters. The 475th hadn't lost a pilot in weeks. It was even longer since one of the experienced flyers had gone down. It was evening by the time briefing officers came across the field from Colonel MacDonald asking each pilot to write out their missions and note the last time they saw my plane with O'Brien in it. Mostly the pilots hadn't noticed the switch and just assumed that O'Brien was in his own plane but somewhere behind or above them when they heard his commands.

I was in my tent, on my bunk trying to read a trashy novel by Erskine Caldwell under a dim light when they came to talk to me. It was a major and a clerk who took stenographic short hand. I rose as the major entered.

"As you were." He pointed back at the bunk and they sat on the cot next to mine. "How come you switched planes?"

"Captain's orders, sir. He couldn't get his ship started and wanted to lead the mission."

"That ever happen before, Lieutenant?"

"Not to me, sir. I don't think it's happened to anyone since I got here."

"Why do you think he did it, take your ship?"

"Mine was the closest to his is all. He must'a really wanted to fly with Lindbergh. Our squadron hasn't had much chance to do that." Did they know O'Brien had not liked me very much?

"Did you see Captain O'Brien go down, Lieutenant?" The major's eyes were drilling into mine.

I held his gaze by looking hard at the tip of his nose. "Nope. I was so late taking off and so slow getting over target that I missed the entire raid, dropped my ordinance and came home alone." The trick worked. He rose.

"That's all Thurlow."

The major left the tent, his corporal behind him. They passed my crew chief, coming in with a GI haversack. Suddenly I worried whether he'd heard their questions and my answers. What I had told the debriefing major wouldn't make much sense of my interest in Lindbergh's gun camera. But either he hadn't heard what I said or he didn't care. He held out the pack with one hand, and rubbed the thumb against the fingers of the other. I pulled my locker out, opened the padlock, and found the cigarette cartons and the Johnnie Walker.

"Cash?" He asked

"Major Rankin holds my folding money, Sarge. I'll get it to you as soon as I can."

The man looked doubtful, hesitated and then let the pack fall on my cot. He'd probably calculated that there wouldn't be a higher bidder and that I'd be easy to betray if I didn't get him the money.

————

I was still on my cot, in the dark, with a service .45 pistol under my pillow, when Rankin came in and turned on the light. His look showed how surprised he was to find anyone awake in a dark tent. I spoke.

"John, I need a hundred bucks from my stash."

He pulled off his hat. It was where he kept his money, and mine, counted out five twenties, passed them on, and moved to his bunk. He stripped down to shorts and skivvies, then he turned off the lights. "Don't expect the other guys for a while. Craps game over at 433rd Squadron." He was right. I was still awake, looking into the dark for Lindbergh when my bunk mates stumbled in at almost four o'clock in the morning.

In spite of myself, I must have nodded off. But I was still alive when the sun began to filter through the jungle canopy a few hours later. There was enough light to write a note on a piece of paper small enough to palm.

Lindbergh,

If you still want to kill me, I'll take you to a spot where you can get away with it. Meet me at 1500 hours behind the headquarters latrines and showers.

Thurlow

Then I dressed in khakis neat enough not to look out of place at headquarters and made my way across the field walking slowly enough not to work up a sweat. I needed to look like I belonged, at least until I found Lindbergh and passed him the note.

It was too early for breakfast. I stood at the headquarters assignment board for twenty minutes pretending to be interested in its minutiae, worried I'd already missed him, or that I'd be spotted and asked my business. But then he turned up, ambling over to the mess tent, hand over his eyes to cut the glare, looking over at the tables to find someone he recognized, a companion for breakfast, I suppose. I'd hoped he'd want to eat alone. I moved to intercept him before he reached the chow line. He was still looking across the tables under the canopy by the time I crossed his path. Intentionally I cut him off, he looked up slightly annoyed. That was the moment I put the note in his hand and walked away. Then consternation spread across his face. Probably he had not even heard about O'Brien's loss. Why should he have? Twenty feet beyond I looked up to see him unfolding the note and reading it.

————

Everyone knew about the cave system the Japs had occupied a mile from the field. It had started out a tourist attraction for base personnel, one where a little rooting around decaying corpses was rewarded by finding short Samurai knives, an occasional Rising Sun flag, and some Japanese Yen-banknotes in denominations large enough to be souvenirs. By now it was a charnel house of skeletal shapes filling fading and tattered uniforms that interested no one. When I told Lindbergh we were headed there, he stopped.

"Must we? It's revolting and when I think of how our own people did that, with flame throwers and grenades…makes me ill."

"Only place you can kill me and get away with it."

"Why's that?"

We began walking, side by side. From behind anyone would have thought we were just two pilots out for a stroll beyond the base perimeter.

"Way you feel about the place, that's how most people feel about it now, Lindbergh. So, if you kill me there, no one will find the body for weeks."

There were several questions I wanted to ask, but I didn't think I'd get any answers till I'd laid my cards on the table and he was sure they were the high cards.

We walked in silence for about ten minutes, till the dirt road gave way to a track, pock marked by mortar impact craters and the tree branches were burned to the trunks. Suddenly a hill loomed and behind shrubs already growing in the damp earth, rich with munitions-nitrogen, the mouth of the cave loomed up.

We had to crawl for about seven feet but then the space opened up quite high enough to move about comfortably. I pulled a flashlight from my pack and handed it to Lindbergh, then retrieved another one for myself. We turned them on and allowed them to play over the walls, then down to the floor of the cave where they picked out the bodies of the dead.

I spoke first. "Search me. Lindbergh. You'll find I'm not armed."

He turned to face me and patted my shoulders and torso down. It wasn't a very good job and he stopped before he'd reached my waist.

"Okay, you're not armed." My flashlight was turned towards his head. Lindbergh paused, weighing his next words. "Well, I am…armed." He pulled his shirt flap up from the trousers to reveal a small leather holster. "And you're right. This is a good place to kill you, Thurlow. So, why'd you bring me here?"

"I wanted to have a conversation. Ask you some questions, get some answers, figure out my life the last five years or so."

"But if I'm going to kill you, Thurlow, I can say anything I want. In fact, I don't have to answer any of your questions. So, I'm guessing you think you can stop me killing you, force me to answer your questions, and walk out of here…without any anything to protect you."

"Right." I nodded. He'd sized up the situation pretty well. "So can we begin?"

"Shoot." Lindbergh smiled at his choice of words. We were standing in a sort of ellipse of light, facing one another, flashlights pointed chest height, so our faces were visible in their penumbra.

I began. "Just so you know where we stand, here's some history. You won't remember, but we met first in 1924. You were barnstorming in Iowa, took me for a joy ride. I was thirteen. But we met again five or six years ago, didn't we?"

"Don't think so." He shook his head in emphasis of his recollection.

"Maybe you're right. We didn't exactly meet. But you shot me down—flying a Condor Legion Me 109 and then took a photo of the plane with my name stenciled on it below the cock-pit."

"Prove it?"

"I took pictures too—you, in a German uniform, with a German soldier, in a staff-car, gloating over the Russian built P-16 you shot down that day. My P-16."

"They don't exist."

"How do you know? Been looking for them?" I waited for an answer. It didn't come. "They've been sitting somewhere in occupied Paris for five years. Friend of mine will be getting a hold of them as soon as Paris is liberated." Did he believe me? Maybe, maybe not. But it wasn't the only wild card in my hand.

"You, or some friend of yours knew about those pictures back in 1940." I thought for a moment. "Initials O.R.?"

Now I had Lindbergh's attention. "Ogden Reid" He volunteered.

"Who?"

"Publisher of the New York *Herald Tribune*. Friend of mine. Heard a rumor. By the time he tried to buy the negatives, Paris had fallen and they'd disappeared."

"One more question. This Ogden Reid, is he a friend of Henry Stimson?"

"You mean Roosevelt's Secretary of War? I suppose so. They're both New York Republicans."

"That's about all I needed to know to figure out the last five years of my life, thanks."

"Huh?" It was a one-grunt request for amplification. It deserved to be honored.

"That's when you, or this fellow, Reid, or someone decided to get rid of me. Couldn't get the negatives so you tried to get me killed—in China, then Burma, then in the Flying Tigers, the Eighth Air Force. Nothing worked, so you had to come out here to do it yourself, right?"

It was then Lindbergh lunged at my flashlight, still held chest high a yard in front of him. He pulled it from my hand, then switched both flashlights off. In the sudden dark we were completely blind, but he had a gun and both flashlights. Then I heard one of them skitter across the cave floor till it hit a wall. He couldn't hold on to both. He'd need his right hand for the pistol.

"Well, they started out to have you killed. But when I found out, I wouldn't let them just kill you, Thurlow. You had to die from an Axis bullet. But you just wouldn't. No matter how long you were kept in the firing line."

Would he say any more before he pulled back the pin on his .45? The noise would at least warn me it was time to play my last card. He spoke again.

"Jimmy Doolittle wouldn't cooperate, not after you were captured and escaped. All he'd do was have you shipped out here." I heard the firing pin pull back on his pistol.

"Before you shoot, there's one more thing you need to know, and something I'd like to know."

He switched on his flashlight. The pistol was aimed at my chest, just where the light was brightest. "What do you want to know, before you die?"

"My question?" He nodded. I went on. "Why've you gone to such lengths just to get rid of a guy with some embarrassing photos. Your people know about them already. Hasn't made a difference to them."

"Look, Thurlow, I am going to want to get my life back, do something for my country. Save it from the people who got us into this war, fighting against our own race on the same side as Stalin's Asiatic hordes."

Suddenly I was hearing those radio broadcasts back before Pearl Harbor. It was time to pull the plug, turn Lindbergh's plans into pipe dreams.

"MacArthur and Lindbergh in '44? "The Lone Eagle in '48? Not going to work, even if you shoot me now." I paused. "It's not just those pictures of you flying for the Nazis I've got. There's more now. That's what you've got to know." I stopped for a moment. It had to sink in. "I've got the film from your gun camera. Took it from where your crew tossed it. I knew you wouldn't want it processed."

"Why, what's in it?"

"Don't you get it? I was late to the party over Amboina Island. But that's where I watched you shoot down O'Brien, thinking it was me in that ship. Last thing you'd want was proof you'd downed a P-38. Might even have the markings of my plane visible. Everyone in 431ˢᵗ Squadron knows O'Brien commandeered my plane. Anyway, that canister of undeveloped film is heading Stateside right now in an APO sack." It was a safe assumption Lindbergh couldn't get an Army post office ransacked to find the right bag.

"Any proof it comes from my P-38, Thurlow?" Lindbergh sounded genuinely curious.

"Of course. Every canister is marked with the identification letters of the plane that carries it. The first ten frames of every film cartridge do the same. Didn't you know that?" I was shaking my head in mock dismay. He dropped his arm so the gun was no longer pointed at me.

Now, empty handed, I was holding a gun to Lindbergh's head. It felt good.

"Here's what you're going to do, Lucky Lindy. You're going to go home to America, and live a quiet life. You're going to stay rich and famous, grow old, and honored in your country. But when it comes to politics, you're going to become as invisible as…Alf Landon." This was the governor of Kansas who'd run against Roosevelt in '36 and lost every state but Maine and Vermont. "If I or the people I've sent the film to, ever see your name on the front page, there'll be pictures all over the next day's paper. Understood?"

Lindbergh didn't speak. He simply turned and began walking towards the cave entrance. Without a flashlight I had to follow him. No one could see my smile. But I couldn't help it. What I'd done was better than killing him. He'd live a life, maybe even a long life, blighted by his thwarted ambition. I'd enjoy it myself as long as I lived. And for once, maybe the good guys would win.

37

The rest was history, without further interference in my life. But it wasn't immediately obvious.

Lindbergh left the 475th Group three days later. No one ever heard about his combat missions till he published his diary twenty-five years after the war. And two decades after the war a civilian shooting Japanese pilots out of the sky still wasn't murder anyway. The public never got to hear about his shooting an American out of the sky. He'd done as I demanded, and I kept my word.

A week after Lindbergh left Hollandia, I got a transfer order. It had all the marks of Lindbergh's 'friends' back in action.

TO: Operations Officer, 475th Fighter Group

FROM: Kenney, Officer Commanding, 5th Air Force

SUBJECT: Thurlow, William, 1st Lieutenant, serial number 08426880

This officer is separated from 5th Air Force with immediate effect. Officer is transferred to

Headquarters Squadron, XX Air Force

Hsinching Airfield

Jinzin, Szechuan, China

Officer will transit by priority means.

Report directly to C. Le May, officer commanding.

Rankin was on his cot in our steaming tent when the orderly came in to hand me the telex.

"What gives?" he asked. I passed him the sheet. He whistled in a way that showed he was impressed. "Report to Le May himself. Know what that means?"

"I know what Le May means—Iron Ass. Served under him in England, till he personally got rid of me." I didn't add that it was after he stole my ideas about bomber formation. It would have made me sound delusional, I knew.

"Don't you keep up? Means you're going to be staff officer in Le May's new B-29 group." I knew. I just hadn't read the telex closely enough or all the way to the end. The paranoia Lindbergh's departure lifted had just returned. Rankin's voice broke into my thoughts.

"Where is Jinzin, Szechuan anyway?"

"Middle of nowhere in China." I took the telex back. "I'd better start packing."

———

Three weeks later I reported to headquarters squadron, XX Air Force at Hsinching. It took that long, from New Guinea through Australia, Ceylon, India, and over the Himalayan "hump" where I had lower priority than fuel and ordinance. Coming out of the C-47 I saw my first B-29. It was the first airplane I ever saw that looked like a malevolent death machine—a long silver tube unencumbered by any structure needing human control. I handed my orders to an officer with a clipboard, checking each man coming out of the C-47. He looked up at me.

"Le May's been waiting for you. I've got orders to get you to headquarters soon as you arrive. We'll get you to your quarters later. He pointed me at a jeep a hundred yards away with two stars on the signal flag above the hood.

Rural China looked pretty much the same as when I'd left it. The deep ruts and broken road surfaces felt the same too, as the jeep bounced its way an endless five miles while I contemplated my fate back in Le May's hands again.

He looked me over, trying to place me while I held my breath and hoped he couldn't. Le May had evidently seen too many faces and hadn't learned enough names to put both of mine together. He gave up the effort, looked at a file on his desk and spoke.

"Thurlow, I plucked you out of the Pacific 'cause you're the single officer in the entire Army Air Force with the qualifications I need. You drove four engine bombers for me in England, you served in China with Chennault and you've got some Chinese lingo, so I figure you know this here…" he was searching for an adjective he could use, but gave up, "…country." I remained at attention, inwardly breathing again. He looked at my wings. "No more flying for you. You're going to spend every moment of your waking life on the ground, scrounging everything you can out of Chiang Kai-shek's gangsters so we don't have to fly it in from India. Got it?"

"Yes, sir."

"One more thing. Take those first louey bars off your collar. Nobody's going to listen to a lieutenant. You're a light colonel now. Get yourself a couple of eagles for your uniform…and remember, it's temporary."

POSTSCRIPT

Most Secret

March 21, 1972

From: Martin Furnival Jones, Director, MI5

To: James Callahan, Home Secretary

Subject: Possible role of Charles A. Lindbergh in death of MI5 agent

I provide the information herewith. Whether any action should be taken in light of this information is evidently a political matter.

From about 1955 this office had raised concerns about Charles A. Lindbergh that HM government communicated to US intelligence agencies. These concerns were based on:

1. Lindbergh's active participation in the US Air Force Intercontinental Ballistic Missile Scientific Advisory Committee.

2. Lindbergh's frequent and unexplained annual travel to several cities in West Germany. There he would assume an alias—Careu Kent, and disappear only to surface weeks afterward and return to the US. These travels continue into the present time.

The US Intelligence Agencies, including the CIA and FBI, to which Lindbergh's repeated travel and aliases was reported, declined to act on this intelligence in any way, or at any rate told us they were not authorized to do so.

In 1959 MI5 assigned one of its agents, William Thurlow to investigate the matter. Thurlow had US citizenship, a qualification we thought useful to investigations that might involve travel to that country. The choice of Thurlow was singularly unfortunate as we subsequently had reason to learn. (Details available on request.)

It is worth mentioning that Thurlow had been recruited to MI5 in the period after the Second World War, having been brought to our attention by Sir Solly Zuckerman. The need for agents with American passports, who could act in the US and with its agencies abroad, made this recruitment expedient.

Having tracked Lindbergh from the US to Germany on several occasions over the period 1958 to 1964, Thurlow discovered the reasons for his repeated *incognito* visits. It transpires that this travel had nothing to do with missile technology, espionage, or any matter of obvious American national security. Thurlow had discovered that Charles A. Lindbergh was living a double life, fathering children with three different German women, whom he visited for fortnightly stays three times a year.

After he reported these findings Thurlow was ordered to cease further enquiry into the matter. Thurlow argued that continued surveillance was warranted. He believed that Lindbergh was a member of a secret society, established in the 1930s by one Alexis Carrel, to practice positive eugenics and otherwise advance notions of racial superiority later associated with the German Nazi party. Carrel had won the Nobel Prize in Medicine in 1912, and Lindbergh worked with Carrel on scientific experiments in the US and France before the war. Carrel expressed fascist sentements and subsequently was a scientific advisor to the collaborationist Vichy government of France. He died in 1944. Lindbergh is the executor of his estate responsible for his papers.

Thurlow held that Lindbergh's extra-marital relations and resulting children in Germany reflected his continuing participation in some sort of more dangerous political conspiracy. He argued that further work could uncover deeper involvement of Lindbergh with underground networks possibly ones aiding Germans still in hiding, whether in Europe, Latin America or even the USA.

It was determined by this office that Lindbergh's illicit personal life did not evince any national security concerns and Thurlow was assigned to other duties.

Evidently he did not obey this order. The circumstances surrounding Thurlow's death in Frankfurt last month suggest Lindbergh was the murderer. Thurlow was repeatedly run over near an address our records show was occupied by one of Lindbergh's German "wives." The vehicle seen by a witness was a late model Volkswagen. 'Pampas Green' paint fragments were found near Thurlow's body. Rental records indicate that this is the color of car Lindbergh's alias, Careu Kent, was driving at the time. Our belief is that Lindbergh detected the surveillance and when he recognized Thurlow, concluded there was a real threat of exposure and so killed him.

Actual historical persons among the Dramatis Personae

Charles A. Lindbergh
Benjamin O. Davis
Robert Capa
Dan Goulie
Byron Glover
Claire Chennault
Clayton Bissell
Harvey Greenlaw
Olga Greenlaw
Paul Tibbets
Frank Armstrong
Ira Eaker
Curtis Le May
Solly Zuckerman
Wilhelm Carnaris
Walter Cronkite
Thomas MacGuire
Charles MacDonald
William O'Brien

About The Author

Alex Rosenberg is the author of five historical novels, three non-fiction trade books and more than a dozen academic titles in philosophy. He holds a distinguished chair in philosophy at Duke University, where he teaches courses across a range of subjects from biology to economics and public policy. Alex has been a visiting professor at universities from Oxford to the Australian National University as well as a permanent faculty member in several American and Canadian universities. He has won several distinguished national and international awards in philosophy, including the Guggenheim fellowship, The Lakatos Award in philosophy of science and the Phi Beta Kappa Romanell lectureship. His op/eds have appeared in the *New York Times* and other publications. Alex's historical novels are all thrillers, linking the dots of real history into webs of danger, intrigue, espionage and mystery. His non-fiction brings contemporary science face to face with the human search for meaning in the world.

Warpath Press is dedicated to publishing the very best in military writing from around the globe.

We believe that writing that is rooted in the human experience of war and conflict, even when written by non-veterans, allows us as a society to examine how human nature responds under extreme pressure. It also gives us a means to ask the big questions about life.

"Military stories" aren't all action-adventure novels. We are committed to finding ways to push the boundaries of "military writing" in new directions, bending it into new shapes that serve society in better ways.

Many of the literary greats of the early to mid-20th century wrote about war and its effects. But Hemingway, Remarque, Dos Passos, Faulkner, Wouk, Greene and Waugh, only had the impact that they did because they were published.

Today, they would likely have been ignored by the major publishers.

And that is why we do what we do.